BLOOD WILL TELL

A LACEY BENEDICT NOVEL

ELIZABETH BASDEN

Blue Muse Books

A DIVISION OF BLUE MUSE PUBLISHING GROUP

For Deborah

PROLOGUE

"Now watch your step, miss. They've not done any renovation up here."

I followed the appraiser, Jerry Freeman, up the stairs from the second floor to the third-floor attic of the Tarantino house and watched his steps, if not my own, in the murky darkness there. The wooden plank stairs were in pretty bad shape, and they were covered with a thick layer of dust. I hadn't needed to come with him for the interior property inspection, but I was interested to see what he thought of the partially remodeled Tudor in Dallas's sought-after Lakewood neighborhood.

I was also glad I'd worn my old boots for it, even though they'd felt distinctly out of place in the upscale luxury of the renovated first floor. As we passed beneath an overhead light fixture with only one lit bulb remaining, I realized I was unconsciously placing my feet where Jerry had already disturbed the dust. There was no rail on the sides of the narrow stairwell, and the opening itself was only a bit wider than my shoulders. I steadied myself against the plastered side wall, wondering miserably if I was that much larger than someone living in the 1930s.

We crested the stairs on a small unlit landing, and then the stairs doubled back for the second half of the flight. The air seemed thicker up here, musty and warm even though it was only the 26th of February, and I felt sorry for those hardy domestics who might have lived up here when the house was built in 1937. We finally emerged onto a larger landing with doors on either side. Bare bulbs inserted directly into sockets shone brightly in the rooms that led off the landing, but there was no fixture at the top of the stairs. Mr. Freeman had stepped to the room on the left, so I followed.

"See here on this side, you go in and there's this closet here?" He showed me a closet just to the right of the door opening, the door off-centered on the wall. The room itself was longer than it was wide, perhaps 14 feet long and 8 feet wide, the ceiling sloping down pretty dramatically to about three feet above the floor. These two rooms were over the kitchen section that protruded out the back of the main house. The walls were covered in a cabbage-rose printed paper that curled at the top and bottom where it met plain white-painted wood moldings.

This would have been a bedroom for several maids or a house-keeper, twin beds, perhaps, with maybe a dresser or chair. I thought of my own sparsely-furnished apartment, and winced, realizing I had about the same amount of furniture that someone in a *Downton Abbey*-type attic bedroom would. I resolved to get online and buy something frivolous right away.

I dutifully looked in the closet, a small space measuring about two by eight feet and built of bare wood planks, with a sloped ceiling to match the one in the main room. A few empty wire hangers dangled from the wooden pole.

"Now come over here, miss," he invited, as he moved across the hall to the other room, a space that matched the other down to the wallpaper and closet. In this closet, however, Mr. Freeman told me, he'd found something different. "Look in this closet—do you see it?"

Aside from a lack of hangers, this closet looked no different from the other, and I told him so. He tsked under his breath and unhooked a large, square metal measuring tape from his belt. He slid out the metal tape as he stepped inside and measured the length of the closet, and then showed me. Five feet. He looked expectantly at me, and I felt like I'd missed a math lesson.

Then it clicked. This room, like the one across the hall, was about eight feet wide, but this closet was short almost three feet, and the ceiling slope downward ended at least six feet above the floor, not three like the other closet. He nodded approvingly as I looked out in the room, and then back in the closet. There was no light inside, but it looked like any other closet except for the size.

He hooked the measuring tape back on his belt. "I was checking the wiring up here—it's the original Romex wiring from when the house was built in 1937 in these two rooms. It's not a real fire risk, but it needs to be replaced." He continued to chatter on, throwing miscellaneous building terms around like I throw legal ones. I have to admit I wasn't listening.

He picked up a heavy flashlight and a screwdriver, and then he stepped back into the closet, motioning me in with his other hand. I reluctantly crowded into the closet with him. "This made me curious, so I felt around in here for a minute." He pointed the end of the screwdriver to the wooden board that the 'socket' for the dowel rod was screwed into. "Lookee here, miss." He slid the end of the screwdriver up the corner to just below the board, and then dug in. The wall was divided at that line, and as it swung toward us like a door, I could see dark space behind.

Mr. Freeman clicked on his flashlight and shone it inside the space. It was a small, windowless room, and it woke up every latent bit of claustrophobia I didn't know I had. I tried to peer over his shoulder, but he moved back and handed me the flashlight, so I bravely stepped to the entrance and ducked down to see inside. The smell was unpleasant, the air inside stale, and I began to breathe through my mouth. There was a small box on the floor—a blue metal lockbox, it turned out—and nothing else. I don't know what I was expecting, maybe a skeleton or a valuable painting locked away for 80 years, but 'nothing' wasn't it. I shone the light around the floor, but there were no footprints in the thick dust. Like the closets, the walls inside were bare wood, with no wallpaper or plaster.

"I wonder what's in the box?" I asked, as much to myself as to Jerry Freeman, and started to reach down for it. He stopped me with a hand to my shoulder.

"You see that, miss?" He took the flashlight from me and pointed at some discolorations on the wall. They were about three feet from the floor on the back wall, faded brown spots and streaks and smears, and I leaned forward, struggling to see the area clearly.

"What is it, mold or something?" I asked, a bit troubled. Mold is a four-letter word you don't want to hear when you're considering a potential house sale, even I knew that. I started to reach out to touch it, but his next words stopped me.

"That's blood, miss."

CHAPTER ONE

There's no such thing as a friendly divorce.

I've heard there are 'bloodless' ones, but I think those are ones where the anger and the passion have drained away over the years until both parties are simply relieved and anxious to get it over with. I've seen a few of those, and while they're less bitter than the usual ones, they're much more depressing to watch unfold.

The Tarantino divorce was neither friendly nor bloodless. Both Trisha Tarantino and her husband, Jules Tarantino, were lawyers; they both practiced in finance, with Trisha specializing in international transactions, while Jules was corporate general counsel for a small, regional bank. They both knew enough about litigation to be very, very dangerous to each other and their respective divorce counsel. They also despised each other after eighteen years of marriage, the multi-million-dollar purchase and partial renovation of a historic Lakewood home, multiple affairs, and a very public torching of a vintage Jaguar. I couldn't decide which movie divorce this looked like, but it was worse than anything I'd ever seen in real life.

As an attorney, I'd considered practicing family law—divorces, custody, and the like—for about ten minutes. Five years ago, when trying to decide the focus of my new firm, I'd sat in on some proceedings and realized I didn't have the stomach for it. I sat through one hearing where the parties ended up shouting at each other over their counsel's arguments, and the bailiff intervened as the judge walked out. Don't get me wrong: I like the way there's a lot of data in divorces, like inventories, forensic accountings, or detailed testimonies of the parties, but there's a fine line divorce counsel must walk to keep some objectivity through it all. The turbulent emotions of divorce and custody disputes made me want to go hide my head.

While sitting in on some hearings and considering family law five years ago, I'd watched Trisha's counsel, Karan Sullivan, calmly cross-examine a cheating wife in a divorce hearing. She'd been precise and detailed in her questions, never veering over that fine line into melodrama or contempt, even while asking questions about the wife's sexual activities in the couple's marital bed. Her demeanor was reserved and formal, and she paused politely when the wife sobbed during the telling of the sordid story.

I could tell the judge appreciated Karan's restraint too. While it was clear that Karan's client in that proceeding five years ago felt the marriage was over, he sat at the plaintiff's table, pale and frozen, and allowed his attorney to do her job. Afterwards, I happened to be in the bathroom washing my hands when Karan stepped in to throw up. I waited until she came out to wash up and asked her if she was all right.

"I will be," she said, a bit shakily. "I'm leaving for a vacation as soon as this case is over." She looked at me in the mirror as she dabbed her face with a wet paper towel. "Or at least, that's the plan. Do the dirty job, selfcare before the next one."

I asked her for her card that day, and since then, I've referred to her all the many requests for divorce counsel that came my way. Last year, she referred something to me: one of her divorce cases needed a receiver to sell the couple's home and furnishings because the husband was active military deployed overseas and couldn't be a part of the process. It was the easiest money I'd earned as a lawyer. I worked with a real estate agent to list the house, which sold within thirty days, and then the proceeds were split between the couple by the judge. Easy peasy, and I got a check for my time when the house closed.

So, when she asked me to be the receiver for the Tarantino house sale, I assumed it would be more of the same. You know what they say about assumptions, right?

———

KARAN STIRRED THE CHICKEN SLICES INTO HER SALAD. "IT'S NOT that I don't like my client." She must have caught my skeptical look. "Okay, I don't like my client very much. She's not someone I'd ever call a friend."

"I've learned that some clients just aren't people you'd want to go to lunch with." I checked the tomatoes on my cheeseburger: pale pink and hard. I slid them off onto the plate. Tomatoes in February—you take your chances. I cut the burger in half with all the best intentions, thinking I'd eat half now and save the rest for dinner. Biting into it, I smothered a moan of happiness and reevaluated the 'saving half for dinner' part.

"Yes, well, Trisha and Jules have spent the last couple of years tormenting each other, hoping the other one would file first." She speared a bit of chicken on her fork and contemplated it. "I should have gotten the grilled chicken instead of the fried. We're going diving in Belize next month, and this chicken will still be showing up on my thighs."

I had a vivid mental picture of a live chicken attached to her thigh, holding tight with its wings. Instead of laughing like I wanted to, I happily dipped a fry into ketchup. For the last few days, I'd been living pretty frugally. My purse got stolen last week, and I'd been stretching out the $25 cash I'd pulled from the bank while waiting for replacement credit and debit cards. The debit card came in today, and this burger and fry combo at the fancy uptown Texas Steakhouse was my reward for being good.

Karan was giving me the same look my sister-in-law Sara gave me when I ate. Both of them are pretty and petite, and, while they both eat like birds, they claim that everything they eat goes right to fat. I'm not convinced, but I let them have their protests. I've determined to ignore my body—for better or worse—and I simply eat for pleasure when I remember. Maybe I have a strong metabolism, I don't know, but I refuse to buy into the constant diet hype. I nudged my metal cup of fries closer to the middle of the table, and she snagged one.

"What will the receivership hearing be like tomorrow?" I took a sip of water. Splurging I might be, but I can't handle paying four dollars for a soda, even when I'm flush. "Last time, I didn't have to go to the hearing."

She adjusted her scarf, a pretty-patterned pale green wool thing tied in a complicated knot I couldn't have managed, before picking up her fork. She'd finished with her hearings for the day, but she still looked like she could step back into court at any time. "Jules and his attorney are fighting about having a receiver appointed. They know there's no way this is ever getting resolved without one, but I think they're hoping we can get one of Jules's banker buddies appointed." She chewed meditatively. "I didn't even ask: You don't know either of them, do you?"

I snorted. "Like I would know those people. They may be attorneys, but they're not attorneys anyone like me knows."

She tilted her head, her big green eyes narrowing. "Why do you say things like that? I'm not a socialite, but I know other lawyers. You might have met them in a CLE seminar or something."

I rubbed my nose, a sure sign I'm feeling embarrassed or having springtime allergies. "You're right. I don't know why I'm being such a snob today." I did, actually. Someone recently dressed me down for not getting involved in the legal community, and I'd realized that I was waiting for everyone else to come to *me*. "No, I don't know either of them." I leaned in and lowered my voice. "But I don't think anyone in town doesn't know about the divorce. It's been really public."

She rolled her eyes at that. "High profile divorces get a lot of press in the *Observer*, if not the *Dallas Morning News*. The Jaguar incident didn't help." She sipped her iced tea and shook her head before picking up her fork again. "I'm still trying to recover from that hearing. Yoga and massage didn't really do the trick."

Right before Christmas, Trisha and Jules had tangled in their temporary orders hearing, where the parties decide on rules that go into place while their assets get divided up. They'd had a massive fight in the hearing about a restored 1965 Jaguar they'd owned together, which Jules was driving—at least he had been until he'd been at a fancy steakhouse not too far from here and valet-parked the Jag, only to come out a couple of hours later to find the fire department hosing down what was left of it. The valet had left in it an unmonitored parking lot a few blocks away, and someone had doused it in gasoline and set it on fire. At that exact moment, Trisha Tarantino had been at a charity gala with 1,200 of her best friends, but no one really thought the socialite had torched it herself.

I noticed Karan looking at my left eyebrow, where a still-purple scar bisected my eyebrow from the injury I'd received last week during the mugging. Call it a purse snatching or a mugging if you want, but what I remember most was the moment my face hit a brick wall. I'm not sure why injuries to the face hurt so much. I'd gone back to the ER yesterday to have the stitches removed, and now I just had a dark pink train track about an inch and a half in length, neatly splitting the eyebrow. My cheekbone bruises were clearing up too. Considering the mugger's other victim had ended up dead, I considered myself lucky.

I arched my right eyebrow at Karan, which unfortunately caused the left one to prickle and burn. "You're not going to ask?"

She raised her own eyebrows. "What is this? My first day on the job?" She shook her head and picked out another piece of chicken to dip into dressing. "Lacey, I was around for the sprained shoulder from the foreclosure fall and the broken headlight from the divorce petition service fiasco." She wrinkled her nose. "Still sorry about that one, by the way." I acknowledged the apology with a gracious wave as I chewed cheeseburger. "Until I met you, I didn't know that practicing law was such a dangerous profession."

I didn't either. When I started practicing law eight years ago, I expected it to be a cushy job at a law firm, with a six-figure salary and all the benefits they talk about in law school. What I got was a job at the firm of a man helping his clients perpetrate a fraud, and I was the whistleblower who helped catch him. After that particular fecal matter hit the fan about five years ago, I've pieced a law firm together by practicing—for the most part—real estate and other minor business litigation, which unfortunately involves collections, foreclosures, evictions, and people unhappy about whatever you're taking away. The smashed headlight came when I'd agreed to find and serve divorce papers on the husband of one of Karan's clients, who'd sought safety in a shelter for battered women. He wasn't too happy about the divorce and decided to bash in my headlight to exhibit his displeasure after he realized what I'd handed him inside a 'you won a new camera' envelope.

These days, my practice is somewhat more on target, with some foreclosures and evictions tossed in, and I was able to put money into savings for taxes or unexpected insurance deductibles at emergency rooms after muggings. My heart was still pounding a bit at the $1,000 I just put down to pay the hospital on last week's ER visit.

"I've asked Trisha not to come to tomorrow's hearing," Karan commented as she checked her phone, "but she's just said Jules texted her to let her know *he* was coming, so she'll be there." She put the phone down with an unhappy thump.

"They're still talking to each other?" I regarded the second half of my cheeseburger. *Maybe if I eat it now, I won't be hungry for dinner,* I thought, and then got myself under control. The second half of a burger isn't nearly as good as the first half anyway. The server dropped off our checks in black leather folders, and I asked her for a box as I tucked my new debit card inside mine.

Karan asked for one as well, and then she massaged her left temple. "Yes. Well, they're still texting. Evil, angry, bitter texts that Trisha screenshots and sends to me. Late at night, during the day, it doesn't matter." She sighed and took the box from the server with a nod of thanks. "I'm surprised either one of them still has a job. They spend most of their time trying to find ways to jab at each other. Or they're on the phone with their lawyers, talking about it."

I loaded the small container with the remaining half of the burger and decided not to add the fries. They never reheated well. I took one more and dipped it into ketchup. "Yet another reason not to practice family law." The server returned the card folders. I added a tip to the check and swallowed hard as I signed and tucked my new card away. These places were so expensive, but this was Karan's choice, and I was getting new work. "Can you turn your phone off?

She poured the rest of her salad dressing into the little plastic ramekin the server had left for her and capped it. "Oh, absolutely. Most clients don't have my cell phone number, but the friend that referred Trisha gave it to her." She made a face. "Maybe former friend." I laughed as she put the container in the box with the rest of the salad. "Seriously, Lacey, there may be some unpleasant moments tomorrow. Jules and his attorney are playing pretty dirty because Trisha makes so much more money than he does. He's trying to get whatever he can."

I dusted the bit of salt off my hands and tried to look confident. "Hey, I'm wonder-lawyer, remember? I can handle it." I mimed ripping a suit off and stood up with my hands on my hips in a classic superhero pose.

She stood too and smiled at me as she gathered her things. "I do want to know you're okay—that scar looks painful. Are you going to get it worked on?" I watched her with a little envy as she adjusted the scarf over the collar of her wool coat. Like so many Dallas women,

Karan had style and the money to indulge it. I'd never be able to wear a scarf like that.

I shook my head. "My insurance won't cover plastic surgery, but I think it's okay anyway. It looks worse than it is." I smoothed a finger over the tiny line. Truthfully, it itched a bit, but it didn't really hurt much anymore. The bruise on my cheek was fading, but it still ached whenever I bent down. "I think once it heals it will barely be noticeable." I hoped. "So...I'll be at the courthouse at 4 tomorrow."

"Be there about 15 minutes early, and we can visit outside the courtroom." She hugged me, careful not to press my head into her shoulder. "Try not to damage yourself before then, okay?" She handed her ticket to the valet.

I laughed and waved as I veered off into the pay-by-the-hour lot across the street, where the rest of us park.

———

I LIVE IN DALLAS—THE EAST SIDE OF DALLAS—WHICH ISN'T AS glamorous as Highland Park, a small city within a city not too far from Southern Methodist University. Highland Park is home to some of the most expensive real estate in the country, with palatial homes and sparkling, well-manicured parks. One of them runs beside Turtle Creek, a natural waterway that's been a part of Dallas lore since the late 1800s. On the east side of the creek, a protected greenbelt forms a series of lush and lovely parks; on the west side, developers have built homes for the very wealthy. In the winter, you can walk on the paths in the park and get a peek of how the 1% live on the other side. By late spring, the trees at the water's edge form a natural screen, and the lower classes can't gawk.

I parked my car on the street next to the park and got out to walk off those fries. Aside from dodging dogwalkers and jogging stroller-parents, it was a lovely and peaceful walk, especially on a winter weekday. The sun had come out from behind the clouds, and I debated leaving my jacket in the car, but took it just in case. The ducks and geese drifted in the lazily moving water, and I could even see a fish or turtle surface quickly to nab a bug. The path curved to the water's edge, and I paused for a minute to look across the creek at the houses on the other side. They're enormous, some with their own tennis courts, water features, vine-covered trellises, and stone pavilions and pergolas, and they're made to look old, even if they're not. I've seen a wedding or two held in a backyard, and I imagined the bride or groom was a daughter or son to the homeowner. In the summer, there'll be garden parties, and the tinkle of glass and laughter carries across the creek in the warm air. Watching one of those makes me feel a bit like Nick Carraway in *The Great Gatsby*, observing the rich in their playtime, destined to be always on the outside even if he's invited in.

Walking helps me think calmly and rationally, and I needed both of those today. I really wasn't trying to be a snob with Karan. Back when I worked for Bill Stephenson—my dishonest former managing partner—I rubbed shoulders with some of Dallas's upper class. Bill would help his clients inform—and sometimes *under*-inform— investors about projects, and the wealthy would open up their pocket-books to invest their trust funds and maximize their returns. The projects ranged from technology to real estate to pharmaceuticals, and the amount of money raised for investment staggered me back then. Since then, I've seen a bit more of Dallas and its wealthy citizens, and I know all that was just business as usual.

I was born and bred north of Dallas, mostly by my grandmother, on a farm that had been in the family for over a hundred and fifty years. My father's family was what they call in Texas 'land-rich/dirt-poor,' which means that we own land that's valuable for agriculture or development but don't have a lot of money. In our case, we had enough cleared land for some farming, and for years, we've kept just enough agriculture going to get an ag exemption on property taxes. Now, with my grandmother gone for more than 10 years and my father in a facility with Alzheimer's disease, my brother and I were considering selling off the farm. The farmhouse was leased to some relatives and some of the farmland was leased to nearby farmers, but that didn't bring in much more than the property taxes, even with the exemptions.

I shook my head to dispel those thoughts; I wasn't ready for that just yet. I raised my face to the sun and enjoyed the faint breeze. Live oak leaves rustled, and I could hear geese squawking somewhere. For a moment, I decided that life was good. Nice and easy and uncomplicated. Who needed money? I had fresh air and beauty, and that was enough for right now. Spring and better days were right around the corner.

I should have known better.

CHAPTER TWO

The sun went behind some clouds and the breeze suddenly felt cold, so I got in my car and turned on the heat as I headed for home. It was still early enough to get a bit of work done before my meeting in the morning, and I wanted to duck my head into the office space being remodeled for me while it was still light.

I had a missed call when I turned my phone back on, and I frowned when I saw the name. Rob Gerard. Gerard had been the defense attorney for my former managing partner in his fraud trial, but just recently he'd helped me maneuver my way through some aspects of criminal law for a case. I wonder sometimes if we're friends or enemies, or if he belongs anywhere in my life at all. He's sort of dashingly piratical, with prematurely silver hair and black eyebrows over icy blue eyes, but he's a reminder of a part of my life I'm not sure I want to think about. *Like I could ignore him.* He has a way of insinuating himself into my thoughts when I'm not paying attention, and I still have a Mont Blanc pen of his that I need to return. I checked, but there was no text or voicemail. *Figures*, I thought, *he'll just drop a reminder that he's there, but no information with it.* I put him out of my mind and headed home.

Almost five years ago, after things went really bad for me in the legal world, I rented a tiny one-bedroom apartment in an old mansion on Gaston Avenue, one of the oldest streets in Dallas, and, at one time, one of the most expensive places to live. The street was a part of Munger Park, built in the early 1900s and bounded on either side by streets filled with the mansions of the very wealthy in Dallas's history. A few of the original homes are still there, for the most part meticulously restored and maintained. This street, along with several others like Swiss, Live Oak, Munger, and Ross, were where the mega-wealthy Dallasites of the late nineteenth and early twentieth centuries lived, before Highland Park and Lakewood became the streets for the city's elite. At one time, there was a railroad spur at the end of Swiss Avenue, so the wealthy could keep a railroad car at home.

Hattie and Sallie Shelton's grandfather bought two lots facing on Gaston and the two behind those, and he built this mansion on the full acre to house what he hoped would be several children and many grandchildren. It wasn't to be. Both he and his son died young. The Shelton sisters grew up in this house in the 1950s without their father, and it was sold out of their family in the late 1960s and split into apartments like mine. When the Shelton sisters returned to Dallas years later, they bought it and began renovating the house back into its original conformation, in part—I think—to get a historic designation of some type. Sallie is a member of several historic associations here in town, and there's apparently a pecking order of sorts. I think my apartment is endangered, but they've never mentioned anything to me.

Last week, Hattie showed me the old butler's pantry in between my space and theirs, and we negotiated a deal for me to rent the small space from them for an office. Since I moved in five years ago, I've used the dining table as my desk and office, but my practice has outgrown the table. Books and paper usually spill on to the floor when I'm in the middle of legal matters heavy on documents. The butler's pantry always had an outside door on the back side of the house, which Hattie explained made it easier for them to bring supplies in from the cold storage in the back garden. The cold house is long gone, but that separate entrance is still there and will be the door to my office—when it's all finished.

I parked under the side overhang that shelters my 'front' door and walked around the house. The back garden, which Hattie won't let me call a 'backyard,' is huge—almost a half-acre—and it's beautiful, with trees and flower gardens, an arbor with a very old grapevine, a working fountain, and a detached carriage house that matches the main house. With spring still a few weeks away, the flower beds were covered in some kind of cloth and the fountain was off and drained, but even so, it's a beautiful space.

There were piles of lumber and sheetrock cluttering the lawn and up on blocks, waiting for the construction guys to finish out the new room. Tomas Gutierrez and John Adams (no relation to the second US president) were Hattie's contractors for their residential property management company. The 'Shelton Shelters Management' signs are all over east Dallas, so I think they're pretty busy, but they've made time to oversee the remodeling of the pantry into an office.

I'd peeked around the corner yesterday, and since then the guys had finished reframing the doorway. Turns out back in 1917 when the house was built, they'd had two smaller doors instead of one (for the big stuff they wanted to bring in, maybe whole boars or calves to roast, I don't know), and then replaced them later with one larger door and wide, thick beams on either side to fill the space. Hattie was replacing those with one French door with glass panes and two side panels with smaller glass panes to fill the space. Because the room was an interior one with no windows, this would let in some natural light while also keeping the house's brick exterior intact, something that I guess is important to the historic preservation police.

The door hadn't been hung yet, so I stepped in between the bushes that Atencio had cut back and looked inside. Sallie was trying to research what kind of steps had been placed in front of the door, so nothing was there yet except a two-foot square flat piece of concrete Atencio had laid to protect his flower beds. I stood there now and peered in. The room looked awful and cluttered with supplies and dust, but I hugged myself and tried to see it as Hattie had described it, the floor-to-ceiling shelves on one side filled with books and family photos or knick-knacks, a small desk in the middle with a desk chair in back, maybe a comfortable chair in front. It was hard to envision all that right now, with two sawhorses and all kinds of tools lying around.

John was talking to someone who was hidden in an opening in the ceiling, but he came over to the doorway to block my view. "Miss Hattie told me not to let you in, Lacey."

I frowned at him. "What? Why? It's going to be *my* office."

He stepped outside and down to the concrete square, forcing me to back up to the grass. "She wants it to be a surprise."

That was like Hattie, and I really appreciated the sentiment, but I was hoping to get some ideas of what I should bring from Ryan and Sara's house this weekend. It wasn't John's fault though, so I let him put an arm around my shoulder and lead me away, talking to me about lighting and ducts and drywall. Then I went looking for Hattie.

———

THE CONNECTING DOOR FROM MY APARTMENT LED INTO THE Sheltons' laundry room, so I took the opportunity to start a load of laundry as I passed through to talk to Hattie. Access to the laundry room was a great perk to living with the Sheltons. The machines are top of the line, there's a table to fold laundry so I don't just dump the clean laundry in my bedroom chair—which I could live out of for a week or so—and I can usually find Hattie or Sallie in the kitchen with something to nibble on when I come over.

This time, the kitchen was empty, but there was a plate of chocolate chip cookies on the counter, as if Hattie had known I might be coming by. I nicked one as I went by and hallooed. I've been—in my opinion—an unwelcome intruder into the kitchen before, interrupting Sallie with a gentleman caller. Okay, Sallie had called him her boytoy, but since he was a smidgen past 60, I prefer to think of them sharing a cup of tea or something.

The Shelton sisters are in their 70s, fraternal twins who don't look a thing alike, and they are both absolutely the women I want to grow up to be someday. Hattie is tall and thin and reminds me of Katherine Hepburn with her tailored and masculine-styled clothes, while Sallie is shorter and curvy, with a socialite's sense of style and a youthful attitude, complete with boytoys and a love for hip hop. They told me that they'd deliberately cultivated different habits, hobbies, and style when they were teenagers back in the 1950s and 60s, and it stuck. They'd moved back to Dallas together, and intended to live that way till the end.

Hattie came down the stairs as I came in, looking—as always—calm and collected. She saw the remains of the cookie in my hand and smiled. "You found the cookies."

I swallowed and hoped I didn't have chocolate smeared all over my face. "I did. I should have been able to smell them baking, but I had to catch sight of them instead." I laid on the plaintive tone, hoping for some pity.

She shook her head with a smile. "I baked them yesterday." She tilted her head. "John texted me that you'd tried to look in the office."

I'd hoped to catch her first and convince her this 'surprise' thing was ill-advised. "I did." I cleared my throat. "I need to go in and take some measurements." That sounded plausible.

She smiled again. "I have them for you." She took her phone out of her pocket and tapped a few times. "There. Now you have a text with the room measurements and the different shelf dimensions."

"You know how curious I am." I tried to look winsome and innocent.

She lifted her eyebrows and looked pointedly at the pink scar bisecting my left eyebrow. "Lacey, dear, we *all* know how curious you are. How is the cut, by the way?"

"Dr. Shalev said it's healing well." She stepped closer to look, and I tilted my head so she could see it better. "Hattie, really, I just wanted to see it, you know, to decide what I need to buy to fit in there."

She looked concerned, and I wondered if I'd laid it on too thick. "Do you *want* to buy furniture?"

Her concern immediately made me uncomfortable. I didn't talk much about money issues to the Shelton sisters, but I was pretty sure they knew I wasn't flush with cash. Since the whistleblower trials that ended my relationship with my former boss, I'd created a law firm from practically nothing, one client at a time. While I was slowly building up my savings and was happy with my small nest egg, the thought of buying office furniture so soon after paying an insurance deductible was enough to strike fear in my heart. "Maybe a desk or chair." I thought about it. "Ryan might have something I could borrow." I realized I had melted chocolate on my hands and looked around for something, considering wiping them on my jeans.

Hattie led the way to the kitchen, then wet a paper towel and handed it to me. "You know, we have a large storage section in the warehouse just filled with furniture. Why don't you come see if there's anything that would fit?" Her voice was casual, and I looked at her suspiciously.

"I'd just borrow something from you?" I wiped my hands on the paper towel and considered this, wondering if it was charity that I should accept. I heard my grandmother's voice in my head, contradicting her 'neither a borrower nor a lender be' with 'charity begins at home.' "I'd be grateful to use something until I can afford my own." There. That sounded gracious. Hattie nodded without looking at me.

We passed pretty close to the plate of cookies. I debated another one but decided it was too close to dinner and my leftover half burger. Then I realized that I'd left the takeout box sitting on the table at the restaurant. *Damn.* I took the cookie.

Hattie glanced at me. "No dinner plans?"

I shook my head. "You cooking?" I asked hopefully through the mouthful of cookie.

"Not tonight, but why don't you come to see the storage on Saturday and then to dinner on Saturday night?" She smiled slightly. "Unless you have a date. If not, Sallie could invite someone for you."

I looked at her suspiciously, wondering if she was teasing. Sallie had tried to 'hook me up,' as she called it, more than once, and the poor men were ones she found at society events. I'm not sure what she promised them when they came to dinner, but—given their expressions when presented with a younger, less-fashionable and less-wealthy alternative presented to them—it wasn't me.

"What are you cooking?" I asked Hattie.

She patted my arm and smiled as she walked past. "Does it matter, dear?"

Not at all. I finished the last bite of cookie, thanked her, and went to measure my books to compare to Hattie's measurements.

———

My brother Ryan and his wife Sara live up in Plano, a fairly innocuous suburb north of Dallas. Our father had lived with them until recently, when we helped him move to an assisted living and memory care facility a mile or so from their house. He has Alzheimer's disease, and needed more care than Ryan and Sara could give him. The move meant we'd be further consolidating the furniture and other things we had in storage with what we'd kept out for him. We'd started going through the families' joint belongings after my grandmother's death a few years ago when we cleaned out the farmhouse up near Honey Grove. None of the three of us liked to do anything permanent with my grandmother's carefully hoarded furniture and collectibles. We'd stored a lot of items in one of the barns up on the farm, and, when he'd moved in with Ryan and Sara, we put most of my dad's things in a small storage unit not too far from their house. Ryan let me know last week when my dad moved to Landover Avenue that the lease expiration was coming up on the storage unit, and they planned to spend spring break next month getting ready to sell the extra items.

I'm not a nostalgic person. I spent most of my young life surrounded by family antiques with attached stories, which is how my unromantic grandmother connected herself to her ancestors. She kept genealogy records and pictures of dead people, and my memories of childhood were mixed up with stories I heard her tell too many times of people and places and things. For years, I had a distinct memory of learning to sew at five years of age on the black iron Singer sewing machine in the guest bedroom—even though it hasn't worked for years—until my brother and father both finally convinced me that it was a story my grandmother told about *her* childhood.

The apartment I lived in now was very small—really two rooms and a bathroom, with very little room for furniture or knick-knacks, so I didn't have much. Or at least that's what I told myself. I really wasn't someone who felt a connection to people through *things*. I looked around the main room, which was sort of a combined living room, dining room, and kitchen. There was a small navy sofa—maybe a love seat, when it came down to it—and my grandmother's old rocker, a gracious brocade and wood piece that made me feel good when I sat in it. I did that now, stroking my hands down the wooden arms that curved into the necks of carved swans, their heads lowered until their beaks met their bodies. I was struck with a memory: did my mother rock me in this chair? The mental picture was faint and tantalizing, like the scent of perfume that lingers in a room when someone passes through. I concentrated on it, but the memory was gone, and I felt queasy and uncomfortable in the void left behind.

I shook it off. I needed to think about books for the office, so I stood in front of my one tiny bookcase, stuffed full of law books and nonfiction hardbacks I kept meaning to read, with a few often-read paperback romances and dog-eared mysteries stuffed into the crevices in between. There were two boxes of my books in Ryan's garage I wanted to get Sunday when I was up at the farm, and I might have to make a trip over to R&D Booksellers for some new-old books. Just the thought buoyed my spirits.

I spent a couple of hours prepping for my meeting the next day with Tom Terry and Carla Gutierrez of Handlebar Properties, the company that owned the small apartment building giving rise to my current most-troublesome case. An older woman named Sophia Barnstead had refused to pay her rent for three months running, and I'd successfully evicted her—only to find she'd appealed the writ granting the eviction, and we were bound for new eviction proceedings in Dallas county court in the coming month. When an eviction is appealed, you start from scratch, and this time she'd warned that she was going to be bringing up a lot of complaints she says she reported to management. Tom and Carla wanted to discuss next steps and the complaints, so I was meeting them for lunch tomorrow to talk about it.

I also looked up the house at issue in the Tarantino hearing set tomorrow afternoon. I felt restless, and I finally decided that was why. Starting something new was exciting, but it was also a bit nerve-wracking. I'd learned so many new things over the last year that I felt like I was back in high school trying to remember algebra equations for an exam.

According to the Dallas County Appraisal District records, the house located at 7224 Lakeway Circle was built in 1937. The deed had been transferred in 1980 from Jack O'Toole to the Estate of Jack O'Toole and then in 2015 to Trisha and Jules Tarantino. Last year's tax valuation was $1.4 million, just $100,000 higher than the purchase price in 2015. I whistled through my teeth. Tax valuations are notoriously low for renovated property. I wondered what the appraisals would look like now that the Tarantinos had spent money to renovate. I pulled the deed records from the Dallas county clerk's office and found they'd taken out a bank loan to finance the $1.3 million purchase, and a second loan from another lender for $1.5 million for the renovations.

I downloaded the documents for use later if I needed them and opened a blank document to make notes while I processed the facts. *Wow*. Almost three million dollars for an old house. I couldn't even imagine what that would be like. Was there silk on the walls? A gold toilet? I snickered. The lives of the rich and powerful always made me laugh. You'd think everyone put their pants on the same way—or peed the same way—but maybe not.

I was still snickering at my own joke when my phone dinged with a text from my friend Melinda. Did I want tacos and a margarita? She'd had a date with a guy she met online, and she wanted to tell me about him, tacos on her. I considered: online dating stories with Melinda were always pretty funny, but in about three weeks, she'd be crying over the guy. I never knew what to say when the tears started. On the other hand, free tacos were always...free.

I hit *save* and grabbed my jacket as I headed out the door. As usual, I'd worry about the crying later.

CHAPTER THREE

It started raining during the night, an off-and-on spitting rain that just deepened the moderate cold we'd been experiencing. The nighttime temperatures were hovering above freezing, and it never got quite warm during the day. So much for spring. Every place I went, heaters were on, but it really wasn't cold enough for them, and it wasn't quite warm enough for air conditioning. I just left my thermostat switched to 'off' at this time of year and hoped for the best.

Calls from clients looking for the answers to questions they hadn't even asked yet kept me hopping past noon, and, when I finally looked up at the time, I knew I was going to be late to lunch. This always served to make me fret, no matter how nice the client was. And Tom Terry was one of the nicest, even though he looked like the head of a television biker gang. You know, the guys who look really tough, with tattoos and muscles, but are a bit too clean and good-looking for a sleazy biker dude.

In reality, he had been a pretty heavy-duty biker in his younger years but saw an opportunity for a different way of life. He'd started a garage in east Dallas when his son was born back in the 1990s, settling down and curtailing real gang-like habits. That had morphed into a successful business called Handlebars that customized both street bikes and touring motorcycles, and I know Tom was still riding the best bikes available at that point. That ended a few years ago when his 17-year old son was killed in a motorcycle-car accident. As far as I know, Tom hasn't taken a ride on a motorcycle since then.

Life changed a lot for Tom after the accident. He and his wife divorced—amicably, they say—and he started looking for other places to put his money. According to him, the motorcycle customization business is pretty much recession-proof. People are either buying new bikes or fixing up the old ones they have, and Tom had cash and time. One of his employees who'd shown promise as a businessman became a partner in Handlebars, and Tom started investing in residential real estate after the recession, when so many properties came up for sale. I've never asked how he and Carla Gutierrez got to know each other, but it was an introduction from Carla's dad, the Tomas Gutierrez who works for Hattie and Shelton Shelters, that brought me into the mix.

Handlebar Properties, the residential real estate company that Tom founded eight years ago, buys and flips residential real estate. To make the money to do this, they keep some of the properties they renovate and rent them out in the thriving residential rental market of east Dallas. Tom's the money guy, while Carla has a real estate broker's license and decides what they buy and sell. They have a third partner, Greg Martinez, who's a construction whiz. I keep telling them they should have one of those house-flipping reality shows, but Tom would rather die than go on television.

For the most part, they've had a string of really good luck in the properties they've had. I've helped with some closings or filings or evictions when the tenant wouldn't pay rent or move out, but for the most part, everything has been positive. Eerily positive, you might say, given how crazy real estate can be sometimes. And Handlebar Properties is a well-run and successful company, which has given Tom the idea he might go ahead and sell most of Handlebars—the motorcycle shop—to his partner, while he concentrates happily on the real estate company.

Until the *issue* that is Sophia Barnstead arose.

I met Tom and Carla for a late lunch at a salad place not too far from my apartment—not my choice, I might add. While I will eat salads, they're not my favorite thing. Oh, I like them with a lot of stuff on top, but true health nuts like Tom frown on all the dressing and croutons and toppings that make lettuce taste good to me. Sure enough, when he saw the bowl the server put down in front of me, he started clucking like an old hen. I held up a hand to stop him before he really got going.

"Isn't it enough there's green underneath all this?" I asked him.

Carla leaned over. "It's never enough for Tom." Her own salad bowl had fried chicken pieces and ranch dressing, so I didn't feel too bad.

Tom forked up a piece of rare ahi tuna and some kind of spiky green and pointed it at me. "This is what you should be eating, Lacey. Eat enough of this, and you'll live forever."

I poured the whole ramekin of honey mustard dressing onto the salad and stirred the chicken, chopped boiled egg, and avocado into the lettuce to mix it all up, looking at Tom with a raised eyebrow—the unbruised right one—as I did so. "I'd think the preservatives in my food would keep me around long after all *you* health nuts are gone." Carla snickered.

Tom saw the scar bisecting my left eyebrow and frowned again. "What happened to you?"

I smoothed the eyebrow a little self-consciously. "I got mugged and crashed into a brick wall." He kept frowning, so I elaborated. "I'm fine. I'll just have a barely-noticeable scar."

Carla leaned over to look, then shrugged. "I've got a great plastic surgeon you could talk to." She took a bite of salad. "He's amazing with scars, I've heard. Does great stuff with Botox, too."

I really doubted Carla, who was an absolutely gorgeous woman with long, shiny black hair and liquid brown eyes, needed Botox or plastic surgery, and I said so. She shrugged again and winked at me. "I keep my options open, Lace."

We ate for a few minutes and exchanged a bit of small talk, but I could see Tom getting antsy. I finally took pity on him and started the Barnstead conversation by going into detail about the two hearings we'd had in front of Justice Laughlin in the last couple of weeks. The elderly judge was a stickler for protocol and procedure, and he had not appreciated Ms. Barnstead's ignorance of either. In the end, though, all that mattered was that she was subject to a lease and required to pay rent, and she hadn't paid her rent for three months. He'd issued the writ of possession for the apartment to Handlebar Properties.

"I just don't get it," Tom interrupted. "How can she appeal it and stay in the apartment without paying rent?"

"She can't," I explained. "She has to pay the rent into the registry of the Court while the case is pending. She's filed the case *in forma pauperis*—or as a pauper—so she avoided paying a bond, but she has to pay rent, or the appeal gets dismissed."

Carla impatiently pushed her salad aside. "We know she can afford the rent. We were careful to make sure her social security payment would more than cover the rent when she applied."

Tom nodded. "We were considering getting Section 8 approval for that property, but we hadn't decided when she applied. We just needed to get some people in there to pay rent so we could make the loan payments." Section 8 housing is rental housing where the government pays a portion of the rent payments for low income tenants, and the tenant makes up the balance. "We've got some renovations to do there, and we thought we'd do them as the tenants left, one apartment at a time. Sophia Barnstead was the first tenant in there."

"So...what about her complaints?" Ms. Barnstead had told the judge the place was a 'shithole,' an earthy expletive Justice Laughlin had not appreciated in his courtroom.

Carla rolled her eyes as she sipped her iced tea through a straw. "She makes a complaint about once a week or so. The water heater isn't heating her water hot enough, now it's too hot. The air conditioning isn't cold enough, then she's cold and wants the heat on—in July." She shook her head and dabbed at her lips with a paper napkin, careful not to smudge the dark red lipstick she'd reapplied after finishing her salad. "Sometimes it's something legitimate—this is a 1950s duplex, after all—but most of the time it's just her unhappiness with her situation." At my look, she clarified. "She's old, she's in ill health, and her children can't stand to be around her."

Tom chimed in with a growl. "At some point, she got my cell phone number. I get a voicemail from her about once a week calling me a 'slumlord' and telling me that I'm going to hell for tormenting her." He'd finished his salad, and he nodded when the server came to clear the table. I was still making my way through all the green stuff at the bottom, but I let her take mine as well, a little relieved not to have to forage anymore.

I started digging in my bag for my pad and found Gerard's pen. "Are her complaints valid?" Tom didn't immediately speak, and I looked up from unscrewing the cap to look first at him and then at Carla. They both avoided my eyes. "What?"

Carla looked over at Tom and then sighed. "We've been hoping she'd just move out." She gave a shrug. "You know, if the situation was bad enough. We're getting ready to do some reno over there, but we didn't want to make the place more attractive."

Well, this wasn't good news. "You couldn't wait till her lease expired? Isn't that in May?"

Tom spoke up. "When all this started, she'd just renewed last year." He frowned, a truly beetle-browed glare, and scratched his elbow through his long-sleeved Metallica t-shirt. "The first year, she'd seemed okay, maybe somewhat needy, but not really a problem. Then the other tenants started leaving, and we got this current group in. It's like she has an audience. None of them seem to want to move on."

I'd seen that audience in the courtroom last week: two very old ladies and an equally old man. I'd thought of them as her 'chorus,' since she spoke to them or about them for much of the hearing. They'd nodded whenever she did, egging her on. Justice Laughlin had not been amused.

Carla leaned forward, taking the lead as always, speaking in a low voice. "What's the bottom line here, Lacey? What's it going to take to get her out? We've got plans for that property." She sat back, looking annoyed.

I tilted my head. There seemed to be more here. "What are the plans?" I looked over at Tom, who was looking out the window. "Tom?"

Carla answered instead. "Lacey, the property that quadruplex is sitting on is a gold mine. Just the lot is worth over a million now. We haven't decided whether to sell it or build some really nice town-homes on there and either rent or sell them. But we have a lender willing to get the process started right now, and interest rates are due to climb higher. We need to get that loan locked in *now*." She inhaled deeply and looked at Tom, who was still looking out the window. "Normally, it wouldn't be a problem to get the loan approved early. But to get a loan while the tenants are still there will require them to sign estoppels saying they have no pending claims or issues with the property." She looked at me and raised her perfectly-arched eyebrows. "See the problem now?"

———

I DID SEE THE PROBLEM. IT WAS HAPPENING ALL OVER MY neighborhood and others in east Dallas. Call it gentrification or renaissance or reclamation, but older houses were being torn down and new ones put up left and right. The Dallas residential real estate market was hot, and homeowners with old thousand-square-foot wooden-frame houses were able to sell their properties for far more than the market value. Some people argued they were forced to sell, since their property values had skyrocketed, or worse, the land value increased quickly, while the structural value continued to decrease. If you sell your house, you can do all right; but if you want to keep it, your property taxes will continue to go up until you can't afford to. Try to get a loan to renovate the structure, and you find out the appraised value of the house itself won't support a loan. Take your money and move, and you may not be able to qualify for another loan somewhere else. Renters—like the elderly or low-income working families—may be forced out when their landlords see profit potential in selling the properties to get in on the upswing in prices. For investment property owners, it was a no-brainer: sell when the market is ready to pay top dollar.

It wasn't a popular topic in conversation unless you're the one developing property. As I told Tom and Carla as we walked to our cars, I was just hoping Sophia Barnstead didn't get wind of their plans, or she might get press coverage for her complaints that we really didn't need.

I'd never had an eviction appealed before, so I offered to step aside if Tom and Carla thought they needed someone more experienced. Tom waved the offer away. I encouraged them to do everything they could to fix the legitimate problems the property had—doing so was an obligation under the tenant leases. I also wanted access to the entire client file, including all her complaints. Tom promised to put them into our shared e-file, and then suggested I meet them next week to talk to the other tenants without Sophia Barnstead there, which I thought might not be the best idea, given Sophia's closeness with her chorus. But sometimes the client is right.

I checked the time as I headed downtown to the court and then looked at my reflection in the visor's mirror. Carla had noticed that I was dressed up a bit, and when I told her I had a hearing that afternoon, she insisted on loaning me a scarf she had in her car and whisking my cheeks with a bit of powder stuff to even out the fading bruises on my left cheekbone, showing me how the matte powder covered the bluish tint completely. I had to admit that I looked a bit more even, and the silky blue scarf did make my gray eyes look a bit bluer—was that a good thing, or not? I flipped the visor back up and determined not to think about it. I had 20 minutes to get there and park before I needed to meet Karan and worrying about makeup and scarves was distracting.

———

I MADE IT TO THE COURTHOUSE WITH TEN MINUTES TO SPARE—A record time, given that it had started misting, and Dallas drivers can't drive in the rain. I made sure to protect Carla's scarf as I dashed across the plaza, which gave me enough time to take the three escalators to the courtroom floor rather than ride the elevator. At just before 4 pm on Friday, the courthouse was practically empty, with no jurors thronging the halls and most lawyers preferring not to set hearings this close to the weekend if they could avoid it. Generally, the only hearings set at this time were ones that are set short—that is, with only the minimum three-day notice required—or temporary restraining order hearings that only require two-hour notice to opposing counsel.

Karan was already there, pacing outside the courtroom, phone to her ear. I could tell by my side of the conversation that she was talking to Trisha, and things were tense.

"Trisha, we cannot ask the court to wait. I've told you, neither you nor Jules will be asked to testify today, so the court won't hold the hearing for you." She paused, listening. Even from a few feet away, I could hear Trisha squawking. Karan cut her off. "You've got 10 minutes. Concentrate on driving instead of arguing and get here. I'll see you then." She disconnected, even though Trisha was still talking.

I gawked. "Aren't you afraid she'll get mad at you and fire you?" I was only half joking. I had yet to be even a tiny bit rude to my clients.

Karan rolled her eyes as she put her phone on silent. "I should be so lucky." Before she tucked the phone away, I could see the 'ringing' screen with Trisha Tarantino's name. "How are you feeling?"

I smiled, trying to look brave. "I'm good." She continued to look at me, and I wondered if I had the green stuff from lunch in my teeth. I ran my tongue over my front teeth to be sure before speaking again. "What?"

"Lacey, it's going to be a pretty messy and heated hearing. I'm not sure what's up, but Jules and his lawyer brought a guy with him that I think they're going to proffer as receiver in place of you." She paced beside one of the couches outside the courtroom, but I just watched her walk. "I don't know him, but I suspect he's a banker or someone who can give Jules an advantage over Trisha."

Was she warning me off, or egging me on? "Do you want me to step out of the running?"

"No, not at all. Just wanted you to be ready." She checked the clock on the wall. "Okay, let's go in."

We walked into the courtroom where two lawyers I didn't know stood at the wide, wooden raised desk we call the judge's bench, talking to each other in low voices. Off to the side, the court's bailiff was talking to a short, nattily-dressed man Karan told me was Cliff Clark, the attorney for Jules Tarantino, while a tall, dark-headed man I presumed was Jules Tarantino was seated on the left side of the gallery, mostly blocking my view of the man sitting beside him. Their heads were together as they spoke quietly.

Karan went to the bailiff's desk to check in, and I moved into the gallery on the right side to sit behind the plaintiff's table, next to where the jury would sit if they were in session. I felt something nudge my brain, and then a prickle started at the back of my neck. I turned to look at Jules again, craning my head to see around him. The bailiff saw the door from the judge's chambers begin to open, and he called out, "All rise!"

I stood, watching Jules and the man beside him, the prickling on the back of my neck becoming a gnawing itch. It was Rob Gerard.

CHAPTER FOUR

I could not decide how to feel about Rob Gerard. Given that he was the white-collar defense attorney who represented my former boss and tried to make the jury think my whistleblower complaint had been the result of an unconsummated crush, the fact that I still speak to him is pretty gracious on my part. At least, I think so.

The case we had until last week threw us together, and that was completely my fault. I'd gone to him for help when I was asked to defend a young man wrongfully accused of murder, but—instead of just taking the case and leaving me out of it—Gerard had used me as a sort of associate to do research and interviews. We found the real killer, and that was gratifying, but spending time with Gerard wasn't really comfortable. I knew the basic public facts about him— longtime criminal attorney that had started as a Dallas assistant district attorney and then moved to a defense firm after three years, mid-40s and divorced—but that was about it. He's an enigma, and I really don't like mysteries. Okay, I like to read them, just not *live* them.

Even worse, for a long time, I blamed Gerard for everything that happened after I filed my whistleblower complaint—the depositions where I was grilled for hours, the long, drawn-out trials when my motives were questioned, and my inability to get a job immediately after the trials ended, all capped with my relative poverty when my savings ran out. I would dream of his voice asking me *why, why, why,* and I usually had no answer. Add in that I had a crazy tingle every time he and I met and, well, you can probably understand why seeing him in the middle of all this might not be a good thing.

As I looked across the courtroom to where he stood next to Jules Tarantino, all of that came rushing back, and so did the nausea that used to affect me when I was in the midst of the whistleblower trials. Our eyes met, and only the fact that he looked as shocked as I felt— well, that and the judge coming into the courtroom—kept me from running out. But he did look surprised to see me, and that fact amused me enough to keep me standing there.

Judge Hernandez told us all to be seated, and I could see Gerard and Jules speaking furiously before Cliff Clark rejoined them, and then the three of them hustled out of the courtroom. Karan watched them leave as she walked back over to me. The judge was busy dealing with the two attorneys at his bench, so she kept her voice down as she spoke to me.

"What was that about?"

I shook my head. I had an idea, but I didn't want to speculate. I did want information, though. "Where did Jules go to law school?"

She stared out the little window in the door to the lobby. "UT Austin. With Trisha. Why?" She looked back to me. "What are you thinking?" I started to shake my head, but she frowned. "Lacey, dish it. What's going on?"

"That's Rob Gerard. You know, the criminal defense attorney." She started to shake her head, so I finished in a low voice. "I think he and Jules went to law school together. Jules is what—45?" She nodded. "So is Gerard. I think Gerard's agreed to be the receiver."

We both turned to look through the narrow window, where we could see the three men talking, each of them gesturing vigorously. Karan kept her eyes on them and her voice quiet. "And Rob Gerard is...?"

"He represented Bill Stephenson." I looked at Karan, to see if she got it. She did.

"Oh, shit."

———

It didn't take Judge Hernandez long to deal with the two attorneys in the matter preceding our hearing, but it was time enough to allow Trisha Tarantino to sweep in, her leopard-print coat billowing around her, her black Louboutins stabbing the carpet between the pews comprising the gallery. She was a tall redhead, her hair curling in long, loose waves that looked complicated to me. Her eyes were the usual green you see on some redheads, but her expertly-applied makeup made them seem large and luminous.

She knew enough to keep quiet, but her voice still seemed loud in the courtroom when she whispered. "What is Rob Gerard doing here?"

Karan shushed her, and then said quietly, "You know him?"

"Of course, I know him. He and Jules have been friends since college." She turned to me and was a bit more gracious. "You must be Lacey." She proffered her hand. "Trisha Tarantino. Nice to meet you." She turned back to Karan, and her voice rose. "So, I'll ask again: What is Rob Gerard doing here?"

I felt, rather than saw, the judge and bailiff looking our way. We couldn't really go outside right then, with the hearing before us wrapping up. Karan leaned in close to Trisha. "I don't know, Trish. But if you don't keep your voice down, we're going to piss the judge off before we ever get in front of him."

Trisha stiffened, clearly offended by Karan's tone. She whispered tersely. "I don't like this. Rob's an attorney, a litigator, and he's been Jules's best friend forever. There's no telling what he might do."

Oh, I could tell some stories about what he might do, but I wasn't going to. I did know one thing. Rob Gerard might be a skillful litigator, but I could attest that he was an honest man. The knot in my stomach eased as I recognized that this was true.

Jules and his attorney came in, followed by Gerard, who didn't look in my direction. I'd seen him angry a few times, though, and I could tell by his frozen, hard face that he was beyond livid.

The judge finished up with the attorneys at his bench and excused them from the courtroom. "Tarantino versus Tarantino," he said, and I thought I heard a bit of resignation tinged with exasperation. Judge Hernandez was a really good judge, fairly young and even-tempered with a sense of humor, which I think you'd have to possess to work with family court cases. He'd been the judge who'd appointed me as receiver in the case last year, but I doubt he remembered me.

Karan and Cliff Clark moved forward to the counsel tables and opened the folders they had with them, taking a few moments to get documents set up. The judge checked some things on his computer screen and then faced forward, waiting. When both attorneys looked up at him, he nodded to Karan.

"Counsel, this is your motion. Begin."

Karan spent a few minutes outlining the history of the case so far, detailing some of the problems the Tarantinos had in working through the issues of their divorce. They'd attempted to start what's called a 'collaborative divorce,' where the couple utilizes some common professionals and tries to work through the issues of the divorce together, but that failed spectacularly when Trisha threw a full glass of water in Jules' direction in a joint session (she'd missed). They'd tried one mediation session, where the spouses are split up into separate rooms with their attorneys, and a neutral third party goes in and out of the separate rooms trying to get them to agree on specific terms. That had gone downhill when Jules came into Trisha's room to shout at her for showing the mediator pictures of him kissing another woman. They'd ended the day arguing in the hallway between the rooms, with the mediator going into his office and shutting the door.

Both wanted the house they were renovating, both wanted everything of value from inside, and neither wanted the other one to have it even if they themselves couldn't. Karan described this situation to the court, who summed up her presentation: "So you want the receiver to split the baby," in a reference to the famous story of Solomon in the Bible.

Karan nodded. "Your honor, Petitioner has filed this motion and proposes real estate attorney Lacey Benedict as the receiver to list the property with an appropriate real estate broker, oversee any negotiations for the property and the non-personal items inside, and bring any contracts for sale to this court for approval."

The judge nodded. "Fairly standard." He turned to Cliff Clark with a skeptical expression. "I suspect Respondent has an objection?"

Cliff, a tanned and fit man in his sixties with a pompadour of silvery blond hair, nodded as he rose, smoothing his silk tie down and buttoning his jacket. "Several, your honor. First, my client doesn't believe a receiver is merited in this case." He indicated Jules, who sat a row behind the divider, with a wide hand motion that revealed a gleaming gold watch on his wrist. I could tell from his gestures and expression that Clark was a showman, one of the older, more theatrical attorneys who believed more in their powers of persuasion than in procedure, research, and case law. Jules nodded soberly as the judge looked at him. Clark continued his argument. "Respondent believes that, if the couple could but agree on the broker to list the property, they could set this process on its way. The parties would, of course, have to work together." He spread his hands, all genial bewilderment and television-preacherly *bonhomie*. "Respondent cannot comprehend how Petitioner and Respondent could fail to agree on something as simple as this."

Beside me, I felt Trisha stir. Before I could look at her, however, Cliff continued, congeniality leaking from every pore. "In fact, I have with me today a draft agreed motion appointing a real estate broker, which I could file at this very moment, if Petitioner would but agree." He passed a copy of a document to Karan, who looked only at the first page before shaking her head.

"Your honor, I don't think this broker would be agreeable to Petitioner."

The judge looked at her over his reading glasses. "You don't want to run it by her?"

Karan shook her head again. "I'm pretty certain this won't work, your honor." Trisha moved again, her coat and something crinkly rustling together. The judge heard the noise and looked her way, as did I. Trisha was puffing—there was no other way to say it—and her face was alarmingly red. Karan turned around, and Trisha rose to meet her at the bar.

"It's not..." she started. Karan nodded, and Trisha turned toward Jules and—I'm not kidding—she hissed at him.

Jules stood, and for a moment, I thought I might have to either step in, or more likely, step back out of the line of fire, but Gerard reached a hand up to Jules's arm. Jules turned away and sat down abruptly, and, when Clark looked back at him, he shook his head.

Cliff turned back to the court and shook his head sorrowfully. "It seems that solution isn't amenable to Petitioner." He sighed theatrically. "It's a shame that Petitioner cannot be reasonable about this when Respondent makes a suggestion that could resolve this matter, but we've come to expect this level of intransigence."

Trisha puffed up again, and I think she muttered "reason this" under her breath, but she sat down heavily beside me, her right leg crossing sharply over her left, her spike heel almost jabbing me in the leg. I moved it out of the way.

The judge looked back at Cliff, and I thought I could see a bit of annoyance on his face. "Counsel, do you have any *actual* objections before I rule on this matter?"

Cliff put his sorrowful expression on again. "We do, your honor." He looked back to the gallery again, but this time he looked at me, and my stomach began to twist. "I'm afraid we cannot agree to Ms. Benedict as receiver."

Judge Hernandez looked at us over his half-glasses, from me to Karan to Cliff Clark and back to me again. "Counsel, sidebar."

———

APPOINTMENT OF A RECEIVER IS PROVIDED FOR BY TEXAS statute. A receiver is put in place for a specific reason and is answerable to the court for his or her actions. He or she has no power to do anything that isn't included in the Order Appointing Receiver, and the procedure is pretty simple. When a party files a motion asking the court to appoint a receiver, the judge holds a hearing to determine if a receiver is warranted by the situation—something that's left to the discretion of the individual judge. Then, the judge gets to decide who will be appointed, whether it's someone suggested by the party filing the Motion for Appointment of Receiver, or someone else the judge thinks is appropriate, including a nominee of the other party. Once the receiver is appointed, he or she swears an oath and then posts a bond in an amount the court decides. It's a straightforward procedure, unless no one in the courtroom is agreeing to anything at all. And then it's a nightmare, like the one I was living in at that moment.

I watched Karan and Cliff huddle with Judge Hernandez at the side of the judge's bench, each of them at one time or another looking in my direction. They spoke in whispers, and next to me, Trisha shifted in her seat, clearly straining to hear and, every few minutes, sending a withering look across the aisle at Jules. I kept my head still, facing the front, determined not to look to the left where Jules and Gerard sat. Truly, I felt frozen, much as I had during the whistleblower trials, when remarks about me from the witness stand would cause jury members to look my way as I sat in the gallery.

But as I sat there, ice water chilling my veins, I was convinced more than ever that I had changed, that I was no longer that young girl who was so terrified of what her life would be like when there was no one to tell her how to live or practice law, no one to judge whether she had succeeded or failed. I won't say it was a lightning strike of an epiphany because the realization had been dawning for a while, aided in part by the man sitting a few feet to my left. I still wasn't too sure how to feel about Gerard, but I was getting over my anger at him. I moved my feet and began to thaw.

And then I was called by the judge to come to the witness box.

The judge explained the change in procedure. "Ms. Benedict, receivership hearings aren't really evidentiary hearings, but Mr. Clark has questioned your ability to function as receiver, and I'd like to hear from you. Because you're not counsel in this matter, I need to swear you in. Do you understand?"

I did. The ice had started to form again, but this time it was accompanied by a slow burn in my belly as I walked toward the bench. I was sworn in, and for the first time in more than five years, I was back on the witness stand.

———

THEY'D AGREED ON A PROCESS FOR THIS, CLIFF AND KARAN AND the judge. Karan started first after the judge asked me to swear to testify truthfully, and I swore I would.

"Ms. Benedict, could you state your name and occupation for the record?"

"Lacey Benedict, and I'm an attorney, licensed in the state of Texas."

"And for whom do you work, and for how long?"

"I have my own firm, The Benedict Firm." I swallowed. "I've worked for myself since 2014."

"Where did you work before you opened your own firm?"

I breathed in and out steadily, calming myself, a trick I'd learned not too long ago. "I worked for Stephenson and Associates.

I was an associate for Bill Stephenson. Before that, I was in law school."

"You went to work for Mr. Stephenson directly after law school?"

"Yes."

"What is the focus of your law firm now?"

I felt myself relaxing just a bit. "I mostly practice real estate law now. Some of it deals with transactions, and some of it is litigation. I have a few non-real estate matters, such as collections or other financial transaction work."

"Have you been a receiver before?"

"Yes. Last year, this court appointed me a receiver in a divorce case." I snuck a look at Judge Hernandez, who regarded me in a grave but not unfriendly way.

"And what did that matter entail?"

"I engaged a real estate agent, oversaw negotiations, inspection, and appraisal, and brought an offer to the Court to approve before signing a contract and monitoring the process through closing. I was then discharged by the Court." There. That was a successful receivership and resolution. Let them poke holes in that.

Karan smiled at me, but her eyes looked anxious. "Pass the witness."

Cliff Clark stood and straightened his papers before looking up, his eyes on me as he smoothed his tie down and buttoned his jacket again—a ritual of his, I guess. I felt the ice tingle in my fingertips. "Ms. Benedict, you mentioned you had worked for Bill Stephenson before opening your own firm." He smiled at me, a snake's smile, self-satisfied and smug. "What were the circumstances surrounding the ending of your employment with Bill Stephenson?"

I froze, staring at Clark, willing myself not to look past him and slightly to the right, where Rob Gerard sat next to Jules Tarantino. What was this about? I swallowed over the lump that had formed in my throat and answered him.

"I left Stephenson and Associates when the firm came under

investigation for securities fraud and other criminal violations." I stared back at him.

He raised his eyebrows as his smile twisted nastily. "And why did the firm come under such an investigation?"

I raised mine in response, my left eyebrow tingling. "I reported the firm to the authorities."

His smile slipped away as he dove in for the kill. "And in doing so, you violated client confidentiality and privilege, did you not?"

My gut clenched, and I couldn't help myself. I looked at Gerard, who was staring back at me, his face grim and closed. Was he where Clark had gotten this information about the case? Most of the case pleadings had been sealed to protect the confidential information of the innocent investors.

I looked back at Clark. "Federal securities law trumps state ethics rules." I'd told myself that phrase so often that it barely made sense in my head anymore, like a word you've re-written too many times. I breathed in and out, in and out.

"You didn't exactly answer my question, Ms. Benedict. Did you or did you not violate client confidentiality and attorney-client privilege when you reported Mr. Stephenson to the authorities?" He leaned forward, his hands on the table on either side of his file. He seemed angry, his nostrils flaring and his eyes wide. His expression sparked something in my brain, and I seized on the issue to solve, my mind spinning. *Why was he so angry?*

I felt a calmness come over me in the face of his anger, and I breathed in and out once before answering. "I suppose that I did, Mr. Clark. When I saw the investors of Bill Stephenson's clients being harmed during securities transactions, I reported Mr. Stephenson and his clients to the authorities, and I declined to assist Bill Stephenson and his clients in fraudulent activity." I looked at Judge Hernandez, who was still regarding me with very little expression. "Everything I did fell under exceptions to confidentiality and privilege, and a state bar ethics complaint was resolved for that reason."

"But the fact remains that you violated both of them to draw attention to yourself and what you *believed* was illegal activity, didn't you?" I looked back at Clark, whose face was reddening, and out of the corner of my eye, saw Karan rise to her feet. "And Bill Stephenson wasn't convicted of *any crimes*, was he, Ms. Benedict?" The words were an angry staccato, the tone was triumphant, the question thundering in the almost-empty courtroom.

Karan spoke softly but firmly in the echoes of Clark's question. "Objection, your honor, relevance. While Petitioner agreed to allow Ms. Benedict to answer questions regarding her suitability as a receiver, we've veered far off topic here."

Clark turned to partially face Karan, his eyes hot and angry, his left forefinger pointing in my direction as he spoke about me as if I wasn't there. "Her honesty *is* relevant. She'll be required to handle confidential information of Petitioner and Respondent, and to perform tasks for their benefit in a fiduciary capacity. Respondent does not believe she is a suitable candidate." He turned back to face Judge Hernandez, his voice rising to his own personal crescendo. "Respondent would propose attorney Robert Gerard as receiver, and we have a draft Motion to Appoint Receiver ready to file."

I saw Gerard's head shake slightly as he turned to Jules Tarantino, and I felt my face flame. Was that what this was all about? How could Gerard let Clark use me this way?

Judge Hernandez spoke quietly, and I realized he didn't need to shout to make himself heard. "Mr. Clark, Ms. Sullivan, be seated." He cleared his throat as they complied, and I turned my head slightly to see him, my neck feeling as though the vertebrae had been welded together. "Petitioner's objection is sustained. Mr. Clark, this line of questioning is neither relevant, nor is it what the court agreed to allow Respondent." Cliff Clark started to stand, but the judge waved him down with a slight motion of his hand. "I've heard enough, Mr. Clark. While Mr. Gerard is an able and respected attorney, Ms. Benedict is as well. She's served this Court before, and I think her honesty and willingness to sacrifice her own livelihood to bring an end to criminal activities speaks well of her integrity, not the opposite." I felt my hands clench and realized my fingers were stiffly intertwined. I eased them apart.

"Ms. Benedict, raise your hand please." I faced him fully and raised my right hand, straightening the fingers with effort. "Do you swear to serve this Court as receiver, faithfully discharging your duties as receiver and implementing the orders of the Court?"

"I do, your honor."

"Thank you, Ms. Benedict. Ms. Sullivan, do you have an Order for me?" Karan stepped up to hand the judge a document, giving Cliff Clark and me a copy as well. We walked through the Order Appointing Receiver with Clark objecting occasionally, and the judge making a few notations and then signing at the end. I really couldn't hear or see a thing. There was a roaring in my ears that blocked out much of the sound, and my eyes felt like they were on fire.

The judge excused us all, and I walked past Clark, Jules Taran-tino, and Rob Gerard, straight out of the courtroom and to the bath-room, followed by Karan and Trisha. I splashed cold water on my face as Karan watched me worriedly, Trisha twittering angrily in the background. Karan finally ground out, "Trisha, stop talking," and, blessedly, Trisha stopped talking.

Karan put a hand on my shoulder. "Are you all right?"

I nodded. "Just a bit of an unexpected shock."

Trisha stepped over to look at me. "Where did all that come from?"

I shrugged. "Rob Gerard represented my old boss in all that stuff. I guess he told Jules and Clark." I struggled to breathe deeply. The bathroom seemed really crowded.

Trisha gawked. "Rob? I can't believe it! Of all the people...he's probably the most honest and nice of all of Jules's friends." She snorted. "Not that it's much of a contest." She dug in her purse for lipstick and leaned in to the mirror to apply the vivid shade that matched the maroon silk blouse under her black suit, still talking. She was a gorgeous, tall woman who wore the deep color well. Karan and

I stood there as she chattered on. "He and Jules have stayed friends all these years, and I thought Rob was a steadying influence on Jules." She wound the lipstick back down and tucked it into her purse. Watching her, I had vague memory of my mother putting on lipstick when I was very small. She'd put a folded tissue between her lips afterwards, I guess to get some of the color off, and then she'd give me the tissue. I'd unfold it, and there would be her mouth on the tissue, as vividly colored as my crayons, and I'd try to open my mouth wide to match hers, a kiss I rarely received from her. Trisha didn't do the tissue thing, I noticed numbly.

I realized she'd stopped talking, and she and Karan were looking at me with a bit of worry in their eyes. I felt tired, and I knew what I wanted. "I'm going home."

Karan patted my shoulder. "Let's file the oath and bond, and then meet next week to talk about it all." I nodded, and we all went out in the hall to the elevators, where only Rob Gerard stood waiting. Trisha clicked her tongue at him, and then went over to hug him. Karan pressed the elevator button, and she and I stood there, facing the doors and not speaking, as Trisha and Gerard talked behind us. When the doors opened, we stepped in and Trisha joined us, facing the opening as you do, waiting the interminable moments for the doors to close. Gerard stood there, his hands in his pants pockets, looking at me.

Trisha continued to chatter, but then stopped and looked first at me and then Gerard. "Aren't you coming?" she asked him.

He continued to look at me, and I stared back at him with my chin held high, daring him to say something. He didn't. He just shook his head slightly, and then the doors closed with him on the other side.

CHAPTER FIVE

FRIDAY, FEBRUARY 22 (CONTINUED)

I posted the cash bond required, and we got a couple of certified copies of the executed Order, and then I must have driven home. I know I got there, and my car was outside, but I had no memory of the drive. I was sitting on my couch when I realized I was home. I'd skipped stopping off at the grocery store—which was unfortunate, since I still had nothing to eat in my apartment—and I was in one piece.

Well, I felt a bit shell-shocked. You know how you can be sitting there thinking, and another part of you is sitting off to one side, screaming internally? That was me in that moment.

Finally, the screaming part got to me, and I stood up and stretched, my muscles aching from holding myself so tightly. I began to pace the small room, my mind replaying the hearing, Cliff Clark's questioning, and my feeble answers. How dare he? How dare he twist the fraud committed by Bill Stephenson and his clients into something that deserved protecting with privilege? How dare he try to make me the villain? And how dare Rob Gerard give him the ammunition to fire in my direction?

I paced from my couch to my kitchen, examining my empty refrigerator, and then to my bathroom, noticing some soap scum in my shower. I checked under the sink and realized I needed cleaning supplies as well as food. I couldn't remember the last time I'd gone to the store. My pacing took me to the front door, where I'd apparently stepped over my mail as I came in. I picked up the small stack and went to the recycle bin, absent-mindedly sorting through the catalogs, flyers, and envelopes, and flipping the junk mail in. I stopped at a white envelope with The Gerard Firm on the return end. What the...?

I slid a finger under the flap and then stopped, my heart pounding. Inside was a check, made out to me, with 'Parrish Defense' on the information line. I pulled it out and, as I saw the five figures in the amount box, my head joined my heart in the drum section. An entry on the check stub showed the total amount of hours I'd reported to Gerard a couple of weeks ago—with 40 more hours added—when we were in the middle of representing Todd Parrish. I'd tried to refer Todd and his grandparents to Gerard, but instead, Gerard had guided me in doing the research and investigation myself. We identified the killer and passed the information on to the district attorney, who'd dropped the charges against Todd a few days ago. And his grandparents had told me that Gerard had returned their *entire* retainer.

So, what was this? A pity payment? I went to my bag and dug for my phone to call Gerard and give him a piece of my mind. It was still on silent from the courtroom, but I had several missed calls. One of them was Karan, with a voicemail I was sure was her checking up on me. Four were from Gerard, with only one voicemail. I selected it, and listened to Gerard's low, gravelly voice.

BENEDICT, CALL ME, PLEASE.

· · ·

THAT WAS IT? HIS GOOD FRIEND JULES AND HIS SMUG SNAKE OF a lawyer ambush me and malign me on the stand, and all I get is a 'call me?' My stomach burned. I checked the time. 5:50 pm. Gerard wouldn't be at his office this late on a Friday. I hesitated for a moment, and then I pulled up the browser and typed in Gerard's name and 'Lawther,' the street that circled White Rock Lake, where I knew Gerard lived. His address came up, and I swallowed hard. Did I dare?

I mentally punched myself. Of course, I dared! Didn't Gerard himself compare me to Don Quixote? I glanced at the framed art I'd received from him just yesterday, a small black and white lithograph of Picasso's famous *Don Quixote and Sancho Panza*, windmills whirling in the background. He'd called me a justice warrior last Sunday—how did that square with supplying his friend with information against me?

Before I could change my mind, I grabbed my keys and the check and headed out the door.

———

THE DRIVE TO GERARD'S WASN'T LONG ENOUGH TO GIVE ME TIME for second thoughts. In fact, it was just long enough to allow me to whip my righteous indignation into anger. He lived only ten minutes from me, right next to White Rock Lake, which is my favorite place to walk—a fact that seemed to make things inexplicably worse.

I scanned the house numbers for Gerard's address, and then I slowed down and simply gawked. I'd seen this house from the walking path across the street, and I'd wondered who lived there. It looked like three gleaming glass boxes had been dropped by a giant, landing in a fanned-out jumble, each layer jutting out for a gorgeous view of the water only a hundred feet away. The property itself was on a curve of the road, and a more traditional house would have faced only the trees directly across the street. Instead, the bottom layer was turned slightly to face the lake across the curve, and the floors above turned a little less, so that the topmost layer faced more of the trees at the side of the lot and had more privacy while still providing a view. The driveway led up to the left side, where a boxy garage set against the property line was attached to the house with a covered walkway. As I looked, small recessed lights came on above the windows in the house, shining brightly in the gathering twilight.

I parked in the graveled area in front and tucked my keys into my suit jacket pocket. A pair of doors were set into the bottom box, off-centered to greet the walkway from the garage and to keep a car from blocking the view of the house. The landscaping was modern and minimal and very low-maintenance, with ground-cover vines covering much of what yard there was. From where I stood, I could tell the lot itself was narrow and not very deep, and the placement of the house made the most of the space. There might be a yard in the back, but it wouldn't be very large. Clearly, this house was designed for someone who would enjoy the view and not much else about home ownership.

I walked up the stone-paved path, seeing myself in the reflection of the glass and belatedly realizing that I was still in my going-to-court clothes, Carla's once-beautiful scarf hanging limply around my neck. Any makeup that I'd had on was likely gone by now, and somewhere between the courthouse and home, I'd found a clip in my car and dragged my long hair up into a scraggly bun. I started to smooth the wisps hanging around my face, and then I realized anyone inside the house would see me preening and stopped.

I steeled myself and knocked sharply on the gleaming black-painted door, bruising my knuckles. I heard a dog begin to bark inside, and then Gerard opened the door. He'd had a chance to change clothes from court, and his faded blue jeans and soft gray-blue sweater made me ache for my own comfy jeans.

He didn't speak, just opened the door wider and stepped back to let me in. I took only a few steps before a large golden retriever bounded up to me, tail and tongue wagging. I held out a hand and she licked it, then slid her head underneath so I'd be rubbing the top of her head. I scratched behind her floppy ears and bent over to croon sweet doggie nothings for a moment—and to hide my flaming cheeks. Just her adoration and willingness to accept the caress comforted me.

When I looked up, the space and the view swamped me, and I fell in love. It was twilight outside, the cloudiness of the day lifting a bit over the lake. The view was to the east, and, though the moon was almost full and would rise later, a sliver of deep clear sky beneath the clouds on the horizon reflected darkly on the lake's surface. It was cold this evening, so most of the walkers were already gone, but a few hardy souls were bundled up and walking with their dogs in the gloom.

The view through the glass was the artwork in the room. No, that's not quite right. There was art on the walls, but to my mind, the glass wall facing the lake was the most beautiful piece. The floors were wide wooden planks burnished a deep golden brown, a huge deep fluffy rug in the center. The wall opposite the door was stone, huge jagged chunks of it, a large fireplace centering the wall. There was a fire, a real fire, burning there now, and part of a long, low sectional in tan suede faced it. The whole room was very modern, but it wasn't austere or uncomfortable—just the opposite. I wanted to lounge on the sofa and be warm.

Instead, I dug deep for the anger that had brought me there. I turned to see Gerard watching me examining his home, his hands in his jeans' pockets. The dog left me when I stopped petting her and went to Gerard, rubbing her nose on his leg, but he didn't look down.

I dug in my pocket for the check and held it up. "What is this?" With effort, I kept myself from hurling it at him.

He simply raised his dark eyebrows. The move infuriated me, but I held my tongue.

The dog nudged him again, and this time, he crouched down and stroked her golden head, ruffling her ears a bit. She looked up at him with adoration, and he smiled down at her. This was Bella, the dog

I'd heard him talking to when I was on the phone with him, the Bella I'd imagined was a girlfriend. I didn't let the smile I felt show—it did look like a love match. Against my will, I felt myself begin to relax.

Finally, he spoke, still looking down at the dog. "Benedict, you spent hours working that file. An *excessive* number of hours researching and interviewing people." His voice was quiet, the tone reasonable, but it did nothing to calm my anger. "That had to have affected your firm's revenue. That check is payment for the work you did."

"*You* didn't charge the Parrishes anything. *You* returned their retainer." I felt tears bite at my eyes, and I clenched my fist, hoping the pain would distract me. Anger usually made me cry, and I didn't want to cry in front of Gerard. "I don't want or need your money." I swallowed the lie, making it mine, daring him to contradict me. "If you didn't get paid, I shouldn't get paid."

He looked up at me, still stroking the dog's head. "Benedict, I have people to keep billing while I tilt at windmills. You don't."

His reference to the *Don Quixote* sketch reminded me of my own doubts about the wisdom of this visit, and I pressed my lips together. I had the moral high ground here, and I was determined to keep it. I said nothing.

He continued to rub the dog's ears while both he and Bella looked at me. "All right, Benedict. You don't have to keep the money." I handed the check to him, and he folded it and put in his back pocket. His voice seemed a bit more gravelly than usual. "But you didn't come here about that."

The tears were back in the corners of my eyes, but I blinked hard to keep them at bay. I didn't even know where to start.

Gerard gave the dog a final pat and rose. "Benedict, let's sit down. You look exhausted." I started to protest, then realized how silly that would sound. I *was* exhausted. I sat on the section of the sofa facing the window and felt warm for the first time since the hearing started earlier that afternoon. The dog didn't jump on the couch as I thought she would; instead, she settled herself on the fluffy rug next to my feet, resting her head on my shoe.

Gerard sat in the deep leather chair next to the fireplace and regarded me with more composure than I felt.

"The bruises are fading, and that cut looks like it's healing," he said, surprising me. I reached up automatically to smooth the scar. "But this was a tough day, Benedict." He tilted his head, and the sympathy in his voice almost undid me. I dredged up as much of my earlier anger as I could find.

"Why did Cliff Clark choose to attack me? Why were you there? How could you have *told* them?" My voice sounded plaintive, and, the moment the words left my mouth, I was appalled. Gerard owed me nothing. We meant nothing to each other. But the truth was, I felt betrayed.

He leaned forward, his hands clasped loosely between his legs, his forehead creased. "Benedict, I didn't tell them anything about Stephenson's case. Jules and I have been friends for a long time. When he asked me to come and be appointed as a receiver to sell the house, I jumped at the chance. I thought it might ease what's happened between him and Trish if someone they both knew was the receiver." He looked down at his hands. "As for Clark, he let me know afterwards that he and Bill Stephenson have been friends since they graduated from SMU law school forty years ago. He saw his chance for some revenge for Bill." He sat back and sighed, sliding a hand over his short silver hair. I felt some of my tension ease at the gesture. I knew he only did that when he was thinking or was anxious.

"I didn't know, Benedict. I didn't know it was you that they were talking about until I saw you walk into the courtroom." He looked steadily back at me, and I imagined my eyes looked as miserable as his. "I hope you believe me."

I breathed out and in. "Oh, I saw your face when you caught sight of me. I'm pretty sure it was a mirror of mine." I tried to smile, but I couldn't muster one. "I'm so tired of Stephenson and that experience intruding into my life."

He didn't say anything, his eyes locked on mine.

My throat ached from unshed tears, and I swallowed hard, searching for something to say. My hands ached, and I realized I'd folded them together, as I had when I was on the witness stand. I eased them apart and decided to throw him a bone. "Trisha said you went to college with Jules?"

He nodded, his face relaxing. "We met our freshman year. We were both at UT, and we decided to boycott the whole frat thing. Instead, we threw ourselves into intramural sports. We did them all: soccer, baseball, basketball, flag football, you name it." I could tell it was a good memory.

"I should have known you were a jock," I teased, my voice coming out hoarse, and he flashed a grin at me.

"What can I say? I'm flexible *and* coordinated but mediocre where the talent is concerned." He laughed. "We both applied to law school, and both got in at UT Law. He met Trisha there." He shook his head, still smiling. "There was a group of us that studied together, and we were an unwilling audience to that house fire. Get the two of them in a room and before long, it would go up in flames. They're so passionate—about life, love, law—about everything." He sighed and stretched his arms over his head, the gray sweater riding up to show a strip of tanned skin before he relaxed. I looked away with effort, my face flaming, and hoped he hadn't seen me ogling him. "They'd break up and be devastated for a few weeks, then get back together and disappear for a couple of days." He grinned and waggled his eyebrows at me. "They'd show up, exhausted and starving and burned out from all the make-up sex, ready to see anyone but each other for a while." The smile faded. "We all thought that's what was going to happen last year, but instead, this time they've burned it down. They seem to hate each other now, constantly at war."

"'Love and war are the same thing'," I said, quoting *Don Quixote*, and he grinned, recognizing the quote. I grinned back, but then his smile faded again, and he slid his hands down his thighs to clasp his hands again.

"Yes, but usually it's just the two of them in the crosshairs—we've all learned not to take sides when they fight." He looked at the dog, who caught his glance and got up to go sit at his side. "That had to have been awful for you today. I'm so sorry you had to go through that." He looked down at Bella and fondled her ear gently. "The really bad thing is Jules knew about my connection with you and Bill's case, and he let it happen anyway. I don't want to defend him—but he feels desperate in this whole divorce. It's not an excuse, but I know he meant nothing malicious. Clark has no such excuse." He sat back, and Bella gave him a betrayed look before coming back to flop down at my feet with a deep doggy sigh.

I shrugged, trying to act as if I had people attack me on the witness stand every day. "I'm sure Cliff Clark has only heard Bill's side of the story," I said lightly. "And most people haven't even heard that. I'll bet Bill has made himself pretty innocent in the story he's told to get the most sympathy from his audience." Just saying the words made me feel nauseated. I reached down to slide my hand over Bella's silky golden head, a move that allowed me to surreptitiously hug myself. Bella stretched her head up to give me better access, and for a moment, I let myself be comforted by the simple act of petting a sweet, beautiful animal that trusted me enough to expose her neck to me. She looked at me, her big brown eyes serene and unconcerned, and I wished that for a few minutes I could wallow in the peace I felt there in that room.

But this wasn't my peace—it was Gerard's. I looked up to see him watching me, his face a picture of concern, and I wondered for the space of a few moments if he could read my mind and see the chaos and hurt there.

I sat up and slapped my hands lightly on my thighs, a move that made Bella sit up expectantly. I leaned forward to pat her head, and she panted, her mouth stretched in a doggy smile. "I'm sorry I came loaded for bear, Gerard," I said as I rose with effort from that comfortable, happy space. He rose too, and, for the first time, I realized his feet were bare. For some reason, the sight of his naked feet on the soft wool rug seemed extraordinarily intimate, and I felt a bit of increased warmth spread.

"Benedict, won't you change your mind about the check?" He pulled it out from his pocket, still folded and now creased.

I shook my head before I changed my mind. He sighed and frowned.

"You keep refusing money that would help you. There's no dishonor in taking money you've earned." He looked directly in my eyes. "This isn't like the whistleblower award, Benedict. Even though I think you earned that, too." He held it out again. "I would have paid an associate more than this to do that work, you know."

I smiled. "Your associates make too much money."

He laughed, and, to my relief, finally tucked the check back into his pocket. Temptation averted again.

I started to turn to the door, but then I gave in to my desire and took a few steps toward the windows. Darkness was setting in now, and, across the lake, lights began to appear in houses as people went about their lives. The land the house was built on was about ten feet above the lake level, and I could see the lake was still a bit restless, small waves lapping at the shoreline. I wanted to go to the glass to press my face up against it like a child and stand there looking at the water, but I resisted the urge. I turned back to see Gerard and Bella watching me again, and I tried to smile and look sophisticated and worldly, as if a beautiful room like this had no effect on me. I should have known better.

"You're welcome anytime, Benedict. Bella loves you already." At her name, the dog got up to go stand next to Gerard, who leaned down to smooth a hand over her head. He laughed. "She's ready for a walk before dinner."

That reminded me. "By the way—speaking of *Don Quixote*— thank you for the sketch." I walked toward the door, where Bella was stretching and starting to dance around. We both laughed as she slid on the tiles in front of the door.

"You're welcome, Benedict. It's you."

I shook my head, smiling. "Not me. I was shaking on the stand today." At least I could smile about it now.

He looked skeptical. "Didn't look like it from where I was sitting. You were staring Clark down, as if you were daring him to come at you." He slid his feet into a pair of soft leather shoes sitting just inside the door, not looking at me.

"I was?" Hmm. So that's what being frozen in fear looks like to someone else. I stifled a yawn, suddenly even more tired than I'd been before.

"That's what it looked like to me." Bella, impatient for someone to give her a signal, danced around us. "Bella, go get your leash." She dashed off to the kitchen, and her absence left the space between us a bit awkward. I rocked up on my heels as I watched her running and sliding on the tiles, reluctant to leave the beautiful home but anxious to get to mine and my bed.

"Benedict," he began, and I turned to see him really close to me, his blue eyes serious. "You know I like you, don't you?"

I smiled. "Yes, you told me. You called me a justice warrior."

He smiled too, his eyebrows winging up. "Yes, that too." His face grew serious and earnest. "But you know I like you, too." At my look, he clarified. "*Like* you."

What was he saying? My heart began to beat faster. "*Like* me?" I gave it the same inflection he had.

He nodded, starting to grin. "You seem shocked."

I swallowed, stung a bit by his obvious amusement. "For god's sake, Gerard, up until a few weeks ago, I considered you my worst enemy."

His smile died. "As bad as that, hmm?" The eyebrows came down, and I felt ashamed I'd used that phrase. Bella came running back, her leash in her mouth with the end trailing behind her.

"Well, maybe not quite that bad," I said, as he turned away and opened the door. Bella danced through the doorway, and I followed. She immediately began to snuffle at the bed of ivy at the side. Gerard came out and shut the door behind him.

"How bad then?" He tilted his head, looking at me seriously.

I looked across the street to the lake, remembering all the times I'd walked there, hearing Gerard's voice in depositions and at trial asking me about my actions in deciding to report Bill Stephenson for fraud, and then later hearing his gravelly voice inside my head, questioning my choices about my own clients and the work I'd done. My friend Dr. Amie, a psychologist, suggested that I'd given Gerard's voice to my own doubts about my actions and choices, and I thought she had a point. This man was kind and generous and fair, and while I might not agree with his legal specialty, I had to admit I liked him. A little.

"Not Satan," I said as I looked back at him over my shoulder. "Maybe one of the lesser demons."

A corner of his mouth quirked up. "Would you ever go to dinner with one of Satan's minions?"

His easy tone made me look at him again. Was he asking me out? I decided to play it casual. "Hey, I'm a lawyer. Anything's possible."

Bella, clipped onto the leash, began dancing out to the sidewalk, but Gerard tugged her back. "Benedict, I'm serious. Would you say yes to dinner?"

My heart pounding, I looked across at the lake and pulled my keys from my coat pocket before answering as casually as I could. "Try me sometime and see."

From the corner of my eye, I could see he smiled and nodded. "Be safe, Benedict," he said, and then gave Bella her head to dash across the street to the walking path next to the lake. As I turned my car onto the street, I looked in the rear-view mirror to see him and Bella standing there on the path, watching me drive away.

CHAPTER SIX

I woke up at seven on Saturday morning partially dressed and lying across my bed, the cat purring next to me. I'd fallen there the night before when I got home, lying there on my face for a few minutes and wondering if it would be hard to sleep after the day I'd had. Clearly, that hadn't been a problem.

I untangled myself from the covers I'd pulled over me, dislodging the cat, who jumped down, meowing crankily. She wasn't really my cat—the Shelton sisters had given her to me about six months before, and she migrated between my apartment and their house at will. A glance out the windows showed a low, gray sky that promised rain, so a walk probably wasn't going to happen. I have to say I wasn't disappointed. I can take or leave exercise, even though I knew it was good for me.

I was starving, but I hadn't grocery shopped for a couple of weeks. As I showered, I noticed a healthy harvest of mold starting in the corner of the shower and tried to remember the last time I'd scoured the tile. My grandmother, who cleaned every Saturday, rain or shine, would be spinning in her grave—if she hadn't been cremated.

After drying my hair and clipping it up high, I dressed in my oldest, softest jeans and a Dallas Cowboys sweatshirt I should have thrown out years ago, chucked a load of laundry into the washer, and headed out.

Two hours later, I'd picked up some essential groceries and cleaning supplies, eaten a quick bacon-cheddar omelet at the Purple Pig Diner, and was ready to clean.

I was halfway through scrubbing the shower when my phone dinged, letting me know there was a voicemail. It was my second from Karan, which worried me slightly. I played the one from the day before that I'd skipped over to get to Gerard's.

LACEY, HOPE YOU'RE DOING OKAY. YOU WERE GREAT UP THERE, *really showed Cliff Clark to be the asinine Neanderthal in a silk tie he truly is. So, listen, we already have an issue. Cliff left me a voicemail telling me that he was emailing you Jules's appraisal on the house. Jules wants to sell the house as-is, and not pull any more funds off the line of credit, but Trisha wants to use the funds and finish the renovations. She thinks the house will go for peanuts if it's not finished. Call me back, and I can explain.*

KARAN'S SECOND VOICEMAIL, THE ONE FROM THIS MORNING, sounded a bit more concerned.

HEY, LACEY. DIDN'T HEAR BACK FROM YOU, AND I'M SORRY TO *call you on Saturday. We got Jules's current appraisal and it's really high. We don't think it will get anything near that if it's not finished, and Trisha is freaking out. I'm sending you Trisha's as-built appraisal so you'll have some context. If you want to discuss it all, we can, but I also don't want to do anything unethical in trying to sway your opinion. Thanks, and I'll talk to you soon.*

A QUICK CHECK OF MY EMAIL SHOWED EMAILS FROM CLIFF Clark and Karan, with attachments. The summary statements showed the figures, and I whistled when I saw the difference between the two—almost two million dollars. I sat back in my chair, wondering what the right path was here. I knew pretty much nothing about historical houses or the differences between a partially-renovated architecturally significant home and a fully-renovated one, but I could imagine how one would be more attractive to some buyers than the other.

I decided to call Jerry Freeman, the appraiser I'd used on the last receivership, who also worked on a house purchase I'd worked for an out-of-state buyer last year. In Texas, unlike in other states, you don't have to have an attorney represent you in a real estate purchase, but it's a good thing to have, especially if you're not going to be present during the process. I'd been hired by a couple from New Jersey to represent them as they purchased a home in Dallas—one that they'd seen only once. Freeman had been the appraiser hired by their real estate agent, and I'd liked the older man the moment we met. He had a crusty, weather-beaten outside and a soft, sweet center, and he carried around square, cinnamon-flavored suckers that reminded me of the cinnamon Jolly Ranchers my dad always had in his pockets when I was a kid. Jerry rocked from his heels to his toes when he talked, and I imagined he was like the grandfather I'd never known.

A quick call later, and Jerry and I had agreed to meet early Monday morning to take a look at the house and the status of the renovations. I was lucky he'd been able to squeeze me in, but it was supposed to rain on Monday, so he'd postpone the appraisal he'd had scheduled. It was at least a place to start. I also had an email from

Judge Hernandez's court coordinator, setting a status hearing on the docket for Friday, March 8 at 9 am to give the judge an update on where things stood on the house sale. Unusual, but not unheard of, and probably due to yesterday's drama. I put it on my calendar with a bit of a worry about where this matter would be by then.

———

By 3 pm, I was sick of cleaning and laundry, promising myself—as I always did—that I'd be better about cleaning daily instead of saving it up. I'd even cleaned out my car, and I took the opportunity to sneak around the house to my new office. I found that the new French door had been installed—complete with lock—and brown paper covered all of the windows in the multipaned door and sidelights. I couldn't see a thing. A circular stair of bricks matching the kitchen entrance on the other side of the house had been roughed in.

I let myself into the Sheltons' side of the house with a halloo and found Miss Sallie in the kitchen stirring something in a huge Dutch oven on the back of the stove. The warm room smelled of red wine and onions.

"Are you cooking tonight?" While Miss Sallie was an artist and an amateur architect, it was Miss Hattie who was the chef in the family, so Miss Sallie's presence in the kitchen was a bit of a surprise.

"Oh, good lord, no," she trilled, laughing. "Hattie made the base for boeuf bourguignon last night, and I've taken it out to warm to room temperature. She said it's bad for the meat to warm it up from cold." She rolled her eyes at me and shrugged. "Do you mind giving me a ride to the warehouse? Hattie said she'd meet us there." She took the apron off and shook back her thick gray hair, settling it into large, heavy curls that just brushed the collar of her white t-shirt. From the heels of her black leather tennis shoes to her perfectly-made up face, this was Sallie's Saturday chic, and I felt grungy next to her.

"Of course not. This is the one on Haskell?"

A denim jacket was draped over a kitchen stool, and she pulled it on over the t-shirt, tucking the front of the shirt into the waistband of her black jeans like I'd seen models do. At 74, she looked casually hip and stylish. And, I should add, better than I did at 34. "Nope. We moved everything to a new place Hattie found over on Live Oak."

"Smaller?"

She rolled her eyes again, and I had my answer. Bigger. Always bigger, with Hattie.

———

When the Shelton sisters moved back to Dallas in the mid-2000s, they bought the home their grandfather had built in 1917 and began to renovate it, restoring it from the disastrous 1960s apartment configuration to a mostly single-family home. According to Sallie, this gave Hattie the bug to do more residential real estate. After the recession, they began to buy up properties much like Tom Terry did, except the Sheltons absolutely loved multi-family properties, preferring them to the single-family homes that Tom and his partners flipped. As a result, the 'Shelton Shelters Management' signs that popped up around the neighborhood were usually in front of duplexes or small apartment buildings.

Sallie was also very active in Dallas society and philanthropy, and, as we dodged a bit of traffic on Ross, I asked her if she knew Trisha or Jules Tarantino.

She wrinkled her nose. "Heavens, yes. She and I have served on a couple of committees together. The two of them have had a few fights at charity events." She shook her head. "This divorce has become very public and dragged in a gaggle of the socialites they both run with."

"Gerard said they've been passionate in one way or another since they met in law school." I saw Sallie look sideways at me at the mention of Gerard. She's made no secret of the fact that she likes him.

"So, *Robert* knows them?" The tone was casual, but I knew her interest was not.

"He and Jules are friends." I thought about his comment last night, how Jules had known about Gerard's history with me and had still set Clark loose on me, and I wondered how that would affect the years-long relationship—if at all. "Well, they *have* been friends."

Sallie adjusted the heater vent. "And of course, they bought the O'Toole house." At the casual comment, I swiveled my head around.

"That's the Lakeway house?" She nodded. "I've been appointed as receiver to sell it."

"*Really?*" She teased the word out, and I could tell her interest was piqued.

I nodded. "I haven't even seen it yet. I drove past it this morning, but the gates are locked, and I won't get the keys till Monday morning. Have you been in the house?"

"Oh, of course." Sallie looked out at the neighborhood we were passing. "That was years ago, though. Right after old Mr. O'Toole died. 1980 or 1981, I think?" She shook her head. "Mother was still alive, I know. I was here visiting her when the obituary came out, and she insisted we go."

"Was he the one who built the house? I saw from the records that it was built in 1937."

She nodded. "Mother said he built it for love. She was a teenager when he married his wife, and to her, him building the house was a romantic gesture. It was such a shame she died so young." She pointed out the warehouse on the east side of the street.

I pulled in. "When did she die?"

"A year or two after they moved into it, I think." She sighed. "This is all so long ago—I wish I remembered more about them, but I can't even remember her name."

I put the car in park and looked up at the large warehouse with six truck loading bays and a discreet Shelton Shelters sign on the side. "Sallie, this is massive. Did you guys need this much space?"

She snorted and unbuckled her seat belt, rearranging her jacket as she got out. "You know what they say. Get more space, and you'll fill it. I'm sure we will need this much space soon, if we don't already."

————

HATTIE WAS TALKING TO HER GENERAL MANAGER, WILL Parker, and my renovating friend John Adams while she waited on us. As always when working, she wore what she once told me were men's 'duck' trousers, an off-white fabric that's a bit stiffer than denim (apparently popular in the 1920s), a soft white long-sleeved safari shirt with the sleeves rolled and buttoned up just below her elbows, and leather boots with soft soles. All she needed was a pith helmet to look like a nineteenth-century explorer giving her crew directions on where to set up the tents and start the fires. Of course, there would never be any doubt that she was in charge.

We toured the renovated warehouse, the organization of Hattie's mind clearly evident in every corner. It was a huge old place with multipaned windows on every wall, but Hattie had also installed large skylights in the roof, so even on this gray and cloudy day, natural light shone in to assist the lights in illuminating the entire place.

Every pair of bay doors on the side had a long room made out of wood and wire attached to them, so that a crew backing up a truck to a particular set of doors didn't have access to the rest of the warehouse. There was a landscaping room, complete with mowers, a small backhoe, and other assorted tools and machinery I didn't know the purpose for. Next to that was a room with construction equipment, tools, wood, moldings, and other interior materials. Beyond that was a room with shiny new appliances waiting for installation into new apartments in their complexes.

The space beyond the bay door rooms was filled with furniture, much of which I presumed were valuable antiques organized by type of furniture. When the Shelton sisters' mother passed away in 1995, they'd come home only to put her things into storage, and then had returned to their homes outside Dallas. There were multiples of everything, though, and I felt certain the items Mrs. Shelton had left behind had been supplemented at some point.

"What kind of furniture do you have in mind, Lacey?" Hattie locked up the gate we'd just walked through and turned us into the aisles of furniture.

I shrugged. "Just a desk and chair, I guess. I don't need much." I ran a hand over a beautiful, massive mahogany dining table. The furniture Hattie and Sallie had in their home now was lovely, and I couldn't imagine how they'd decided which to use and which to store. I restrained myself and put my hands into the pockets of my jeans. "All this looks really nice. Do you have anything that's a bit more —used?"

Hattie crossed her arms over her chest and watched her sister heading for metal shelves stacked to the rafters with boxes. "Sal, what are you looking for? We have all those boxes inventoried."

Sallie turned back to her sister. "Lacey was talking about the O'Tooles, and I know Mother had some old society invitations she'd saved from things. I was trying to remember what Mrs. O'Toole's first name was."

"Eleanor," Hattie promptly supplied. "Eleanor Hartsfield." She checked her phone for a moment, then took down a box marked 52 from the lower-level shelves. I moved quickly to take it from her— which she allowed with a smile—and set it down where we'd come into the open area. Hattie moved on, setting aside a dining chair covered in a lustrous peacock blue upholstery, and I followed, sliding a finger along the top of the chair back, which seemed to be curved like a moustache. I realized that there were 11 more just like it against the wall, with two chairs that had arms alongside. This entire area seemed to be dining tables and buffets.

"Absolutely right. I should have remembered that. Leona O'Toole lived with her aunt Delia Bock—remember her? She always used her full name, 'Delia Hartsfield Bock'." Sallie wrinkled her nose. "I think 'Delia Bock' was too short and un-elegant sounding for her." She put her hands on her hips and looked around. "Hattie, where are the desks?"

"Around the corner here," Hattie said as she walked. "Awful woman."

Sallie nodded. "She was. Arthur Bock cheated on her their whole marriage, and no one seemed to blame him." She stopped to stroke a small round table. "Hattie, is this the table from grandmother's bedroom?"

"It is," Hattie replied. She bent and ran a hand around the top, which had a curved pie crust edge that reminded me of something my grandmother had used in her bedroom. "I still think of her every time I see it." She walked around the shelves, her voice echoing in the space. "Sallie, do you remember Mother's writing desk?" Sallie disappeared around the corner as well, and I could hear an indistinct murmur as they talked.

I turned the corner to see four desks, lined end to end. They ranged from a huge, imposing wooden desk with feet made of lions' paws over globes to a fancy, gilt-edged one that looked like something I'd seen in a palace in France. Hattie had stopped next to something beyond those that looked like a five-foot-long table, with legs carved in a twisting design from the floor up to where they met the base. The table itself was a dark wood, almost black, and it looked old. On the top, someone had painted swirly leaves, but the gold paint had faded long ago. I traced the leaves, my finger leaving a new trail in the dust. Something in me whimpered, then sat up and begged.

Hattie turned to see the look on my face and laughed. "It's not a typical desk, but our mother loved it. She would spread out her materials on here—what she called her 'little work'—and just work for hours when we were teenagers."

"What did she do?" I was curious, since we'd never had an opportunity to talk much about their mother. I stepped back from the table and put my hand back in my pocket.

"She organized committees," Sallie said shortly as she sat in a huge, oxblood leather desk chair. "She was really in charge of the boards for the charities she was involved with, but women didn't get to sit on the boards then. They might have a 'women's auxiliary' committee or something, but they didn't have the foresight to put women on the big boards in those days." She sighed heavily, and for a moment, she looked closer to her age than mine. "Mother ran everything but got none of the credit. But that was par for the course in the 50s and 60s, and for women then. She broke the mold."

Hattie leaned against a desk near her sister and clarified. "When Father died in 1951, we were financially secure, but Mother wasn't confident at all about how to keep it that way. Her sister's husband stepped in to 'help'"—and she made the hand gestures for air quotes here—"and by the time we graduated high school in 1963, much of her ready cash was gone due to poor investments. We both had trusts out of Father's will, so we were fine, but eventually she had to sell the house." She walked to their mother's table and stroked the edge.

Sallie picked up the story. "She sold it, bought a few life insurance policies and a small house in Highland Park, and invested the rest pretty wisely—all on her own. And then spent the rest of her life working for the charities she loved." She blinked a few times. "I miss her every day." I was next to Sallie's chair by that time, and I patted her shoulder. She covered my hand with hers for a moment, and then I saw her nod at Hattie before she spoke again. "You liked the look of the little library table, Lacey?"

My brain stuttered. I knew nothing about furniture, but I knew about family sentiment. "I did, but it looks valuable. I'd be afraid I'd scratch it or something."

Hattie snorted. "That thing is old and tough, and it survived our mother. *Her* mother said that 'Grace' was the most inaccurate name she could ever have given her child." She brushed her hands together to remove the dust, smiling at the memory. Sallie chuckled softly.

"We'd love you for to use the table, Lacey," Hattie said. She and Sallie exchanged a look I didn't understand. "And I think I know a few other things that will be perfect for the office." She rose and held out a hand for her sister, who took it and rose. "Will you give Sallie a ride home, and I'll see you a bit later at dinner? Shall we say 7?"

I found myself hustled out of the warehouse with Sallie, who texted on her phone like a teenager the whole way home.

———

I SHOWERED AND PUT ON REAL PANTS AND A NEW RED SWEATER I'd found at a consignment store a few weeks ago, drying my hair with a round brush and actually putting on some makeup. I entered the Shelton side of the house exactly at 7 pm, feeling a lot cleaner and a bit prettier despite the little gap in my eyebrow from the scar, to be greeted by the most handsome man I'd ever seen. I'm not kidding. He looked like a model who'd stepped down off the runway into the Shelton sisters' kitchen. He was tall, tanned, and much better looking than the all other men Sallie Shelton had dragged to their home to meet me over the last four years—combined. He was laughing at something Hattie had said as she pulled a baguette from the oven, and he took my breath away. Men like that aren't supposed to exist in real life—only in airbrushed magazine photos.

I stopped just inside the doorway. He turned toward me, and I literally felt my thighs quivering as I kept myself still. Everything inside me was poised to run back through the door to my apartment.

"You must be the *famous* Lacey Benedict," he drawled as he approached, hand outstretched.

"Must I?" I asked weakly. If he was gorgeous at a distance, he was devastating close up, his blue eyes twinkling at me.

"You must." He took my hand with both of his and drew me into the kitchen. "Hattie was just telling me about your recent adventures." His voice had a distinct Southern drawl, Louisiana perhaps, and I could clearly see him in a white suit and planter's hat instead of the open-necked pink dress shirt and navy blazer he wore over pressed blue jeans.

I looked over at Hattie. She was clearly enjoying this, but she decided to save me anyway. "Lacey, meet Gray Powell."

He was still holding my hand, but he shook it anyway, his eyes dancing. "Nice to meet you," I managed.

He looked at Hattie. "She's just as you described."

I gave Hattie a look. "And how was that?"

Hattie smiled mysteriously, but Gray Powell answered. "A perfectly lovely young woman with absolutely no pretension or arrogance." He leaned in. "A rarity in Dallas, I might add."

I gave Hattie a dark look. There was something going on here I didn't understand, but I was going to keep my mouth shut and listen.

He tucked my hand into the crook of his elbow, clearly intending to keep me attached. "Hattie, can we help with anything?"

She shook her head as she arranged the crusty, steaming baguette in a snowy napkin on a silver server. "Everything's ready." She led the way through the swinging door into the dining room.

Then the penny dropped.

Sitting with Sallie at the table—the white tablecloth-draped, candlelit table, decked out with the best silver and china and crystal—was another handsome man. He and Sallie were laughing about something, and he turned toward us, his eyes finding my companion and stopping there for an intense moment. I looked up at Gray Powell, who was looking back with the same expression. And I began to breathe again.

"Lacey, may I present—"

He stood. "No, no, you don't have to introduce me. Miss Benedict, I'm Martin Dove. I've *so* looked forward to meeting you." He came toward me, and like Gray Powell, he took my breath away. Where Gray was tall and model-perfect, Martin was smaller, more compact, and just as attractive, his blue eyes bright and joyous, and his smile infectious. He liberated my hand from Gray's arm and took it in his, leaning in conspiratorially. "I see you met my—*my husband,* isn't it strange to say that?—and isn't he gorgeous?" He laughed, his eyes twinkling.

I leaned in too, my face serious. "He scared me to death. I thought Miss Sallie had caught him for me."

Martin laughed. "Oh no no *no*. She caught him for *me*." He looked over at Gray. "And I reeled him in."

Gray smiled at him. "How do you know I didn't reel you in?"

Martin's mouth curved up in a Cheshire cat smile. "I know what I know." He pulled me to the table. "You must sit here next to me, Lacey. You don't mind if I call you Lacey, do you?" His accent was more Texan than southern, with flat vowels instead of Gray's soft drawl.

I told him I didn't mind and let him seat me to his left. Miss Sallie sat at the end of the table, while Hattie joined Gray on the other side and served us the rich beef stew over buttery noodles.

Sallie explained that Martin and Gray owned DoveGray Productions, an event-planning firm that organized all the best events in Dallas society, which led to a post-mortem of the last event at the Dallas Country Club for a large local charity. Both of the men were in their forties and had gotten married the year before. Martin was raised in Dallas, while Gray had come from New Orleans about five years before.

Talk over our delicious dinner was light and frothy, with dishy gossip on the Dallas social scene, but I could tell Sallie was saving something. Over coffee, liqueurs, and a small (too small) dish of a very light raspberry sherbet, she opened the ball. "Lacey, Marty is an expert in Dallas history, and I thought he could tell you about the O'Tooles and their house." She waved toward Martin Dove, who pretended to cough over his tiny glass of port.

"Sallie, dear, I wouldn't call me an expert."

"I would," Gray broke in. "We spend enough time and money on Dallas historical documents, artifacts, and antiques to qualify you."

Martin frowned at him across the table. "I think we both know who all those antiques are for." Gray just shrugged and smiled at his spouse as he sipped his coffee.

Martin toasted him with his port glass. "Dallas just has so many wonderful stories. It really has been a place of accidental glamour, intentional graft, and unabashed greed over the years." He rolled his eyes. "And that was just the 1970s!" We all chuckled, knowing the years of the *Dallas* television show weren't that far away from reality in that time of glitz and gluttony. He turned to me. "Sallie tells me you've been dragged into the 'Tarantino Tornado'." I could tell he'd coined the term for that maelstrom of passion. He sighed. "Such a shame. Those two had really great plans for that beautiful old house."

"Martin and Gray bought a house in Lakewood last year," Sallie told me as she poured more coffee for herself and gestured to Gray.

He nodded at her and turned to me as she refreshed his cup. "Nothing so grand as the O'Toole house, of course." He added a half spoonful of raw sugar and stirred it in. "Trisha and Jules wanted to restore some things, especially the exterior and grounds, while making the inside look much more modern."

"That's not easy to do," Hattie said. "Were they wanting to try for a designation?"

Martin shook his head and sipped the ruby-red liqueur in the delicate crystal glass. "They really didn't care about that. It was solely an investment for them." He sighed. "No one's been able to see what they'd done so far." He looked at me with a sparkling smile. "You'll be the first, Miss Benedict."

I shook my head and hid behind my coffee cup. These two men might be playing for the other team, so to speak, but their smiles were still pretty devastating on little old me. For a moment, I thought of Gerard's grin last night when he asked me if I'd date a demon. I mentally shook myself. I'd managed not to think of that too much all day. I put my cup down and gave Martin my best lawyer look.

"I'm just the receiver. And I haven't even gotten in to see it yet." I grinned. "And I thought I was Lacey."

He toasted me with his small glass. "Well, if you need someone to come in and see it with you, Miss Lacey, I'm your man." He grinned at his turn of phrase.

Sallie leaned over to pat his arm. "Martin, I was trying today to remember about the scandal surrounding the O'Tooles. I remember my mother talking about the family, but I'm afraid I never paid much attention. What do you know?"

He looked down into his now-empty glass, but I thought I saw a twinkle in his eye. "Oooo, let's see. There were several scandals. Do you mean the one where he came to Dallas with a huge fortune and maybe he'd been a war profiteer, or the one where he killed his wife?"

CHAPTER SEVEN

The stunned silence was enough reward for Martin. He kept the innocent expression for a few seconds, and then grinned hugely at us. "I looked through a few things when Sallie texted me this afternoon." He placed his glass on the table and sat back in his chair, and I recognized a storyteller settling in for a good tale. He adjusted his shirt cuff down over a large watch with a silvery blue face.

"The Hartsfields and the O'Tooles seemed to attract scandal and mystery. The Hartsfields were an old family, maybe Jewish—Hartsfeld, you know—but no one knew anything about them when Edward Hartsfield arrived from New York with his young wife and set up their household. It was a different time here in Dallas. I suspect he didn't want to be stereotyped. He was already wealthy then, and he started the Trinity Bank and Trust with his own money." Martin nodded to Hattie and pushed his glass forward as she held up the port decanter, and we all watched as she poured the ruby-red liquid into the crystal glass. "Thank you, Hattie." He sipped, then set the glass down. "The turn of the century was a crazy time to be in Dallas—land was going for pennies, no one knew oil was going to be important, and the railroads weren't even interested in this area. The Trinity river flooded all the time, and land south of the river was still empty except for Kessler Park. But Edward Hartsfield had money, a lot of money, and the war—World War I—just increased his fortune.

"The Hartsfields brought their New York society habits to Dallas. They hosted parties and balls and garden parties at their home in Highland Park. They had two daughters in the next few years, Eleanor and Delia, and those girls attended Miss Hockaday's school for girls—the original one, over off Greenville. They were introduced into society, debutantes, you know." We nodded, since we did, indeed know how Dallas society went. "Delia got married to Arthur Bock almost immediately after graduation—you know the Bock family here in town—but Eleanor was quite the flapper in the late 20s, I've heard. Very independent. Apparently wasn't going to get married at all. And then the crash of 1929 happened, and somehow the Hartsfields were broke. Not just stretched, but downright destitute. Quite the come-down. And Edward Hartsfield put Eleanor out for sale." Sallie made a noise, and he turned to her. "That's the only way to put it, dear Sallie. She was engaged to a young man within a couple of months after the crash, but apparently *he* broke it off." He grinned.

"And then Jack O'Toole came to town in the summer of 1930. No one knew anything about him—except that he was wildly rich, *still* wildly rich, after the crash. To everyone, that seemed to mean there was something shady about him. Was it dirty money? Did he profit from the war? Was it inherited? No one seemed to know, and he wasn't telling. They didn't know whether to be attracted or repelled. But Eleanor married him, and then suddenly he and Harts-field are partners, and Hartsfield doesn't need money anymore." He sighed, and his face was suddenly sad. "You can draw your own conclusions."

Sallie sipped her coffee and shook her head, her curls bouncing softly. "It wasn't unusual for that time. Our grandmother married our grandfather after she'd only known him a few weeks. It was an arranged thing."

Martin exchanged a glance with Gray. "And there were many reasons those things got arranged back then." Gray smiled a bit ruefully, and then Martin continued. "So, Jack and Eleanor got married. And then a few years later, Jack decided to build that house on Lakeway, but Dines and Kraft wouldn't let him design it. They insisted on architect-designed houses." He turned to me. "Do you know about Dines and Kraft?"

I shook my head. The names sounded familiar, but I wasn't sure where I'd heard them.

"Albert Dines and Lee Kraft. They took what was rolling land—some of it just farmland—north of Lakewood Country Club and developed what we now know as Lakewood. Dines and Kraft had started in Munger Place in the 20s, building according to the requirements of old man Munger—deep lots and architect-designed homes, rare in that time, and something only the rich could afford." He spread his hands, and we all nodded. Many of the houses in the Munger and Swiss areas still stood, and they were elegant and extravagant even compared to homes built now.

"Ever drink Dr Pepper?" I nodded. "One of the men who developed Dr Pepper into a brand, Robert Lazenby, built a house there in the 20s when they moved Dr Pepper from Waco to Dallas. There wasn't even a road up there at that point—they had to get donated land to extend Gaston. But Dines and Kraft—and the other wealthy country club people—wanted the development to be special and a place only the truly wealthy could afford. Dines has been quoted many times saying the houses had to be built in the 'right manner,' and that meant they controlled what plans would be approved. They called it 'Westlake Park' back then, and if you were friendly with those men, you got a beautiful homesite and a luxury house."

Hattie offered me a coffee refill, but I shook my head. Gray accepted a refill, and Martin stretched as they busied themselves with the *cafetiere* and the sugar bowl for a moment, and then he continued.

"So, when Jack O'Toole—Black Jack O'Toole, they called him, because of his black hair, I think—decided to buck Dines and Kraft and demand a design they didn't approve of, they told him they wouldn't sell him a lot in their development. But apparently no one told Jack O'Toole what to do and not do." He raised his eyebrows and took a sip of his port, a bard spinning out his tale. "There was a small dairy farm on the far east side of the development, next to the lake, and Dines and Kraft had tried to buy it when they were buying up land. The family had refused to sell, and then, when O'Toole was looking around, the father died suddenly, and the mother and sons changed their minds. O'Toole swept in and bought the land before Dines and Kraft even knew anything about it. He cut it in three lots around a cul-de-sac and kept the biggest piece for himself. He built the streets and had electricity put in, and the city let him do it all. He offered the rest of the land to Dines and Kraft, but they refused, so he donated it to the city for a park."

I sat up, remembering a wild and beautiful piece of land with a hill that swept down to trees and bushes and a path to a lovely little meadow at the bottom. "Do you mean Chapel Park?" Martin nodded. "I love that place."

"Apparently he left a small trust that pays for the park's upkeep and everything else. O'Toole's son is the trustee." He took another small sip of the port.

"And he built that beautiful house for his bride." Like her mother, Sallie clearly yearned for the romantic side of the story.

"And then she died," Hattie added flatly, her voice punctuating the reason for the story.

Martin nodded. "Mysteriously. I don't know the details, but there was definitely some feud between O'Toole and his wife's family when she died. Everyone knew you didn't invite O'Toole to anything the Hartsfields or Bocks were invited to. And Delia Hartsfield Bock wasn't shy about telling anyone who asked why. She claimed O'Toole had killed her sister." He shrugged and looked at the liquid in his glass, seeming a bit sad. He swirled the dregs of liqueur in the glass. "No one else accused him. For a while he was the wealthiest and most powerful man in Dallas, and nothing came of it. It was true that O'Toole refused to have his wife autopsied, and so she wasn't autopsied. Just like that. Dallas was quite the tight society then, and the wealthy were *ultra*-wealthy and *ultra*-connected. The law didn't quite apply to them." He raised his eyes to mine, and the twinkle reappeared as he raised his glass in a small toast to me. "Not like these days, of course."

Ah, he knew my history. I looked over at Miss Sallie, who smiled gently at me as she sipped her coffee. No, she wouldn't have discussed me with someone else. He must have heard it from someone else. Quite a bit of that going around.

"The O'Toole house had one of the first residential air conditioning units in Dallas," Hattie said quietly, and the tension broke, just like that. I looked at her, but she was sipping her tea, watching Martin.

He finished his port and set the glass carefully on the table. "This is true. He could afford it, so he did it. He also had some of the earliest advanced plumbing, electrical wiring, and a private cistern just in case there was a fire at the house." Martin sighed. "I remember my mother talking about him. By the time she and my father moved here, he was a very old man, and he had become a recluse in that house. It always seemed very lonely and sad." There was a pause as we all thought about the bit of loneliness in all our lives.

Gray pushed his coffee cup forward, and then turned to Hattie to speak quietly, his voice firm but soft. "Miss Hattie, this was a wonderful meal. You are quite the best cook—may I say chef?" His southern accent reminded me of *Gone With The Wind*, and called to mind trees draped with Spanish moss and warm, humid afternoons.

Martin took Sallie's hand. "And your home is beautiful, as always,

Sallie. Thank you for showing me the renovations. By the way, Hattie, the little office is going to be a jewel."

I sent Hattie a shocked and hurt expression, which she ignored as she answered him. "Thank you, Martin, dear. It will look lovely when it's finished."

Martin turned to me. "Lacey, I was serious about the house. If you have any questions going forward about its history or anything to do with that, I'm happy to help. And I can usually find the right expert for restoration."

I made a face. "There's already a question about finishing the house to sell it or leaving it half-done and selling as is." I tilted my head. "Do you have an opinion?"

Gray made a gentle snorting noise, but when Martin and I looked over at him, he just looked back with wide, solemn eyes. Martin rolled his own eyes and turned back to me. "I do, my dear, but perhaps we could talk about it another time, after you've seen the house and grounds and are ready to talk?"

We agreed to talk in the next week, and I said my goodbyes to Gray and Martin before slipping into the kitchen to start washing up.

Hattie joined me a few minutes later, and, as always, we worked in harmonious silence as we washed and dried the beautiful china, crystal, and silver. She took the clean items to the dining room, and Sallie would put them away as she hummed and sang with the Bluetooth speaker in the other room. It was a comforting ritual, and I realized as we worked that I missed my grandmother, who, like me and Hattie, couldn't rest for the night without the kitchen cleaned and everything tucked away.

As Hattie filled containers with leftovers and I wiped down the counters, I asked her about Martin Dove and Gray Powell.

"Our mother knew Martin's mother back in the 70s." She found lids for the containers and snapped them on. "Gray came to Dallas after his divorce." She smiled tightly. "After he came *out*."

"He was married before? To a woman?"

She nodded. "As you can imagine, it didn't go well or end well."

She handed the containers to me, and then patted my arm as she passed by to switch off the lights. "But then Martin and Gray found each other, and I've never seen two people more happy or in love. And that's what matters—the happiness you find, and what you hold on to."

———

I checked my phone after putting the containers in my fridge. I'd be out tomorrow for lunch, but these goodies would more than take care of me for dinner tomorrow night. I wouldn't even need to dip into the groceries I'd bought that morning. I did a little dance step in the kitchen, loving the savings.

I had a text from Sara, my sister-in-law, confirming us all meeting tomorrow at Sepulveda's in Bonham, where we'd go in one car to my grandmother's farm. Sara's parents lived in Sherman, a town just a few miles south of the Oklahoma border, and she and Ryan would go there after we finished for a visit. I planned to come back through Plano for a visit with my dad.

I also had a voicemail from Gerard, his voice raspy and deep, and also slightly annoyed:

Benedict, do you ever actually answer your phone?

Big sigh, and I could see his eyebrows raised high, and I smiled to myself.

I'm calling to see if you'd like to go with me to my sister's annual Texas Independence Day party—extravaganza is really a better word—next Saturday. It goes from about 1 pm till they're done, which is usually midnight, if not later, but I thought we could go about

6 pm if you'd like. I know what you're thinking, my family and all, but I thought perhaps there would be comfort for you in the masses of people Claire invites to these things. There are children running all over the house, movies playing, games happening—it's insane. And fun. It's definitely fun.

ANOTHER PAUSE.

LET ME KNOW. BE SAFE, BENEDICT.

THE MESSAGE ENDED WITHOUT A GOODBYE, BUT I PLAYED IT twice more, telling myself I just needed to hear the details to decide what to do.

CHAPTER EIGHT

I've always tried to live my life in the present moment, you know, like all the greeting cards and memes tell you to. My family didn't believe in 'navel gazing,' as my grandmother famously said to one of my high school teachers, who had bravely suggested counseling for me and my brother the year after my mother committed suicide. My brother had coped with her death by trying to re-envision himself as different from our mother as he could be (including dyeing his hair each of the shades of the rainbow—in order), and I took out my feelings on my studies, trying to improve my grade average in every subject until there was no higher grade to achieve. We didn't discuss our feelings, good or bad. We just put our heads down (both multicolored and not) and pretended they didn't exist. It's what Ryan and I call the Great Benedict Silence (no relation to the Great Silence of the Benedictine monastic order, by the way).

At the same time, we lived surrounded by the past. Our house

was filled with antiques. They weren't the valuable kind, like the
Louis XIV chair or Duncan Phyffe dining table that you'd find in the
Sheltons' warehouse, but instead were a bedstead handmade by an
ancestor, or a milk stool that a great-great-grandmother had actually
used while she was milking, or a lamp that someone liked for its colors
and kept forever. Stories accompanied almost every piece of furniture
or dish or collectible in my grandmother's house, and the rooms of the
farmhouse—as well as most of one of the small barns—were burdened
with a century and a half of history.

The land that made up the original farm where my grandmother's rambling white farmhouse stood had been purchased by my
ancestor, Samuel Dalton, who followed his brother Lamarcus to
Texas. Lamarcus had come from somewhere in Kentucky in 1839 to
fight in the army of the Republic of Texas, and he'd received a patent
for 320 acres of land from the cash-poor new republic in exchange for
his service. Samuel, a year younger, had come to help the fight in the
last few months of 1840, but alas, the Army of the Republic of Texas
was effectively disbanded in February 1841, and Samuel never had a
chance to serve. An older brother, James, had brought his family with
him sometime earlier, and had enlisted in the army to earn land.
When he died of cholera in an army camp in 1840, the brothers and
James' wife sold his 640-acre headright patent to another emigrant to
the republic of Texas, and Samuel used his share of the proceeds to
buy a land patent awarded to another soldier. James' wife disappears
from the story at this point, along with—apparently—at least one
child, never to be heard from again.

Perhaps you see the trouble here. The story of James and
Lamarcus and Samuel Dalton had come down through the generations to my grandmother, who was the first descendant with Internet
access and a desire for truth with no illusions. She was determined
not only to believe all the family stories, but to *prove* them and get to
the truth, whatever it might be. When she retired, she purchased an
RV and set out for Kentucky to try and trace the brothers. And she
hit a dead end.

The brothers had apparently taken the name Dalton from the tiny town in central Kentucky, because try as she might—and oh, she tried mightily—my grandmother could never find a James, Samuel, or Lamarcus Dalton until they appeared in the Peters colony in north Texas in the late 1830s. The 1840 census just showed their birthplace as 'Kentucky.' Even Internet ancestry databases couldn't find the brothers before they arrived in Texas. This fit the time, though, when 'Gone to Texas' was scrawled on abandoned houses in the neighboring United States, as people without means or reputations left to find opportunity and a new life—and sometimes, a new identity—in the young republic.

Their wives, however, were another story. The brothers met and married a pair of sisters, Lucy and Mary Gambill, who had moved to Texas from Tennessee with their father and four siblings in 1840. There was ample documentation for the Gambills, who lived and died with much flair, showing up in birth notices, marriage licenses, war records, and death certificates. The two couples lived next to each other on their matching farms until they died in 1844, when all four adults succumbed to some type of fever, dying on consecutive days in August. Each couple left a child: Lamarcus and Lucy left a son, Marcus Samuel Dalton, and Samuel and Mary left a daughter, my great-great-great-great grandmother, Lucy Jane Dalton. The orphans were raised by Lucy and Mary's brother, and the headright properties were held in trust for each. My great-grandmother would buy the 'Lamarcus piece' from Lamarcus's descendants almost 100 years later, after her husband died on Omaha Beach in Normandy on D-Day and she received his death benefits. Now Lamarcus' great-great-great-great grandson Mark Dalton was our tenant. It's sort of a weird circle of life.

All these generations later, and my grandmother's farm is still in our family, although a few acres have been sold off from time to time. Come to think of it, I'm not sure why I still consider the farm my grandmother's. She left it to me and Ryan in her will, skipping our father at his request, but who she was, the *essence* of Ina Benedict, was tied to that land and still imbues it today. The women in our family have always owned and worked the land, and the men have died young. In my great-grandmother's day, it was a working farm, with cattle and sheep and chickens and hogs, and fields planted not only with cash crops like cotton, but with sustenance crops too, growing corn and alfalfa and all kinds of vegetables, while leasing the other land to their neighbors.

My grandmother came back to the farm when my grandfather died in 1960, a single mother with an infant needing the comfort of family around her. *Her* mother and grandmother still lived on the farm then, and they took care of my father as my grandmother learned to manage the farm and worked a day job at a law firm.

By the time we moved to the farm after my mother left us, my grandmother had hired a pair of brothers in their 60s who lived in a tenant farmhouse on the north edge of the property. They worked the fields that weren't leased and, in exchange for room and board, took care of the few farm animals we had. They were like uncles to me and Ryan, eating dinner at the big farm table in the kitchen, taking us up on the tractors, giving us their attention as we told jokes or performed magic tricks, helping with whatever wild project we wanted to try (for the record, Ryan's were wilder than mine, since they usually involved chemistry experiments), getting us out of trouble when we got in over our heads. We called them 'Uncle Austin' and 'Uncle Henry,' and my grandmother left them a life estate in the small tenant farmhouse when she died, envisioning them living peacefully on the farm when they couldn't drive a tractor anymore. But they died—one immediately after the other—the year after she passed away, their hearts just stopping as great hearts sometimes do.

Through it all, the land has remained, the houses and barns standing as ancient witnesses to the decline of family farms, the inevitable demise of the Dalton line, and the deterioration of wood and soil.

———

THE TAMALES AT SEPULVEDA'S HAVE ALWAYS BEEN PERFECT: they're made fresh every day, and they're sold by the dozen out the front window of an old 1930s frame house: hot, foil-wrapped bundles bagged in repurposed plastic shopping bags. When we lived in McKinney before my mother left us, it was a tradition to stop at Sepulveda's on the way to visit my grandmother at the farm. After we moved to the farm, we'd stop at Sepulveda's when we traveled to Dallas or anywhere else we could convince ourselves was on the other side of Bonham and the small house that smelled like cumin and garlic and peppers.

We hugged and chatted with Ricky Sepulveda, whose grand-mother started the tamale operation years ago to support her grand-children after they'd lost their parents. Old Mrs. Sepulveda had passed away a few years ago, but Ricky and his siblings continued the tradition, cleaning up the kitchen in the old house to comply with some relaxed city ordinances. The product hasn't suffered. We bought a dozen pork tamales and pulled away the foil to each take a corn shuck-wrapped tamale, blowing on the steaming masa tubes for a few seconds before biting off the end, burning our fingers and our tongues. They had a mild version, but we preferred to suffer for the reward of intense heat and flavor. The spice numbed my tongue to the steaming heat of the tamales, and I suspected I might be in trouble later.

Sara had brought along refilled water bottles in a picnic-sized cooler, and we all drank deep in between bites. It was cold sitting outside, but Sepulveda's didn't have inside seating, only a few park benches and lawn chairs in the front or back yard. When we finished, Ryan and Ricky stood by the porch for a few minutes and talked as men do, their hands in their pockets and their eyes to the sky or the surroundings, two men who'd known each other for 25 years, and whose lives had taken different paths. Ricky and his wife had a nice place outside town, but they kept this tiny frame house where he and his sisters had lived with his grandmother. I know that someday the family will sell the house, or they'll give in to the pressure to have a 'real' restaurant, but for now it's still exactly as it was the whole time I was growing up. I refuse to entertain thoughts of the alternative.

I left my car at Sepulveda's, with Ricky's permission, after we'd purchased another couple of dozen tamales and tucked them away in the cooler. Sara's parents loved them too, and she and Ryan would go on to Sherman after we were done at the farm and they dropped me at my car. Sepulveda's closed at 2 on Sundays, but Ricky told me my car would be fine, since his son was living in the old house 'till he grew up and got his act together.' His son was 29, so I commiserated silently in the face of Ricky's disapproval, wondering if I had my act together, and if so, where I'd put it.

I sat in the backseat on the passenger side, where I had always sat when we drove to my grandmother's farm. Bonham and Highway 82 are only 12 miles south of the Red River and the Oklahoma border, and this far north, spring was still a distant hope. I rested my head against the window glass to watch the farms and landmarks as we passed by, the scenes mostly the same from the countless trips we'd taken over the years. Some of the farmhouses were gone, replaced by real estate development billboards touting new homes in the mid-$300s. The highway was being widened, and giant yellow construc-tion vehicles littered the verges and median, orange cones stacked high for tomorrow's lane closures.

Although I loved this drive, even I was a little daunted by the weather and the landscape. The terrain is gently rolling hills and flat, farmed fields with heavy oaks or cedars marking creeks or sloughs. That day, the trees were still bare, and the fields were brown and muddy; as we drove past, my mood darkened with the clouds. It started to mist a bit as we drove into Honey Grove, the tiny town where I attended high school. Local legend has it that Davy Crockett found honey in trees here and his letters home about the beauty of the place were responsible for the migration from Tennessee of one Sam Erwin, a surveyor who moved here, platted the town, and became the town's first founding father. Davy Crockett, of course, continued on to the Alamo, where he met his untimely end defending the new republic (or aiding and abetting the unlawful revolutionaries and squatters, depending upon which side of the Rio Grande your sympathies lay).

Honey Grove, like Ladonia and Ravenna and Windom and countless other towns sprawled across north Texas, struggles on each year, dusty villages with hundred-year old town squares and schools that service not only the residents of the town, but children from the farms and unincorporated communities in between. Honey Grove has the distinction of place, lying along Highway 82 about 15 miles east of Bonham, and it boasts a population of 1,500-plus and a new high school, finished more than a decade after I graduated. We drove past boarded-up businesses and houses whose walls were losing the fight with gravity, and it all seemed sad to me.

Ryan's windshield wipers automatically clicked on as the rain intensified, a rhythmic mechanical sound that lulled me close to sleep. I remember falling asleep in my father's car to the sound of whooshing wipers, my mother and father talking together quietly, Ryan reading beside me. Those were good memories, from long, long ago, and until that moment, they'd been blocked by the more harsh ones from those times: my mother and father yelling at each other behind the closed bedroom door, arguments sometimes punctuated by a slam as one or the other of them left to cool off. All that ended when I was seven, when my mother left for the last time. I don't think she slammed the door that time. I remember only a suffocating silence in the house that day.

I stretched as I felt the car slow and looked out the windshield for the bridge over Sanders Creek, the sign that the farm was just around the next curve. They'd widened this bridge before starting on the rest of the road, and I mourned the loss of the old one, with its low concrete sides and the trees hanging into the road. They had been cruelly pruned back for the construction of the new bridge with its shiny metal bollards and barriers, and the branches seemed embarrassingly naked.

Ryan turned in at the paved farm road, passing the hay barn at the corner of our land, its skeleton bare against a leaden sky. This barn had been built sometime before 1900, but our great-grandmother had taken the (then) radical step of replacing the wooden poles with steel ones and a wooden roof with a metal one, and those poles and metal roof remained even after the rotted wooden walls fell. She was the last real farmer in our family, a woman who studied agriculture theory and seed catalogs with interest, always thinking first of the land and its care. The men who owned the farms around her treated her with the respect she deserved, and many of them attended her funeral, I was told, even though she died in the height of the haying season. My grandmother had grown up here, and she was the first woman in our family to have no interest in the land except its historical and financial value. She took a job as a secretary to an attorney in Bonham as a young widow with a small child, and she worked for him for almost 40 years, finally retiring only to hit the road in her RV for the last few years of her life. The farm represented family to her, and that was probably the only thing that kept her from selling it off completely, piece by piece.

I always thought Ryan would come back to the farm. I could hear the excitement in his voice this morning at Sepulveda's, and I knew it was because we were near the farm. As a teenager, he bored me to tears talking about the science of agriculture, and his frequent chemistry experiments brought nervous chuckles from the neighbors, who just wanted to be sure he wouldn't start a fire that would threaten their fields or hay barns.

We pulled up in front of the farmhouse, a rambling one-story frame structure that seemed much smaller than it had when I was seven and looking to hide from my brother, father, or grandmother. I had reading cubbyholes all over the house and its attic, cupboards that had no purpose then, but must have been useful at some point in time. My favorite the first year we lived here was in my bedroom, a paneled and painted cabinet above my closet, a good three feet deep and the width of the closet below. I outfitted it with pillows and a blanket and a stack of books, and I climbed the wooden ladder attached to the wall below every chance I got. I'd stay there for hours, coming out only for food or to use the bathroom, happy only when I was tucked away in there. My father bought me a flashlight for my eighth birthday, and, since he'd bring me batteries when he came home from working weeks at a time in the oilfields, even darkness didn't get me to come out. We all went our separate ways to read: my grandmother had history books and notebooks of our family's historical records, Ryan read science fiction and fantasy novels, and my father—when he was home for a week or so—would read thick paperback novels with gun sights or knives dripping blood on the covers, books that would interest me only much later in life.

Mark and his wife, Andi, came out of the house to greet us, dogs yapping and dancing around them. I stopped to pet the dogs and was introduced to yet another stray they'd adopted, this one a short-haired puppy that looked like an accidental mix of Labrador and hound. Mark took Ryan into the house to show him a new project, while Andi came to the small barn with me and Sara, the dogs splitting into two camps to follow us all. The new dog, Layla, seemed confused and unsure who to follow, and dealt with the issue by sitting down under the huge oak tree in front of the house, watching the groups heading to the barn or the house with equal longing.

Andi kept up a steady stream of conversation as we walked to what we always called the 'small barn,' a 20x20-foot structure that had the benefit of tight walls and windows, telling us about Amanda, their teenage daughter, who was finishing a weekend sleepover at a friend's house. Andi was such a social woman; she'd owned a catering company out in California where she and Mark met, and she loved people and parties and conversation. I knew it was only because Amanda had been in so much trouble in Santa Barbara that they'd moved out to this lonely spot. Amanda was doing so much better, it seemed, that she might actually be able to go to college after she graduated next year, and I wondered if Mark and Andi would move on as well. I watched her talking, her animated face bright with interest in Sara's answers about Michael and his college studies.

My grandmother's 'antiques' were stored in this barn—at least, what wasn't being used by Mark and Andi or by Ryan and Sara or me in our homes. We had all agreed that furniture was meant to be used, and we shared everything freely within the family, with only a proscription against selling or donating something without offering it to everyone first. Andi unlocked the door, and we ducked in just as it began to rain again. The rain beat down on the tin roof, and, for a few minutes, it was too loud for conversation. I had to admit I wasn't disappointed by that. Sara and I can talk or not, and Ryan and I have been known to spend hours without saying a word, but Andi and Mark are both cheerful, chatty creatures with positive attitudes and a willingness to dig into anyone's life at any given moment. The peace was an unexpected benefit.

What we all called the 'small barn' was actually a tiny old house that one of my ancestors had built, something similar to a 'mother-in-law apartment' these days, I guess, although this one had no indoor plumbing. It was full of furniture and collectibles stacked to the ceiling in some parts of the room, and I couldn't help but contrast the disorder to Hattie Shelton's warehouse. I grinned at the thought of Hattie in this room with its disorganized piles, clipboard in hand and imaginary pith helmet pushed to the back of her head in dismay. A couch had boxes of books and dishes piled on it, while dining chairs and end tables were jumbled together with coffee tables and book-shelves.

I was looking for something in particular that day, a box of used books my grandmother had given me when I changed my major to pre-law and really started thinking of law school. There was a green hard-backed and dog-eared copy of *Black's Law Dictionary* in there, and a crumbling copy of Henry Maine's *Ancient Law*, two old law books that had served lawyers for years before law schools and bar exams had become the norm. There were other books in there, a few of them more than a hundred years old, some a bit newer but no less weighty for their relative youth. Holding them made me feel connected to generations of lawyers who took care of clients as if they were family, minding their duties and responsibilities long before the state bar codified ethical rules. I missed them.

Although she didn't make a big deal of it, I could tell she'd been collecting them for years, and I wondered how she'd known I would practice law before I knew. She died during my first year of law school, telling me before she died how proud she was of me for 'doing the hard things' and not giving up. I wondered, as I stood there in the musty house with the rain pounding on the roof, what she would think of me now.

———

SARA HAD FOUND A COUPLE OF BOXES WITH CHINA AND CRYSTAL odds and ends that she wanted to take back with her and explore, and we all three waited until the rain stopped to carry them out to the car. We loaded them into the back of the Jeep while Ryan and Mark stood on the porch talking, both of them tall men with glasses and shocks of longish hair, Ryan's light brown like mine, Mark's a sandy blond that reminded me of my grandmother's. They were clearly both excited, laughing and talking, their postures familiar to me. I realized, as I stared, that they both reminded me of my father when I was growing up: a tall man who spoke with his hands to tell a story, all big gestures and facial movements. That seemed to be so far away from the man in the memory-care center I was about to visit. I blinked the wetness in my eyes away as I knelt to pet one of the dogs.

Andi was saying something about Memorial Day and a picnic, which made me think about Gerard's sister's party the next week. I'd have to decide what to do about that. As much as I liked him some-times, our shared history was turbulent. I sighed and stood up to stretch my back, noticing that Ryan and Mark seemed to be going strong. Sara and I exchanged an amused eyebrow raise, knowing that

Ryan could stay and talk about the farm for hours, and I felt my left eyebrow itch a tiny bit. Sara looked at her smartwatch, clearly ready to say something about getting to her parents' house before dinnertime, when it began to rain again. Andi ran for the porch, and Ryan said his goodbyes, sprinting to the Jeep and throwing himself in just as it began to rain in earnest.

He tossed something back at me as he buckled in, and I picked it up from the floorboard where it landed. It was a bound pamphlet, with dark blue cardstock cover and back and a spiral binding. A label on the front read "Blackberry Bend Farm: Business Plan," and it was almost an inch thick.

"What's this?" I began to flip through it, stopping when I saw photos of the trees next to Sanders Creek, the dividing line between the Samuel Dalton piece and the Lamarcus Dalton piece. The creek was heavily bordered by trees and blackberry bushes on both sides, and summer blackberry picking figured heavily in my childhood memories of the farm. The picture had clearly been taken last summer, when the trees were in full fruit, and the heavy berries pulled the bush branches down low to the ground. Just looking at the picture made my mouth water. I turned the pages, flipping past pie charts and spreadsheets.

"Mark has a really great idea for developing the farm. We didn't have near enough time to discuss it all, but I wanted to look at that and then come back."

My heart began to pound. "'Develop the farm'? I thought we all were in agreement not to break the farm up for development until we had to."

Ryan laughed as he wiped his hand over his wet hair, his excitement palpable. "It's not breaking it up. That's the great thing. He's got an idea for turning the farm into an organic farming experiment and learning center. Even some B&B cabins and a fresh food market in the old pole barn." He turned the windshield wipers up to high as he turned around in the gravel drive, and I swear I could feel my breathing increase to match as I flipped over a page or two. I stopped at a page with an artist's rendering of the pole barn with stalls and vendors selling vegetables and crafts. I closed the book.

Ryan continued to talk with much accompanying hand motions, and I let his words flow over me. Sara responded, and I hoped she was calming him down, talking him down from this ledge where he was taking flight, but I was very much afraid she was just as excited as she was.

———

Ryan pressed me to keep the business plan, telling me that Mark had already emailed him a copy. Sara was a bit quieter and watched me closely as we said goodbye with a hug. I took a special small package of tamales with me that Ricky had wrapped for my dad. Ricky's wayward son was nowhere to be found when we got there, but my car was still fine anyway.

I tossed the business plan on the passenger seat and drove mechanically to Plano, my hands damp on the steering wheel, trying desperately not to think about buildings and markets and business plans and changes. Ryan had left me with a hug and an ebullient "Grandmother would hate this idea," and I knew he was right. She was forever lecturing us on our responsibilities to the family, to the history of the family, and this farm was a prominent symbol of that history, kept pretty much like it had been when our ancestors had lived there. I'm not sure why the idea of our grandmother disliking the idea was so attractive to him, but, just like it had been when we were teenagers, the idea of her disapproval was like a red flag to a bull.

I got to the memory-care center where my dad lived now, arriving right after their early dinnertime. I sent up a mental prayer to whatever deity might exist that it had been a good day for him. For once, someone seemed to be listening. He was up, his hair combed and his olive-green cardigan neatly buttoned over his pale blue pajamas, watching a DVD we'd gotten him of *Ironside*, one of his favorite old television series, and he greeted me by name when I came in.

Dad had been diagnosed with early onset Alzheimer's disease when he was 57, and the disease had progressed faster than they'd expected or we'd feared. Recently, he'd become combative and confused, as well as physically uncontrollable, and we'd moved him to Landover Avenue a couple of weeks ago. They seemed to be taking good care of him: his room was spotless and so was he. I tucked the three tamales into his tiny refrigerator and made a mental note to let the caregivers know it was there. He patted the seat next to him, and we watched the rest of the episode together.

When the next one started, he asked me to mute the volume. I sat next to him on the love seat and told him about the visit to the farm, and he asked after Mark and Andi—a very good sign. It meant that he was remembering they'd moved there about four years ago, and that meant he wasn't living far, far in the past but was aware of the passage of time and recent events. I told him a few things about Mark's business plan, my heart pounding a bit as I repeated Ryan's enthusiastic descriptions. Dad seemed to approve of the plan—or was at least positive about the idea.

"Your grandmother would hate it," he said, confirming Ryan's supposition, "but your great-grandmother would definitely approve. She loved that place, and she expected everyone else to agree." He smiled. "My mother hated it."

"If she felt that way, why did she stay there?"

"It was home, even though she wanted to get away from it all her life," he said and sighed, focusing on the television for a moment. "She thought she'd escaped when she married my father, but then he died right after I was born, and she had to move back in with her mother."

"It's a great place, or it was to grow up." I resolved to keep a happy tone. "Remember blackberry picking in July?"

He nodded, squeezing my hand. "And you getting your hair tangled in brambles every time. You were fearless, even when you should have had some fear." He yawned, blinking rapidly, and I saw his hands clench, so I took hold of the one closest to me. "My mother had a love-hate relationship with the land. She didn't like the farm, but she knew family was the most important thing." He sighed heavily. "Even though I didn't like it at the time, she was right to have us come live with her."

"That was her idea?"

He nodded, his eyes far away. "She knew there was no way I could be the father I needed to be if we were struggling in McKinney." He looked down at our joined hands. "And I truly had no idea what work I could have done if I hadn't been an engineer. The idea of trying to do something else was almost as frightening as trying to raise you and Ryan alone."

I thought about my grandmother's gift of law books before I'd even decided to go to law school. "I got my law books out of the small barn."

He smiled at me, a dimple flashing, the ghost of my charming father alive and well, the green of his cardigan making his gray eyes look deep and clear. For a moment, I thought perhaps we'd been precipitous about putting him in the memory care facility. He seemed so present, so alert tonight.

"She'd been gathering those for a few years, you know. She just knew you'd eventually get the message." He chuckled and absently scratched a healing scab on the back of his hand.

"I wonder sometimes if she'd be proud of me." I inhaled and watched a silent Raymond Burr talking to his young colleagues. The show seemed a bit forward-thinking for the late 1960s; he had a white guy, a girl, and a black guy working for him. He also seemed really confident, a disabled ex-cop solving a mystery before wheeling back out to wherever he went when he was finished.

The silence stretched for a minute, and I realized he was asleep, his eyes closed and his breathing regular. I shifted on the sofa, wondering if I should leave him there or wake him up, and he opened his eyes, blinking a bit at the soft light in the room.

"Rhonda, would you mind locking up when you're finished watching TV? I'm going on to bed. Very tired tonight." He stretched awkwardly.

I didn't want to remind him that I was Lacey, Rhonda's daughter, so I just assured him I would. I helped him into bed, and then I folded his cardigan, leaving it on the end of the bed when I left.

CHAPTER NINE

MONDAY, FEBRUARY 25

I'd left the business plan on the passenger seat when I got home the night before, so it was there to greet me on Monday morning when I headed out to meet Jerry Freeman at the Tarantino house. Karan had had a set of keys delivered to me about 7:30 am, so I stopped to get coffee on the way.

I sipped a cinnamon latte and avoided looking at the blue booklet as I drove down Lakewood Boulevard. It was cold and looked like rain, but there were still joggers out at 7:45 am. I stopped at a stop sign and waved a woman jogging and pushing a double stroller to cross in front of me. She looked to be in her late 30s, wearing expensive yoga capris and running shoes, talking avidly on a Bluetooth earpiece as she jogged. She waved her thanks to me and never missed a beat as she jogged across. I imagined she was a banker or lawyer getting in her daily jog before leaving her kiddies with the au pair to head off for work downtown. If so, she would be the perfect demographic for the Lakewood crowd these days.

I drove slowly, mindful of the 30-mph speed limit and also the pedestrians and joggers. Lakewood is an area to savor anyway. Like Martin had said on Saturday night, this neighborhood is a beautiful Dallas oddity, all perfectly manicured yards and enormous 60-foot tall trees and houses with stained glass windows. Most of the houses are carefully-renovated and architecturally-significant homes from the 1930s, but there are a few newer ones tucked in here and there, some made to look old and others blatantly post-modern. It makes me itch to buy an old house and spend years renovating it. Luckily, I don't have the scratch for that itch.

I turned off on Lakeway Circle, a cul-de-sac that splits off Lakewood to the south, only three houses around a circle of asphalt. The Tarantino house, at 7224 Lakeway Circle, was flanked on either side by a house as different as could be from the red brick mansion they neighbored. On one side was something that looked like an English country cottage, tidily tan-painted brick with multi-paned windows shining in what little sunlight there was, bookended by two tall chimneys and trimmed in black shutters. On the other side was a yellowish stucco Spanish-style house, with a sloping multi-colored tile roof and a large, stained-glass window on the front, typical of the art deco houses of Lakewood built in the 1930s. Both had beautiful yards with cloth-draped flower beds and budding trees.

The Tarantino house did not.

If the Tarantinos had spent the million-plus dollars they'd gotten for renovations already, none of it was spent on landscaping. The property was surrounded by a rusting iron fence with sharply pointed pickets and a red brick base, complete with heavy, locked gates. Thickly overgrown trees and bushes choked the fence and gates, and what view there was from outside the gates showed that any flowers in the brick-bordered beds had long ago been crowded out by weeds and opportunistic shrubs. I stood for a minute at the gates, looking through at the house and grounds.

According to Martin Dove and the other information I'd found, Jack O'Toole had paid an architect to create the plans for this house, but the design had been his: it was a huge, mock-Tudor mansion with a central main portion and two wings that protruded from the back, one with the kitchen, laundry, and guest rooms, and the other with a library and study and the bedrooms for the family.

It was bricked, like many others in Lakewood, in a dark red brick, and the windows on the front were mullioned with leaded sections. In fact, it looked like many of the houses in Lakewood, but on a scale much larger than those houses. The property information left over on the Internet from the listing a few years ago showed this house had 7 bedrooms, 6 bathrooms, a study, a library, a full laundry, a formal dining room and a breakfast nook, and two living areas. The pictures had been dark and uninviting, but the title on the sales entry was an optimistic 'Renovation Dream.'

I used one of the keys Karan had sent me to unlock the padlock hanging on a heavy chain on the gate and swung it to the inside just as Jerry Freeman drove up in his pickup. I waved him in and then drove in behind him. The brick-paved driveway was deeply embedded with dead grass between the pavers, and it circled around a dry fountain. We both parked in front of the house and, as one, stepped out to look around.

Mr. Freeman pulled on a cap as he exited his truck, his face mournful as always, and whistled through his teeth. "This place is huge." He clucked his tongue like an old hen. "What a shame it's been left like this." He felt in his pocket for a square cinnamon sucker and handed it to me, and I gave him the coffee I'd bought for him. He immediately slurped a sip of the coffee and looked as happy as he ever did.

I held up a finger. "Hold that thought." I used one of the keys on the front door lock, which gleamed like new gold in the old arched doors. It opened the right side of the double door, and we stepped into a foyer, where it became obvious where the Tarantinos had started their renovations. Jerry Freeman whistled again, and this time I silently agreed.

The foyer was part of a grand entrance hall, with a central staircase of deep, rich wood leading up to a central landing, which then split into separate staircases going up to the second floor. Above the landing on the back wall of the foyer was a massive, round stained-glass window that reminded me of the Rose Window in Notre Dame in Paris. It must have been original, because I couldn't imagine what something like that would cost to create these days, but I was sure it would have blown the Tarantinos' renovation budget. The foyer floor had to be marble, but, since I'd never seen marble floors up close, I wasn't sure.

I dodged over to the alarm pad to enter the code Karan had sent with the keys, and then I realized I did not want to be holding a coffee cup around this expensive renovation work. We took a few sips, and then I took both of our cups back out to my car.

When I returned, I stood just inside the door and looked at the place with a more critical receiver's eye. Beside me, I saw Jerry Freeman begin to make notes on an electronic tablet with a stylus, muttering to himself as he noted details. (It always surprised me when he did that; I imagined the crusty little man in his 70s would use pen and paper, but he told me his granddaughter had upgraded him a few years ago. Turns out, he loved the functionality and ability to make notes directly into a form that he uploaded back at the office.)

Beneath each of the staircases were French doors leading outside, but the sky was darkening with rain and I couldn't see from the front door what might be behind the house. On each side of the foyer, graceful arches led into beautiful, sparsely furnished rooms: the one on the left was a formal dining room with what was apparently a barrel vault ceiling (as Mr. Freeman informed me as he followed me into the room) and a fireplace on the far wall, opening into a huge kitchen on the end—clearly updated already. The kitchen was completely outfitted with every appliance or device a cook could ever want, from the huge stainless steel and glass refrigerators (two of them) to a gas range that would have dwarfed my first college apartment. There were two dishwashers, a separate pair of ovens, and an island that was the size of a real island between the kitchen and a generously-proportioned breakfast nook. Beyond the kitchen was a huge laundry room and a large butler's pantry, with a separate bathroom and storage room and a tiny well-lit office that happily reminded me of the space being fitted out for me back at home.

Mr. Freeman was whistling and checking under counters and behind doors, so I told him I was going around to the other wing. On the other side of the foyer, a grand living room was just beyond the arched opening, and I caught my breath when I saw the fireplace on the far wall. Where the fireplace in the dining room was large, with decorous wood carving in the surround and mantel all painted white, this one was enormous, reaching to the ceiling of the room, an art deco masterpiece of mosaic tiles that brought in all the colors of the rainbow beneath a dark wood mantel with carved embellishments. It was fanciful and unrestrained and dwarfed anything else in the room. The floors continued the marble from the foyer, and the furniture was velvet, deep blues and greens, with dark wood that came close to matching the mantel. A large rug warmed the room a little, but the thermostat in the house was set at 60, and none of the rugs helped much with that.

I heard Mr. Freeman going up the stairs, muttering to himself as I dawdled in the living room, looking at the doodads and books on an ornamental bookshelf fitted into one wall. Except for their clothes and personal items, all of the Tarantinos' artwork, furniture, and décor would have to be inventoried and divided, or (if they couldn't agree on a just division) sold and the funds kept in the court for the final divorce disposition. My mind ticked away on a long to-do list, an imaginary precursor to the one I'd make when I was in front of my laptop.

A set of matched wooden doors opened into another room, a large, unrenovated library with empty and dusty shelves and a scratched and pitted wood floor, and it gave me an idea of what the skeleton of the house had looked like before the renovations. I moved on quickly, since I hate seeing empty bookshelves. Perhaps it's the booklover in me, but it always leaves me feeling sad and empty too.

A small study was beyond the library, a modern standing desk in the middle, strewn with plans and documents. I looked them over without touching them. They appeared to be the blueprints for a fairly extensive renovation of the rooms and bathrooms in the kitchen wing, and I wondered again how much of the funds they'd borrowed for renovation remained. The office and library both had French doors leading out into the garden, matching two sets of French doors opposite in the kitchen wing, probably in the breakfast nook and office. I rolled up the plans for Jerry to take with him for the as-built appraisal.

I'm not a very 'spiritually perceptive' person, but, standing there and looking at the empty windows reflecting the gray sky, that house felt lonely and abused to me, and I desperately wanted air. I unlocked one of the doors and stepped outside, where the air was only slightly colder than the inside.

The French doors on the back of the foyer and doors on the wings all opened onto a large patio made of thick rectangular granite stones. Because the house protected the patio on three sides, weeds grew in between the stones, even this deep into the winter. Large planters stood empty at the corners, and the grass was overgrown and scraggly. The yard beyond the patio began to slope down to heavy trees, but a path had been created long ago with irregularly shaped flat stones, and it continued on through the trees. I knew that eventually the path ended at an iron gate that opened onto Chapel Park and then the headlands next to White Rock Lake, but I couldn't see it from here.

The door behind me opened, and I almost jumped out of my skin. Jerry Freeman didn't notice as he crunched down on the last of the cinnamon candy and took the lollipop stick out of his cheek to speak to me. "Miss, there's something upstairs I think you need to see."

———

"BLOOD?" I ECHOED. I SAID THE FIRST THING THAT POPPED INTO my head. "How do you know it's blood?" We stood there in the doorway to the closet, our shoulders touching, looking into the dark space lit only by his flashlight.

To his credit, Jerry Freeman didn't roll out his 30-plus years in real estate to prove he knew what he was talking about. He scratched his chin, then took out another cinnamon sucker and offered it to me. I took it without thinking, but after unwrapping it and popping it into my mouth, I realized the cinnamon and the normality of the activity was just what I needed too.

"I can't rightly say, miss." He unwrapped another sucker and tucked it into his cheek. We stood there for a moment looking at the stains on the wall, the only sounds the particularly unlovely but comforting sucking noises you make when you're trying to get hard candy down to a manageable size in your mouth. Finally, he spoke again. "There's just a rusty brown color that you can't fake with anything else." He sighed. "I've had my share of trying to appraise a house that's had some kind of bad thing happen in it. I always feel a bit bad for the house, since it didn't do anything wrong, but everybody goes on like it will be stained forever."

"Maybe they're worried about ghosts," I said, trying (and failing) to lighten the mood. Suddenly the closet and the attic seemed dark and menacing, and I realized we were talking about a person's blood, the blood of someone who had been confined, probably *involuntarily* confined, to this tiny space, and who had bled enough to have left bloodstains on the wall. The realization made me queasy. "So, you've found things like this before?"

He shook his head. "Most of the time, someone's been killed or died under suspicious circumstances, and—well, you know you have to disclose that for a sale—so they bring me in for a re-appraisal."

He kept talking, but again, I lost track of his words after 'you know you have to disclose it for the sale.' I hadn't even known that, and for a moment, I wallowed in the shame I always felt when I came up hard against my insufficient knowledge in some area of the law. How could I call myself a real estate lawyer if I didn't know that about a house sale?

I shook it off and tuned back in. Mr. Freeman was talking about the lockbox now, and I realized I didn't know if we were looking at a crime scene that should be preserved or not. Could I take the lockbox with me? Should I? Who did it belong to? Was the house sold to the Tarantinos with the box in it? Was it included in the house sale? If not, who did it belong to?

My head was swimming. Distantly, I heard Mr. Freeman say he was going to finish the inspection on the other side of the house. He moved off, but I stood in the closet and wondered what to do next.

Finally, logic reasserted itself, and I realized once I got out of the house, I could make a list of my questions and get an idea of the steps in front of me. I turned the light in my phone on and, from the doorway, looked more closely at the walls. The purported blood stains were reddish-brown streaks, with a couple of spots that looked like splatter. They were all badly faded, about three feet from the floor. I took a few pictures of the stains, then shone the light around the rest of the closet. On the floor were a couple of white spots, and as I bent closer with the phone, I realized they were beads of hardened wax. Above them, the wooden wall boards seemed to be lighter in a pattern. I shone the light and backed up as much as I could without getting into the closet. Was that a cross?

I shivered. There was such an emotional pall over this space. It was cold, and it was dark, and I didn't want to be there. I took pictures of everything: the closet, the walls, the floor, and the lockbox and then I left the lockbox where it was, closed the wall panel, and descended the stairs to the landing in the foyer, bypassing the completely unrenovated guest rooms on the second floor above the kitchen. I could hear Jerry Freeman moving in and out of rooms and muttering to himself, and I followed the comforting noises to the family side of the house. A huge bedroom overlooked the back of the house, clearly renovated and modernized.

A modern platform king-size bed dominated the room, which had been re-plastered in a stark white. The wide-plank wood floors were a light oak and couldn't have been original, and they were covered almost to the edges by an enormous, fluffy, off-white rug. A large bathroom had been added, with a stand-alone tub in front of a window overlooking the backyard, a gigantic open shower with seating for—I counted—six, and a water closet that held both a toilet and a bidet. Through a connecting door, another bedroom had been converted to matching walk-in closets that were each bigger than my living room. It looked like—and felt like—a luxury penthouse master bedroom, and I felt a bit disappointed in its bland modernity. Even the fireplace in this room had been painted over and converted to a shiny black and white glass tile façade.

There had been two other bedrooms on this floor, but they had converted these spaces into the walk-in closets or the sitting area on the end of the bedroom facing the front of the house. I followed in Jerry Freeman's footsteps up a narrow set of stairs to the third-floor attic on this side, which looked like it been used as a nursery or children's rooms when they were originally constructed. Like the rooms on the other side of the house, they had not yet been remodeled, but rather than cabbage rose wallpaper, the walls had been hand-painted with murals.

One room was clearly a boy's room, with faded red, blue, and green boats cruising across a painted ocean, while the other had delicately painted trees with swings where fanciful mice and rabbits and raccoons and badgers and other woodland creatures played. They reminded me of Beatrix Potter book illustrations, and I traced one column of the flowery designs with my finger, still able to feel the strokes where someone had spent hours hand-painting the beautiful images. I could not imagine what artisans would have been paid to do such intricate work in the 1930s, but I knew that these walls would have been re-plastered or painted a bland white in the Tarantinos' remodeling. A part of me mourned their future loss, while a more pragmatic part knew that such outmoded gender-specific decorating would be disfavored by today's wealthy parents. The Tarantinos never planned to live here, raise children here, or grow old here, unlike the people who designed this home and engaged artists to decorate its walls.

I wandered back downstairs and considered braving the jungle in the back garden while I waited for Mr. Freeman to finish. The French doors in the main foyer, like those of both wings, had simple thumb latches, and I made a mental note to have the locks changed to two-sided keyed entries once the house was listed and activity began. Residential construction is notorious for security issues, and, since I didn't yet know whether the house would be sold as-is or as-built with additional construction, I didn't want to be behind the ball on getting security in. We might also want to have cameras installed that could live-feed to a security company. I hadn't made up my mind yet about the decision to complete renovations before listing, but I wanted to see what had been spent already. My list was growing.

Before I could go back outside, Jerry Freeman came down the stairs whistling. Since he wasn't doing a full appraisal yet, he wasn't really concerned about the grounds, but I would need to get a landscape company to come out and do an estimate. I sighed, feeling a bit of a headache starting. The previous receivership had been easy compared to his one, the house needing only to be listed and sold.

"Well, miss, you've got quite a project on your hands!" Jerry Freeman wasn't actually rubbing his hands in glee, but he seemed a bit happier about that 'project' than I did. He proffered another cinnamon sucker, and I hesitated a few seconds before taking it. I could always just tuck it into my purse for later. "I've been thinking about it—why don't I get you the as-is appraisal first, and then you can get me together with their architect or contractor or whatever and we can get the as-built done?"

"That's a great idea. How long do you think the as-is will take?"

He held up his smart tablet. "With this thing? Maybe tomorrow night, maybe Wednesday." We agreed to talk tomorrow after he got all his information uploaded, and perhaps meet for coffee later in the week to go over the next steps. He loved Café au Lait's cinnamon knots almost as much as I did, so we knew exactly where we'd meet.

We walked to the front door and opened it just as a cold rain began to patter on the heavy foliage on either side of the steps. Like most mock-Tudors, the house had no front porch, and I watched as Mr. Freeman ran for his truck, his arms full of rolled-up plans, and then he waved as he drove back through the gates.

I turned back into the house, considering a bit more exploration, but I couldn't shake the cold, lonely feeling that pervaded the old house. To be honest, I was slightly creeped out by the whole thing. I knew what I needed to do: get some distance, a cup of hot coffee, and a pad and paper to make some lists. I set the alarm and locked the doors, feeling a definite sense of relief as I turned the key on the gate lock and then drove away.

———

I SETTLED IN TO ONE END OF A TABLE AT CAFÉ AU LAIT JUST AS most of the early morning crowd left. This place was in my east Dallas neighborhood, a converted warehouse-turned-commercial bakery that was my favorite workspace and lunch venue. Marie Haught and her staff start serving pastries and coffee at 6, and there's a great lull about 10 am, when I'm usually looking for a cinnamon latte and something to eat. Esther, Marie Haught's weekday counterperson, could be your best friend or your worst enemy where special consideration was concerned—depending on her horoscope for the day. Cinnamon knots were sold only by the dozen, but if the astrological signs were favorable, she was known to split a dozen amongst the regular customers. If not, a dozen would be just fine with me. I'd take them home and warm them up for dinner.

Today was a good day to be a Sagittarius, according to Esther, and so I had a small plate of cinnamon knots cooling next to my steaming latte as I pulled out my pad and Gerard's Mont Blanc pen. I'd tucked it into my bag this morning, intending to make sure I gave it back to him if I saw him. I weighed the pen in my hand and decided to attack another Gerard-related problem: his invitation to his sister's Texas Independence Day party this weekend.

A *family* party. I thought about what that might be like—his sister looking me over, silently judging me, his other family members (whomever they might be) wondering about the nature of our relationship. I shuddered at the thought of the emotional pressure.

I wasn't even sure I *liked* Gerard. A part of me scoffed at that, and the more honest part of me knew that there was something there, some chemistry that had grown between us recently as we worked together on the Todd Parrish case. I sighed and tested the temperature of a cinnamon knot with a finger. Still too hot. I licked the butter and cinnamon off my fingertip and considered the truth. I'd found Gerard and his shockingly black eyebrows attractive five years ago when he represented Bill Stephenson. Imagine how uncomfortable that had been, that little *zing* of attraction whenever he was around, as I had been grilled relentlessly by him and others about a supposed crush on my old boss.

It felt like I was just learning to move on from the events of the past five years; would seeing Gerard socially just bring that all back? Did I want to complicate my life in that way? Would it be worth it to get tangled up with him? I realized I was shaking my head. He was like canned whipped cream: you know the fact that it is *an aerosol can of whipped cream* means that, regardless of how good it tastes, it is not something you should ever have in your refrigerator. Gerard represented all of that negative stuff from years ago and dating him would just stir up all those feelings. I took up my phone to decline.

· · ·

G, THANK YOU FOR THE INVITE TO YOUR SISTER'S PARTY. *WHAT CAN I bring?*

I'M SPINELESS AND WEAK AND NOT A GOOD EXAMPLE TO ANYONE trying to ignore the temptations hiding in the refrigerator.

CHAPTER TEN

Monday, February 25 (continued)

By mid-afternoon, I'd put in a couple of hours of list-making for the Tarantino project and several other things on my plate and was feeling pretty smug about my preparedness level. I'd also been the recipient of some testing Marie was doing on chicken and tuna salad recipes that had resulted in a free lunch, something that makes me happy any day.

I got out of my car at home and realized that the construction team had stopped because of the morning's rain. With a canny glance around, I edged into the back to see if the new office door had been left unlocked.

It had not.

One lower pane of the French door was partially uncovered, though, and I spent a minute or so trying unsuccessfully to see inside. I finally stopped. The thought of one of the workers—or worse, Hattie

—finding me crouched over with my face plastered against the wet pane of glass was enough to stop that activity in its tracks.

My mail had been delivered, and I was pleased to find a couple of client checks. Most of my clients pay by check, since until recently you couldn't charge the transaction fee to someone buying something with credit card, and I couldn't afford the transaction fees to accept credit or debit cards. I did have a nifty card reader gadget I could use with my phone if I ever wanted to. Every once in a while, I'd plug it in and play with it. I loved learning new things but risking my income on something I'm unfamiliar with is still a bit hard for me. I'd promised myself that very soon I'd learn to use one of the new money transfer apps I'd heard about.

One of the checks was from Shanna Barry, a class-action litigation attorney in Chicago I'd done some work for over the last six months. Her father, who'd lived in Dallas, had passed away, and Shanna was named executor in his will. She'd had a great probate lawyer here in Dallas, but she'd needed someone a bit less expensive to take care of the more basic issues of dealing with someone's estate: working with the remodeling contractor prepping her dad's house for sale, engaging appraisers for some collectibles, negotiating the settlement of some of her dad's debts or outstanding business matters. That kind of work is a dream for me since it involves list-making and resolution-reaching, two of my favorite things.

Shanna had paid her bill in full, and also included a sticky note with a thank you and a warning that she'd referred me to someone who might be calling in the next few weeks. A bit of money, more good news, and more work to do. I did a little quick step in my kitchen, glad for a reminder that some Mondays are definitely better than others. I spent a happy few minutes depositing the checks with my phone and then tallying up accounts.

Things dimmed a bit after talking to the real estate agent I'd decided to use for the Tarantino house, Suzy Shapiro. She'd confirmed Jerry Freeman's statement that someone dying in the house (outside of natural causes or suicide) would need to be disclosed. But had someone actually died there outside of natural causes? A lot of rumor was out there, but what were the facts? Facts I loved—rumor I could do without. She agreed to meet me at the house on Thursday morning to take a look and help me make some decisions.

I stretched, thinking about the information Martin Dove had found on Saturday and the rumors he'd hinted about. Would he be willing to share his information and sources so I could decide on the need for disclosure? I paced for a few minutes, considering the matter, before getting my phone out. I found his card and sent a text to the mobile number listed there.

Hi, Martin. It's Lacey Benedict. You know you'd mentioned that you were available for more info on the O'Toole house? I might need some help.

I thought for a minute, and realized I had no way to pay him to be an expert.

I know you're probably busy, but maybe I could buy you lunch or something in exchange for some information.

The reply came faster than I expected.

Drinks tonight at the Adolphus lobby bar at 6?

Whew. A little expensive, but I was billing by the hour for this...

. . .

ABSOLUTELY. *THANK YOU FOR THE QUICK RESPONSE!*

GREAT. NOW I'D HAVE TO FIGURE OUT WHAT I'D HAVE TO WEAR for a bar in the Adolphus Hotel. Sallie would know.

———

AT A FEW MINUTES BEFORE SIX, I WAS LEAVING MY CAR WITH A valet at the entrance of the Adolphus Hotel in downtown Dallas and trying to pretend I was cool with an exorbitant valet parking charge. It's hard enough to find parking in downtown, and when you add in rain and heeled boots—well, let's say that the (ouch!) $20 better be worth it.

The Adolphus Hotel is a grand hotel in Dallas's downtown, built in 1912 by Adolphus Busch—yes, of the Anheuser-Busch family— and renovated several times, most recently a few years ago. Walking up the stairs in the main entrance takes you back to an earlier time, a more gracious one, when people socialized in hotel lobbies, rather than hurrying through with your wheelie suitcase to a bland, modern hotel room.

I walked up the marble staircase to the lobby, glad I'd listened to Sallie and worn something nice. She'd pulled this dressy black skirt suit out of the back of my closet and suggested some spike-heeled black leather boots with them. I rarely wear anything with heels, but this *was* the Adolphus. I polished the dust off the boots and took a chance.

Fires were burning in the twin fireplaces on either side of the lobby, and couples and small groups of people in varying levels of business and casual dress sat with drinks in their hands on the velvet sofas flanking the hearths. Some looked like they were dressed for dinner at The French Room, the hotel's five-star restaurant.

Martin Dove was there at the lobby bar before me, holding a martini glass and chatting with the bartender. He was dressed in a light gray suit ('dove' gray, perhaps?), a white shirt with a complicated stiff collar, and a satiny-white tie. If I don't understand women's fashion, I understand men's even less. In some ways, his outfit looked both formal and informal at the same time, but it definitely looked good on his trim build. He beamed when he saw me and stepped forward to greet me, giving me a hug and a double-cheek kiss as he did so. My cheeks heated, and he smiled at me. "Don't you look nice! Is this for me, or do you have a date after we meet?"

"No date," I told him drily, "just trying not to shame you at the Adolphus."

He tsked under his breath. "You could never do that. What would you like to drink?" He tucked my hand under his arm and turned to the bartender—a truly handsome young man himself—with a charming smile. "Thomas here can make you anything you'd like."

I ordered a beer from the bartender (whose nametag read 'Tom'), noticing that he was much more attentive to Martin than he was to me. *Ah well*, I thought.

Martin took a look at my long, slim skirt and skinny-heeled boots and then at the high bar stools. "Why don't we find some place more comfortable?" He looked around, and then pointed out two turquoise velvet chairs with high backs angled towards each other, close to the fire but away from the laughing groups on the sofas. Thomas assured us he would bring us our drinks, so we settled ourselves into the chairs.

"I sense that you are a woman who gets to the bottom line without much chitchat, so I won't bore you with small talk." Martin twinkled at me, but I didn't feel mocked by his statement. It was true.

"Do you find small talk boring?" I sensed I was sitting with a *master* of small talk, and I truly wanted to know.

He looked surprised that I would ask, but he took the question seriously as he settled into the plush velvet. "I would suppose that, by definition, 'small talk' is discussion that doesn't go to the heart of the

matter but is uninteresting and meaningless. If I then find it interesting, or I find it has meaning, then it would, by that same definition,
not be 'small talk.'" He turned towards me, a serious expression on his
handsome face.

"Ah, but what if only one of the people in the discussion is interested or discovers the meaning? Must both people be interested to
kick it out of the small talk category?" Tom brought us our drinks
with crisp white Adolphus coasters and a silver bowl of smoked and
seasoned pecans, almonds, and Brazil nuts, which he set on the tiny
wooden table between our chairs. Martin waited until the bartender
had arranged everything, and then flashed him a 'thank you' smile
and thanked him. I would have done the same, but Tom never even
glanced my way. I watched him leave with what must have been a
rueful look and turned to find Martin watching me with that same
smile.

"That's another topic for another day, isn't it?" He patted my
hand, and then picked up his drink and sat back in his chair. "So, tell
me, my dear, how creepy was the Tarantino-O'Toole house?"

———

I'd DECIDED, WHEN DRIVING TO THE ADOLPHUS, TO KEEP THE
possible bloodstains out of the conversation with Martin Dove, but I
did describe the house in as much other detail as I could. I ended
with the locked blue metal box, something Martin loved as much as
I did.

"Oooh, hidden treasure," he enthused. "But to whom does it
belong?"

I'd wondered the same thing, so that afternoon I'd put in a call to
Callie Deal, Shanna Barry's probate attorney, and asked some questions in exchange for a lunch to be named later. She agreed that it
would hinge on who was awarded the remainder of the contents of
the home in Jack O'Toole's will, and whether any 'contents' had been
sold to the Tarantinos by the estate. Martin threw in another wrench.

"You know that house was leased for several years after Jack O'Toole died." At my grimace, he nodded. "I know. So...unless you're sure that box was there when Old Man O'Toole left this earth in 1980, it could belong to some tenants as well."

"Well, I'm going to start with Mr. O'Toole. Callie said that probated wills are a matter of public record, so I'm going to see if he had one, and if so, what it said, and who inherited." I took a sip of beer.

"My mother remembered the O'Tooles very well, it turned out," Martin slid into the tiny silence. He toyed with the stem of his martini glass. "She was a bit younger than Patrick and Leona. The children," he added, at my look. "She said everyone knew that Leona O'Toole Franks didn't speak to her father, but she died a few months before the father did—not even 50 years old yet. Cancer," he said with a sigh and a shake of the head.

We sat in silence for a moment, the way you do, thinking of murderous diseases and lives lost before he spoke again. "So that means that his living relatives were his son Patrick, and his grandchildren Peter and Judith."

Hmmm. "I wonder if they live here in Dallas."

Martin eyed me over the rim of his glass. "Oh, my dear, you're joking."

"What?"

"Well, I'm not sure where Patrick O'Toole and Peter Franks are, but Judith Franks Jensen is very much here in Dallas." He made a moue of distaste.

"What aren't you saying?"

He ate a few spicy pecans and took a sip of martini before answering. I got the feeling it wasn't him wasting time for effect, but, instead, he was choosing his words carefully. I let the silence steep, watching a couple across the lobby who seemed to be celebrating an anniversary. Finally, he spoke again. "Judith Jensen married well—very well indeed—to a son of the Jensen family. You know, Jensen Electronics?"

I nodded. I did know Jensen Electronics. The small, years-old television in my apartment was a Jensen.

"She's the reason Jensen opened their Dallas manufacturing facility. They met when she went off to finishing school, and apparently Judith insisted they move back to Dallas after they were married, instead of New York or somewhere else."

"Why? Was she that attached to Texas?"

Martin snorted before stirring his martini with the olive-studded swizzle stick. "Ever heard the expression 'better to be a big fish in a small pond'?" I nodded. "Well, Judith Franks Jensen comes from a short line of big fishes in the small pond that is Dallas. And she knows it." He flicked a microscopic piece of lint off his dove gray trousers, his lips pursed.

"You don't like her."

He looked up at me, and I could tell he was about to deny it with some witty evasion. He didn't, though. He dipped his head in acknowledgment and agreed. "I don't like her."

"Why not?" I picked a smoked almond out of the silver dish, crunching down on the nut with pleasure. I love a good story.

He sighed and sat back. "Do you know anything about my family?" I shook my head and washed the spice down with a sip of beer. "Both my mother and father's families come from good, solid, middle-class stock, my mother's from Illinois and my father's from Colorado. They met when they came to Dallas for college in the 1970s. And then my father used his business degree to make some good decisions on oil and gas investments in the early 1980s, and my parents became very wealthy almost overnight." He looked down into his glass and gently swirled the liquid there. "New money in Dallas isn't unusual—there have been a lot of overnight oil millionaires over the years—but my father's job as a bank executive meant they were in society a bit, both socially and philanthropically. My mother has a good heart, and she doesn't allow anyone to speak negatively about anyone else in her presence. On the other hand, Judith Jensen is the *queen* of negativity. Apparently, her mother and aunt were the same way. So, my mother just avoids her, doesn't invite her to events if she can help it. That has come to Judith Jensen's attention, and it has been remarked upon." He took a sip of the martini.

He shifted in his seat and looked at me with a calm but closed expression. "It would have just been something to laugh about, but a few years ago, Judith made a comment about me to someone, knowing it would get back to my mother." His shrugged with one shoulder and fixed his gaze on something over my left shoulder. "You see, unlike my dear spouse, I've known I was gay since high school. I'm not exceptionally flamboyant, but I've learned not to hide who I was, nor do I give people who don't like me or my lifestyle any satisfaction by feeling—*anything*. My mother is not that sanguine about it." His eyes met mine again. I tried to school my expression because I didn't think he really wanted my pity or sympathy, but something must have flitted across my face. He patted my arm. "It's all right, my dear, but thank you for that. If I feel anything, it's a bit of resentment that my mother has had to give it any time or attention or thought over the years."

He started to take a sip of martini but realized his glass was empty. "Goodness, it's lucky Gray will be driving home tonight!" He laughed with me, and then the twinkle returned to his eyes. "And I have my revenge. Judith's daughter Paige and Gray are *very* good friends."

"Is she like her mother?"

"Oh, dear me no," he said, shaking his head vehemently. "Not at all. She's a lovely girl, works for the family business, does good works in the community. Gray adores her." He looked at me out of the corner of his eye. "I try not to be jealous." Then he turned fully to me, his smile and his eyes widening. "Gray can introduce you!"

I swallowed the sip of beer I'd just taken too fast, and I coughed while Martin watched me with concern. "That'd be great," I choked out.

"If you want some background about Lakeway Circle, you should talk to Dorothea Allred. Her family has lived next door to the

O'Toole house since it was built." He tapped his chin, thinking. "I don't know how old she is, but she would have known Jack O'Toole. She's a lovely woman—Gray and I met her at one of the Lakewood annual parades. I can call her for you." His attention was diverted, as was mine and everyone else's in the room, when Gray appeared at the top of the stairs leading up from the street entrance. He saw us and smiled, and this time I was able to appreciate the warmth without the fear that he'd been set up for me. I got up, and he hugged me, then leaned over to greet his spouse with a kiss on his cheek. He smelled wonderful.

"Lacey, are you joining us for dinner?" he asked.

Martin turned to me. "Yes, Lacey, please do. We cannot waste your lovely outfit."

"No, no. I couldn't." I had no idea what food at The French Room cost, but I was pretty sure I couldn't afford it. "I'm sure you have a reservation for two, not three." I turned toward Tom at the bar to get the tab paid.

"Already taken care of, my dear," Martin said as he and Gray each took one of my arms and turned me toward the entrance of the restaurant. "And we always sit in the side booths, where there's plenty of space for three. You must let us treat you, while you tell us more about your plans for the Tarantino house." He leaned forward to look past me at Gray as we walked through the lobby, and his grin was devilish. "Lacey needs you to call Paige Jensen. And this time, it's not me who's the troublemaker."

CHAPTER ELEVEN

Haute cuisine, while expensive and (I would assume) exquisitely prepared, is not filling. I woke up late and ravenous the morning after dinner with Martin Dove and Gray Powell, but luckily there was food in my refrigerator. I cooked scrambled eggs, to the amazement of the cat, who sat at the edge of the kitchen watching me warily, as if unsure why I was in the room. I slid the eggs on a real plate and sat at the desk/table to eat, feeling like the chefs I'd watched the night before.

Tuesday was a day much like many of the days I've had as a lawyer. You do some research, prep some letters, you do more research, prep a report, do more research, and then you decide what needs to wait until tomorrow. After a bit of that, I went and stood in line at the post office, which is always my least favorite waste of time. The Lakewood post office is not a bad one, as post offices go. The staff is courteous and efficient, and many of the patrons know each other, so they talk in line. I usually check emails or communicate with clients by text while I'm standing there and try to learn patience from the experience. It amazes me how impatient Americans are about standing in line. The rest of the world expects lines (or 'queues') and are not annoyed by them, but pretty much every time I'm in a line here in Dallas, someone is volubly complaining about the line they're standing in. (I contrast this with the British, who will silently fume about the line, but will soldier on through the time spent in line with their upper lips stiffened—and shut.). I will not talk on the phone while I line, though—some lines are meant to be drawn.

I was pleased to be sending out several certified mail letters, most of them demand letters for my first commercial foreclosure taking place on the first Tuesday in April. I was a week or so ahead of the mailing deadline, but I was so apprehensive about doing something outside my comfort zone that I wanted to make sure they were in the mail early, just in case I screwed them up and had to re-do everything. The lender was hoping one of the guarantors would step in to save the property, so I was sending out demands to everyone. I whistled silently when I paid the total, happy my flat fee didn't cover postage.

I got in my car to find that Martin Dove had left me a voicemail in his slightly effusive tones; he had spoken with Dorothea Allred, and she would be pleased to share a cup of tea with me and have some conversation about Lakeway Circle, her family home, and Eleanor O'Toole the next day at 10 am, unless I couldn't make that time. I noticed the lack of mention of Jack O'Toole, and I wondered if Dorothea Allred, like everyone else mentioned so far, had a particular disdain for the man. Martin left me her phone number, and said she had mine, just in case she was having a bad day tomorrow. He also let me know that Gray had been in touch with Paige Jensen, and she would be contacting me. He ended with a plea for more to do if I needed it.

If I hadn't been sitting in my car at that moment, I would've done a quick happy step. There's nothing I like more than research and information gathering. I mentally added some heavy-duty research to my very empty evening to-do list as I steered the car out of the parking lot to run more errands.

By early afternoon, I was headed downtown to the Dallas county clerk's office to see if I could pull Jack O'Toole's will from the county probate records. The day had turned exceptionally warm and humid for the tail end of February, and, while I didn't want to turn the air conditioner on, rolling the windows down for a breath of fresh air in the concrete canyons downtown was a futile exercise. I pulled into a lot near Renaissance Tower and rode the elevator to the 24th floor.

The Dallas county clerk had been relocated a couple of years ago to this downtown office building while the building that had origi-nally housed the county clerk was renovated. While I appreciated the need for the move, I had to admit that the office building didn't have the same legal 'feeling' as the one adjacent to the courthouse where I'd researched documents and asked stupid questions when I first started practicing on my own.

I'd found the probate case for Jack O'Toole online last night. He'd died in October 1980, and the family's probate attorney had filed an application for probate the next week. I presumed that, since he had to be pretty old when he died, his death hadn't come as much of a shock. Wills that old weren't imaged online, so I needed to visit the clerk's office for a copy. About half an hour later, I walked out with 40 pages of an application for probate and the Last Will and Testa-ment of Jack O'Toole. The will had very ornate print on it, letting me know the estate attorney was probably old school—even in those days —so I was looking forward to reviewing it later.

I had a voicemail from Sonja Winston, a client of mine who buys investment residential real estate. She was planning on doing a few 'flips,' where an investor buys a property, renovates, and sells the property for (hopefully) a profit—usually within 45 or so days. She needed a new contract for a builder who'd be working with her, and could I review one she'd gotten from a friend who does house flip-ping? I texted her and said yes, making a mental note to review an article I'd seen in an online continuing legal education seminar about the pitfalls of house flipping in Texas.

I also had a voicemail from Gerard.

VOICEMAIL AGAIN, BENEDICT?

HE SIGHED, AND I SMILED, A CLEAR MENTAL PICTURE OF HIS eyebrows lowering in annoyance.

YOU DON'T NEED TO BRING ANYTHING SATURDAY EVENING. THERE will be enough food and drink for an army. Claire can't help herself.

A PAUSE, THEN HE CONTINUED, HIS VOICE GRUFF.

THANKS FOR AGREEING TO GO. I WAS PRETTY SURE YOU'D SAY NO. Be safe, Benedict, and see you at 6 on Saturday.

I ONLY LISTENED TO IT TWICE MORE BEFORE I CHASTISED myself sternly and started the car.

———

DINNER WAS LOOKING LIKE A RESEARCH FEST, SO I STOPPED BY Taco Time, a local food truck stationed near Greenville, and got a dozen street tacos. Don't judge—they're tiny corn tortillas, filled with extra-spicy shredded chicken or beef, a sprinkling of cheese, chopped cilantro, and a sliver of lime to squeeze. And they're wonderful. Messy—but wonderful. And who knows, I might save a few for later.

I ate a few of them watching an episode of *The Andy Griffith Show*, the one where it's Aunt Bee's birthday, but Andy is too clueless to know she'd rather have a frilly bed-jacket than a set of dish towels, even though she'd dropped some broad hints in his hearing. Everything would be all right by the end of the show, I knew, but I turned it off before it finished, disquieted to know that men were just as imperceptive back in the 1960s as they are today.

I had an email from Jerry Freeman's granddaughter, who acts as his office manager, with the as-is appraisal attached. She'd also copied a message from Jerry:

MIZ LACEY—ALL THE DISCLAIMER STUFF IS IN THE APPRAISAL, *short story* $1.2MM *as-is. Pulled some strings to get city info, and there are some big problems. It was never tied into the Dallas sewer, so it still has the old septic system, maybe upgraded in the 60s, looks like. Plumbing and electrical still need to be worked on, and some structural issues too. Doesn't look like they were informed about the best order for renovation. Call if you need more info.*

YIKES. I DIDN'T KNOW WHAT HAD BEEN PULLED OFF THE Tarantinos' line of credit, but I had a feeling that appraisal wasn't going to make them or their banker happy. I downloaded the appraisal for a later review.

I took the copy of Jack O'Toole's will out of my bag and paged through it. I'm not a wills and estates attorney, and my one property law class in law school had not prepared me for such a legal document. It looked very old, and I flipped over to the back. Jack O'Toole had signed the will in 1940, the year after his wife had died, but a codicil had been added in December 1979, less than a year before he died. The codicil dealt specifically with the Lakeway house, leaving the house and all its contents to his son Patrick O'Toole, and an amount from his estate equal to the value of the house and its contents at his death to his daughter Leona. Since she pre-dated him in death, did that mean that was left to her heirs? I had no clue. I could have checked online, but the thought of learning yet another area of law this week was daunting.

I went back to the will, where there were sections thick with legalese that I didn't understand, and various charitable bequests. The will itself had specific provisions with property left to his son and his daughter, and, in the original document, the house had been left to his heirs. I finally gave up and texted Callie, begging a coffee or lunch date and a review of the document. She replied immediately and we scheduled coffee on Friday afternoon to confirm what I thought about contents, and I made a mental note to scan the will and email it to her in the morning.

I turned on my laptop and checked my email, then opened a search engine and typed in "Jack O'Toole Dallas" and let the results scroll down. An hour later, and I knew a bit more about the man than I'd started with—but not much more.

Jack O'Toole had been born sometime around 1900, it seemed, although no one was quite sure. The application for probate simply said he was 80 years old when he died, and the *Wikipedia* entry was very short, with the standard '[*needs additional information*]' disclaimer prominently and repeatedly displayed. He was listed as an 'American entrepreneur, oil financier, and businessman' who died in 1980. He—along with Edward Hartsfield's Trinity Bank & Trust— had apparently been responsible for financing the wild and unfettered exploration and production of the East Texas oilfield in 1930 and 1931, before the National Guard was sent in to keep production levels artificially low (something I knew nothing about until reading these articles). Later, he and Trinity had financed exploration of the West Texas oilfields in the 1930s and 1940s. I followed a few links and whistled when I saw the numbers for production in those fields. I could only imagine how profitable those investments had been.

There were also entries that theorized that he had been involved in the exploration of oil fields in the Middle East between World War

I and World War II, but those sections had '[*needs citation*]' notes and seemed to be based more on rumor than fact. A picture at the top of the page showed a tall, rail-thin man with thick, dark eyebrows and deep-set, light-colored eyes that seemed to bore right into the viewer. He wasn't ugly, but it wasn't a comforting or handsome face either. He had a hooked nose and a thin-lipped mouth that seemed cold and unhappy to me. The only other sites on the Internet mentioning him were for histories of the oil and gas industry, but aside from mentioning him in connection with the financing of exploration, they had no other information.

In the "Personal Life" tab at the bottom of O'Toole's page, the *Wikipedia* entry said that Jack O'Toole had been married to Eleanor Hartsfield O'Toole until her death in 1939. A click on a hyperlink for Eleanor's name brought up a *Wikipedia* page with two black-and-white photos: one showed an old biplane with a woman in an old-fashioned aviator's outfit standing next to it, her hand resting proprietarily on the wing strut. I tried to zoom in on the photo, but it was already grainy, and I couldn't see her well at all. The caption identified her as Eleanor Hartsfield—'the Soaring Socialite'—but the other picture was a close-up of a very young woman laughing into the camera, her shiny dark hair wreathing her head in a cap of loose curls. Her eyes were dark brown and hard to read, but the joy in them was infectious and real.

The entry was a short one, and focused mostly on Eleanor's flying, listing all the contests and derbies she'd flown. It was a surprisingly long list, given that she really only flew for about five years. Following a trail of links revealed that she and Amelia Earhart flew together in several derbies or exhibitions, and also, sadly, that several of their contemporaries died or were seriously injured in accidents. They were a fierce and valiant group of young women, many of them pictured leaning against their planes, cigarettes in hand (which seemed unnecessarily risky to me), dressed like Eleanor in fatigues or leather flight jackets with white silken scarves draped carelessly around their necks. Looking at the pictures, I could feel their exuberance and eagerness to be in the air, and I felt a bit pale and listless next to such vivid and vibrant women.

I shook myself and decided to have one more taco before wrapping up the rest of them. Then I changed course, performing some searches for Jack and Eleanor O'Toole together, finding a few pictures of Jack O'Toole at society events in the 1950s and 1960s, after Eleanor's death. I typed in 7224 Lakeway Circle, Dallas, and pulled more pictures of the house and its interior prior to the start of the Tarantino renovation.

I stretched, knowing that all this research wasn't really necessary to get the lockbox at the house taken care of. I was curious—curious about the bloodstains, the house, even the miniature sailboats painted on the nursery walls. I knew that my curiosity was a live thing, guaranteed to get me in trouble, but I still felt the sadness in that house, the despair, and I wanted to know what had happened there.

My phone dinged with a text from an unknown number that turned out to be Paige Jensen's, confirming that she and her mother would be pleased to meet me at the Jensen home in Highland Park at 2 pm the next day. I put my laptop on its charger and went to bed to dream about houses and planes and women who fly.

CHAPTER TWELVE

I f I'd dreamed up a picture of someone living in a mock-English cottage, she'd be Dorothea Berenson Smith Allred. She was a diminutive woman with gray hair piled in a neat but complicated bun, wearing a flowery dress and low-heeled brown oxfords that looked as if they'd come straight out of the 1940s. She was 90, but she still lived alone, needing a caregiver only on her 'bad days.' She'd buried two husbands, she told me, and had seen all of her friends, both of her children, and two of her grandchildren pass on, so she welcomed visitors. We sat at her dining table where she'd placed a photo album of her family, sharing hot tea and a few Café au Lait snickerdoodle cookies I'd brought with me.

"I'd show you pictures of my children and grandchildren and great-grandchildren, but I know that's not what you're here to see, so I've got the photos of my very *first* family here." Her blue eyes twin-

kled at me, and I smiled back but assured her I'd be happy to see her
family photos.

I'd called her this morning just to make sure it was still okay to
visit, but, since she'd already received a recommendation from Martin
Dove as to my character and mission, she'd invited me right over.
She'd also accepted my offer to bring the cookies with an explanation
that, at her age, she ate every cookie offered. She'd chuckled when I
told her that, at my age, I did too.

Unlike the house next door, 7212 Lakeway Circle had the lower
ceilings and smaller rooms typical of the English cottage it was
modeled on. The day was humid and cloudy and windy, but she had
several lamps on and a gas fireplace burned cheerfully, if not necessarily. The effect was cozy, but not claustrophobic. Chintz
dominated.

I'd towered over her as she walked slowly through the living room
to the dining room where she'd prepared the table for tea. In anticipa-
tion of my meetings for the day, I'd worn a navy pantsuit from the
back of my closet, pairing it with some navy chunky-heeled short
boots and a flowy white blouse my sister-in-law Sara had bought me
for Christmas last year. As a result, I topped Mrs. Allred by at least
eight inches. She waved my help away as she poured water from a
steaming kettle over loose tea into a flowered china teapot that
matched the delicate cups at our places, and then covered it with a
knitted sky-blue tea cozy as we arranged ourselves at the breakfast
table.

She leafed through black-and-white snaps with a few pauses to
show me baby pictures of herself or her brother David and a black-
edged photo of her mother holding her sister Gladys, who'd died
suddenly of a fever before she reached a year old, all attached to the
pages of the album with black triangles at the corners and labelled
carefully at the bottom in faded and spidery handwriting. After a few
reflective minutes, she reached a picture of four people playing
croquet, obviously staged for the photograph: a tall, smiling man in a
flannel suit and funny-looking two-tone oxford shoes; a woman in a

flowered, calf-length dress with short sleeves (much like the one Mrs. Allred wore now); a tow-headed teenage boy in blousy tweed pants to just below his knees, a flat cap pulled down over his eyes; and a young girl with long, wheat-colored hair and a large bow perched precariously on the side of her head.

We laughed when she told me her bows were forever unraveling as she ran around the neighborhood, until the day she decided glue might be the answer and had ended up with a boyish bob haircut as reward. Then she showed me another, later picture of David in a dark blue naval uniform, a few months before he left to take up his station at Pearl Harbor in the fall of 1941. We agreed that he was very handsome, and she told me her mother never did recover from hearing that he had died in the bombing on that awful Sunday morning in December that year.

She poured us cups of hot black tea and, as we added sugar and cream, told me about moving to their new house on Lakeway Circle in 1937. "Father was one of several vice-presidents in Trinity Bank & Trust, working under Edward Hartsfield, Eleanor's father. You know about the problems Jack O'Toole had with Dines & Kraft?" I nodded, making a note on my pad. "Well, no one was willing to buy the other lots on the Circle from Mr. O'Toole and risk the displeasure of some of the most important men in Dallas, but he didn't want to be the only house here. We were living in a house down near Munger Place —oh, not the nice streets like Swiss or Junius or Gaston—but my mother was insisting we move to a house that didn't have bugs just walking in through the cracks under the doors."

She turned the page and pointed out another picture that showed the family in the garden behind the house, where the tall trees I'd so admired were mere saplings. "Mr. O'Toole offered my parents the lot on this side of his property, and Mr. Hartsfield arranged for a mortgage for the house. None of the builders wanted to buck Dines and Kraft, so Mr. O'Toole had builders brought into town for his house, and they built ours as well. The Hermanns across the street moved in from back east, and they didn't care about powerful Dallas men.

Once Jack O'Toole made something happen, that was all it took!" She laughed and sat back in her chair, smoothing her skirt over her lap. "Our neighbors on Lakewood were all so grand, with their big houses and fancy cars. They all had maids and gardeners, and they had garden parties and dinner parties and summer outings at the lake— even boating and houses on the shore."

"These are pretty big lots." I added more sugar to the strong, fragrant tea. "Did someone help with the yardwork?"

She broke off a small bite of cookie and ate it with pleasure, wiping her fingers with the delicate linen napkin she'd laid at our places. "Not at first. I think it was all my parents could afford to make the mortgage payment, but then my father's work meant extra money coming in. We were able to hire some people to help with the yard and house. And after Eleanor died, Father worked for Mr. O'Toole." She sipped her tea and smiled sadly. "Both Mother and Father died in 1961, and Father had worked for him all that time—over 20 years."

I perked up. No one seemed to know how Jack O'Toole had made his fortune, or what he did with it. "What were his businesses? Do you know?"

She laughed and shook her head. "Oh, my dear, no. At that point, all I cared about were my studies and my friends and then, of course, boys. And Father would never talk about work at home." She smiled mischievously. "I didn't start caring about business until much later, when I met my second husband." She laughed softly, her mind lost in memories. I had second thoughts about another snickerdoodle, and then decided to emulate Mrs. Allred and seize the cookie while I let her remember. I broke off a piece and ate it as she thought.

Finally, she looked back at me. "You're a very patient young lady. My great-grandchildren would be on their phones and bored by now."

I smiled. "I love information, and you're what I like to call a 'treasure trove,' Mrs. Allred."

"That would make you a treasure hunter," she said, smiling back at me. "Are you?"

"That I am." She held the teapot over my cup, and I nodded for some more of the lovely tea. As she poured, I asked, "Do you remember much about Jack and Eleanor O'Toole?"

She added a bit of the warm tea to her cup and replaced the tea cozy before answering. "I had a bit of a girlish crush on Eleanor O'Toole. I was nine when we moved to Lakeway Circle, and she was quite famous in Dallas." She added a tiny bit of cream to her cup and stirred. "Did you know she was a pilot?" I nodded my head, thinking of the picture of the excited young girl with a proprietary hand on the old plane. "When she was 20, her father gave her a flying lesson for a birthday present, and then she took to the skies and found her home, she told me." She cradled her cup in her hands and stared out the window to the garden. "She paid for more flying lessons herself and then convinced her father to let her buy a plane. She flew in several races. The most famous was a cross country race with only women pilots. In 1929, can you believe it?" We both shook our heads in amazement.

"Women had only received the right to vote in 1920," I said, "so I can't believe what that must have been like."

She sighed. "She was my hero, so strong and brave. And I thought perhaps she would fly again. But then she died less than two years after we moved to Lakeway Circle."

I took a small sip of tea as I carefully chose my words. "I'd heard there was something mysterious about her death, that Jack O'Toole refused an autopsy."

She made a face and set her cup in its saucer with a click, seeming slightly disappointed in me. She paused, then looked in my eyes and asked me, "Have you lost someone close to you, my dear?" I nodded. "Then you know that people deal with grief as their minds and hearts allow. My mother dealt with the loss of my brother by just —softening. I don't know how else to describe it. In that one awful moment when my father read her the telegram, it was if all the bones in her spine had been stolen from her body, and she could no longer fight gravity. For weeks, she didn't seem to have the strength to stand.

Even after that, she seemed smaller. And she stayed that way for 20 years." She folded her hands together in her lap and sat back in her chair. "Mr. O'Toole—I can't think of him as Jack O'Toole, even now— he was just the opposite. He seemed to become less human, harder than steel. When Eleanor became ill, he closed that house off to everyone. He let all the staff go except for Mamie and Alton Hardwick, their housekeeper and yardman. He and Mamie took care of Eleanor, and the Hartsfields were only allowed to see her once a week, on Sundays." She sighed.

"That would have been difficult." *And that would be an understatement,* I thought.

"Oh, it was, it was. I remember seeing them drive up in their big car on Sundays after church. Mr. O'Toole would have the gates shut until right before they arrived. The Hartsfields had a driver, a big black man named John Saturday. John would pull the car up and into the drive, and then help Mrs. Hartsfield out of the car. They would stay for an hour, and then they would leave, Mrs. Hartsfield weeping, and John would drive them back home. And Alton Hardwick would shut the gates for another week." She fingered the pearl necklace she wore as she thought about those Sunday visits so long ago. "Except for her doctor and the Hardwicks, no one else came in or out until Sunday. I went around through the back gate one day, trying to see in, and Mr. O'Toole came out and chased me away." She laughed softly. "I was terrified of him. He was tall and had very dark hair, with heavy black eyebrows over these cold, cold blue eyes, and I think my imagination made him much bigger and darker and ferocious. He probably just told me to go home, but I was embarrassed to be found peeking, and I cried for an hour after I got home and locked myself in my room."

"Why did he shut everyone out? I would have thought having her family around her would make her feel better."

She shrugged and shook her head. "That was a different time. Visiting hours at hospitals were limited, and people still didn't understand about how diseases were transmitted. Even so, his behavior was extreme." She paused. "I think he knew she would die, and he began to grieve even before she did."

"What was wrong with her?"

She sighed, her eyes glistening. "I'm not sure anyone knows. It was probably cancer, but there's no way to know. The last time I remember talking to her was at a garden party at the Hermanns' house." She looked off out the windows at the gray day. "It was May—spring, when everything seems so new." She shook her head. "She looked pale even then. She seemed to sicken very rapidly, and by August of that year, she was gone." She wiped away a tear, and I felt sorry to have brought her sadness. "And then Mr. O'Toole seemed to turn to granite. An autopsy—" she shook her head sharply "—there was no way he'd have allowed that."

"Did he love her that much?"

She was still for a moment, remembering, and then she surprised me. "I don't know. Looking back at how he seemed after her death, I'd say yes, but I don't know what he felt for her when she was alive." She looked out the window at the trees moving slowly in the wind. "They were a golden couple in Dallas for a few years. The newspapers loved them: they'd attend the theater or a party or event, and there they'd be in the society pages the next Sunday. They were such an attractive couple, him tall and dark with those startling silvery-blue eyes, and her so pretty with her hair cut in a curly bob, always so fashionably dressed. But..." Her voice trailed off as she paged through her memories. I stayed quiet and waited.

"He always seemed to be next to her, but never with her." She looked back at me and grimaced. "The words don't describe it well. He was always careful to treat her well, but he didn't seem to be very affectionate." She smiled. "My brother and I would catch our parents kissing or holding hands or laughing quietly together all the time, and so we were very comfortable with adults showing love for each other. But not all couples were that way in that time before the war, and Eleanor and Jack O'Toole were never affectionate in front of anyone. What they were in private, I don't know."

She offered more tea, but I declined. I could tell she was tiring, and I didn't want to overstay my welcome. I had one more question, but I didn't know how to ask it, so I quietly made a statement.

"I've heard there were rumors that he had a hand in her death."

Dorothea Allred snorted derisively, a sound that made me hide a smile as I made a note on my pad. "Hogwash, my dear. That was Delia Hartsfield's bitterness over her sister's death and her envy of her sister's life. She started that rumor, and kept it going until she died."

"Are you sure?"

She hesitated and then stood, and I noticed she wobbled slightly. I immediately felt bad for keeping her talking so long. She steadied herself on the table, and I stood as well. Her voice was strong, her distaste of the subject clear. "I'm not sure of anything. Could Jack O'Toole have poisoned Eleanor for months or years until she sickened and died? It's possible. But I don't believe that Eleanor—that smart, strong, capable woman—would have stayed with a man who was threatening her life. And she would have known." She sighed heavily, and I felt ashamed to have caused her distress. I began to gather my things, and she turned to the doorway, moving with more difficulty this time. "I know he was never the same."

We walked slowly to the front door, and I thanked her for her time. She murmured pleasantries, but before I could open the door, she put a hand on my arm. "Have you seen the chapel next door yet?"

For a moment, I thought she meant the secret closet in the attic, but before I could answer, she went on to describe a small stone building in the back corner of the property that shared a boundary with her own. She looked troubled. "I've never told anyone about this before, but I heard Jack O'Toole in there crying and praying one day the winter after she died, begging God over and over to forgive him for his sins, speaking a phrase in Latin I didn't know then: *mea culpa, mea culpa, mea maxima culpa.* I never thought he'd killed Eleanor, but I always wondered if he'd prevented her from getting some help that might have saved her."

CHAPTER THIRTEEN

After a quick leftover taco lunch (see, I told you), I headed into Highland Park to meet with Paige and Judith Jensen. The Jensens' home was located on Beverly Drive, a wide and beautiful street once considered to contain the most expensive per square foot real estate in the United States. Highland Park is a small municipality within Dallas itself that boasts magnificent hundred-plus year-old homes, acres of parkland, and the first shopping center in the United States, but had remained a *de facto* 'sundown' town until 2003, when the first African-American actually purchased property in the community. Most people in Dallas know it for the beautiful parks and homes but are unaware of its segregated past—or present. It's a lovely place to drive all year round, with immaculate lawns and huge old trees, but, during the holidays, the homeowners decorate with unusually heavy hands, and horse-drawn carriages take gawkers through the choked and crowded residential for an exorbitant fee.

The Jensen home was a huge white Greek-revival home with enormous columns and forest green shutters on the lower floor windows, placed far back from the street on a huge corner lot and surrounded by mature oaks and alders. Terraces edged the lower floor on both ends, and the tall old trees screened the house from view on the side street. I'd seen it on that corner for years, but I'd had no reason to know who lived there. They had an antique lawn jockey, carefully painted completely white, on the sidewalk a few feet from the street, so I supposed the house dated back to a time when someone would need to tie their horse's reins to the ring at his side. (It seemed a bit small to have ever acted in that capacity, but what do I know?)

I sat for a moment in my car after pulling up, considering my approach. At every turn for the last few weeks I'd been thrown together with people who lived in places like this, and I wondered when I would become more comfortable with the extreme wealth of the people I met. I was still in my navy suit and white blouse, but the temperature was heading quickly to a non-wintery 80 humid degrees today, and I was already beginning to steam. I doodled around on my phone as the clock inched its way to 2 pm, fingering one of the gold hoops I'd remembered to wear and trying not to give in to the urge to pull my hair up into a ponytail.

While I sat there, I looked up the phrase Dorothea Allred had told me she'd heard Jack O'Toole say in the stone chapel: '*mea culpa, mea culpa, mea maxima culpa.*' The first entry on Google sent a chill through me: 'Through my fault, through my fault, through my most grievous fault.' The words were part of a medieval Latin mass:

I confess to almighty God
    and to you, my brothers,
    that I have greatly sinned,
    in my thoughts and in my words,
    in what I have done and in what I have failed to do,

through my fault, through my fault,
through my most grievous fault;
therefore I ask blessed Mary ever-Virgin,
all the Angels and Saints,
and you, my brothers,
to pray for me to the Lord our God.

WHAT HAD JACK O'TOOLE DONE—OR FAILED TO DO—THAT HE
would confess in such a way?

Troubled, I tucked my keys away in my bag and got out of the car,
reaching down to brush some dust off my navy boots. Martin's only
advice for this meeting had been a text this morning: '*Be careful*' and
a tiny red heart. I took that for the cautious encouragement I assumed
it to be. The internet research on Judith Franks Jensen yielded little
more than bare facts. As I already knew, Jensen Electronics had relocated its North American headquarters to Dallas in 1980, around
the time Nils Jensen had married Judith Hartsfield Franks. The
company had flourished here, adding subsidiaries and dominating a
large campus located conveniently north of Dallas in Richardson
along the Highway 75 Tech Corridor. Judith and Nils Jensen
featured prominently in Dallas society, sitting on philanthropic
boards and volunteering their massive home for galas and other
events. They regularly made large donations in their family's name to
the opera, the symphony, the ballet, and the school for the performing
arts, and the Jensen family had a private foundation that supported
other charitable endowments, mostly in the arts and humanities.
Judith Jensen had attended TCU in Fort Worth for only a year
before leaving school to marry Peter Jensen, but she remained active
in support of the university, and they apparently attended many of
the school's alumni events. Paige Jensen had followed her mother to
TCU, then SMU for law school.

In the photos appearing in the society pages and magazines, Nils
Jensen was flanked by his wife and their daughter Paige—Gray's

friend—who was their only child and was now in her late twenties. All three of the Jensens were strikingly blonde, a fact I found highly suspect since only about two percent of the world's population is blonde. While I didn't look too closely, I suspected some artifice was involved somewhere.

Other than those bare facts, I really had no information on Judith Jensen, except that she was the granddaughter of the couple who had built the home at 7224 Lakeway Circle. Judith's uncle Patrick O'Toole was probably the patriarch of the remaining family O'Toole, but, while he was mentioned frequently in society pages as a trustee of the foundation that Jack O'Toole had begun in the 1950s, he appeared to live outside the country. The only people that might have any contact information for him were Paige Jensen and her mother, and they'd not volunteered it to me. It seemed I would start with Judith Jensen first, and then take it to the next step if she suggested or offered additional information.

At exactly two o'clock, I finally stood before the massive double doors and pressed a button discreetly placed to one side. The doorbell echoed in the house, and, after about 30 seconds, the door was opened by a young Hispanic woman dressed in khakis and a button-down shirt, who seemed to be the maid. She clearly expected me, addressing me as 'Miss Benedict' and showing me into a foyer with gleaming marble floors and a curving staircase. She took my card and laid it on a beautiful wood round table in the center of the foyer that reminded me of pieces in the Sheltons' warehouse. She took the opportunity to straighten a white rosebud in an enormous vase centered exactly in the middle of the table, and I realized what I thought was an exuberant confusion of white flowers was in truth a very carefully constructed arrangement, with the rose stems placed at exact intervals among the other beautiful white flowers and greenery. I don't know why, but her attention to the wayward blossom made me a bit more nervous than I had been.

She showed me into a living room decorated mostly in white and off-white, and I began to see a pattern emerging. In my navy suit, I felt like an embarrassing ink-stain on the upholstery of the white side chair she directed me to. I perched there uncomfortably for a minute or two before my natural curiosity and nervousness pushed me to cross the thick white rug and stand at a decorative bookcase on one side of a white marble fireplace. I think everyone is curious about the books people have, and we take advantage of moments alone to check out what other people read. Judith Jensen's books were all covered in an off-white paper, hiding the spine and leaving me frustrated.

I was contemplating taking one or two off the shelves to see if they were real books or 'books by the yard' that had been purchased for effect when I heard footsteps. I turned but didn't have time to dash back to the chair before Judith Jensen and her daughter entered the room.

Like her home, Judith Jensen wore only neutrals, an off-white designer outfit of soft fleece pants and what anyone else would consider a hoodie, but which I suspected cost more than my rent payment. I recognized her flat ivory velvet mules with gold embroidery as Gucci, perhaps casual shoes for her day. Her hair was an artfully-assisted platinum blonde worn in a smooth short pageboy style that made me think of Doris Day in one of her Rock Hudson movies, but there the resemblance ended. She was tall for a woman and very slender, her nose long and aquiline, her mouth colored in a dark pink that even I could tell made her lips look thin. Her eyes were a dark brown lined in a smoky charcoal, and they were cold as she assessed me standing there at her fireplace—rather than the side chair where I was to have been placed—and dismissed me just as quickly.

Behind her, her daughter Paige seemed to be a pale reflection of her mother. The smooth hair caught up in a bun was clearly a natural blond, and her eyebrows were a light sable that she didn't bother to darken. Her eyes were lighter than her mother's, a hazel perhaps, and she didn't wear lipstick or much makeup at all. Her light blue coat-dress highlighted her slender build, and she wore low navy heels with —surely not—nude panty hose. I tried not to let my dismay show (I don't even own a pair of panty hose), and I quickly flicked my eyes up to her face. Where her mother's eyes were cold and unfriendly, Paige looked worried, as if she was already regretting arranging this meeting.

I stepped forward and took the limp hand Judith offered me, and then sat in the side chair she again directed me to. She sat on the very edge of the sofa to my left, Paige perched uncomfortably on the cushion of the sofa just beyond her.

I thought I'd be direct. "Mrs. Jensen, I appreciate you giving me a moment of your time today. I'm sure you're very busy." As the words left my mouth, I realized that good manners meant I should have allowed Judith Jensen to speak first, and I watched as her lip curled at my presumption, her eyes a bit hard. I unfairly compared them with the soft and vibrant brown of her grandmother's eyes in the online photo.

She spoke firmly and clearly, with none of the Texas accent most of us who live here possess. "I am, unfortunately, very busy today, Miss Benedict, or I would offer you refreshment. My husband and I leave early tomorrow morning for New York, and my daughter and I are trying to get errands taken care of before an event this evening." Her mouth twisted with what I presumed was distaste. "I'm told by my daughter that you have some questions about the house on Lakeway Circle." She checked the rose gold smartwatch on her wrist and folded her hands together in her lap. "The house hasn't been in my family for some time. I'm not sure how I can help you."

Her words made me decide to skip some of the small talk I'd planned, and so instead, I laid the facts baldly between us. "I've been appointed receiver by a court in the Tarantino divorce to list and sell the house." Her eyes narrowed at the words, and I thought I knew how she felt about Trisha and Jules Tarantino. "While an inspection was being performed, an attic room was discovered with a small lock-box. Since it appears likely that the room and the box were there prior to the sale of the house to the Tarantinos, I wanted to consult with your family about the box and its contents." She checked her watch again, and I felt annoyance stir. I paused and then forged on. "And the state of the attic room."

I saw Paige stir in my peripheral vision. Judith's chin raised, and she looked down her nose at me. "What do you mean by 'the state of the attic room'?"

I wanted to see how Judith Jensen took the news, so I watched her eyes as I spoke. "There appear to be bloodstains on the wall." Judith's dark eyebrows lifted, and then her nostrils flared as she took in a breath before speaking.

"What are you trying to say, Miss Benedict?" Ice dripped from the words. "Surely you're not accusing my dead grandfather of something untoward?" She was clearly daring me to do just that.

My heart was pounding; this hadn't gone exactly as I'd planned. I'm not sure what about Judith Jensen had gotten my back up, but I had let myself become confrontational right away. I gentled my voice and tried belatedly for diplomacy. "Of course not, Mrs. Jensen. I'm merely trying to find out the best way to deal with personal property that is in the house but was most likely not a part of the sale to the Tarantinos."

She rose from the sofa, and I stood automatically. Her words were a bit louder this time, and I realized that she was furious. "Miss Benedict, as I said, my family has nothing to do with that property. As you may know, my uncle Patrick was left the house and its contents when my grandfather died." Her lips flattened, and her tone was sharp. "The only time I was in that house was after my grandfather's death, and I have no idea what *was* there, what *is* there, or what you should do with that property." Her eyes narrowed, and she inhaled sharply.

Paige rose to stand behind her mother, her hand reaching out for her mother's arm. Judith ignored her daughter and continued to speak directly to me, her voice loud in the quiet room. "But let me make this clear, Miss Benedict: If you or anyone else should disparage my family's name in any way by making your *suppositions* public, I will bring whatever legal action necessary against you or those disgustingly common people that purchased that house." She ended in a hiss, the acid in her voice taking my breath away.

She raised her chin again. "Paige, please see Miss Benedict out." She turned and left the room without another word, the heels of her expensive mules clipping the marble floor as she crossed the foyer.

Paige looked at me, her face troubled and her eyes sad. I could tell she was considering apologizing for her mother's attitude—something that would be so insincere—so I apologized instead.

"I'm sorry for upsetting your mother, Miss Jensen."

She shook her head. "I'm Paige," she said, surprising me. "And my mother is completely capable of being upset without input from anyone else." She turned towards the door. "I'm curious—what was in the box?"

"I haven't opened it yet." She turned back to me, clearly surprised. "I wasn't completely sure who it belonged to." I followed her into the entry, where she picked my card up from the table in the center of the foyer.

"I can email my great-uncle if you'd like, and let you know what he says." She looked at my card, presumably making sure an email address was on the front.

"That would be great. All the documentation points to him owning the box, so I'd appreciate his approval to open it and make sure it wasn't left there by a tenant or someone else." I guess I'd gotten what I needed from this interview, but it felt like it'd been a complete waste of everyone's time.

The woman who'd let me in was nowhere to be seen, so Paige opened the door for me, holding out her hand to shake. I took it, and she shook it firmly, clearly more of a businessperson than her mother.

"It was a pleasure to meet you, Miss Benedict." She smiled, a perfunctory and polite smile that didn't reach her worried eyes. "I'll be in touch."

I thanked her, and then found myself back on the front porch, less than ten minutes after I started there, none the wiser.

I WENT HOME AND CHANGED OUT OF MY SUIT, TRADING NAVY traditionalism for my comfiest jeans and a thin, decade-old Dallas Mavericks t-shirt, finally feeling comfortable and cool for the first time that day. I almost took a shower, just to try to wash away the embarrassed feeling I had after the Jensen interview.

I stood in my living room, looking at my table/desk and crowded white board and sighed. Time to get organized and do some billable work. It was the next-to-the-last day of the month, and I had some projects to wrap up before month end. I also had the first county court Barnstead hearing on Friday, and I wanted to be ready for that. In my head, I catalogued all the things I needed to do, the tasks I needed to accomplish, the end of month reports I needed to provide to clients. It was a long list I should attack right away.

Instead, I followed the smell of baking to the Shelton side of the house.

I tapped on the kitchen door before sticking my head in to say hello—you only have to learn that lesson once with Sallie Shelton, who has a very active social and love life. Hattie was the only one inside, though. Her professional stand mixer kneaded away, the dishwasher rattled dishes as it worked, and Hattie hummed along with the swing music playing as she mixed something in a big bowl. She smiled at me and nodded toward the kitchen table where a warm orangey-brown loaf had been sliced and fanned on a plate. I plucked a paper napkin from a stack in the holder and inhaled cinnamon and nutmeg and something I didn't recognize, but I trusted Hattie. I slathered on the soft honey butter in the dish next to the plate and bit into pumpkin bread, the top brown and a bit crunchy, the moist inside tasting slightly of orange.

I sat down at the big kitchen table and pushed the papers strewn across the top aside so I wouldn't get butter on them. One of the ones on top looked like architectural plans, and I leaned over to get a better look, careful not to spread crumbs. When the mixer finally stopped, I looked over at Hattie and gestured with a finger shiny with butter, not touching the paper, of course.

"What's this?"

She gathered the dough from under the hook in her flour-covered hands and transferred the ball to an oil-slicked glass bowl. She'd dampened a thin towel, and she carefully covered the dough before answering as she set the bowl near the stove. "A new project I've got in mind. It's a co-living space." She went to the sink and washed her hands, drying her hands and then smoothly moving around the kitchen, putting everything back into its place as she talked. "We have some property already zoned multi-family that has to be razed, and we were thinking about doing a more cooperative model." She measured coffee into a French-press coffeemaker and poured hot water from the kettle in, then brought it to the table with a small cream jug frosty with moisture and two small cups.

She arranged everything to her liking and then sat, sighing heavily as she did so. "This heat," she said, shaking her head. "Climate change, I suppose. February seemed colder when I was young." I murmured agreement through a mouth of pumpkin bread. She pulled the plan I'd been looking at over nearer to herself. "We've been looking at several footprints. This one allows for separate one-bedroom spaces with a small sitting area, a bath, and a miniscule kitchen." She gestured to a large square with what looked like an apartment in each corner. "In the middle is this circle atrium, with a large communal kitchen and eating area on one side, and a large living space spread around the other side, with small working carrels on each end." She turned the plan to show me the other end. "The atrium has sliding doors from each side."

I looked at the plans as she pointed out features like an herb and vegetable garden on one side, parking in the back for ten cars, and various outdoor seating areas, then I sat back and took another bite of pumpkin bread while I watched her, the light of enthusiasm bright in her eyes. When she finally stopped, she saw my smile. "What?"

I shook my head, smiling back. "I love to see someone excited by what they do." I licked some cinnamon butter off my thumb. "Are you building a housing project?"

She started to shake her head, and then she stopped, considering. "I might be. It depends on how you'd define that." She pulled a thick packet of papers over and flipped to the middle to show me some numbers on graphs. "We purchased a survey a few months ago of apartment dwellers who were asked about what features they'd like to see in an apartment complex. A significant number—especially in the two ends of the age demographics, Millennials and over 65—responded favorably to co-living spaces and places where they could work from home. It's a trend that is just going to increase as housing costs climb."

I looked at the numbers, thinking. "Did you know that Section 8 housing allows for payments for co-living areas, as long as the land-lord isn't related?" I'd done some research after meeting with Tom Terry last week.

She nodded. "Because this footprint would fit well within the old quadruplex or small apartment complex sites we already have, we could build a new building up to code from the beginning, with two co-living spaces on one site." She showed me a rendering of a snazzy modern décor, with concrete countertops and mid-century modern details.

"How do you deal with people living in such close quarters? What if they're terrible at living with other people, or the others hate them?" I couldn't imagine having people around all the time.

"We've been talking about that. I think perhaps short leases at first, with an option to extend at the same rate." She plunged the coffee and then poured us each a cup of the dark, rich brew, nudging the cream jug toward me. "But senior living centers sometimes have much closer quarters, and they seem to be successful." She turned the plan back toward herself and looked at it. "We've even talked about two floors, since most of these sites were zoned for two-story complexes. It means we could move quickly to get some things in place and not have to wait for re-zoning or other foolishness." I poured cream into my coffee as she penciled a new mark on the plan.

"You didn't wait for the survey results before planning this," I guessed. I got up to get a pair of teaspoons from the drawer and handed her one before sprinkling raw sugar into my cup.

She took the spoon with a raised eyebrow, and then smiled as she stirred her coffee. "No, I've been thinking about this for years. It's something our mother said often, that she wished she and her friends could have a personal compound like this, where they could spend time together when they wanted, or apart when they didn't. Of course, some senior facilities have something similar to this, but we believe young people would like it too, and it might be suitable for disabled adults." She broke off a small piece of pumpkin bread and nibbled at it as she thought. "On a development side, the savings on appliances alone help with the cost, so the finishes can be upgraded. The finish style could vary complex by complex." We both chewed for a long few moments looking at the materials spread before us, and then she turned to me with a smile.

"Your office will be ready tomorrow afternoon."

I choked on my last bite of pumpkin bread, and Hattie watched me cough with that little smile still in place.

CHAPTER FOURTEEN

I woke up to four texts.

From Paige Jensen:

My uncle Patrick said you have his permission to open the lockbox. I've forwarded his email to you, just in case you needed it in writing. Would you have any time to meet today? There's something I'd like to discuss with you.

Intrigued, I suggested Café au Lait at 2 pm, since I was to meet Hattie at 4.

From my brother Ryan:

Could you meet me Saturday morning? I'd like to talk to you about Mark's business plan and I have some good news. I'll meet you at TBB at 10 if you can.

I ran through all the excuses I could make and found none plausible in the face of possible biscuits and gravy at The Buttered Biscuit, a great breakfast and lunch café about halfway between here and Plano. With a sigh, I agreed with a thumb's up emoji. Guess I'd need to get that business plan out of my car and actually read it.

From my friend, Dr. Amie Pascal:

Lunch tomorrow?

No excuses needed. *Yes!* I texted back.

From Tom Terry:

Fitzhugh. 1030.

And that was vintage Tom Terry. Succinct. Since I was feeling so emojinal, I gave him a thumb's up too.

———

I'D LEFT A MESSAGE FOR KARAN YESTERDAY, ASKING HER TO check with Trisha about the room in the attic and the lockbox. This morning, I put in a call to Cliff Clark to ask the same thing. He wasn't 'available' to me (fancy that), but I left him a voicemail, explaining that there was a lockbox in a closet in the attic that I believed to have belonged to the previous owners, and asking him to let me know if Jules believed it belonged to him. I carefully did not ask for permission to deal with it as I saw fit. I clicked 'disconnect,' feeling a breathless relief that he hadn't taken my call.

I pulled up Paige Jensen's email. She'd simply asked Patrick O'Toole to confirm her permission to me to open the lockbox and see what the contents were. His reply was just as succinct as Tom Terry's text: 'Yes.'

I gave his reply another look. His email address was patrick@journeyman1934.com, and the domain name triggered a faint memory. I typed it into my browser and remembered seeing it when I searched for a gift for my brother a couple of years before.

Journeyman1934 was a website with everything adventure and travel for the discerning man—as long as he could afford it. The site itself reminded me of the J Peterman company that Elaine worked for on *Seinfeld* (and which was modeled after the real J Peterman catalog company), with small stories about the products, but on Journeyman1934, the clothes and bags and boots and gear were all in photographs and selfies and stories by their users, showing how rough and hardy the products could be, while also being very fashionable and expensive.

I'd wanted to buy Ryan a leather-and-canvas backpack for his birthday a couple of years before, but the hefty price tag was a definite no-no on my budget. My friend Sean let me in on a Journeyman1934 secret: every day, one item went on sale on the site, but there appeared to be no method to the choice—it seemed totally random and there was no warning or sale button. If you happened upon the item, the discount would be especially deep, and, once the item ran out or some previously-appointed number of sales was reached, the discount was no longer available. If someone mentioned the sale on social media or a chat on the internet, the sale suddenly disappeared. Users got the message, and no one shared the information publicly.

Sean—who works as a CPA from January through April 15 and then August 15 through September 30 each year so that he can travel all of the other days of the year—went on the site every day, and I assumed many, many more people who loved the company's products did as well. I thought it was a stroke of marketing genius, but even with a really deep discount, I couldn't afford the merchandise.

I went through the website pretty carefully, but there didn't seem to be any mention of Patrick O'Toole. There were a few pictures on the site of a tall man past middle-age, with startling light gray eyes, dark eyebrows, and white hair and beard, whose penetrating look was very familiar.

I glanced at the time and had to leave my web searches to get ready to meet Tom and Carla at their Fitzhugh residential property. I showered and dressed, keeping in mind that—even though it was already warm and a bit humid right now—the weather-people had predicted a cold front that would sweep through late morning, bringing rain by mid-afternoon. Jeans and boots would do, but I'd add a navy-blue blazer on over my long-sleeved gray t-shirt to meet later with Paige Jensen. I dried my hair carefully, added a little mascara and some silver earrings, and felt quite stylish.

Until I got to Fitzhugh Fields and saw Carla Gutierrez. As always, she looked like she'd just stepped out of a magazine showing what the fashionable Dallas businesswoman should wear. She liked pantsuits with slim legs paired with high heels or boots, which usually gave her a height advantage over the builders and contractors she worked around. She'd told me once that she figured if she dressed more formally than they, she'd have the upper hand over the less-formally dressed. It would work with me, which was why I was usually glad we were on the same side.

Today, she wore a gray pantsuit with a black blouse, silver hoop earrings, and thin chains that winked from within the folds of her silky blouse—no t-shirt there, of course. She also liked to wear multiple bracelets, but she didn't have any on today, just her thin smartwatch. How she put things like that together, I'll never know— or learn. I brought her back the blue silk scarf I'd borrowed the week before for court, and we talked for a minute at our cars about how the scarf would have enhanced the t-shirt I was wearing.

A silk scarf with a t-shirt. Who'd have thought?

―――――――

CARLA POINTED OUT THE NEW CONDO BUILDING ON THE property to the west of Handlebar's property, a slick three-story industrial modern fourplex with rooftop patios facing downtown. New construction was just getting started on a similar building to the east, making the most of a long, narrow lot about half the size of the one where Handlebar's quadruplex stood. "Those condos are going for just under half a million each." She quirked an eyebrow in my direction. "The developers bought the lot itself for less than half of the price one of those condos."

I had nothing to contribute, so I just looked at the high gloss windows and iron railings on the balconies. They reminded me of the high-rise apartment I'd lived in when I got my first job out of law school, an uncomfortable and unhappy memory.

"We might as well go look for Tom. His truck is here, so he is too, but there's no telling where." She led off into the small complex, a 1960s brick quadruplex built with two apartments facing the street in front, and two apartments facing the small parking lot in back. The cars in the lot were a pretty sorry sight, a couple of 1980s Chevys and an even older Ford, but there was a newish Dodge Charger, lime green, parked in the handicapped spot. Carla rolled her eyes as we walked past. "That's Sophia Barnstead's car," she ground out as she clipped past on four-inch heels.

I ducked to look inside. A Christmas tree air freshener hung from the rear-view mirror, and the black seats looked to be leather. "That's funny. It doesn't look like her." A naked green-haired troll doll appeared to be adhesive-taped to the dash, its fluorescent hair coming close to the color of the paint on the car.

"It's her grandson Julius's car. He's living here with her, even though she denies it."

Mrs. Barnstead had testified that her grandson, who was 19 and had been served on her behalf with the eviction suit I'd filed for Tom and Carla, wasn't—in her opinion—an adult. I also remembered that the lease for Sophia Barnstead's apartment had provided for guests, but only for no more than 10 consecutive days. "Has he overstayed the 10-day provision?"

Carla turned and waited for me to climb the three steps to the sidewalk and join her. "He stays for 10 days, and then apparently goes and stays with a friend for a few days, and then comes back and stays for another 10 days." She looked at me with a frown. "Is there any way to revise that in the lease?"

"Sure. You can put a total number of days per year that guests are allowed." I raised an eyebrow. "But we may not need to worry about that for this property, right?"

Her mouth twisted. "Given the trouble this property is causing, I'm not sure of anything anymore. But let's make sure to revise the form lease for the future, okay?" She turned to continue to the apartments, but I put a hand out to her left forearm to stop her.

"Wait, let's—" Her indrawn breath stopped me. "What's wrong?" I let go of her arm as if I'd been burned.

"Just a bruise on that arm." She rubbed her forearm through the suit sleeve, her face pale and her lips flattened with pain.

"I'm so sorry! What happened?" I didn't like the look on her face.

"I live in a construction site, remember?" Carla and her boyfriend Joe were on their third flip in Kessler Park, a section of Oak Cliff in south Dallas where home values were soaring for renovated historic homes. They'd buy a house as their 'principal residence' and get the low interest rate, live in the house while they renovated, and then sell for a hefty profit six to eight months later—all perfectly legal, and the cheapest way to finance a flip. The first two had almost doubled in value when they were finished, Joe doing most of the construction work himself and Carla doing the design, marketing, and sale. "I'm always tripping over some materials or tools in the evening that weren't there when I left in the morning. So clumsy." She smiled tightly.

"But you're okay?"

She focused on me, her color returning to normal. Her smile relaxed a bit. "Yes, Lace, I'm okay. Thanks for asking."

"Well, I'm just sorry for manhandling you."

She patted my arm, much like Sallie Shelton does. "You're just fine. Let's find Tom."

———

WE FOUND TOM UNDER THE KITCHEN SINK OF ONE OF THE tenants. Or at least we found his backside. The tenant, a Mrs. Violet Trenton, was a tiny woman with a cloud of silver hair and purplish eyes that I suspect were the reason for her name. She hung just behind Tom, her hands twisting together. Her front door had been open, and Carla and I had followed the sound of Tom's rather booming voice coming from inside the cabinet.

"Yes, ma'am, I can see a bit of a drip under here. Do you have a pan or something I can put under here for right now, until I can get someone over here this afternoon?"

Mrs. Trenton began rummaging in another cabinet, unearthing an enormous stock pot that none of us believed would fit into the space under the U-bend of the sink trap.

Tom looked at the pot she'd thrust in front of him. "Perhaps a saucepan, Mrs. Trenton. That pot would be too large to fit under there," he said patiently.

Violet Trenton rummaged again and brought forth a battered turquoise and copper pan with a handle on each side, something I was pretty sure was a 1970s fondue pot.

Tom took the pan with a serious air. "Thank you. I'll make sure Angel gets over here right after lunch, so we don't have your pan under here for too long at all." He carefully maneuvered the pan to the right place under the trap and then got up from the floor, brushing off his jeans and Sturgis Harley-Davidson t-shirt. Mrs. Trenton helped him, fluttering a bit as she realized just how much dust could accumulate under a sink. Tom gravely allowed the assistance and then overrode her dismay about the dust with a story of how much dust and gravel he's used to when he does mechanic work.

I could feel Carla's impatience next to me, and I understood, but I also admired Tom for his patience with the elderly woman. He listened to her with complete eye contact, giving her the impression (probably truthfully) that—for that moment—she and her concerns about her apartment were the most important things in his world.

She detailed another couple of issues: a toilet that seemed to keep running sometimes, a spider she saw in her bedroom, and the thermostat that seemed to be in a warmer part of the apartment than her bedroom, and thus had a faulty perception of how cold it truly was. Tom listened to her attentively, promised to have Angel look at the toilet while he was there for the leaky pipe, and noted that pest control was due around again in March when the temperature warmed. On the thermostat, he promised to have it checked, but gently warned her that sometimes the temperature was just different room to room. When he teased her that he might start calling Mrs. Trenton 'Charlotte' if she kept spiders around for pets, Carla's impatience erupted in a puff of breath that Tom clearly heard. He shook Mrs. Trenton's hand and we bid her goodbye. Carla led the way as we exited the apartment, and Tom closed the door gently behind us.

We had much the same visit with the other two non-Barnstead residents, a tall and gaunt elderly black man with a stoop named James Fields who was a retired schoolteacher but still did math tutoring, and Alice Garcia, a former nurse who looked like she might be ill. The yellowish cast on her skin reminded me of my grandmother's right before she died. Both had small complaints about their apartments that Tom either resolved or promised to have an employee resolve later that day.

As we left Alice Patterson's apartment, I noticed a curtain move in Sophia Barnstead's front window, and I knew we were being watched on our survey. Carla went to the door and tapped firmly, but no one answered. She found a sticky note in her bag and wrote a note that we had visited to discuss any issues Mrs. Barnstead might be having, leaving it stuck to the door just above the lock. I took a picture of the note with my phone.

Our small group moved to the parking area just as a stiff breeze began to blow from the north, bringing with it the cool scent of rain. I kept some space between me and Carla, afraid I would bump her arm again, but we huddled together, our backs against the north wind, to talk.

"Are those issues typical of the ones Sophia Barnstead brought up to you?"

Tom nodded. "The issues were the same, the complaints much more dramatic." He ran a hand over the stubbled hair on his head. I'd never seen him with anything but a buzz-cut, but it looked especially fresh today. "Lace, I've got to tell you—I feel really bad about this."

Carla interrupted him, her hand on his arm. "Tom, don't start this again. She hasn't paid her rent in three months. She needs to move."

She turned to me. "Did she pay her rent into the registry of the court like you said?"

I nodded. "All three months."

Carla inhaled sharply, her nostrils flaring. "So, she's got the rent money, she just refuses to pay it. Tom, don't you lose a minute's sleep over that woman." He shook his head, looking at the three-story new construction next door. "I know what you're thinking, but she is not your mother, aunt, or grandmother. She's decided she's entitled to consideration no one else is." She stopped and took a deep breath, and I recognized an effort to calm down because I did the same thing. "Tom, we have taken care of everything she complained about, and that's us just pouring money down the drain."

He looked at Carla for the first time since we'd left Alice Patterson's unit. "Carla, it may be a good economic decision to sell the property, but this is their home. Dallas is getting more and more expensive, and their income is fixed—it's not going up with cost of living or anything else. Don't we have an obligation as humans to take care of each other?"

Stung, Carla crossed her arms over her chest, an action that caused her some pain, I saw. "I do take care of other people. My aunt and my *abuela* live in good places because of me."

Tom pressed on. "And what about the people that don't have a niece or a granddaughter like you? What about them?" He put a hand on Carla's arm, and I heard her indrawn breath. "Carla, I just want to have some empathy for them—Sophia Barnstead included."

Carla shook her head angrily, and I could see the shine of tears in her eyes as she carefully moved her arm away. "Tom, this property is the best chance we've got of a real windfall. Can't you see that? I don't know about you, but I can't just give that up."

He nodded. "I know. But evicting her isn't going to help. The other three have leases that aren't up till fall anyway." He turned to me. "Lace, can you see if you can resolve this with Mrs. Barnstead? I know she's pushing this because she knows her lease is up in a few months and she doesn't have any place to go."

I looked at Carla, whose eyes were fixed on the new building next door. "I can try. Let me see if I can get her to talk to me." Carla still didn't say anything, but she wouldn't look at me or Tom. He nodded and smiled at me. "Go get 'em, tiger. Let us know."

———

THIRTY MINUTES LATER, I LEFT THE FITZHUGH FIELDS Apartments with a little more hope than I'd had when I knocked on Sophia Barnstead's door. A young man had opened the door dressed in what I knew to be a sub-sandwich shop uniform, and he'd seemed a bit alarmed when I told him who I was. He stayed while we talked, although he looked at the time on his phone several times.

Mrs. Barnstead seemed a lot older and more fragile than she had in court. The coonskin cap she wore was gone, and so was the slightly gamey smell that had surrounded it—and her. The apartment was painfully clean and almost bare, the only furniture in the living room a threadbare sofa with a bedroll tucked neatly behind one end and a recliner with a light blue sheet covering the back.

We sat at the kitchen table to talk, and I wrote down a list of the issues she said she had with the apartment, mostly having to do with the oddities and idiosyncrasies of the HVAC system. She too had an often-running toilet, so I warned her that someone would come by that afternoon to check it, and she needed to let them in. The young man, who was indeed her grandson Julius, admonished her to let them in as well since he would be gone, and he took me into the bedroom to see how the window wouldn't shut completely any more, letting cold in during the winter, and bugs in during the rest of the year. I took a picture with my phone and promised Tom would look at it.

I left after promising to return the next week to check on the issues we discussed, and I agreed to postpone the Friday eviction hearing until we could check on the progress of fixing them. I told her I would keep the case on the docket, however, which meant her rent would stay in the court's registry. Julius helped her to understand why that was, and I realized as he carefully explained the situation to her that, while he might be staying there because of money, he was also acting as her caretaker and contributing to the bills. It might not be the ideal situation Carla had envisioned, but it was necessary for this little family.

I left when Julius did, after shaking my hand gravely and assuring me he'd talk to his gramma, rushing off to work in the Charger with the troll doll on the dash, roaring out of the parking lot like any young person would.

———

I set up my laptop at one end of a long table at Café au Lait and stretched happily. Marie Haught loved bringing her native French cuisine to our part of the world, and today's lunch special was what I love to think of as 'real' French onion soup. I had a huge tureen of the beefy broth with onions, topped with a crunchy cheese-topped heel of bread. It was warm and lovely and comforting on such a cold afternoon—which it was, now that a 'blue norther' (as my grandmother called it) had blown into Texas. I'd put my blue blazer on, but it was absolutely not going to be enough when I stepped outside to go home later.

Both Karan and Cliff Clark had left voicemails for me. Neither Trisha nor Jules knew anything about the lockbox or the room in the attic. Both were more concerned that their spouse might wrongfully claim the item than they were with any curiosity about its contents.

Paige Jensen slipped inside as some people left a minute or so before 2 pm, and, like everyone else did on their first visit to Café au Lait, she stopped for a moment just inside the door to take it in. The old windows stretching to the ceiling, the glass cases full of baguettes, croissants, eclairs, crème puffs, and everything else wonderful from the bakery, the huge old copper-and-steel espresso machine, the long dark wood tables and benches—the space tended to delight visually, and, even without the wonderful scent of baking bread that permeated every inch, the place made people happy.

"I think this must be what heaven smells like," she said as she shrugged out of her coat and put her large bag on the bench. "Be right back." This was a different Paige today. Her pale blond hair was loose, curling loosely past her shoulders. The jeans she wore fit well, and her turtleneck sweater was an olive color that brought out the green in her hazel eyes. She charmed Esther at the counter and came away with two chocolate frosted crème puffs and a cappuccino, eating one of the crème puffs and then the other with evident pleasure. She wiped her mouth with a paper napkin and missed a bit of chocolate, and I pointed it out with a tapped finger on my own mouth. She laughed and wiped it off, and I realized she was really very pretty.

We exchanged some small talk, and I sensed some intentional delay as she felt me out, asking about who I knew or socialized with. We didn't exactly run in the same circles, but we did know some people in common besides Gray Powell and Martin Dove. She'd graduated from SMU's law school a few years after me, but we'd had some of the same professors. Finally, she pushed the empty plate forward an inch or so and took a sip of cappuccino. "I need to apologize for my mother." She waved away my protest. "No, I do. She was awful to you. I wish I had some excuse, but there isn't one."

"It was an upsetting subject, I could tell."

She nodded. "She doesn't like to talk about her mother's family at all."

I nodded, agreeing to the understatement.

"So, what kind of an attorney are you?" There was some reason she wanted to talk to me, but she was going to take her time to get to it.

"Mostly real estate, but general business too." There was a bit of an awkward pause, and I took pity on her and filled it. "What about you? Are you practicing?"

"Sort of. I work in the family business right now, Jensen Electronics." She adjusted the handle of her cup, making it line up with the tiny spoon in the saucer. "But not for much longer." This was a surprise. There'd been no indication from anyone that she was leaving Jensen.

I tried to keep my voice light. "Is it a big secret?"

She smiled, a tight smile that didn't reach her eyes. "Well, there's been no announcement yet. And my mother doesn't know."

"Where are you going?"

She leaned back, looking at me for a moment, perhaps trying to decide if she could trust me. "I'm starting a foundation."

"Oh yeah? What are you going to do with it?"

She smiled again, and this time it reached her eyes, a full and happy smile that brightened her face. "I'm going to help women make their dreams come true."

———

SHE EXCUSED HERSELF TO TAKE A PHONE CALL, AND I GOT another latte, this time a decaf, since I was pretty sure another full-caff one would keep me up all night. She finished her call and her cappuccino and set the cup and saucer aside, as if clearing the decks, before launching into her story.

"You know part of my family's story, I believe." I nodded. "We're more about who we shut out of our lives than who we let in." She sighed. "My grandmother Leona died of cervical cancer before I was born. My mother was only 19 when her mother died—she'd made sure her wedding happened in February before her mother died a few months later, but she didn't invite my great-grandfather O'Toole to the wedding. He was old then, and I think the story was that he was in ill health and couldn't come. But he wasn't invited." She twisted a ring on the pinkie of her right hand, a small gold ring with a pearl surrounded by diamonds. "I've asked my mother about him and my great-grandmother all my life, but she won't tell me anything." She grimaced. "Oh, she gives the 'family line' all the time: Jack O'Toole's family came over from Ireland, everyone else died, he made a fortune in the oilfields, he fell in love with my great-grandmother Eleanor, she died tragically young, and he survived her by more than 40 years." She sighed. "That's the story she tells, if she's asked."

"But that's not the truth?"

She shrugged, her eyes on the table. "It may be, for all I know." She raised her eyes to mine. "She doesn't want me to know anything else."

That was a surprise. "Why do you believe that?"

Her mouth twisted. "Because she's told me so." She turned and dug in her bag, bringing out a thick brown accordion envelope with an attached elastic band holding it closed. She opened it and began to pull out black and white photographs and photocopies of newspaper articles, laying them out between us.

She spread out the photos first, carefully placing them side by side on the table facing me, as if she was the dealer in a game of high stakes poker. I recognized the first one, but this was her show, not mine, so I just waited. "This is a photograph of my great-grandmother Eleanor with her plane, a few months after she bought it in 1925. And this is a photo of Jack and Eleanor leaving Eleanor's parents' house after their wedding." I dutifully examined the photo of the two young people, Eleanor in a fitted cream-colored suit with a matching cloche hat pinned to her curly dark hair. They both looked terrified and overwhelmed, but I imagined I would too if I'd just gotten married. I followed along as she showed me the other photo of Eleanor that I'd seen before, and I realized that I was sitting across from the author of Eleanor's *Wikipedia* page.

"Here they are in front of the Lakeway house—that's my great-uncle Patrick on Jack's shoulders, and my grandmother in her arms." The couple stood proudly in front of the house I'd seen on Monday, the grounds manicured beautifully, blurry water jetting from the fountain. She laid out another photo, all four of them posed formally, Eleanor in a suit with a cloche hat on her head and Jack in a suit and tie, the children both dressed in frilly white outfits. The little boy had his father's eerily light-colored eyes, and he stared at the camera with a similar penetrating look. "That's a photo they sat for a family photo just before Eleanor's death. And this is my great-grandfather in 1959, when my mother was born."

She swallowed hard as she laid the last picture on the table, and I picked it up to look at it more closely. It was a black and white photo, but it looked like a candid shot of an older man, his eyebrows now as white as his hair, sitting at what was obviously a Parisian café, his attention drawn to something near the camera. "He was in Paris, and Uncle Patrick called him on the telephone to tell him she had been born. But he didn't come back." I laid it back on the table, and her finger nudged the photo straighter in line.

"I don't know why he hated my grandmother and my mother. But he had nothing to do with them at all." She slumped on the bench, misery etched on her face. "After Eleanor died, my grandmother and Uncle Patrick went to live with Eleanor's sister Delia and her husband Arthur. And Jack went away—for almost ten years. Uncle Patrick was a teenager when he came back. Even then, Uncle Patrick told me that his father was distant and removed from their lives." She touched the most recent photo again, then folded her hands together in her lap. "He doesn't resent his father, but I could tell—it hurt him."

I thought of my own father, who spent weeks at a time in the oilfields after my mother left us. When he came home, the three of us would spend days together roaming over the farm and playing games or reading, until my brother and I became teenagers and became too busy with friends and school activities to spend hours with him. I don't know why I felt the need to defend Jack O'Toole, but I thought Paige Jensen was a little naïve, even though I found I liked her a bit. My left eyebrow twitched once where the scar crossed it as I looked up at her. "Every family is different."

The look she gave me was reproachful. "I know that. Believe me, *I* know that." She shook her head. "From what my mother said, my grandmother hated him. *Hated* him. I'm not sure why."

I was still mystified about this whole meeting, but I went along with the story. "Does your mother feel the same way?"

"She just pretends he never existed. Maybe that even Eleanor never existed." She seemed near tears about this, and, while I could tell the emotion was genuine, I wasn't sure why she was telling me all this. "But she's angry about it. And afraid." She began to bite the edge of her thumbnail, and I saw that it was bitten to the quick, while the rest of her naturally manicured nails were grown to the ends of her fingertips. "She doesn't ever want to talk about it or have any reminders of it." She put her hand in her lap with some effort.

"The Tarantinos have courted the Dallas press about their mysterious renovation of the Lakeway house, and, every time something is printed in the papers or someone mentions it to her, we have days of my mother's anger spilling out everywhere."

I watched her frown and worry at her thumbnail, and I realized we were getting to the heart of whatever was coming now.

"I want to hire you. Gray told me that you're like a bulldog about finding out the truth. He told me about the murder of that girl last month, and how you got to the truth about it."

Well, this was a bit of a turn. "I'm a lawyer, not a detective."

She focused on me, her lovely face pinched with whatever she was holding back. "Well, maybe I need a lawyer then. The only attorney I have is the one for my family, and there is no way he's going to help me."

"Why do you need help?" My head was starting to ache, and my left eyebrow was taking on a life of its own with the twitching. I wondered if it was noticeable. I smoothed a finger over it. "Look, I'm always happy to work with new clients, but I don't really know what we're doing here. What is it you think you need a lawyer to do?"

She blinked at my tone, and I realized my impatience was coming through. I held my tongue anyway, assuming she'd need to be able to handle at least that if she wanted to hire me.

"I was in a wedding over the Christmas holiday two years ago. In Scotland, in a castle. I went to Ireland on my way back—even went to

County Cork, to Cork and to Cobh, to see where Jack and his family came from, according to Uncle Patrick. I didn't make it public, just went on my own. I've always been curious. It was beautiful—so green and lovely, and the people were so friendly and kind." She stared off out the window to the clouds scudding by on the wintry wind. "And when I got home and told my mother where I'd been, she flew into the most awful rage. She told me she forbade me from ever discussing Jack O'Toole or Ireland again." She looked at me with a rueful smile. "She really thinks she can do that." I smiled back but didn't say anything. She seemed cowed in her mother's presence—but I think everyone was.

She straightened the last photo of Jack O'Toole again. "She said something, something unusually negative, about our 'roots' and Ireland, and when I defended the country, and tried to tell her how wonderful it had been, she told me that we probably weren't even really Irish, that it had all been a story cooked up by Jack to cover his crimes."

I thought back to my own ancestors, and considered saying something, but I didn't want to break into her flow. "So, I took a DNA test a few weeks later. One that shows everything—genealogy, demographics, country of origin—all of it. And there wasn't an ounce of Irish in me."

CHAPTER FIFTEEN

I looked at her with my mouth open for a few seconds. Then logic reasserted itself, and I shook my head. "Those tests are notoriously inaccurate sometimes."

She nodded. "I know. But I tried three more, all the most reliable companies." She swallowed hard, and I realized this was really bothering her. "I even went to a friend who works in genetics at a university, and she had a more specialized test performed." She leaned forward. "My father is Danish—pretty much full Danish, born in Denmark, and both of his parents are too. My mother's father was Bavarian, and Eleanor O'Toole's parents were both the children of Lithuanian Jews who came to this country before the turn of the century. All of this—*all of this*—was pretty clear and accurate in all the tests. And there was some Iberian Peninsula and even some French in there, but nothing Irish, nothing they could point to." She sat back.

I felt like I needed to get something out of my head and into this confusing discussion. "Why is this so important to you? Are you afraid of being a mutt?" The word came out a bit harsher than I intended, but there it was.

She inhaled, and glared at me for a full five seconds, and I saw a bit of Judith Jensen in her. Then she smiled. "That's my mother. She's terrified of being someone plain and uninteresting." She leaned back and continued to breathe deeply, closing her eyes. "I've spent my life in her shadow. And most of the time, I don't care. Being underestimated has worked for me, for the most part." She opened her eyes and smiled again, and I thought once more how pretty she was. I realized she wasn't as forceful as her mother, but, in her own way, she had presence.

"I'll ask you again: why is this so important to you?"

She looked down at her hands clasped in her lap. "I don't know how to explain this." Her blond hair shone in the pale light coming in the window. "So much of my family history has been kept from me. But I've always idolized Eleanor and her independent spirit. Every time Uncle Patrick came to Dallas, he and I would get together, and I would ask about her." She looked in her empty cappuccino cup, and then, finally at me. "I just want to know about her and what happened to her, how she lived and how she died. That's not a good reason, but it's the one I have."

I willed my eyebrow to stop twitching as I smiled at her. "That's good enough. But you may not find out everything you want to know, and you may not be happy with what you learn."

She looked at me steadily. "I can deal with whatever I learn. Will you work for me?"

I looked at her and considered. "This has nothing to do with the Lakeway house, or a claim of ownership?"

She frowned quickly and shook her head. "Not at all. I just want some help finding out about my family—who I am, and what happened to them all." She looked at me, a bit of concern on her face. "But I need the privilege to apply—I don't want my mother to know about this, I don't want anyone in my family to know I'm doing this, unless I decide to tell them."

I sighed, my eyebrow twitching. "All right."

"Don't I need to give you a dollar?" She dug in her bag. "I've got a five." She held it out to me. "It can be a down payment on whatever retainer you require."

I smiled. "That's mostly symbolic, but okay." I tucked the five away. "I'll get you an engagement agreement tonight."

"Good." She stood up. "I need more coffee. You?"

"No, I'm good." I watched her walk back to the counter and checked my phone, smoothing down my twitching eyebrow with my finger. Depending on how long this took, I'd be late meeting Hattie about the office. Ah well. I texted her quickly, got a pad from my bag, and started a new page.

———

"ELEANOR WAS ONE OF THE FIRST WOMEN IN DALLAS TO TAKE flying lessons. Did you know that?" I nodded as she sprinkled stevia into her cappuccino and stirred it. "She was amazing—flying in air races, living her own life." She picked up the photo of Eleanor Harts-field standing next to her plane. "In 1929, her father lost almost everything—not because of the stock market crash exactly, but because some of his employees had embezzled money from the bank and used it to invest in the stock market, and in the crash, they lost it all. He had to use his own money to repay depositors. It took almost everything they had. He tried to sell their house in Highland Park, but no one was buying houses that expensive. Eleanor sold her plane and her mother sold all her jewelry, and neither of them got what they should have out of the deal." She unfolded the photocopied pages from her envelope. "And then Jack came to town, and he and Eleanor married, and then everything just—ends. He must have forbidden her to fly again." She swallowed hard and looked at me. "Do you know about Eleanor's trust?"

I shook my head, and she passed a single sheet to me. It was entitled 'Certificate of Trust' in large, Old English calligraphy that looked much like Jack O'Toole's will, and named as beneficiary "any unmarried female direct descendant of Eleanor Hartsfield O'Toole upon reaching the age of 21." The trust was called the 'Eleanor Hartsfield O'Toole Descendant Trust,' and the initial trustee named was Eleanor O'Toole herself.

"What is it?"

"It's a Trust fund that any female descendant of Eleanor receives —as long as she's not married." I felt my eyebrow twitching again, but I didn't touch it. "My uncle Patrick is now trustee, and I'm the only beneficiary. As long as I stay unmarried, it's all mine. And I can use it however I want, but I can't give it to a potential husband."

I didn't want to ask, but she volunteered. "She started it with five million dollars in 1937, just after my grandmother was born. As far as I can tell, it's what he paid her to marry him."

I put the page back on the table. "Back up. What do you mean?"

She opened another sheaf of pages and handed them over. "The trust accounting—which Uncle Patrick is happy to share with me— shows a bank account in Eleanor's name that was opened with five million dollars deposited on Monday, June 30, 1930, a little more than one week after their wedding. Eleanor never touched it. She started the Trust just after my grandmother was born and used the money in that bank account as the first Trust deposit. She was the grantor of the Trust—she started it herself." She sipped her cappuccino, but her face was tense.

"My grandmother Leona married before she was 21, so she never became a beneficiary. My mother married at 20, so again, she never became a beneficiary. I came into the trust at 21, and—as long as I don't marry—it stays mine. The only criteria for a beneficiary was that the funds, whole or divided equally, be available to all direct female descendants who are unmarried."

We stared at each other. "She wanted to make sure her daughter never had to marry for money." Paige nodded. "Wow." I thought about it for a few seconds while Paige sipped her cappuccino. "And you were the first to draw from it?"

She nodded again. "It's been invested over the years. She named Jack as substitute trustee before she died. And while Jack was trustee, he added to it a few times, ownership of stock in companies or percentage interest in energy projects." She shrugged. "It's lost money a few times during these years, but the bottom line is that it's been invested well over the years."

I flipped to the last page. "Holy crap." The trust was worth well over two hundred million dollars.

Paige looked steadily at me. "Uncle Patrick has left his estate to the Trust, including shares in his company." She leaned forward and spoke clearly. "I'm not *ever* getting married."

"I guess not." I flipped the pages over to the front, folded them back in half, and handed them to her. "You don't think you will, truly?"

She shook her head, a bit of a frown on her face. "I'm not sure I see a point." She looked at me. "Do you?"

I shrugged. "No one's asked yet." I tilted my head, considering. "And no one else shares it with you?"

She smiled, a lively grin that lit her eyes. "My mother's brother had a son, but he died very young, so it's mine alone unless I have a daughter—but no husband, of course. If I get married, it skips me to wait for my daughter. If I have a son, it waits for his daughter, and so on." She quirked an eyebrow. "Of course, I wouldn't have to be married to have a daughter or a son."

I raised my eyebrows, my left prickling. "Oh, your mother would *love* that."

She laughed. "I just might do it, if for no other reason than to see that explosion." Then her smile faded, and she picked up the photo of Eleanor with her plane. "I feel so sorry for Eleanor. She seemed to be such an independent woman, and then she married and gave up flying. And then died so young."

"Have you talked to Dorothea Allred?"

Paige shook her head. "Who is that?" I told her about the woman who had been Eleanor's neighbor, and she perked up immediately. "I'd love to meet her!"

I smiled at her enthusiasm. "I think that can be arranged. She'd love to meet Eleanor's great-granddaughter."

"That's it, exactly," Paige said excitedly. "I want to know about her, about Eleanor. What happened to her? Why did she give up flying, give up her life, for a man she didn't love?"

"Are you sure she didn't?"

She made a face at me and then held up the picture of Eleanor and Jack leaving their wedding. "Does that look like a picture of a happy couple?"

I stared at the picture, then reached across to take it. True, they looked shell-shocked, but I'd seen a few of my friends get married, and the wedding day was anything but joyous. In fact, it was high stress from sun-up to the final, grinding moments of the reception and wedding night. Jack and Eleanor might have just been really stressed by the situation. Then I remembered what Dorothea Allred had said about Jack and his guilt after Eleanor's death. I put the picture back on the table in its space.

As if I'd drawn the thought from her, Paige blurted out, "Tell me about the bloodstains." I looked up at Paige, who was staring down at Eleanor's picture. "Do you think it was Eleanor's blood?"

"I'm not sure we can tell anything about it at this point."

She looked up at me, shock on her face. "Surely there are forensic tests that can be done!"

I felt a little sorry for her. "Paige, if they are bloodstains—and I only have my appraiser's opinion for that—the property isn't ours to test. And that substance has been there for years." She started to protest, but I shook my head. "I've gotten confirmation that the Tarantinos didn't leave the lockbox there, so we can check out the contents." The frustration was clear on her face, but I couldn't help her deal with this. "That's got to be enough for right now." She looked like she was going to argue with me, but she nodded tightly.

The screen on my phone flashed, and I saw I'd received a voice-mail from a number I didn't recognize. She saw my glance and sighed.

"Go ahead and get that. I'm going to take a break." She went off to the restrooms as I accessed my voicemail.

MISS BENEDICT, MY NAME IS LEWIS MENDENHALL, AND I *represent the Jensen family. Please give me a call back at your earliest convenience.*

HE RATTLED OFF A NUMBER, AND I WROTE IT DOWN AND STARED at it, wondering what he wanted from me. Paige returned, sniffing her hands.

"I swear that lavender soap is handmade. I've never smelled something like that." She sat down. "Is everything okay?"

My eyebrow was twitching again. "That's the number for your family's attorney."

"Lewis?" She stared at me. "Lewis Mendenhall called you?"

"He did. Any idea why?"

She nodded, her mouth twisting. "I can imagine. My mother probably called him before she left town." She made a face. "He's been my family's attorney since my grandmother's time—probably 40 years. He still calls me 'little Paige.' What'd he say?"

"He asked that I call him back."

"Are you going to?" She sat back and crossed her arms over her chest. I couldn't tell if she was afraid I would, or afraid I wouldn't.

"Are you worried about me calling him back?" We stared at each other for a full ten seconds before I relented. "Paige, we've not formalized things yet, but what you've told me is privileged. Does that make you feel better?"

The stress on her face eased. "It does, actually." She smiled and shook her head. "My mother the other day—that was mild compared to how the mention of her mother's family usually gets her going."

"Are you worried about her being angry with you?"

She shrugged. "I know I shouldn't be. I'm a grown woman, and I can deal with her tantrums. But I worry about her—and I also don't want to be cut out of her life."

"I can understand that." I looked back down at the number and then around the Café, which was fairly empty. "Let's call him back and see what he's got to say." I frowned at her. "You're not here, ok?"

She nodded, grinning at me.

I put the phone on speaker, dialed the number, and asked for Lewis Mendenhall when the receptionist answered. After a few moments, he took the call, talking on a speakerphone himself. I identified myself and waited.

"Miss Benedict, I appreciate you calling me back so promptly."

This was his call, so I simply murmured agreement.

He paused, as if waiting for me to speak. "I know that you spoke with Mrs. Jensen yesterday about a subject she found incredibly painful, her grandfather's house on Lakeway Circle." He paused again, but I said nothing. "It's possible that she may have expressed herself forcefully in an attempt to make sure you sufficiently understand her desire not to be connected with the unfortunate situation unfolding with that property." Again, I said nothing, but I was coming to understand that Lewis Mendenhall would never use one word when he could use two. I looked over at Paige, who was listening, but looking out the window next to us, where a light rain was beginning to fall, drops blowing into the old glass panes. As the watery light began to fade outside, Esther turned on the lights inside the café, but this close to the window, little light penetrated the shadows in this corner.

"Mrs. Jensen has asked me to make sure you are clear that neither she nor her family wish to be involved in any way with that property, nor do they want to have any further contact with you or the owners of that property, nor should there be any mention of her family in regards to that property or its owners." He cleared his throat, obviously a bit uncomfortable with his message. "This is not meant to offend you in any way, of course. It's simply the course of action she wishes to pursue." He waited, and I took pity on the man.

"I see." And I did. Paige kept her eyes on the streaks of rain on the window. "And if any of the Jensens or their family wish to contact me?"

Lewis Mendenhall harrumphed. "I sincerely doubt such an occurrence will take place, Miss Benedict."

I pressed, irritated by this man and his condescending attitude. "But if they do?" Paige turned to look at me, her eyes luminous and her expression unreadable in this light.

"Well." He cleared his throat again, patently uncomfortable with the hypothetical I'd posed. "If the Jensens decide to contact you, Miss Benedict, I would hope you would treat them with all due courtesy and consideration. But there is no doubt in my mind that the Jensens wish to be left alone." He was beginning to sound as irritated as I felt. Perhaps he disliked this errand as much as I disliked being spoken to as if I was a child. "I do not believe you would benefit from a disagreement with such an old and respected Dallas family." He cleared his throat one more time. "Especially someone with a history such as yours."

I was suddenly tired, tired of men like Lewis Mendenhall and Cliff Clark and Bill Stephenson, the old guard lawyers from 'silk stocking' firms in Dallas, who did business over cigars and whiskey at the country club, who thought young lawyers could contribute nothing to the law or its practice besides billing hours for their bottom line, who thought nothing of using us to whatever end they felt was just or right. The law, like anything else, loses its relevancy when it becomes disconnected from the people it serves. Across the table from me was a woman who needed real information, who wanted to understand her family, who wasn't interested in the soft, easy answers the past was willing to give. *This* was the law I practiced.

"Thanks for your call, Mr. Mendenhall. Good day." I disconnected without waiting for a reply. Paige stared at me.

"Let's find out what happened to your great-grandmother," I told her, and watched her face bloom into that beautiful smile.

————

WE TALKED FOR ALMOST AN HOUR AFTER THAT, AND SHE TOLD me everything she knew about Eleanor and Jack O'Toole from her Uncle Patrick or anyone else, even the tidbits of information she'd gleaned from her mother over the years. Once we began to put things together, she realized how much she knew. She also didn't know a few things: how to access information or records from websites and archives online, or how much information could be found about that time in Dallas from the library or historical society accounts online. For my part, I told her what I could about the whistleblower trials, and found out she already knew, from Gray or someone else, and wasn't concerned. I also shared with her what Dorothea Allred had told me about her experience with Eleanor and Jack.

She was upset but excited. "That's it! He must have done something to her and felt guilty about it!"

I was shaking my head before she even finished the sentence. "Following a line of inquiry is one thing; making assumptions is another." I checked the time on my phone. "I've got to go. But tomorrow I'm meeting the real estate agent, and I'll get the lockbox then. I'll speak to Mrs. Allred about visiting with you."

"Can I see the house?"

I shook my head again, hating to disappoint her. "I don't think that's appropriate. I'm the receiver, and it's not listed yet."

She tilted her head. "Maybe I'll call the agent and book a showing."

I raised my eyebrows, my left one tingling, as I packed my pad and pen in my bag. "Well, I can't keep you from doing that once it's listed."

She was still for a moment, and I turned to look at her. Her eyes were open wide, as if a thought had just occurred to her. "Maybe I'll buy it."

I thought of all the work that needed to be done on that house—that huge, family-sized house. "That's up to you, but I think I'd see it first."

———

I HAD A TEXT FROM HATTIE, LETTING ME KNOW THERE WAS A key on the bar in my kitchen. I'd thought she was going to look at the office with me, but she was clearly letting me do it on my own.

I parked under the overhang and went in my apartment to drop off my bag and snag the key, nervous about what had been done on my behalf, uneasy with the favor I knew she was doing me. The rain was still lightly falling, so I was careful to walk on the stone path Atencio had laid from my door to the back of the house.

A brick step half-circled the door, a tiny double to the huge one on the front of the house, and when I stepped to the top, I could see inside the French door. A lamp sitting on a gleaming wood table glowed, and I felt my breath leave my lungs as unlocked the door.

The hardwood floors had been cleaned until they shone in the lamplight. The walls and moldings had been repainted their original white, but this warmer tone reminded me of real cream. They'd cleaned up—and maybe refinished, I couldn't tell—Grace Shelton's little table so that the delicate gold of the flowers painted on top was clear, and a small Tiffany lamp sat at one end, casting a luminous multi-colored light. The table sat squarely on a thick blue floral-patterned rug centered in the middle of the small room, and one of the dining chairs I'd admired stood behind it, the lamplight reflecting off the peacock blue upholstery covering the back and the arms of the chair. Two more of the chairs, these without arms, stood against one wall, a tiny table between them. On the other side of the room, bookshelves painted the same creamy white covered the entire wall, floor to ceiling, and I realized that the books I'd brought from my grandmother's farm had been unpacked and left on the shelves. They'd been dusted off and stacked neatly for me to arrange, and I felt hot tears start as I realized Hattie had planned this surprise for me and left me alone to find it and enjoy it. A tiny vase of pale blue flowers sat next to them on the shelf, and I hoped they were silk, since everyone knew I couldn't keep plants alive.

I stepped around to sit in the captain's chair and was distracted by a shine on the wall behind it. I moved closer and was stunned to realize the entire back wall was covered by glass. A holder with dry erase pens was discreetly attached to the side next to the bookshelves. I uncapped the blue one and tried it out on the glass, a tasteful and— I'm sure—expensive alternative to a white board. I erased the mark and sat down in the chair, still unable to believe what I was seeing. The table had no drawers, of course, so a wooden tray sat on one of the bookshelves immediately adjacent to the desk, complete with cubbies for paper clips or pens or highlighters. Some investigation showed that a hole had been cut in the rug and a cord threaded through it, snaking up the inside edge of one of the front legs, and a surge protector had been attached to the underside of the desk, solving the problem of how to get power to the middle of the room. I was appalled to think someone had cut a hole in the rug or put screws into this beautiful table, but both things had already been done. Me being upset about it wouldn't undo it, so I let it go.

I wandered around the room, turning the lights on (recessed lighting above the bookshelves and a brass-and-frosted glass sconce on the opposite side) and then back off, loving the warm glow of the lamplight. A small note on the table listed a wi-fi password and an alarm code to the unarmed alarm box at the door.

I dashed outside and around to my apartment and got my laptop, then plugged it in and sat at my new desk. It felt so warm and right, and I knew I could never—never—repay Hattie and Sallie for this favor. I created an engagement agreement for Paige Jensen, asking for a moderately large retainer, and emailed it to her before shutting off the lights, setting the alarm, and locking the door on my beautiful new office.

Then I went to find my landladies. I had no idea how to thank them for giving me space to be the lawyer I wanted to be, but I'd start with a hug and dinner.

CHAPTER SIXTEEN

I woke up in an awful mood. The night before, I'd offered to take Hattie and Sallie to dinner as a thank you for the loan of the furniture, but Hattie had already prepared beef stroganoff with buttered noodles for dinner, and a plate and a beer were set for me. Over dinner, I told them about the business plan for the farm. Hattie had me fetch the booklet, and we spent a couple of hours going through it. By the end of it, two things were miserably clear.

It was an excellent business plan, and—if the needed investment could be obtained—the chances were pretty good it would work.

I woke up late after dreaming about my grandmother and the farm all night. Some of my strongest memories of her were evenings on the farm, when she and I would walk down to the big barn after dinner, her dog Ham trotting along behind us, so she could 'check on everything.' 'Everything' might be bags of feed tucked away for winter feeding or one of the cows brought in for calving or just a quiet walk through the barn, our footsteps echoing on the concrete floor. For someone who supposedly hated the farm, she loved to walk over the land, but I think for her, it was an exercise in making sure everything was tidily in the place where she'd tucked it away.

At one point during the evening, Sallie—who'd kept quiet for much of the conversation about the business plan—spoke into a lull in the conversation. "Lacey, dear, why are you so afraid of the farm changing? Of all the people in your family, you're the one who's moved the farthest away from it. Or is it that you are afraid of changing yourself and not having the farm as a constant?"

I made some answer, probably tried to make a joke, but her questions bothered me, and they followed me home later to echo in my head as I tried to sleep. Why *did* this bother me so much, the idea to change the farm to an actual, thriving, and profitable concern?

Because it did. Don't get me wrong: the business plan and the business it described were amazing. Mark had done an excellent job of remaining true to the history of the farm, while also hitting every single one of the modern elements that would bring profit to the land. There would be six luxurious cabins of varying sizes all up and down Sanders Creek, tucked into bends where individuals and couples and families could stay with quiet activities for each; the farmhouse would be expanded to provide a few rooms for people wanting a bed-and-breakfast experience; the kitchen would be upgraded to allow Andi, a classically-trained chef, the space to hold cooking lessons and 'epicurean weekends'; the pole barn would be added to, partially enclosed, and outfitted to provide for a real farmer's market on the weekends—right there on the newly-expanded Highway 82, where it would have the perfect exposure; they'd build an outdoor wedding and event space and utilize the big barn for the kind of country-barn weddings so many people wanted these days; the unleased acreage would be turned over to organic produce and a hydroponic greenhouse; and they'd already talked to a nonprofit about hosting an agriculture center that would work to save heirloom seeds and keep the history about farming and ranching alive and available for young people on school trips.

It was absolutely, completely perfect. Enough of the ideas would be profitable streams of income that—according to Hattie, who apparently knew these things—investors would be crawling all over, if they weren't already. Mark had even calculated negative hits from Acts of God, like extreme weather and swarms of locusts, into his bottom line.

Reading it made my heart pound, and I was swamped by memories of my father and my grandmother and Uncle Austin and Uncle Henry, and even my traitorous brother. I lay in bed for hours last night, wondering why this was affecting me this way. I finally drifted off to sleep only to wake to my phone's alarm far, far too soon. I had a busy day today, and I didn't need to feel this tired or anxious. I showered quickly and bypassed coffee on the way to the Lakeway Circle house. I wanted to get in and get the lockbox out before Suzy Shapiro, the real estate agent, and the security company got there.

The day was cold and rainy—March had come in like a lion—and I bundled up. If I had time, I wanted to walk around a bit in the back and see if the chapel Dorothea Allred had described was there.

I'd asked Paige to wait for a call before coming over, and I was happy to see she'd listened to me. Mrs. Allred's lamps in her living room were lit, and I hesitated before walking up her path to knock on her door.

I'd almost given up when she opened the door, looking much like she had three days before, with a different pretty flowered dress and a cardigan with needlepoint daisies neatly buttoned over it.

"I don't have snickerdoodles today," I said with a smile, "but I was hoping for a minute of your time."

"You're welcome anytime, young lady." She looked tired, to be honest, but her eyes were bright and so was her smile as she ushered me in. "Do you have time for tea?"

I hesitated, but then I smiled and nodded. My self-imposed timeline and its attendant anxiety shouldn't rob me of good manners. I

followed her back to the kitchen where she had water boiling in a
kettle. In the drainer next to the sink was a small pan, and a lonely
bowl and spoon, and I was suddenly glad I'd said yes.

This time she let me set the table with a much more plain and
serviceable china, just the cups and saucers, and she poured water
over the loose tea in the pot and brought it over with a tiny pitcher of
cream.

She sat back to let the tea steep. "I was going to call you today."
She paused, but I didn't speak. She sighed heavily. "Would you go
into the living room and get the blue notebooks on the table beside
my chair?"

"Sure." I felt concerned about her tiredness, and I wondered if
someone was coming to check on her. In the living room, I found the
notebooks. They were four light blue composition notebooks, the
lined paper inside filled with a spidery handwriting in faded pencil.

I placed them in front of her when I returned, the tea steaming at
both our places. I added a spoon of sugar and a splash of cream to
mine and enjoyed a sip while I waited for her to begin.

"These were my father's," she said, resting a hand on top of the
notebooks, "and I'm pretty sure he intended to destroy them before
he died." She paused. "Had my mother not been taken ill right after
he died, she would have done it for him."

"Why?"

She tilted her head and looked at me. "They're a record of his
work activities."

My heart began to pound harder. "For Jack O'Toole?"

She nodded but said nothing.

I sat back in my chair, thinking through the issue. John Berenson
had not been an attorney, so the notebooks would not have necessarily contained privileged information, but it certainly might be
confidential. But the notebooks were unquestionably the property of
Dorothea Allred, and she had the right to show them to whomever
she chose. I took a deep breath.

"I have some news for you today too. I met yesterday with Paige

Jensen, Eleanor's great-granddaughter. She would love to meet you, if you feel inclined."

Her eyes widened. "Leona's granddaughter?" I nodded, and her look softened. "Does she look like Eleanor?"

"She has that same stubborn chin." She laughed softly. "She's blond like her father, but she has Eleanor's spirit. She hired me to help her." I paused. "She wants to know about Eleanor."

She smiled. "I'd love to meet her."

I was still concerned about the weariness on her face. "Perhaps next week?"

"Oh, my dear." She shook her head with a sad smile. "At my age, I never put anything off till later if I don't have to."

"Forgive me, but you seem a bit—tired. Is someone coming to check on you today?"

She patted my hand and smiled at me. "You're very sweet. My granddaughter will come by this afternoon, and I can call Mavis too." She took a sip of tea. "I didn't sleep well last night. I went up to the attic yesterday and found these books, and I read enough to be worried about what to do with them."

She straightened the composition notebooks, so they stacked squarely atop each other. "As far back as I can remember, my father kept notes for himself about what he did every day. Sometimes they were to-do lists"—she smiled as she looked out the window and remembered—"even though he was terrible about completing those. Sometimes they were where he recorded his thoughts or what he'd done about something." She rested her hand on the notebooks again and looked at me. "But these aren't what I remember. These are notes of what he did for Jack O'Toole. And I think you should read them."

I held my tongue, not wanting to interrupt.

"Father started working for him not too long after Eleanor died— early 1940, I think. And worked for him until he died in 1961. And no, there's no record of confessions of guilt or anything." She hesitated. "But he was troubled by Jack and Jack's state of mind, and I think you should read them."

She sat back in her chair, her hands gripping the arms, and I worried again. On Tuesday, she'd seemed so active and alert, but today she seemed to have faded and aged. "Are you sure your grand-daughter shouldn't come early?"

She made an impatient motion with her head, a tiny shake, and I realized she didn't want me hovering. She probably felt the same way about her granddaughter. I looked at the clock on the stove and real-ized Suzy and the security company would be getting to the house next door in a few minutes.

"Would you feel like seeing Paige this afternoon?"

She nodded. "I'll be better by afternoon." She slid the books closer to me. "Read those before you show them to her." She looked steadily at me. "And prepare her."

———

I TUCKED THE COMPOSITION NOTEBOOKS INTO MY CAR AND opened the gates, driving in and parking moments before Suzy drove in behind me in her Lexus SUV. Suzy Shapiro is a powerhouse agent, in her 60s now, one of those agents who win the multimillion-dollar sales awards every year, and one who loves her clients so much they refer her and use her again and again. Her son was now her partner, and together they were taking the Dallas real estate market by storm. They were busy, but Suzy would have killed me if I hadn't pulled her in for this property.

She hugged me hard when she got out of her car, dipping back in to get a paper cup to hand to me. "Cinnamon latte," she said with a wink. She smoothed back her naturally curly gray hair and looked around.

"Bless you." I sipped for a minute and watched her assess the house and grounds, her long legs eating up space as she walked. She was wearing skinny jeans and boots with chunky high heels that made my feet ache just looking at them. Finally, she came back to me, her big brown eyes sparkling.

"This place is just fabulous. *Fabulous.* We are going to have so much fun!"

We chatted for a minute as Lakewood Locks and Security pulled in. Amber and Harry Blake had owned a locksmith company in Lakewood since the 1980s, and they saw the writing on the wall when alarm systems became affordable in the 1990s. One of their sons, Freddie, now in his late 40s, had trained on the systems and was expert in the area. The house's original alarm company—from back in the 1990s when the house had been rented—was long out of business and the alarm system had not been replaced by the Tarantinos. Given how they'd spent the loan funds so far, I wasn't surprised.

I wanted to get a quote from Freddie Blake for an upgrade to the entire system, but for now I just wanted to get some better window and door security in place and get new locks installed all around. Freddie got out of the van along with a young man that I thought might be related, since he had Amber's curly reddish hair, and Freddie introduced him as Kobe, helping me place him at about 20 years old. They offered us blue shoe protectors to put on our shoes, which I thought was an excellent idea. Suzy replaced her boots first with flats she had in her car, and we all covered our shoes before entering.

I'd put my coffee safely in my car, so I handled the locks, but I let Freddie and Kobe deal with the alarm while I watched Suzy take in the marble floors and soaring ceilings. She stood in the foyer, turning around slowly to take it all in, her fingers twitching as she took notes in her head, then she moved into the dining room, and I let her go. I ducked back outside to take a final sip of cinnamon latte and to get the flashlight I'd brought with me. It was Hattie's, one with a very powerful and bright lamp that she kept charging in the laundry room. This time I was going into the darkness upstairs prepared.

Suzy came out of the dining room tapping notes on her phone, and she flashed a smile as I let her know I'd be up in the attic. I mounted the stairs slowly, this time taking in more about the unfinished sections of the house. In reality, the Tarantinos had only redone the foyer, the dining room, kitchen, one living area, and the master bedroom. As Jerry had pointed out, in their enthusiasm to have renovated areas to live in, they'd skipped a lot of 'unseen' remodeling that was still necessary and might even result in re-renovation of the living areas. I wondered if they'd had any guidance from professionals other than an architect. By now, the builders had removed all their tools from the rooms above the kitchen, but there were still boxes of bathroom tile, hardwood floor planks, and plumbing and light fixtures in a haphazard staging area. Large plastic containers of paint and solvents sat atop the piles.

I continued up to the third floor, wondering again at the narrowness of the stairwells and feeling breathless as I reached the top landing. I turned on the overhead light and then the flashlight, setting it on the floor facing the secret room. The door to the room was hard to recognize even though I knew it was there. The closet, like the one matching it on the other side, was made of unpainted shiplap, a rough-hewn pine that had a thinner edge on one side in order to allow it to overlap its neighbor. Something was bothering me as I looked at it, and I finally realized that the shiplap was installed vertically, rather than horizontally. As far as I could remember, the other closet had the same feature. Shiplap is usually installed horizontally, but the vertical installation here fooled the eye, making the room look larger. It also hid the edges of the door to the secret room. I remembered how tall the door had been, so I felt around under the socket of the closet pole. Sure enough, there was a lip where the door edge met the wall. I got my keys out and used a thin one to get underneath the lip, working it into the gap until I finally felt it give. I wiggled my fingers underneath the lip and pulled, and the door swung out.

The hinges had been installed on the inside, I could see in the bright light, and a tiny handle had been attached to allow someone to pull it closed. The shiplap boards had been staggered in length, hiding the top of the door. Had they all been cut to the same length, the outline of the door would have been more apparent. It didn't surprise me at all that no one had found it before this. Perhaps the tenants and anyone else after O'Toole's death just assumed the closet was small because of the pitch of the roof.

Everyone said that Jack O'Toole was responsible for the design and construction of the house, and I could only surmise that this room was built by or for him. Had Jack O'Toole done the carpentry work himself, or had he taken some builder or worker into his confidence? I thought about the harsh-looking man who'd left the wedding with Eleanor in her cream-colored suit. He didn't look like the trusting type. I had to believe that it was he who placed the lockbox inside the room.

Before moving it outside of the room, I sat on my haunches and studied it. The lockbox was metal, painted a deep blue, with a sticker on the front under the combination lock, the kind that had three wheels with numbers on them. The blue box sat exactly in the center of the floor, obviously placed there on purpose. The dust all around the box was thick and undisturbed.

I moved the lockbox out of the closet and used the powerful flashlight to look around the tiny room. I'd been right about the cross on the wall. The walls themselves were covered with a light, sooty dust that I recognized as candle soot. Most people don't realize it, but candles give off carbon soot to such an extent that it even resembles mold in unventilated areas. I'd worked on a case a couple of years before with a woman who'd gotten very sick from breathing candle soot. She'd worked in a candle shop for years, lighting the candles every day, and the expert reports about the amount of carbon in candle soot helped to get her a settlement from her employer, who'd had to acknowledge both the lack of ventilation in the work area and his knowledge of the conditions.

From the outline of soot on the wall, it was clear there had been a large cross hanging on the wall opposite the door. I shone the light on the wall and found small nail holes where the crossbar had hung. It looked like the vertical bar had been about 18 inches tall, and the horizontal crossbar had been at least 12 inches wide. *A very large cross,* I realized. The small drops of wax were on the floor directly under the outline of the cross, so I assumed someone had put candles on the floor. That didn't leave much room. Two feet by three feet—six square feet, with the door closed, and I couldn't imagine someone who needed this much privacy would do whatever they did in here with the door open.

I pulled the flashlight in with me, took a deep breath, and pulled the door closed—almost. I put my keys in the space between the door and the edge of the doorway, just in case, and turned around. The presence of the outline of the cross on the wall made me think this had been a secret space of worship, so I got on my knees as if I was praying to the wall where the cross had been.

For a moment, my head swam, the lack of air in the closet making me feel slightly nauseated. With my foot, I pushed the door open just a bit more and felt better. The bloodstains were on the wall to my left, so while I was down there on the floor, I turned the light on them and looked closer. Did they look even more faint this time? I got close as I could to try to see more clearly, but they were still just small spots and streaks of a very light reddish-brown. Blood. Human blood. Suddenly, I felt like there wasn't enough air in here, and I wanted *out*. I picked up the flashlight and moved to grasp the edge of the doorway when I saw the inside of the door. I shone the light right in front of my face, where the reddish-brown spots and streaks were densely spattered. It wasn't just one wall with this substance on it—it was two. And I still didn't really know what I was looking at.

I was a few inches from the door when Suzy opened it, and I almost fell on my face.

"So, *this* is what you were telling me about?"

———

WE SPENT A FEW MINUTES LOOKING AT THE LITTLE ROOM, BUT Suzy got right to the point.

"You don't know if anyone died here?" I shook my head. She stepped inside to inspect the rust-colored stains. "If you hadn't said they were blood, I wouldn't have even known." She shook her head. "I can't advise you about the disclosure—if you have no knowledge, you have no knowledge. What you disclose, or what the owners disclose, is up to them." She looked back at me, her eyes concerned. "Why are you so worried about some fading stains that are going to get remodeled away?"

It was a good question. Why *was* I so worried about them? I didn't like unanswered questions, and I'd always just considered them an invitation for a solution. But this wasn't my problem, and this closet wasn't something I had enough knowledge to make a disclosure about.

We went down the stairs, talking about the more pressing issue: would the house sell as-is, or did it need to be finished? Jerry Freeman was meeting the Tarantinos' architect later in the day, and I expected the as-built appraisal soon after that, something I needed to make a decision and update the court about at next Friday's status conference.

We stood on the first landing under the spectacular stained-glass window and discussed the issue, Suzy with her hands in the back pocket of her skinny jeans, the blue shoe covers looking better on her than they did on me. She was still pretty stoked about the potential, either way.

"It's either a great 'finish up the project' Lakewood architecturally-significant home, or it's a beautifully remodeled addition to the Lakewood neighborhood." She slid a look at me and grinned. "I can sell it either way."

I laughed. "I know you can."

———

After setting up the electronic key box with the new key and alarm code, Suzy went off to meet another potential client, and I put the blue lockbox in my car with the composition notebooks. Freddie and Kobe would be changing out thumb latches for keyed locks and wiring additional window alarm points for at least another hour, so I took the opportunity to text Paige and let her know that Dorothea Allred would be waiting for her at 2 pm. I reminded her of Mrs. Allred's age, and asked her to keep an eye out for her being tired.

Then I put on the old hiking boots and peacoat I'd brought with me and headed to the back of the house. It was cold, so I pulled a navy beanie down over the tops of my ears. I could scrape my hair back into a ponytail before lunch with Dr. Amie.

Now that I was close enough to see, I could tell that the flower beds in the front of the house had at least been cleaned out and cut down in the last few years. The ones on the rest of the grounds had not. Huge trees had grown up all around the house, some five or six feet across their trunks, reaching 50 or 60 feet into the air. They'd originally been circled by the same bricks that comprised the driveway, but most of the bricks had been displaced by thick roots that had come up through the ground. I picked my way carefully through the forest on the right side of the house, choosing to start on the side closest to Mrs. Allred's house, so I could check out the chapel she'd mentioned. I pulled some knit gloves out of the pocket of my jacket and put them on, hoping to keep frostbite at bay. It was cold and damp, very unusual for March in Dallas, but I was determined to see what was back here, and I told myself it was better now than when it warmed up and the snakes and bugs would be out.

Rounding the back of the house, I fought my way through some smaller trees that had grown up between the larger ones, and I could see the remains of some kind of pool or fishpond, the ceramic tiles cracked and littering the edges of the concrete. I bent down and picked up a largish piece of one and brushed it off. An art deco lily was painted on a tan background, the lines delicate and the colors still beautiful, if faded. I tucked it into an inner pocket of the coat and forged on.

The path from the back patio into the forest beyond was choked with vines and trees, but it could still be seen. I followed the path, wishing I'd brought a machete with me. I stopped for a breath and listened. Even this deep in winter I could hear some birds twittering away, and I was glad there wasn't a creepy silence to freak me out. I started up again, but something startled off to the right—a squirrel maybe—and I stopped, my heart pounding as I peered into the darkness to see what it was. A break in the trees revealed what seemed to be a path branching off to the right of the main path, so I headed into the darkness. The trees were thicker here, the young volunteers grown more densely together, the ground soft and damp where the late winter sun hadn't reached. Pushing through the lower branches on the young trees was difficult, but I worked to move them aside, sweating in my heavy coat even in this chill. I wished I'd brought Hattie's flashlight with me, but I hadn't realized the growth would be so thick or the day so gray and dark.

I pushed a thin branch aside and then lost hold of it as I tripped on something. It whipped back and I ducked, but it caught me on the forehead just below the edge of the beanie. My duck took me off balance, and I caught myself on the trunk of a young tree, ripping my glove and the skin underneath. I said a few curse words and checked the cut on my hand with the light on my phone, but it seemed okay. At least it was my left hand this time. I used the light to look down to see what I'd tripped on, and realized the whole area was littered with fairly large reddish-colored stones, big ones. I shone the light around and caught sight of the iron fence that formed the boundary of the property about fifteen feet ahead, with piles of those large stones in between. This had to be what was left of the chapel.

The trees all around were relatively young, mostly volunteer hackberries and mulberries whose seeds were brought in by birds eating the berries, the thickest only about five or six inches across. These would all be removed when the grounds were re-landscaped and whatever shape had been roughed in for the chapel's base would be revealed. I don't know what I was hoping to see when I hacked my way back here, but there was nothing left at this point. I shone my phone's light around in the dimness, but, other than piles of the reddish-brown stone, I couldn't see much.

And then I dropped my phone. There was an alarming crash as it hit a stone, but the light stayed on. I cursed again, feeling foolish as I thought, *Of course, you dropped it, you idiot. You were holding it in a cotton knit glove, swinging it around like you were some kind of Lara Croft, looking for treasure. What did you think would happen?*

I dropped to a knee, praying I hadn't broken it—there was no way I could afford a new phone right now—but knowing that had been a glass-breaking crunch I'd heard. It had a supposedly unbreakable case on it, but you know how often those fail.

I picked it up and examined the back. The 'unbreakable' case had cracked, but I didn't want to take it off in the dark to see if the back of the phone was damaged. I turned it over to look at the front. The hard, plastic screen cover looked broken, but I didn't think the glass beneath it was. I started to rise, but the light was shining off something on the ground just under the edge of a stone. I shone the light more directly on it: it was metal, perhaps jewelry. I kept the light on it and pulled it out from beneath the stone, scrabbling for it in the soft dirt.

It was a medal of some sort, an inch or so across, maybe silver under the encrusted dirt, with a woman on it, and a broken chain still threaded through the loop at the top. For a moment, I just looked at it in the glow from the phone's light, feeling like I had indeed found something priceless and rare, then I tucked it into my coat pocket with the piece of tile and turned to fight my way back to the house.

———

I'D NOT LEFT A GOOD TRAIL WHEN I WENT IN, BUT AT LEAST I knew where I was going this time, so it took a lot less time to get out. I was hot and sticky, and my hair was matted to my head under the beanie. The cut on the palm of my hand was bleeding, but not too bad, so I didn't think I needed stitches. With my bad luck in getting scrapes and cuts, I stayed up on my tetanus shots, so I wasn't too worried.

I'd pulled a brush out of the center console in my car and was trying to fix my hair in the reflection on the stainless steel and glass refrigerator when Freddie and Kobe finished up. I'd borrowed the sink in the kitchen to wash up, and I'd cleaned the cut on my hand and put a couple of band-aids on it that I'd found in a kitchen drawer.

Kobe shook his head at the splendor of the renovated kitchen. "With the price of copper and the bad security in this house, I'm surprised these copper fixtures are still here."

He was right—and that made me even more nervous. "How quickly do you think we can get the rest of the house wired and the new system in?" Copper was as valuable than some of the harder-to-move appliances, and the house hadn't been too secure since the Tarantinos had moved out. Even with the keyed locks, the doors wouldn't be much of a deterrent.

Freddie scratched his chin and showed me his plan for the new security points, which he'd scribbled on the back of a flyer for Chubb locks. He'd pretty skillfully drawn the main house and the wings and noted where all the windows and doors were. "The upper floors wouldn't usually be an issue, but with this overgrowth and the walls, there's no line of sight anywhere. A guy could just climb one or two of the trees out there and open a window." He added a mark or two on the windows on the back.

I set the alarm with the new alarm code, and we walked out together. I took the opportunity to show them the blue lockbox and ask for some advice. I hadn't wanted to break it open, but I had no idea what the three-digit lock's combination was.

Freddie handed it to Kobe, who took it and headed to their van. "He's practically an expert at this now. These are the kinds of locks on guitar cases, old luggage, old insurance lockboxes like this." He looked over at his son proudly. "He even did a YouTube video explaining the technique."

Curious, I followed Kobe and watched as he took a thin, pointed shim out of a tiny case. He held a small flashlight in his mouth, pointing at the lock, while he inserted the shim to one side of the three wheels and spun them slowly as he held the shim steady. They reached 9-1-0 and then the lid of the box popped open. He handed it back to me and took the flashlight out of his mouth.

"Thank you." I tucked the box under my arm and shook his hand. "You looked like a jewel thief there for a minute." He gave me a toothy grin and reached in his pocket for some gum.

I resisted the urge to look in the box and spent a minute talking with Freddie about next steps. He suggested a better lock on the front gate, so he rattled around in the back of the van and produced a chain and a strange round lock, handing me one of the keys and suggesting he make a couple of extras for the key box for agents showing the property, once it was listed. He also agreed to send me a proposal for the new security plan by Monday.

I let them out and locked the gate, feeling relieved to be off the property—not a good sign, since this project looked like it'd be around for some time. I wondered when I would get used to the dark feeling that seemed to hang over it.

CHAPTER SEVENTEEN

I stopped at Café au Lait, telling myself I needed to put in the order for two dozen snickerdoodle cookies for Gerard's sister's party, but really, I just wanted to be warm and in a happy place when I opened the lockbox and looked inside.

I took a few minutes first, ordering a cinnamon latte and wheedling Esther out of a couple of cinnamon knots (which was alarmingly easy and unfortunately explained when I went to the restroom much later and realized I looked like I'd been mugged out there in the woods), then checked out the damage to my phone in the light. The 'unbreakable' case was beyond saving, but it seemed to have done the job and protected my phone. I decided to stop by my phone carrier's store on my way home to have them take a look and make sure.

I ate the cinnamon knots and sipped the latte, finally warming up and feeling the darkness slip away. I went and washed up, and then I gave into the urge.

I opened the lockbox carefully, wondering what the '9-1-0' combination meant, if anything. My experience showed me people set combination and passwords locks to something that had meaning —so they'd remember what they were. A thick-stuffed envelope sat on the top, 'Patrick' written on the front in a shaky, old-fashioned style, sealed, with yellowed strips of scotch tape still holding firm. I set it aside. The rest of the contents were all paper, mostly photographs and newspaper clippings.

Then, like Paige had done yesterday, I carefully laid the other contents out on the table, spacing them out evenly. There were ten small photographs, all but one black and white, and five carefully cut pieces of newsprint, as well as a postcard and a booklet. The newspaper cuttings had been folded for so long that the creases had whitened away the news ink, so I left them folded for safety's sake. I didn't want to be the one responsible for them falling apart, so I'd be careful opening them up.

I took out a pad and searched for a pen, unearthing Gerard's Mont Blanc at the bottom of my bag. The sight made me smile. I was trying not to think about tomorrow night too much because I still wasn't sure about all this, but I couldn't help being excited by the thought of him. I shut that down pretty quickly—this little treasure trove was enough excitement today.

I uncapped his pen and started a list, describing each item in turn:

1. Colorized photo of Eleanor Hartsfield with her plane, a date written in pen on the back: July 5, 1928
2. Newspaper clipping of a photo of Eleanor Hartsfield with her plane, dated Sunday, September 1, 1929
3. Black-and-white photo of a small boy dressed in what

looked like a sailor outfit with a huge ball in his hands, 'Patrick, 1939' written on the back

4. Newspaper clipping of a story on the Lakewood Theatre's opening night, October 27, 1938, a photo of the theatre with 'Love Finds Andy Hardy' on the marquee

5. Newspaper clipping of the obituary of Eleanor Hartsfield O'Toole, the newspaper's date on the top: August 10, 1939

6. Black-and-white photo of Eleanor O'Toole in a white dress and cloche hat, stepping out of a doorway, no date or writing

7. Black-and-white photo of Jack and Eleanor O'Toole in formal wedding dress, a date written in pen on the back: June 21, 1930

8. Black-and-white photo of Jack and Eleanor O'Toole outside the Lakewood Theatre, a date written in pen on the back: December 22, 1938

9. Newspaper clipping with a photo of a posed group of children, nuns, and priests on the steps of a wood building, undated and ragged at the edges, no date was visible

10. Black-and-white photo of Eleanor O'Toole at the gate of Fair Park, a sign with 'Texas Centennial Exposition,' at the front and a date written in pen on the back: August 16, 1936

11. Black-and-white postcard with 'The Midway at Texas Centennial Exposition' at the top

12. Black-and-white photo of Jack and Eleanor O'Toole with a small boy and a toddler, a date written in pencil on the back: March 16, 1939

13. Black-and-white photo of Eleanor O'Toole asleep in a lounge chair on the patio of 7224 Lakeway Circle, no date

14. Black-and-white studio photo of a young woman, 'Leona, Graduation 1955' written in pen on the back
15. Savings passbook in the names of Jack and Donal O'Toole at Texans Merchant Bank
16. A newspaper clipping from April 4, 1980 with the obituary of Leona O'Toole Franks
17. Sealed envelope with 'Patrick' written on it

IN THE BOTTOM OF THE BOX WAS A PLAIN WHITE ENVELOPE, unsealed, with two white gold rings inside, one small and thin, the metal slightly tarnished—a woman's wedding band—and the other a matching man's band, the gold shiny from use, the edges worn smooth. I added it to the list.

I rearranged everything by date order, with the undated items off to one side, noting how much more tattered the photos were than the ones in Mrs. Allred's albums had been. The ones of Eleanor were the most ragged, the one of her asleep on the chaise longue almost worn away in places, and the snapshot of her stepping through the doorway of a brick house—the Lakeway Circle house?—creased across the middle as if it had been tucked inside a wallet. I was still looking at the passbook, noting multiple deposits between opening and closing —and no withdrawals—when the alarm on my phone beeped. I checked it and realized I was about to be late for lunch with Dr. Amie. I carefully scooped up the lockbox contents and stacked them neatly back inside. They'd waited for almost 40 years—they'd wait a few more hours.

———

DR. AMIE PASCAL BECAME A FRIEND OF MINE A FEW YEARS AGO when I represented her as a witness in a heated divorce case. She was the therapist that had worked with the child trapped firmly between two wealthy and angry spouses. She was a voice of calm that was respected—and listened to—by the court, and she'd made my job pretty easy.

She had a rare Friday afternoon appointment, so we were meeting at a small soup and sandwich shop not far from her office in Lakewood for lunch. While it wasn't in glitzy Highland Park, the small café did seem to draw in its share of the bright and beautiful set. I'd learned the first time we came here that a modeling agency around the corner had an account here, and models came in and out for coffee on a regular basis between shoots or castings. I'd just about gotten used to sitting next to extraordinarily tall and gorgeous men and women—trying not to stare too often.

When I came in the door, she was chatting with the owner about soup, which resulted in big bowls of potato soup for lunch. I didn't mind. I'd still not warmed up from my exploration of the Lakeway Circle jungle, and the hearty potato chowder, topped with cheese, bacon, and chives, was perfect. The soup was served with thick slabs of sourdough bread, baked fresh that morning, according to Amie.

We sat at a table near the back, and the warmth from the busy kitchen was welcome. The shop occupied a small end unit in a very old shopping center near the Lakewood Theatre, now sadly out of business. Amie, of course, looked all business, her red-gold hair drawn back in a low ponytail and secured with a gold clasp. She wore a light pink sweater with gold chains today, pairing them with dark fuchsia slacks and dark maroon leather boots. I was just happy I'd had a ponytail holder for my hair.

She looked me over as I sat down. "Should I ask about the bruise forming on your forehead, Cherie?"

I shrugged as I sugared my hot tea. "A tree objected to me," I said after taking a sip.

She smiled and shook her head as she sat back so that our soup could be placed before us. "I'm having a few people over tomorrow evening for wine and cheese. Would you like to come?"

I eyed her skeptically as I slathered butter on my sourdough bread. Amie and her husband Robert had invited me over on more than one occasion to make up numbers for a dinner party, and, like Sallie Shelton, had found it convenient to invite a man for me. "Is this a setup?"

"Nooooo," she said soothingly. "But why shouldn't I want you to meet people?" She winked as she scooped up a small spoonful of soup.

"Well, I have a date, thank you very much." I waited for the expected shock, and I wasn't disappointed.

Amie carefully placed her spoon on the plate under her soup bowl and sat up in her chair, her delicately shaped eyebrows raising high. I raised mine back, feeling the left one prickle slightly, my forehead stinging with the movement.

"And who might this date be with?" She stirred honey into her hot tea and picked up the cup to sip.

This was sticky. The last time I'd told her about Rob Gerard, I'd told her that Gerard's voice was the critic in my head who questioned my actions on a regular basis. "Rob Gerard."

If her eyebrows could have climbed higher on her forehead, they would have. "Oh?" She set her cup down in the saucer with a click. "I thought last time you seemed a bit—." She broke off and tilted her head with a smile.

"Annoyed by him?" I supplied.

"Attracted to him," she said smoothly as she picked up her spoon again. I felt the heat rise in my cheeks. I'd hoped that wasn't apparent.

"Maybe." I spooned up some soup, making sure to get some bacon and cheese in the bite. She let the silence steep as we ate for a minute or so. "He's taking me to his sister's Texas Independence Day Party." Amie delicately dipped a piece of sourdough bread in the soup and didn't respond. "I think it's a date." She nibbled the sourdough and watched me with a raised eyebrow and a hint of a smile on her face. "Okay, it's a date."

"You like him."

I grinned and scooped up another bite of soup, watching the melting cheddar cheese string a little. "I like him. And he seems to like me."

"Why wouldn't he? You're a bright and beautiful woman." She arched an eyebrow at me, daring me to disagree.

I felt my face warm. "Beautiful?" I looked deliberately around the room at the current crop of models gracing the place and lowered my voice dramatically. "Let's not throw that word around, okay?"

"Lacey." Amie's voice was stern. "You should be old enough—and graceful enough—to accept a compliment when it's offered."

Chastened, I wrinkled my nose. "That's not easy to do." She frowned at me. "It's not."

"Try just saying 'thank you.' You'd be surprised at how easy *that* is to do. And perhaps you come to believe it as you accept that someone offers it as a truth."

"You mean accept it even if I don't believe it?" I scoffed. She tilted her head at me, and I thought again how beautiful she was. I'd wager *she* never had to worry if someone was offering a sincere compliment or not. "What if they don't mean it sincerely?"

"How do you know they don't?" She wrinkled her forehead, as if she truly had never considered that people might mock you by talking pointedly about your appearance. She refilled her teacup from the pot on the table and then dripped a little honey from the pot into the cup. "You assume they don't mean it? Why?" She took a sip of tea, her eyes on me as she stirred it a bit more.

"Why would you assume they do?" I knew I was just being argumentative, but sometimes I couldn't help it.

She set her spoon in the saucer, this time distinctly annoyed with me. "Lacey." I felt ashamed at pushing the point at her. "Why did this man ask you out?"

"I guess he likes me." I rubbed my nose, and my hand ached a little as I flexed it.

"Well, of course he does, or he wouldn't have asked you out." She took a sip of tea and sighed, and I recognized some resignation in the sound. "So, when you texted, you said you wanted to ask me something."

I recognized the change of subject and tried not to look as sorry as I felt for pushing at her. I tore off a piece of bread and swiped up the last bit of soup in my bowl, chewing the bread deliberately before swallowing. "I think I'm ready to get counseling."

Amie stared at me for a few moments before returning to her soup, spooning up a bite and eating it slowly. "Why now, Cherie?"

I told her about the farm and Mark's plans and Ryan's enthusiasm —and how I felt last night talking it over with Hattie. "When Sallie asked me why it bothered me so much, I didn't really answer honestly."

"And why does it?"

"I don't think I've ever dealt with it all—the farm was such a drastic change from our life with our mother, that it felt like a complete—" I couldn't think of the word I wanted.

"Repudiation?" She supplied softly.

"Yes." It wasn't the word I was searching for, but it was better. "Like we had shut a door on everything before. And I was glad about it."

"It was very traumatic, that time, yes?"

I shrugged. "Before she left, there were all the fights with my father." I began to feel queasy, as I always did when I thought about my mother. "My father worked weeks at a time in west Texas, and he had to take us to his mother at the farm." I thought back to the memories of hiding from everyone to read. "It was peaceful there." I sipped my water, letting the coolness ease the tight feeling in my throat. "I don't want to stand in the way of my brother's happiness because I can't come to terms with everything." Just thinking about all the changes made my heart pound uncomfortably.

"That's very brave of you." I looked up, and the sympathetic look on Amie's face was almost more than I could bear.

"I love Ryan and Sara." I swallowed hard past the tears that threatened. "They should have the opportunity they want." I sighed. "And it is a really good plan. I want to be able to talk about it with them without having some freaky anxiety thing every time it comes up." I nudged the handle of my cup around in the saucer. "So maybe some counseling. But don't you think sometimes all the looking backwards in your life, talking about it endlessly, slows you down?"

She nodded. "Sometimes. For some people. But more often, we can't move forward because of all the things weighing us down from our past."

"I don't feel weighed down." She didn't speak, but honesty compelled me to qualify that. "I don't. Well, much. I don't feel weighed down much." I frowned and the scratch on my forehead ached. "Well, not too often."

Amie laughed and smiled at our server, who came to clear our bowls and plates away. "I can recommend someone for you."

"Okay. I'll have to check to see what my insurance will cover." The thought of digging through my insurance company's website to find someone in my plan was almost too much to think about, but I resolved to be strong.

She leaned over to touch my hand. "We'll figure it out. A problem shared is a problem half-solved."

I smiled at her, feeling lighter just talking to her.

———

I LEFT DR. AMIE FEELING A BIT MORE UPBEAT. MAYBE counseling would be a good thing after all. I checked my phone and had a text from Callie Deal, the probate attorney, who'd had a family emergency and needed to substitute an email update on her review of Jack O'Toole's will for our coffee together.

I waited until I got to Pegasus Coffee and had a cinnamon latte in front of me to open Callie's email. I wanted to have Jack's will open on my laptop as well—and I was glad I did. According to Callie, the will wasn't an unusual one, but even for 1940, it was a bit old-fashioned. As I checked out the provisions she discussed in her email, I noted that he had appointed John Berenson as his executor, and his son Patrick O'Toole alone as a successor executor when Patrick obtained majority. Not just old-fashioned, but sexist as well. He left bequests to various charities, including the Red Cross, and to any 'private foundation created during my lifetime.' Hmm. *Might be interesting to see if that had happened,* I thought. I made a note.

Callie had also pointed out that the only provision the codicil had affected was one leaving things to his children, or 'heirs of his body,' as the archaic language in the will stated. In the original will, he'd left the house jointly to Patrick and Leona or their heirs, and in another clause, he'd also left extremely large sums—even in 1940s dollars—to each child. The codicil would modify the clause about the house but wouldn't have affected the huge sums of money left to Leona or her heirs—Judith and her brother Peter.

He'd left another large amount to the Eleanor Hartsfield O'Toole Descendant Trust—which got me thinking about Eleanor's will. She had to have possessed some significant assets after being married to a multimillionaire; where did those go? If he had something to do with her death, he wasn't rewarded with the money he'd given her, but he clearly knew about the Trust. I made a note to get a copy of Eleanor's will when I was downtown the next week. He'd also left $100,000 to an organization called 'The Ninety-Nines.' When a quick Internet search revealed that it was an organization started by 99 female pilots in 1929, the year Eleanor was forced to sell her plane, I had to blink away a tear. Maybe he had cared for her after all.

I closed my email and added a spoonful of sugar to my overly-strong latte, stirring the cooling liquid and trying to think. Why had Jack O'Toole changed his will to leave the house—and, presumably, this box of photographs—only to his son? Why did he make sure that neither Judith nor her children would have access to the house? Callie said that the language of the *original* will would have meant that after Leona's death, the house would be left jointly to Patrick and to Leona's heirs, presumably Judith and her brother Peter. In contrast, the codicil didn't include that statement; in legal terms, that meant that, since Leona pre-deceased Jack, her heirs weren't meant to receive the 'house value amount' that Jack had provided for Leona when he left the house to Patrick. Why? Had Leona—or presumably Judith, since Leona was apparently dying of cancer when the codicil was written—so angered Jack in some way that he didn't want anything regarding the house going to Judith?

I finished my latte, remembering something my property law professor had said in law school about wills: Looking at a will provides you with information about the emotional connections or state of mind of the decedent only at the moment the will was signed —not before and not after. It's a snapshot of what he or she was thinking or feeling *at that moment*, and it can be the harshest or the cruelest thought possible when someone with wealth chooses a will's provision to single out a family member. Had Jack used his will to punish Judith and her brother? Why?

A text popped up from Paige, who let me know she'd be at Pegasus at 4—it was almost 330, and she had an errand to run. I texted back, asking her to bring the 'Eleanor envelope' with her; I wanted to look at those photos again.

I laid out the photos and clippings from the lockbox in chronological order as I had that morning, careful to move my empty cup aside just in case. I picked up the photo of Eleanor and Jack at their wedding and looked closer. Something stirred in my mind, and I opened the Application for Probate for Jack's will again. It mentioned in paragraph three that Jack died at 80 years of age. That would have made him 30 when he and Eleanor married, only four years older than Eleanor. I looked again at the wedding photo. I wasn't buying it. Even in black and white and even accounting for the way young people looked older then, Eleanor looked much younger than Jack. I opened a magnifying app on my phone and looked closer at the wedding portrait.

The couple stood in front of a beautiful staircase, a few inches of distance between them, Jack slightly behind Eleanor, who held a large, trailing bouquet of flowers. They stood rigid and unsmiling, staring into the camera. Eleanor was dressed in white, an elegant net of pearls with a long, trailing lace veil covering her short dark hair and shoulders. Like most socialites of the time, she was very thin, and her long, slim wedding dress was satin with short lacy sleeves. She really was a beauty, and she'd clearly decided to forego the heavy makeup many brides chose in those days of the silent movies. As a result, her large, dark eyes seemed liquid and soft, and her mouth seemed tight—was she close to tears?

Jack was dressed in a tie and tails, his shirt front and bow tie brightly white against his tanned face. He was tall, much taller than Eleanor, and his light-colored irises stood out eerily in contrast to his dark hair and eyebrows. His hooded eyes seemed to be glaring at the photographer—or perhaps that was my imagination—but I had the distinct feeling he didn't like to be photographed. I leaned closer. There were clear signs of age on his face, and the hair at his temples was lighter, as if it was graying.

I pulled up the oil history website's entry on Jack I'd found the night before, scrolling to the bottom, where the photo credit showed a date of 1943 and placed the occasion as an oil exploration meeting in Venezuela, the photo owned by a university collection. Jack stood several inches taller than most of the men there, his head swiveled around, the photographer clearly catching him by surprise—and not a pleasant one. His scowl intensified the effect of his light eyes, and he was truly striking, but not in a necessarily pleasant way.

Perhaps it was his expression, but his unsmiling face seemed lined, his eyes wrinkled at the edges. If he was born in 1900, he would be 43 in the Venezuela picture, but he was clearly older than that—his hair seemed very light in the black-and-white photo, probably mostly a dark gray by that time instead of the black in the wedding picture. Sure, men were prematurely gray—look at Gerard, who I think was gray in his early 30s. But Gerard had been clearly young with gray hair. Jack O'Toole wasn't. So... *what the hell?*

I rearranged the items on the table into chronological order. The first was the savings passbook, showing that Jack and Donal O'Toole had over $301,124.16 in the account when they closed it in 1909. A quick internet check gave me a calculator for figuring the buying value of money from 1909 to 2019. I gaped in shock when I entered $301,124.16 in the program and realized the buying power of that money would be over $8.66 million today. The account started in 1904 with $10,000—or almost $300,000 in today's money—and, regardless of how old Jack O'Toole had been in 1904, that was a lot of money at the time. The information on the cover of the passbook was written in a careful, old-fashioned adult hand. Paige had said Jack's family all died when he was young, so who was Donal O'Toole? And was Jack O'Toole effectively a millionaire at nine years of age?

The photos of Jack from the lockbox were from his life with Eleanor in Dallas from 1930 to 1939, where he seemed to be middle-aged. When viewed with the one in Venezuela in 1943, where he was definitely aging, and the one Paige had, from Paris in 1959, he appeared to be a much older man. I pulled the photos I had together and moved the non-Jack pictures to the side, moving the two obituaries aside as well. That left the Jack photos, the passbook, and the newspaper clipping with the class photo. Was that possibly a school picture with Jack included?

There were no identifying marks on the photo in the clipping, like a school name or grade, and any caption had been trimmed off. I carefully unfolded the clipping and flipped it over to the back, where an advertisement for 'McShan Florist' announced a second anniversary sale with '2-cents off each rose stem.' The name sounded familiar. A quick Internet check showed that McShan Florist had been in business in Dallas since 1948, so the clipping was from a Dallas newspaper in 1950, but the photo on the other side of the clipping was clearly from an earlier time. I would have put it at the turn of the century at least. The girls in the photo were wearing long skirts, as were the nuns.

I got as close to the newspaper clipping as I could and took several pictures with my phone. The newsprint was faded and the edges badly yellowed, but the pictures came out pretty good. I flipped through them and selected the best one, then sent it to my laptop. Once on the hard drive, I opened up an image reverse-lookup program from the Internet and uploaded the image. The screen cleared and a webpage loaded slowly. The line at the top listed 'about 25,270,000,000 results,' and I groaned so loud a woman at the next table looked over. The first entry, however, showed the exact same photo with 'possible related search: Galveston hurricane 1900 st mary's orphanage.'

I opened the first search result. That webpage told the story of the loss of at least 90 orphans from an 'orphan asylum' run by the Sisters of Charity of the Incarnate Word in the hurricane that devastated Galveston in 1900. According to the website, all of the nuns and almost all of the children in the orphanage were swept away. The photo in the clipping from the lockbox was reproduced on the webpage, showing 60-some odd children lined up as if in a class photo, with two priests and nine nuns behind them. A closer look revealed that the children, girls and boys, ranged from toddlers to teenagers. Another photo showed the two buildings of the orphanage, destroyed in the worst of the storm.

So why was the photo in the *Dallas Morning News* in 1950? Was it from a fifty-year retrospective of the hurricane? If so, why had Jack O'Toole felt it important enough to clip—and keep?

What connection did Jack O'Toole have with Galveston? Was that when his family died? If he was born in 1900, he would have been a baby when the hurricane killed the orphans. The photo had no date, but as I paged through different sites about the Galveston storm, all of them had the photo with the stories about the demise of the orphanage buildings in the storm of September 1900. Regardless of the age of the photo, it could not have been taken after the night of

September 8, 1900, when, according to the accounts of the storm, the steps the children occupied were swept away by the winds and the waves.

The thirty or so boys in the photo were grouped on the right side of the photo, the youngest on the bottom row, the oldest on the back rows, with one small row of younger boys nearest the nuns and priests —maybe the most mischievous, who needed closer minding during the process. Their hair was cut military-short, even shaved, and they all wore white, with the exception of two very young boys in what looked stiflingly like navy-blue sailor suits. The girls all seemed older than the boys, and I imagined that the unhappy expressions on their teenage faces were from living in an orphanage with nuns and priests. Older boys would, I presumed, be more likely to be out on their own, working on ships or farms.

I pulled up the photo on my laptop and used the zoom to examine the boys, starting at the bottom with the youngest. If one of these boys was Jack O'Toole, he would presumably have been very young, but it was hard to actually tell if any of them looked like him. One young boy had his arms down on the shoulders of an older boy, his face bored and a bit jaded for one so young. Many of the boys had linked arms with each other, and the girls held hands or had a reassuring arm thrown around a younger child.

And then I found Jack. Or I thought I found him. At the far end of the sixth row up from the bottom, a boy sat, several inches away from his neighbor, his dark hair shorn close to his head, his hooded eyes eerily light, just as Jack's had been in his wedding photo. I compared the two photos and felt a shiver. The boy in the orphanage photo was perhaps nine or ten, not the baby he should have been in 1900. His arms were wrapped around his midsection as if kept himself apart and didn't want to be mistaken for part of the group at all.

Had Jack O'Toole been an orphan and survived the Galveston hurricane? The story I'd read said that only three boys survived. I consulted the webpage again, but no survivors' names were listed. I tried another and another before finding one that listed them: William Murney, Frank Madera, and Albert Campbell. The website said they'd ended up in a tree together after floating in the sea water for more than a day. So where was Jack O'Toole?

————

THAT'S WHERE PAIGE FOUND ME A FEW MINUTES LATER, obsessively scrutinizing the picture I'd saved on my laptop, my face inches from the screen. I looked up to find her gazing down at the lockbox contents with an expression I usually reserve for tacos.

I closed the laptop as she sat and pulled out the Eleanor Envelope. Without me asking, she laid those photos out separately from the ones I'd found in the lockbox. Once she had them all spread out, she spent a few minutes looking at each one in turn. I'd returned the clipping with the Galveston photo to the rows, and she looked at each one, leaving them lying on the table as she leaned close. She gave the Galveston photo the same attention, and I held my breath. Would she see what I did? But she moved on at the same pace to the other items.

Finally, she went to the counter and got a to-go cappuccino with a secure lid, sitting at the side of the table away from the photos and clippings to drink.

"How was your visit with Mrs. Allred?"

She took a sip and shook her head with a faint smile. "I can't believe how much she remembers." She leaned over and touched the picture of Eleanor at the Centennial Exposition. "This was 1936, and Mrs. Allred remembers her family going to the fairgrounds to see the Hall of State, with pictures from around the state of Texas." She straightened the photo of the Lakewood Theatre, making sure its edge aligned with its neighbors. "She remembers the night that Jack and Eleanor went to this opening. My grandmother was just a baby then." She sat back and seemed to hesitate.

My left eyebrow prickled. "Everything okay?"

"I told my mother I'd hired you."

I raised both eyebrows. "Oh yeah? How was *that*?"

She smiled over her coffee, a tight worried smile that looked like the one she'd given me in her mother's foyer. "Pretty much what you'd expect. She exploded and shouted, and then she went quiet. She ended with a dire threat."

"A threat about what?"

She looked off at the counter, where they were watering plants from all over the shop. "She said my family would be the ones to pay for what I'd done."

"What does that mean?" I couldn't help but be annoyed that Judith Jensen had this much power to make her daughter unhappy.

She shook her head. "I don't know." She sighed. "She said that my great-grandfather hated his daughter and my mother, and no good would come of me raking that up now."

I thought about the will. "Paige, have you ever seen your great-grandfather's will?"

She shook her head, frowning at the digression. "No. Why?"

I pulled it up on my laptop and turned it around to face her. "Take a look at Section III, the section on disposition of the estate." While she reviewed that, I reorganized the photos, including hers, into chronological order. I hesitated over the second wedding day picture, the one where Jack and Eleanor were leaving after changing out of their wedding finery. Jack's age was showing even more in this one, and I could see some gray starting at his temples.

"Oh, the Ninety-Nines..." She looked up at me. "He left money to them?"

I nodded. "Sorta makes you rethink that whole 'he must have forbidden her to fly' thing doesn't it?"

She pursed her lips. "Maybe. Or maybe he felt guilty for making her stop flying."

I acknowledged the alternative with a head nod. "Again, something we don't know. But as I looked at these photos, I realized how much we don't know about your great-grandfather." I pulled my notepad over. "You told me he'd lost his whole family. Do you remember how?"

She shook her head. "I don't think I've ever known. Disease, maybe?" She was still for a moment, clearly thinking. "All I ever remember my mother saying was that they were all dead. Why? Is it important?"

I didn't answer her question; instead, I turned the two wedding pictures around where she could see them. "How old do you think he is here?"

She frowned at me a bit but leaned over to look. "I don't know—35? 40?" She gently touched the posed wedding photo. "Eleanor had just turned 26."

I pushed a bit harder. "Do you think he's 30?"

She immediately shook her head, looking at the second photo. "Four years older than Eleanor? No way. He's a lot older." She looked at me, frowning again. "Why? What are you thinking?"

"One more thing, then I'll explain. Take a look at this." I pulled up the codicil and turned the laptop around. She read it and then looked up at me.

"I'm not a wills and trust lawyer, but something...."

"So, me either, but here's what my expert told me. When the will was written in 1940, he meant your grandmother and your great-uncle Patrick or their heirs to inherit the house jointly, as well as a lot of money. In December 1979, he changed the will to provide that Patrick gets the house, and *Leona* gets a sum equal to the value of the house."

"But not Leona's heirs if she died before him." She sat back in the chair, her eyes wide. "He was making sure that my mother didn't get half the house or even half the house's value."

I nodded. "The will was written in December—when did your mother and father get married?"

"The next February. My grandmother died a couple of months later, in April." She inhaled deeply. "Did he do that to my mother because she didn't invite him to the wedding?"

I shook my head. "Who can tell? But he didn't *disinherit* her. She still received a lot of money. Just not the money having to do with the house." I tapped my fingers on the table while I thought. "Could your mother and he have had a fight? Did they have any kind of relationship?"

She shook her head sharply. "I don't think so. She waves around the fact that he didn't come back when she or my uncle Peter were born as proof that he had no wish to be in their lives." Her lips twisted, but her eyes were sad. "I think it still hurts her."

I silently disagreed. When Judith had mentioned the house, her eyes hadn't been hurt—she was angry. Then I decided to add that to the conversation. "The house makes her angry, not sad." We stared at each other. "Wouldn't you agree?"

Paige squinted at me. "Why did you ask me about how old he looked? What are you thinking?"

I took a moment to answer, rearranging the photos, passbook, and Galveston photo clipping. "Bear with me here. I was trying to reconcile information, but I couldn't get past something."

She leaned over to look as I set things up.

"Okay, here's the first thing. The Application for Probate for Jack's will says he was 80 when he died in 1980, so he was born in or right around 1900." I nudged the two wedding photos. "That means he was 30 when he married Eleanor. And only 38 when these pictures were taken with Eleanor and their children." I forestalled her exclamation with an uplifted finger. "Wait. It gets worse. When this picture is taken in 1943," I said as I clicked on the photo from Venezuela on my laptop, "he would have only been 43." She leaned over to look, and then shook her head, but stayed quiet. "And in this 1959 photo when your mother was born? He would have only been 59. But doesn't he look a lot older than that?" She nodded, looking at the picture of Jack at a Parisian café with a critical eye.

I pulled up one last thing I wanted her to see. On the website for Journeyman1934, the photo I'd found that I was pretty sure was

Patrick O'Toole was of him in Paris. "Is this your Uncle Patrick?" She nodded.

"It's about five years old, but yes, that's him." She pulled the photo of Jack closer. Patrick had a white beard and moustache, but his light blue eyes looked eerily like Jack's, and his thick, wavy hair was white, just like his father's in the Paris picture. Patrick was stylishly dressed in a Barbour jacket with a denim shirt underneath, a handkerchief knotted around his neck, while Jack was dressed in suit with no tie. But they could have been brothers.

"And Patrick is in his early 70s there...just about the age Jack would have been in 1959 or 1960, or so I believe."

She looked up from the photo. "So, you think he *wasn't* born in 1900?"

I pulled out the passbook. "He had this savings passbook in the lockbox. It shows a Jack O'Toole and a Donal O'Toole deposited $10,000 in 1904, made continuous deposits for five years, and then withdrew over $300,000 in 1909. Paige, that's the equivalent of over eight million dollars today."

She flipped through the pages, pausing at some of the deposit numbers, then laid the book down on the table. "So if Jack was born in 1900, then..."

I shrugged. "It's a puzzle. I don't like unanswered questions." I hesitated. "But there's something else." I carefully opened the newspaper clipping with the Galveston photo. "Have you ever seen this photo?"

She leaned over. "No. What is it?"

I flipped it over to show her the McShan Florist advertisement and explained the timing. Then I pulled up the reverse-search I'd saved for the photo and showed her the Galveston tie-in. Her frown grew darker with every explanation, but she leaned in and examined the young boy on the end of the sixth row.

She sat back and blew out a breath. "I don't understand, Lacey. What are you trying to say?"

"I'm still not sure." I can't help but satisfy my curiosity sometimes, and this thing was bothering me. "This whole thing started because I found bloodstains in a tiny room where a cross used to hang on a wall and a locked box that contains pictures of a man who—at the very least—doesn't appear to be born when he says he was." I nibbled on my lip. "Maybe he *wasn't* who he said he was."

I reached into my bag and pulled out the thick envelope with 'Patrick' on the front and laid it on the table between us. "But he's left a message."

CHAPTER EIGHTEEN

Paige stared at the envelope like it was a snake about to strike. "That was in the lockbox?"

I nodded. "There's no doubt in my mind that the lockbox wasn't forgotten in that room. It was left there, with that envelope on the top of the stuff inside, for Patrick." I folded my arms across my chest, suddenly cold. "And I think it's also clear he didn't want your grandmother or your mother to get to it first."

She carefully turned the envelope over in her hands. "I need to let Uncle Patrick know about this. Mind if I take a minute to do that?"

"Not at all. I'm going to take a break." I walked to the bathroom as she tapped out a text, I presumed to Patrick O'Toole. Once in the bathroom, I washed my hands and face, noticing that the branch that hit my forehead had left a red welt. I leaned close to the mirror and saw a bruise forming. *Oh, just perfect. Gerard will think I've been mugged again.*

Paige smiled up at me as I sat down again. "He's coming into town. He'll be here Tuesday afternoon. He said he could probably meet with us Wednesday."

"That's great. Will he let you open it?"

She frowned and shook her head. "He said he wants to be there when it's opened." She sighed. "He also wants my mom to be there."

"Is that a problem?" Surely her mother would want to know what was going on too.

She laid her phone face down on the table. "She and Patrick really don't get along. They never have, according to her. She says he's always been arrogant, but he's never seemed that way to me." She smiled, her eyes focusing on some memory. "He's always been sort of a granddad to me. My grandfather Franks died when I was baby, and so I never really knew him."

"Do you think your mother will come?"

She shrugged. "Who knows? She's angry enough with me now to just stay in New York—or worse, come home so she can freeze me out for a few weeks." She opened the newspaper clipping of the Galveston photo and got close to it to look at the boy again. "Do you really think this boy was Jack?"

I stretched my legs out, suddenly uncomfortable with all the unknowns. "I'm not sure who Jack was." I blew out a breath. "I'm more comfortable with tasks and lists than I am making great leaps of logic."

She quirked an eyebrow. "It hasn't escaped my notice that you're the one who told *me* not to make assumptions."

I laughed. "Yeah, me either. But I can't help feeling that there's some reason he kept this clipping for 30 years, and that he passed it on to Patrick."

"Maybe the answer is in here," she said, tapping the sealed envelope with a finger.

"We can wait for next Wednesday."

She shrugged. "What else can we do?"

I spoke carefully, mindful that John Berenson's composition books were in my car, and that Dorothea Allred had wanted me to look at them before talking to Paige about them. "I have a few leads I was thinking about. And needed your help with."

She sat up straight, smiling that beautiful smile of hers. "I'd love to! What do you need?"

"Only a blood relative can get death certificates, although I could probably get them with a POA from you. But if you could go down to the county clerk's office on Monday and get them that would be great." She nodded, making some notes in her phone. "You might also see if you can pull Eleanor's will at the same time. There are some online probate records for Dallas County, but they don't go earlier than 1930. I think the county clerk maintains records from before then."

She looked up from her phone. "How do you know all this?"

I shrugged a shoulder. "You never know what information you'll need to find someone, a relative or descendant or property. The Internet has made that so much easier, but sometimes you still have to pound the pavement to find records."

"And do you have to find people often?" She seemed fascinated by the effort required.

I nodded. "When you practice real estate law, sometimes you have to find the last owner of a property, or a descendant of the last owner, or companies that might be owned by them." A thought struck me. "What is the name of your great-grandfather's company?"

She frowned. "What company?"

"Well, surely he had a company all those years he was doing business." She continued to stare at me. "Well, didn't he?"

"I have no idea." She rubbed her forehead. "You ask me stuff like that, and I realize I haven't even done the most basic things to find out about my great-grandfather." She smiled, a twisted and sad smile. "Even though I'd wanted to find out more about her—about Eleanor."

"Easily fixed." I opened my laptop and went to the Secretary of

State's website, turning the computer slightly so Paige could see the screen. I entered 'Jack O'Toole' in the 'people' search and came up with nothing. My curiosity aroused, I typed in 'O'Toole' and got 300-plus results. A quick flip through them, however, showed nothing. I knew that the Secretary of State's records went back farther than 1930, the first year I knew Jack O'Toole was in Texas, and—while it was certainly possible for him to have used a company from another state—there should have been some mention of him between 1930 and 1980. Paige watched me as I thought for a minute, and then I typed in 'John Berenson' and got forty results.

One seemed to be someone recent in Houston, but there was one legacy filing from 1941 called the 'Annie O'Toole Foundation' in which John Berenson was listed as a director. I turned the laptop around where Paige could see.

"Who was Annie O'Toole?"

"Who knows? His mother, maybe?" I clicked on the Filing History tab, and then on the Certificate of Incorporation icon that came up. Quickly, I scrolled down the typewritten pages to the directors listed: John Berenson, Mamie Hardwick, and Alton Hardwick.

"Who are Mamie and Alton Hardwick?" Paige asked.

The names pinged a memory. "Hold on." I sat for a moment, then pulled up my notes from my interview with Dorothea Allred. "They were the couple that lived with Eleanor and Jack in the house, I guess a housekeeper and caretaker." I sat back, and we stared at each other. Then I picked another, later filing at random to check the directors. In 1956, Alton Hardwick was replaced with Nan Berenson. I clicked another, then another and another, and then finally, the last one: in 1961, the year both John and Nan Berenson died, the Foundation filed its final report and terminated its existence.

"A dead end," Paige breathed, looking at the final report.

"Not at all." She looked at me with a raised blond eyebrow, so I explained. "We now have another O'Toole—that's three: Jack, Donal, and Annie." I noticed the barista was starting to clean the table next to us somewhat aggressively, so I closed the laptop. "I'm going to start trying to find them tonight." I looked back at the search results. John Berenson had been director of a couple of other companies, but I wanted to read his composition books before I pointed those out to Paige. I didn't know what Dorothea Allred was referring to, but I was a little leery about opening it all up right now.

Paige leaned in, her voice excited. "What can I do?"

Someone's hooked, I thought. "What were you going to do tonight?"

She shrugged. "I had a date."

"Then that's what you should do. Go on your date and let me do my job." I slid my laptop into my bag and pretended not to notice her quick frown. I continued to pack away my pad and Gerard's pen, and then opened the lockbox to put the photos away, when I realized they were probably her uncle's property. She had the wedding photo in her hand.

"Do you mind if I keep the photos over the weekend? I want to scan it all and save it." She looked up from her inspection, and I knew she was about to object. Instead, she agreed.

"You're right—we probably should. But can we get together on Monday after I've gotten the death certificate and will? I want to see it all spread out. Maybe 3 pm?"

"Good idea." I started to suggest Café au Lait, and then I realized: I had an office. My heart skipped a beat, and I had to stifle a proud smile. "Why don't you come to my office? It's in the back of the house I live in."

"The Shelton house on Gaston, right?" She rattled off the address.

I should have known she'd know where I lived, and where the Shelton sisters lived. "That's it." I opened the lockbox and realized the other envelope—the one with the wedding rings—was in there. I took it out and handed it to Paige. "I don't think Patrick would mind you keeping this."

She opened the envelope and slid the rings out in her hand. I should have known the sight of the rings, one bright and worn and the other barely used and slightly tarnished, would make her cry. But then, I've never been able to predict things like that.

———

I STOPPED BY THE PHONE STORE ON THE WAY HOME AND HAD the phone checked. Miraculously, it was still intact and unbroken. I bought a new cover and screen shield, counting my blessings.

I had some of Hattie's stroganoff left over, so I set it on the stove to warm while I went around to my office. The night before, I'd carried my printer and a few essential supplies over, but Hattie had added a small wooden cabinet to the room sometime today, and she or one of the guys had put the printer on top. It was wireless, so I was able to scan the photos with high resolution straight to my laptop.

I decided I deserved a break while I ate, so I piled a plate with warmed-up stroganoff and noodles. I shook some cat food into the cat's bowl, and the miracles just kept piling up—she deigned to join me in the kitchen, eating a few bites before coming into the living room and curling up in her cat bed by the heater vent.

I checked my email and returned a few, and then I found some *M*A*S*H* reruns and spent a couple of hours eating and enjoying watching Hawkeye spar with Frank and Hot Lips, remembering how much my father loved this show. Ryan had sent me a text reminding me of breakfast—which I ignored—and Sara had forwarded me a picture of my dad she'd taken when she went to see him. He'd apparently had a really good day today, if the smile on his face was any indication. Another miracle.

And then I settled in for research.

———

AT 2 AM, I SHUT THE LAPTOP DOWN AND WENT TO BED. THE miracles had kept on coming, but now I was really certain that Jack O'Toole was not who he claimed to be, and I didn't know what effect

—if any—that might have on him or his family. I was also concerned that Judith Jensen seemed to know that something Paige might find would affect their family adversely, and not knowing what that might be, I didn't want to blunder into anything.

I'd started by looking for Donal, Annie, or Jack O'Toole in property records in Galveston, since that was the only place outside Dallas where I had any idea Jack might have been. Annie was a complete zero, but I wasn't surprised, because women weren't usually property owners in that time, so they had no deeds in their names or probates opened for them. There were some exceptions, but Annie wasn't one of them. Donal had nothing in Galveston either. By statute in Texas, birth and death certificates aren't available online, and marriage licenses online are pretty spotty, so no birth records, death records, or marriage licenses for Donal and Annie, assuming they were his parents.

I washed up the dishes and thought it over. The ease of gathering information online made people think that records pre-dating the Internet were hard to find. The reality was that governments love to track people, and that didn't start with the information age. There were deed records, and census records, and licenses, and business records—and amateur genealogists like my grandmother were responsible for getting records gathered and scanned as soon as technology was available to make it happen.

I dried my hands and went to the lockbox, pulling out the Texans Merchant Bank passbook. Inside the front cover, spidery handwriting noted the date and 'Houston, Texas' for the location of the first deposit in 1904. If Jack O'Toole was in Galveston in 1900, where was he between then and 1904? An hour later, I'd tracked Donal and Jack buying and selling properties throughout counties in south Texas between 1900 and 1912, showing Donal as Jack's guardian. They popped up again in property records in Hardin, Victoria, Fort Bend, Liberty, Harris, Duval, and Bexar counties between 1902 and 1908, and then they disappeared from the south Texas counties until 1913, when they showed up on multiple properties in Orange, Harris, and Brazoria counties.

About 11, I made some microwave popcorn and got a beer from the fridge for a break, considering the issue as I paced the apartment to think. The constant buying and selling reminded me of what historical associations said about Texas in the early years of statehood: land was bought and sold multiple times as the state moved to have land occupied (there is no public land in Texas). I assumed Jack and Donal were 'land speculators'—people who swept in and bought cheap, worthless land for pennies and then sold it for large sums to gullible newcomers.

The cat abandoned me to go to the Sheltons' side about the time I came up with an idea. I'd remembered one of the pieces of property they had owned was sold to someone who immediately leased it out to an oil company. Where was that? Harris county? Orange? I flipped back through the screenshots I'd made of the deed records and found it: Hardin county in 1902. I changed my search parameters to include oil terms, and then found a site for the Texas Almanac that had a chronological listing of major oil discoveries in Texas counties. After that, the information came fast and furious. Jack and Donal O'Toole had bought and sold land just before and during all the oil discoveries from 1901 to 1909. The list tracked all the major discoveries and some minor ones all over Texas, including some non-south-Texas counties, and I searched those for the years Jack and Donal disappeared from south Texas, 1910 through 1913, finding them buying and selling land up north in those years. And then, following the trail of oil discoveries, they came back south again in 1913.

All in all, I found almost 300 properties the two had bought and sold between 1901 and 1915—almost 20 purchases a year, and I was doing a very cursory search. More importantly, in a deed for property purchased in Wichita county in 1912, Donal O'Toole and Jack O'Toole were both listed as owners in their own right. If Jack had been born in 1900, he'd have only been 12 at that time—still too young to own property. The last property deed transfers I could find were in July 1915, in Brazoria county, when Jack and Donal O'Toole had purchased acreage from a Thomas Crittenden for $1,000 and then sold a portion of it a few days later for $22,000 to a company called Yellowjacket Oil. A few weeks later, on August 1, 1915, Jack O'Toole *alone* sold the rest of the Crittenden property to Yellowjacket Oil for almost $100,000. I checked all the counties around, and even a few more that were listed in the Texas Almanac chronology as having oil discoveries after that year, but Jack was nowhere to be found in the property records after that month, and neither was Donal.

If Jack O'Toole was only 15 in 1915, he was a minor, and he could not have contracted for anything, much less bought or sold property, and the fact that Donal O'Toole didn't sign off on the sale deed to Yellowjacket Oil indicated to me that he might have died. I continued looking, changing search terms, until I found an heirship affidavit showing that J. O'Toole was D. O'Toole's nephew and heir and that he was 24 years old. The heirship affidavit was filed the day Jack transferred the second deed to Yellowjacket Oil, but it hadn't been attached to that property deed. Assuming this was the same Jack O'Toole—and all the evidence seemed to point that way—he was born sometime in 1890 or 1891, not 1900. So why lie about his birthdate?

I got up to stretch and pace and think, and I found myself standing in front of the open refrigerator, staring at the contents as I thought about Jack O'Toole. There are a lot of reasons people lie about their personal details—as my own family knew very well—and those were magnified prior to the 1930s, when the Great Depression meant social security numbers and more secure banking laws. People who were born prior to 1938 and never had a need for public assistance or bank accounts sometimes died without ever having a social security number.

Jack clearly had developed significant assets by the time the savings passbook was started with $10,000—had that come from property sales? I got out the passbook and carefully paged through it. Several of the dates of the sales of property were near—but not an exact match—to the dates of the deposits in the savings pass-book, and I strongly suspected Jack and Donal withheld cash from their windfalls to make the next purchase. It was obvious that the two men were buying land before a major discovery was made, and then selling it for huge profits when the discovery became known. Were they swindlers? Or simply lucky speculators? If they were just lucky, why hide the source of the funds when he came to Dallas?

I got a surge of energy after that and organized dates and transactions from the deed records. Some of the amounts for the second land sale were not listed with dollar amounts (as is Texas tradition), but all of the dollar amounts listed were much larger than even the Crittenden one in Brazoria county. In between oil discoveries, land was still being bought and sold for enormous profits by Jack and Donal, more so after about 1905. I tallied amounts as best I could.

Just my quick notations of amounts were staggering. Just the records I could find with numbers indicated hundreds of thousands of dollars at play, and those were only a fraction of the deeds I'd found. Jack and Donal rarely withdrew money from the savings account, but, given that they withdrew over $300,000 in 1909—and considering that the years from 1909-1915 were incredible banner years for oil discoveries and for railroads—it was clear that Jack's fortune was based solidly on their work for those years. It was likely they had accounts at several banks, not just the one represented by the passbook in the lockbox.

And all of this started in 1900, the year Jack O'Toole *claimed* to have been born. I was pretty sure now that he'd been lying about that, but I still didn't know why.

I'd wanted to look more into the 1900 Galveston hurricane (it was before they began naming hurricanes, apparently) connection, but much of the records about it were in the Rosenberg Library in Galveston, and only library cardholders could access the records. I had a brainstorm about 130 am and texted my friend Gabby, who worked as a personal injury attorney in Galveston, to see if she had a library card.

I got in bed, my eyes so tired I could barely see, my mind whirling. This day had gone on forever, but all I had to show for it were questions. And in a few hours, I'd get to talk to my brother about the changes he and Mark wanted for the farm. I put the pillow over my head and told myself to go to sleep. That works so well...

CHAPTER NINETEEN

March 2 is Texas Independence Day. Depending upon who you talk to, it's either the day that Texas's first constitutional convention signed its Declaration of Independence, or it's the day the revolutionary Anglo settlers in Mexico's northern colony rebelled against their lawful government. If you're in the first group, it's usually celebrated in Texas with chili, Lone Star beer (if you drink beer, Dr Pepper if you don't) and backyard barbeques if the weather is nice. Any given year, it could be the chilly tail of winter or the warm fingertips of spring.

This year, it was freezing. I left my house to meet Ryan about 945, knowing I'd be late, but a bit too tired to care. Sometimes my habit of satisfying my curiosity is a good thing, but more often, it's not. Gabby had texted me back this morning, letting me know she'd search for her 10-year-old son's library card number, so that was a positive. My appearance was not. I'd faced myself in the mirror this morning with eyes more red than gray, the bruise across my forehead blooming in reds and pinks and purples. My left hand was healing, but the cut needed a new adhesive bandage. Searching through my bathroom—where I usually have enough medical supplies to outfit an emergency room—yielded an empty box. My recent mugging and subsequent stitches had emptied me out, and I didn't restock last week when I went to the store.

I tapped on the Sheltons' kitchen door but no one answered. I let myself in with a quick 'hallo' anyway. Hattie usually kept a small first aid kit in the kitchen, and she didn't disappoint. I could tell from the supplies that Sallie had been the one to restock their kit, and I picked through some Disney princess-imprinted bandages to find one with the young ice queen from *Frozen*, which, of course, resulted in me humming 'Let It Go' all the way to The Buttered Biscuit.

I had my copy of Mark's business plan with me, nicely marked and tabbed from my conversation with Hattie, but Ryan, as usual, disarmed me from the beginning with a huge hug, complete with hearty pats on the back. He's older than I by two years, but we're miles apart in how we deal with things. After a period of teenage rebellion, Ryan settled down to domesticity with Sara as if he was born to it. They tried for several years to have a baby, and then they adopted Michael, a five-year old who'd already been several years in the foster system. Ryan is a great dad, compassionate and firm, but with a sense of humor about everything kids and parents go through. His good news this morning was that Michael, now a freshman at Texas A&M with a communications major, was going to be interning at the *Dallas Morning News* during the summer. Ryan, the proud dad, showed me Michael's text with his acceptance letter, and I ooh-ed and ah-ed and dreamed with him about his son's future.

By the time we got done with that, our orders had arrived, and we dived in. Michael had gotten the Biscuit Benedict, which is a biscuit-based Eggs Benedict loaded with Canadian bacon, poached eggs, and Hollandaise sauce. While I usually avoid things that share our last name, his plate looked really good, the yolks of the eggs soft and a deep orange next to the yellow of the Hollandaise. My Better Biscuits and Gravy seemed a bit plain next to it, but it's my favorite, and it never disappoints: fluffy sliced biscuits topped with thick, handmade sausage patties and covered with spicy sausage gravy. We dug in, still talking about Michael and his internship, but I knew the dreaded conversation about the farm would eventually come.

He finished his breakfast long before I did, but he accepted another cup of coffee and leaned back in his chair, arms crossed over a full stomach. I took a bite of the spicy sausage and stabbed a bit of gravy-covered biscuit to even out the heat, but I'd lost pleasure in the contrast. The moment of reckoning was here.

"So. What'd you think of the plan?" He motioned with his chin at the spiral bound book to my right.

I took a moment to finish my bite of biscuit and sausage before answering. "I showed it to Hattie. She marked it with a bunch of questions and comments." I slid it across the table to him.

He paged through the annotations, nodding and mumbling to himself, then smiling at me. "That's great! She's raised some good points. I'll scan it to Mark." He looked off to the side, thinking. "Or maybe I'll just run up there this afternoon and drop it off." He looked back at me, his green eyes so kind and understanding that I felt a tear bite at my own. "But what do *you* think about it?"

I looked down at my last few bites of biscuit, sausage, and gravy and pushed the plate aside. "It's a good plan," I said, avoiding those kind eyes.

"But?"

I sighed and looked directly at him. "I'm uncomfortable with it. You know that."

He cupped his hands around his coffee mug. "The farm has to change, Lace. You know *that*."

"Why? Why does it have to change? It's been there, just a big old piece of farmland, for 175 years." I put my knife and fork on my plate and used my napkin to brush crumbs off the table for something to do with my hands. "It pays for itself, and it just exists there."

Ryan watched me realign the used silverware on my plate. "It's not paying for itself much longer, Lace. All but one of the leases expire this year, and I know for sure two of them aren't going to re-lease."

I stared at him. "Those farmers have been leasing for thirty years."

He nodded, his eyes troubled. "Both Stubbs and Washburn are selling out. Developers are going to be building homes on Washburn's land. I don't know what's happening to Stubbs, but I think they're moving. Their kids moved north, and they want to be with them."

"When did all this happen? Why didn't I know?"

He snorted. "Lace, when did you want to know anything about that land?" He sat back as our server came to clear our plates away, then leaned forward again. "You always get that glazed expression in your eyes when I talk about it."

"Ha. That's because you just go on and on and on about it."

He grinned briefly. "That's true." His smile dimmed and he looked away. I knew something was coming I wouldn't like. "Lace, Sara and I are going to move out there if we can make this work."

My mouth fell open—I felt it happen. "What? When?" I sat up, my breakfast churning in my stomach. "What about your house? Dad? Your job?"

"We've been thinking about selling our house for a while. You know what the house market is like in Plano. We may have even missed the hot seller's market, but we think a home our size might still do well, if we price it right. That will give us a really good equity check." I started to speak, but he held up his hand. "I can commute for a while to school—most teachers do. Most of them don't make enough to live in Plano proper anyway." He looked away to the table next to us, where three generations of a family brunched, the grandfa-ther cutting a biscuit loaded with strawberry jam into small bites for his grandson. "As for Dad, we can be at Landover in 45 minutes from the farm, even quicker on nights and weekends. Most of the time he doesn't recognize us, Lace." He looked back at me, his eyes full of the same pain I felt when I thought about it. "That's not going to get better." He swallowed hard. "That doesn't mean we're abandoning him. But I'm not putting our lives and future on hold."

"Of course, you shouldn't," I replied, feeling slightly rebuked. "I just didn't know you had these plans. Did you know that Mark had come up with this business idea?"

Our server came back with a coffee pot and our check, and, as he refilled our cups, I could tell Ryan wasn't unhappy for the time before responding. "Not exactly this one, but he and I had been talking at Christmas about doing something that would use the land in a better way." He took a sip of coffee, not looking at me. "You know I've wanted to do something with the land since I was a teenager."

I felt an ache inside. "Yes, but I thought that was just rebellion against Grandmother." I emptied a half-and-half container into my cup and stirred the mixture up.

Ryan laughed, and I felt the ache ease. "There was some of that. But, Lace, I've thought for years about using the land in a better way than just leasing it out year after year for farmland. I hate what that does to the land."

"I know you do." I swallowed hard. "It's just so much change all at once." I took a sip of the coffee for something to do.

He leaned forward. "I know, Lace. Changing is difficult. And it's frightening. But it's also what we do to kids' poopy diapers and think what a relief that must be."

I laughed at that, but I still felt miserable about it. I sipped more coffee. "I can handle it. So is that all, or is there something else?"

He looked down in his coffee cup before looking back up at me. "Sara and I are talking about remodeling the 'Uncle House' and living there."

I was appalled, and I know my face showed it. The 'Uncle House' was where our 'uncles' Austin and Henry Peavy had lived while we were growing up: a two-bedroom shack on the northern edge of the 450 acres we had left, at the end of a dirt road that washed out when it rained too much, with only a septic tank and the most rudimentary electrical hookup. How could Ryan and Sara give up living in a 5/3 split-level ranch in Plano for something that couldn't even be called 'rustic?'

He laughed at the expression on my face. "We'd fix it up, Lace. In fact, we think we could make it be a really cool place with the cash we'd get for selling our house." He grew serious. "But part of what we spent to remodel the house was Dad's savings, and some of that is yours. We need to talk about you getting some of that." I waved him off, but he shook his head. "Yes, we do." He took a deep breath. "And we need to talk about you being a partner in the Blackberry Farm thing. You need to take a share of it."

I closed my eyes and rubbed my forehead, where an ache I didn't think was due to the bruise was starting. "Ryan, I just don't understand how this is happening. And so fast. Where is the money for all this supposed to come from?" I opened my eyes to see a distinctly guilty look on his face—and given my experience with my brother, I knew that look very well. "What? What aren't you telling me?"

He blew out a breath. "We've gotten an offer to sell 50 acres off the northeast corner to a luxury home builder. It's where the creek tails off and goes east, on the land Washburn has always leased."

"Houses? *Luxury* houses? That far north?"

He nodded. "That's where people are moving. That's why they're expanding Highway 82. This builder wants to pave the east farm road, but otherwise keep it mostly rural. The plan is for 30 one-acre lots, high-dollar homes, a community center and park." He inhaled, his eyes on mine. "He's willing to pay $700,000 for the land, and another $200,000 for the right of way for the road."

"Jesus Christ." Even with the inflated amounts for property these days, that number was too much. I narrowed my eyes at him. "And?"

"Well, for that amount, he wants to gate the road."

"*Exclusive* use? Isn't that going to cause problems for the use of the rest of the land? The west road that goes to the 'Uncle House' won't work for anything east of the creek."

He scratched the back of his neck, a gesture that reminded me that my big brother sometimes tended to leap before he looked. "I figured we could put in a new road."

"And how much would that cost?"

He looked pained. "I don't know yet."

I felt some anger stir, and I welcomed it. "How far have these negotiations gone?" He raised his eyebrows at my tone, but I noticed his cheeks were pink. I pressed the advantage. "Ryan?"

"The developer has sent a letter of intent."

I leaned back, gladly letting the anger clear my fear away. "I'm just as much an owner of that land as you are, Ryan. And Mark— who's gone so far as to make a business plan using *our* land—isn't even *that*." A thought occurred to me. "Is that why Sara's not here? She didn't want to get in the line of fire." I snorted and felt better. "How mad at you is she?"

He grinned sheepishly. "She's pretty pissed off. She told me to let you know about this weeks ago."

"So, let me see if I've got the timeline straight. Sometime around Christmas, this developer comes sniffing around. You and Mark get to talking about how all this could be done. Yes?" He looked away, but I pressed harder. "Am I right?" He nodded. "And then Mark, with all his business experience, puts together a business plan that will take into account the 50 acres gone, and use those proceeds in the plan." He nodded and rubbed the back of his neck again. I noted the tips of his ears were now red. "And when it's all done, and you guys have negotiated without me—the only lawyer in the family—and got a letter of intent, you finally decide to let me know what's happening." He opened his mouth to speak, but I waved him off. "Is anything I've said incorrect?" He shook his head, and I noted he looked a bit ashamed now. I felt slightly triumphant.

"Well, I see why Sara wanted to stay home."

He leaned forward, suddenly intent, and more than a little upset himself. "You can 'lawyer' me all you want, Lace. But the reality is that we are losing lease revenue, which means that we will all have to reach into our pockets for property taxes next year. And unless we plant those fields ourselves or find someone else to lease, we will lose the ag exemption too." He pushed his coffee mug forward and placed his palms on the table. "Do you have the money to start paying non-exempted property tax on 450 acres every year? Because Sara and I don't. Even with Michael's scholarships and college fund, we're sending him money every month, and we're still paying his truck off."

He broke off and put his hand over mine, and I realized that my fingers had been tapping the tabletop without any conscious thought on my part. "Lace, I know that the farm was your hiding place after Mom left, but you've moved on. You're an adult now, and none of that has to hurt you anymore. You don't need to hide from the emotions."

I stared at him. "What are you talking about? I don't have anything to hide from." I felt my face redden. "I didn't then either. I was relieved when she left."

He stared back at me, and I felt an uneasiness, the same one I'd had when Dr. Amie and I were talking about my mother. When he spoke, his voice was gentle. "Lace, I don't think you remember that time very well. You were only seven."

I was stung by his tone. "And you do? You were only nine."

He kept his hand on mine, and I didn't struggle to pull it free—even though I wanted badly to. "Lace, there's a lot of difference between seven and nine." He kept his eyes on mine. "You probably don't remember a lot about what happened when Mom left."

"I remember a lot of fights before she left, and how quiet it was after she went." I felt miserable again. "I feel really guilty about how relieved I was."

Ryan looked like he was near tears, and I felt bad that this subject was causing him pain. "Look, Ry, we don't have to talk about this—"

He interrupted me. "Lacey, do you not remember anything else?"

The usual nausea returned, and my stomach threatened to give up the biscuits and gravy I'd managed to eat before this conversation began. "I don't know. I know she and Dad fought a lot, and then she just—left." I swallowed hard. "And it was so quiet. And then we moved to the farm."

His look softened, and I could tell he wanted to hug me again, but we were sitting across from each other at a table. "Lace, it was more than that." He paused, as if afraid of telling me. "You tried to follow her as she left, and Dad had to bring you back into the house. She got in Aunt Pam's car and didn't look back. They drove off and you tried to run after the car. And you screamed and cried until you were sick —literally sick. And then—nothing. I think you slid into some kind of catatonic state. Dad finally packed us up the next day and took us to Grandmother. He didn't know what to do. And it was a few days before you—just sort of woke up."

I pulled my hand free, hoping he'd stop, but he kept going. "It was like you refused to believe anything had happened. You just didn't talk about her at all."

———

I DROVE HOME IN THE LIGHT SATURDAY TRAFFIC, TRYING TO recall what happened all those years ago. No matter what Ryan told me, all I could remember was our mother quietly closing the front door as she left. It seemed now like that quiet reached out and around me, blanketing me from everything happening, and nothing penetrated it until much later, when we were already living and settled into life at the farm. I hadn't ever pieced together the timeline, but Mom had left when it was cold, and my memories of the farm began with spring.

The trip was cold and slow because a light rain had begun to while we were in The Buttered Biscuit. Rain in Dallas seems to bring out the worst driving habits in everyone. I focused enough to avoid multiple collisions, but I felt cold and empty. Ryan hadn't wanted to let me leave alone, but I wasn't able to have a coherent conversation in my head, much less with someone else.

I hadn't been relieved she was gone.

I can't tell you how knowing that affected me. Most of my life I'd worked off the premise that her leaving us was a good thing, and that we'd all wanted her gone. It sounds awful thinking that, but the pain of not having a mother all those years was slightly dulled by the knowledge—or what I thought was the knowledge—that I hadn't minded her going. Now that I thought of it in those terms, of course it was unimaginable that a seven-year-old wouldn't miss her mother. But knowing that I did, that I cried when she left, that the pain had been sickening and awful, made me shaky with the longing to go back and live my life again, to see if everything would be different now.

I lay down on my bed, sure that this shaky awareness would lead to tears, but I found I couldn't cry. Instead, I lay there for hours and rewound my life, to the time before she left, and the time after we were at the farm. What lay between was still as dark as it had been before talking to Ryan. But every interaction after that, every discussion, every event was different, as if I'd snapped a different lens on a camera and retaken every photo of my life. They weren't clearer; they were just *different*. I let them roll through my mind, examining that difference, until I drifted off to sleep.

CHAPTER TWENTY

SATURDAY, MARCH 2 (CONTINUED)

I woke up a few hours later from a dream where I was a princess in an ice castle, singing as the ice around me melted. Just a note: I sing much better in dreams than I do in real life. I stretched and did an emotion check—everything seemed to be steady, a complete surprise given my shakiness a few hours before. I even had enough time to go get the snickerdoodle cookies at Café au Lait, shower, fix my hair, and put on some makeup if I hurried.

Marie had my box of cookies ready, and I bought an extra to munch on as I drove back home. The temperature seemed to be dropping, and it was misting, so it was possible we'd have a bit of ice before the night was out. I hummed the *Frozen* song as I turned in to my driveway.

I was showered and dressed in fifteen minutes. After a few more wondering what the fashionable in Dallas would wear to a Texas

Independence Day party that didn't include 'bring your own keg' on the invite, I'd decided on dark blue jeans fresh from the cleaners, with some fairly decent roper boots and a long-sleeved shirt I'd found at a western store a few years before. It looked like a Texas flag, with a white star on a dark blue field on one side, and red and white fields on the other. I dug around in the jewelry box I've had since childhood for some earrings that look like tiny western-style belt buckles and spent about ten minutes wrestling with my hair. It's long and straight, but I was hoping tonight for something a bit more fancy. I had a curling iron that might be called 'vintage,' but it doesn't heat up enough to really do much more than give me a wave under at the ends. It was frustrating, since I wanted to impress not only Gerard, but his sister too. I refused to think too much about impressing Gerard, but the tingle I had every time he was around couldn't really be denied (trust me, I've tried).

I'm not a virgin, so I understand the tingle. I've had three long-term boyfriends in my life, and I'll date if I'm asked. I find there are more invites to 'hang out' than actual dates these days, but that's okay, too. The infrequent dates have been easier to deal with than the questions about what I've been doing since law school, followed by curiosity about being a whistleblower, or what it's like to testify against your former boss and mentor. But given the dearth of eligible men in my world, relationships have been few and far between.

My first real boyfriend was a senior in high school—I was a junior, and we had two intense months of puppy love before he went away to college. He was also my first lover, and it went as most first sexual experiences do. He had a pickup truck, and I lost my virginity in the back on a couple of blankets under a meteor shower in the June sky. That sounds romantic now, but perhaps that's the filter of time misting over reality. June skies in Texas tend to come with mosquitoes, sudden thunderstorms with intense rain, and older brothers who take a dim view of teenage boys having a romantic rendezvous with their sisters. Or at least, *my* June sky came with all of those. Very dramatic, especially when the brother and the boyfriend happened to be friends as well. The relationship ended, as most of those do, when he went off to college. I found a certain amount of relief both with his departure and the ending.

My college boyfriend was nothing like my high school crush. He was a business major from Boston, complete with preppy clothes, a hair 'style,' and parents who disapproved of a girlfriend without their idea of a family line to recommend her. We dated while he was in Dallas and didn't when he wasn't. My friends couldn't understand how I was okay with that, but I'd found that relationships with the opposite sex come with emotional baggage I didn't understand, and there was no way for me to explain that I knew he was a phase I was working my way through. And I did. He left after graduation with a goodbye kiss, and our contacts grew less and less frequent once the lack of proximity did its job. I missed him—to a point—but then the rush of my own senior year took over, and I missed him less each day.

In law school, I'd decided it was time for me to grow up and find everything I thought I was supposed to want: the perfect law job, a dutifully doting husband, two point five kids. I planned for meeting a future husband the way I plan for court now, a bit of research on the adversary, a script just in case things go wrong, and a healthy fatalistic attitude about the end result. I met Joel at a first-year mixer hosted by a law firm, and we dated all during that first year of law school, hurried and furtive meetings and couplings when we should have been studying. We went to Mexico on spring break that first year and had a miserable time, and, while I should have seen the writing on the wall, I was pretty blind to everything that didn't fit into my world view. Joel was a strong enough student to win a law-firm clerkship the first summer, and he went downtown in an ill-fitting suit every day, entering the law firm party machine with abandon and a fierce determination to schmooze his way to a desk in BigLaw. And he did. He was offered a second-year clerkship with the Chicago office of the same firm, and, after passing the bar, he went on to a partner-track position at their New York office. I think he's still there. I'm sure he's now a partner with a perfect wife and a couple of kids and a house in the Hamptons.

It turns out that I wasn't his picture-perfect idea of a partner's wife, and my average-but-not-overly-spectacular law school grades coupled with my willingness to work in a small firm in Dallas resulted in a moderately-painful breakup right after the beginning of our third year of law school. For the first time, I was hurt and angry that my plans had been interrupted, and there might have been a bit of car damage that resulted from a drunken night with my girlfriends after it was all over. Remembering the experience still brings me a wash of shame, not from the tire damage—he deserved that, given how it ended—but from the explosion of emotions I felt at the time. It was so different from anything I'd ever experienced before, and I was pretty sure I didn't want to feel anything like it again. So I avoided the opportunity.

Saying 'yes' to Gerard was probably the first risky dating maneuver I'd engaged in since Joel. None of the men I'd dated since then really gave me that tingle, and I'd been okay with that. It left me in control of the encounter and my emotions. I would like to have fooled myself about how I felt about this date, but I'm fairly brutally honest about those things, and I'd have known I was lying anyway. Being around Gerard made me feel like the ground had suddenly disappeared from beneath my feet, and, while it was uncomfortable, it was exciting too.

I stepped as far back from my bathroom mirror as I could to try to get as much of a view of my outfit as possible. The shirt was a stiff cotton, and I'd decided to wear it untucked and partially unbuttoned with a red camisole underneath, so I looked a little curvier than usual. My hair was clean and shiny with a bit of a curl under at the ends, and I compromised with my urge to pull it up in a ponytail by just an upsweep of the sides with the rest down my back. I leaned in close the mirror to check out the bruise on my forehead, wishing for a moment I had some of Carla's powder to cover it, but she'd been the one to apply it before, and I didn't have her expertise. I'd managed to apply a little eyeshadow and mascara, but the eyeliner I was sure I had in my makeup drawer didn't surface after a frustrating dig through the disorganized mess. On a recent shopping trip with Sallie, I'd bought some deep nude lipstick that made me feel like I was very trendy (and Sallie agreed), and I was going to apply it at the last minute, so it didn't end up on my teeth. All in all, I wasn't unhappy with the result of my cosmetic endeavors. I dabbed on a touch of perfume and brushed my teeth, checking the time on my phone when I finished. 5 5 0. Ten minutes to go. I tucked the lipstick in my pocket, so I'd remember to apply it right before 6.

I paced the apartment a couple of times, which only used up about a minute. I checked my phone again and saw that a new text from Gabby had come in, with her son's library card number. I'd straightened up the apartment and put everything from the O'Toole case in my office—including my laptop—so I couldn't really do anything with it. I gave it a few seconds' thought and then decided that I'd be pushing it if I got distracted by the research...which I usually do. Pacing was better.

At 5 5 5, he tapped on the door. I answered, feeling shy—not a bad feeling, I decided. He was dressed in jeans and boots with a soft, black turtleneck sweater and a black leather jacket, and was holding another small pot with a weird looking pale green plant in it, much like the one he'd brought me on Valentine's Day. I don't know why, but that immediately made me feel cranky.

"You know, Gerard, you don't have to feel solely responsible for reforesting my apartment." God, that sounded acerbic. He just raised his eyebrows, so I tried again. "Oh look—another little plant thing. How kind of you. Would you like to come in?" I tried out a smile, hoping it didn't look like a snarl.

He grinned, that rakish pirate's grin, and I couldn't help but grin back. "Hello, Benedict. I've missed your sweet tongue." He handed the little plant to me, and I automatically took it.

The double entendre sunk in and I laughed, blushing, remembering this was a date and I liked the tingle. He stepped closer and then leaned forward. I thought for a moment he was going to kiss me, and I felt a bit of panic—was I ready for that?—and then I realized he was looking at my forehead. His smile faded.

"Benedict, what did you do to yourself?" His voice seemed sharp and critical, and I felt cranky all over again.

I turned away, disgruntled that he always seemed to see me when I wasn't at my best. "I knew—I just *knew*—you'd say that, Gerard." I looked at the plant, trying to decide what to do with it, and finally decided to put in on the dining table next to its older sibling.

"And?" He caught my arm gently.

I turned back towards him. "I was walking through some overgrown trees and one whapped me on the forehead."

He leaned in again and looked at the bruise, and the expensive scent of leather and cologne and Gerard overwhelmed my senses for a moment. When *would* I get used to standing this close to him? "Well, at least the skin wasn't broken. And that scar in your eyebrow makes you look like a sexy spy." He wiggled his eyebrows at me, and I wiggled mine back, trying to look arch and mysterious as the left one itched. I also resolved not to show him the cut on my palm if I could manage it. I'd chosen a Disney princess this time, hoping no one would notice I had Cinderella tucked inside my fist.

He stepped back and looked around at the empty dining table and cleaned white board. "What's going on here? Did Hattie finish the office?"

I felt my mouth drop open. "What do *you* know about it?"

He smiled at me, hands on his hips. "Miss Sallie and I stay in touch. How does it look?"

I felt grouchy at his tone, but I was proud of that space. "It's beautiful. If you play your cards right, I might show it to you when we get back." I shrugged on my nicest jacket, an old leather one that had now come back into style, and picked up the cookie box.

"Benedict, I told you that you didn't have to bring anything.

Claire will have so much food..." He took the box from me with a bit of a frown.

I tapped a finger on the Café au Lait label on the box. "Snicker-doodles. You can't ever have too many. And good manners, Gerard. I *do* have them." I picked up my keys and phone and tucked them into my jacket pocket, and then wrapped my best red scarf around my throat. "Just not with you."

He laughed as he followed me out. Before he closed the car's passenger door, he looked at my forehead again. I started to make a snarky comment, but he stepped back. "You look very pretty tonight, Benedict. Thanks for saying yes." He shut the door before I could reply.

———

AFTER GERARD'S COMMENT, THE AIR IN THE RANGE ROVER seemed slightly electric, and we didn't say much during the five-minute drive to his sister's house. He parked down the block, which was packed bumper to bumper with luxury SUVs and expensive sedans, carefully retrieving my cookie box and a cake-sized one from the back seat. He gave me an arch look. "I'm her brother. I have to bring something, or I'll hear about it forever."

I grinned at him, liking him a bit more. "I get that."

We walked up the center sidewalk together, my nerves jumping when I saw which house we were going to. If her brother's modern lake property was the house of my current home-owning fantasies, Claire Gerard Petty's Craftsman bungalow on Belmont was the house of my younger, more traditional dreams. It was only a few minutes west of the Shelton house, and I had driven past it so many times over the last four years, noticing each time the owners had changed the furniture on the wide front porch, approving when they changed the paint from a creamy tan with dark green shutters to the current white with black ones, and mourning the sad day when a bad windstorm took down a huge and mighty oak tree in the deep front yard. A swing had hung there, and it was apparently Claire's children I'd seen playing there, two beautiful small boys with coppery blond hair that matched the man pushing the swing.

Gerard opened the front door and ushered me into a white and navy-blue living room with all sorts of Texas flag-themed decorations. A fire was blazing in a white-painted brick fireplace with swags of red, white, and blue hanging from the mantel. A bored teenager chomping on gum relieved us of our jackets, and I wondered if we'd ever see them again.

Behind all the party trappings, Claire and Caleb Petty had a lovely but sturdy home, decorated to withstand family fights and adventures. The couches were wide and deep, with what I was pretty sure were washable blue denim covers. The floors were the original oak hardwoods, refinished to a deep, distressed dark brown, and the décor on the walls was what I think of as 'family style,' with pictures of the boys from birth onwards, and others of various people I assumed were family members. I wanted to go see if Gerard was in any of them, but he moved us quickly through the room. There were wreaths and window treatments and paintings with inspirational sayings and a big clock, and all of it was homey and gracious and matched seamlessly. I tried not to compare it in my head to my apartment with its mostly bare walls.

I hung back for a moment to look around as Gerard walked toward the dining room with our boxes, and a woman moved swiftly between us to slide a hand up Gerard's back to his neck and then his shoulder. She was dark-haired and beautiful, and I wondered for a moment if she was Claire, but I didn't think his sister would let her hand linger quite so long on his neck. She tucked her hand in his arm and pulled him close as she squealed his name. She was dressed in a dark blue denim dress, form-fitting and short, with a red mock-western belt and matching high-heeled red cowboy boots. Her shoulder-length dark hair had loose curls that my antique curling iron could never have made, and her lipstick matched the belt and boots.

"Robert Gerard, where *have* you been keeping yourself?" She leaned in close and kissed his cheek with those red lips, and the movement reminded me that I'd forgotten to apply my trendy new lipstick, which was even now melting in my jeans pocket. "You never come to the Mansion anymore, and we all miss you!" She laughed with a throaty chuckle and hugged his arm.

Before Gerard could reply, another woman swept in, and, though her hair was silvery gray, she was young, probably only 40, with warm blue eyes that reminded me of Gerard's. "Hey, there, Bucky, 'bout time you got here." She gently inserted herself between the dark-haired woman and Gerard, giving him a brief hug before turning toward the woman. "Lesley, I think I heard the twins arguing over a video game."

Lesley looked off to the living room, clearly annoyed to be interrupted. "Dammit, they can't seem to do *anything* without getting into an argument." She leaned close to Gerard and patted his chest. "Let's catch up in a bit, okay, Robert?" She strode off, her boot heels thumping angrily on the wood floor.

Gerard looked at his sister. "Were the twins really arguing, or were you just trying to save me?" He leaned down and kissed the top of her head.

"Probably. With those two girls, anything is possible, and they're usually arguing over something." She grinned up at him, the same grin Gerard gave me sometimes, full of mischief and fun.

He took a step back and turned toward me. "Claire, let me introduce Benedict." She turned, clearly surprised, but covering it well. "Lacey Benedict, this is my sister, Claire Petty."

"Lacey, so nice to meet you." She stuck out a hand to shake mine and smiled at me, a pretty full-faced smile that lit up her eyes.

We shook hands, a firm, business-like shake I appreciated. "Nice to meet you as well. You have a lovely home I've been coveting for several years."

She burst out into a ringing, musical laugh. "There've been a lot of times over the last few years I'd have let you take it. If you want a tour, let me know."

Gerard hip-bumped her. "Where do you want these, CeeCee?"

"Depends on what it is. Desserts go in the kitchen, everything else in the dining room."

"Kitchen it is." Gerard let his sister lead the way, and I trailed behind, feeling a bit overwhelmed. There were a lot of people in the house, standing in groups or sitting on couches or sectionals, eating and talking. Red and blue plastic cups and beer bottles were held comfortably, people had plates in hand and were eating what smelled like barbeque, and country music played from somewhere in the back of the house. There were adults of all ages, and every few minutes a child ran through the room on an important mission to someone, something, or somewhere. Most of the people were wearing jeans or some type of western wear, but many of the women were dressed in what I'd call 'ironic country' like the outfit Lesley was wearing: a really nice dress paired with a pair of boots and spangly western belts or jewelry. The men, in contrast, all looked really comfortable in jeans and sports jackets or fleece vests—just like they do everywhere in Dallas. Clearly, most of the men felt no need to dress up.

The kitchen was probably a cook's dream, and I recognized a few things that resembled what the Tarantinos had installed in their renovated kitchen—an overly-large refrigerator with two clear glass doors, a big range with gas burners—but there was also a paper towel holder shaped like a really long pig and a hand-lettered sign above the fridge that said 'The family that eats together argues together and loves together,' a sentiment I'd experienced my whole life. The farm-style pine table was covered with all manner of cookies, cakes, and pies, and my mouth began to water. It'd been a long few hours since the biscuits and gravy with Ryan. There were some clearly child-painted pictures stuck with tape to the glass door of the refrigerator, and I stopped to admire one of the Texas flag that looked a lot like my shirt.

Claire came back to stand next to me. "That's Tate's painting. He and Will wanted to help me decorate the house for the party, so they decided to paint flags." She reached out to straighten it with pride, and a bit more of the ice in my castle melted. I couldn't remember a time my mother had posted any of my artwork on the fridge.

I cleared my throat. "He did a great job. How old is he?"

She smiled at me. "Five. But he loves to paint." She turned to Gerard, who'd left the boxes on the counter. "Well, you could at least open them." She opened Gerard's to reveal a square cake made to look like a Texas flag, with blueberries and strawberries carefully placed in the chocolate frosting. "Bucky, you bring this every year."

He rumbled, "And it's appropriate every year."

She laughed, and then leaned close to peer at his face. "Ugh—hold on, let me get that off of you." She pulled a paper towel off the pig holder and wet it under the faucet, then used it to wipe the lipstick off his cheek. "No reason for you to go around marked as Lesley's territory for the next hour." She moved Gerard's box aside to open the box with the Café au Lait label on top. "Oh, wait—this is that place where we met Tuesday!" She turned to me with wide eyes. "And *you're* the friend he mentioned had introduced him to those divine cinnamon knots." She hmmmed, and the look turned speculative.

Gerard stepped in between us. "Benedict, let me show you around a little."

Claire smiled and gave up for the moment. "I'll get these out on the table there and then I'll find you, Lacey, if you want that tour." She turned to take a plate out of the cupboard, and Gerard moved to shoo me out of the kitchen.

"When hell freezes over," he murmured, and I laughed.

"Bucky, hmm?" I asked, and he gave me a quelling look that made me laugh again.

He led me through the rest of the first-floor rooms, a family room where several teenagers—including a pair of identical dark-haired teenager girls that looked suspiciously like Lesley—lounged on a long sectional, a few playing video games and the rest staring into their phones. Through a wall of glass doors, we could see where the men had congregated: the back patio was an outdoor living area, complete with couches, table and chairs, a grill, and—best of all—heaters. About fifteen men stood out there, beer bottles in hand, some staring at a television mounted on the wall, others standing around the huge grill, staring into the flames.

The formal dining room was converted into a buffet, and we stopped and loaded plates with sliced brisket and sausage, hot baked potato salad, cole slaw, and baked beans, avoiding some obviously homemade casseroles with green beans or broccoli. I got a beer, and we found a couple of chairs and ate silently for a few minutes. Gerard's appetite is one of my favorite things about him, since I never feel the need to eat like a dainty bird with him, nor does he seem to be surprised at the amount of food I can put away.

The brisket was expertly cooked, a thick char on the edges and tender, juicy meat on the inside of the slice. The sausage had chunks of jalapeno, and I washed it down with a beer that really didn't do much to cool the heat but paired nicely with the spice. I watched Gerard push the cole slaw around after one bite, and, after I'd tried it, I didn't blame him: whoever had made it had put a lot of dill in it, and it just didn't taste right. I pushed mine aside too, in favor of the baked potato salad, full of bacon and cheese and sour cream. I considered going back for seconds, but I was too full of the delicious molassesy baked beans to attempt it.

We cleaned our plates just before Claire's husband Caleb came in to refresh the trays of meat. He absentmindedly greeted me when Gerard introduced us but was clearly distracted by his duties as grill-master, and he and Gerard began to rumble at each other about college basketball. I excused myself and went off to the guest bath to wash my hands and surreptitiously apply the lipstick I'd forgotten, pleased to find it was slightly soft but hadn't completely melted in my pocket.

I wandered around the first-floor rooms for a while, checking out a laundry room the size of my apartment, a downstairs master bedroom with doors leading outside to miniature patio, and a small office with a huge whiteboard that made me smile and remember my own office. Throughout the rooms were touches I'd never think of adding, like a ladder leaning against a wall with handmade blankets and quilts, or an umbrella stand shaped like a tall giraffe. A picture or two had Gerard in them, one with a much younger Gerard with his arm around a beautiful woman.

I passed a door with stairs leading down and decided—since it was open—that it wouldn't be a bad thing to look around while no one was watching. These basement stairs, like those leading up to the second floor, were dark distressed oak, and turned halfway down on themselves. As I reached the landing, I could see that this was where the smaller children were spending their time. The basement floor was covered in sturdy carpet, and a castle had been built down here, complete with a miniature drawbridge and turrets and swing. Fairy lights were strung from corner to corner across the ceiling. A big Connect-Four apparatus and a giant Jenga set were in full use by groups of boys and girls, and big bean bags were occupied by multiple small children watching a television with the newest *Jumanji* movie playing. A room off to one side looked to have twelve built-in bunkbeds in it, with interesting ways to climb ladders up or poles to slide down, and at least one of the beds was in a cabinet-like enclosure that reminded me of my bedroom at the farm. It looked cozy and fun, and I briefly considered climbing up to hide inside.

A small boy with coppery blond hair caught me snooping. "I painted that flag," he said, pointing at my shirt.

I tried to look mysteriously intelligent as I waited to answer. "Hmmm. Let's see. That must make you Tate, the artist."

His mouth fell open at that bit of brain power, and then his eyes narrowed suspiciously. "You know my mom."

I nodded. "I do, but I know your Uncle Robert better."

He looked at the stairs. "Is he here? He owes me a game of Sequence." He looked back at me. "I'm really good."

"Are you?" I raised my eyebrows. "I'm pretty good myself."

He seemed interested. "You know how to play? I had to teach Uncle Rob."

"I do. I've been beating my brother for years."

He ran off towards the other kids playing Connect-Four, and I thought he'd forgotten me. "Will! Will! This lady says she can play Sequence!"

Several of the kids turned toward me speculatively, and I wondered briefly what I'd let myself in for.

———

I'd won one game against Tate but lost one against both him and Will, his older brother, when I felt a prickle at the back of my neck and turned to see Gerard sitting on one of the sectionals against the wall, scratching the head of a huge shaggy black poodle and watching me. He smiled but didn't say anything. One tiny girl with shiny gold ringlets and a pouty pink mouth had simply laid down on one of the couches and gone to sleep, her small body crumpled in the boneless way children's bodies have of surrendering to exhaustion.

I stretched and moved to let one of the other kids sit in my chair at the kid-sized game table, my knees bumping the underside as I tried to stand. Gerard just watched me struggle out of the small chair, the kids laughing with me at my efforts, and then he patted the couch on his other side. It looked slightly dangerous, a deep soft cushion of risk, but I thought I could handle it. I sat down with a few inches of buffer space, and he smiled, acknowledging but not challenging the bit of distance. The dog finally laid down with a huff at Gerard's feet.

"That's the biggest poodle I've ever seen."

He smiled at me. "Claire is allergic to most dogs, but she let the boys pick out a dog from the hypoallergenic options. They decided on the biggest poodle they could find." The dog seemed to sense it was being discussed and sat up to watch me, so Gerard introduced us. "Benedict, this is Ed."

"'Ed the poodle'? Are you kidding?" Ed, hearing his name, came over to me for an ear scratch. His long, shaggy ringlets were baby-hair soft.

"They were trying for the most masculine name they could give him."

We sat there for a few minutes, taking turns giving Ed attention and watching the kids playing around us, before Tate lost to another boy and decided he was bored. He came over to stand in front of Gerard. Ed happily abandoned our distracted attention for the adoration of one of his boys.

"You owe me some Sequence games, Uncle Rob." His tone was serious and a bit accusatory as he bent down to wrestle the dog.

"I do, squirt." Gerard's tone was mild, but just as serious. "How about I come for dinner soon, and we can play?"

"Okay." Tate looked over at me, calculation clear on his face. "You can bring Lacey."

Gerard looked at me too, the family resemblance plain. "I can do that." He looked back at Tate. "You like her?"

Tate nodded, and then lost interest. On the other side of Gerard, the sleeping nymph had awakened and was sitting up picking her nose. Tate immediately pounced on the fact and called her 'booger baby' as she began to cry. I was about to try to distract Tate when a teenage girl I'd barely noticed stepped over to referee, and I realized that she was there to do just that. She lifted the girl in her arms, and they moved over to a table with drink boxes and snacks, Tate following and still trumpeting the news about Calliope and her boogers, and Ed trailing along, his bit of a tail wagging.

Gerard looked at me with a grin. "He must like her."

"Why? Because he's teasing her?" I smiled. "That's the way it goes when you're a kid, isn't it?" He just looked intently at me, his smile fading. I thought about the lipstick on the teeth thing and wondered if I'd eaten mine off already. "What?"

He leaned toward me, and before I could move, he kissed the bruise on my forehead, so gentle I could barely feel the pressure of his lips. Then, while my forehead was still tingling, he got up and turned to proffer a hand to me. "Ready to go back to the grown-up world?"

I took his hand and let him help me up. "Not really. It's nicer down here. Unless you're Calliope."

He kept hold of my hand as we moved to the stairs, and I felt that lovely tingle where we touched. "Sometimes it is, and sometimes it's nice up there too."

We took the stairs like that, our fingers threaded together as we climbed. At the top, he paused. "Ready?"

"Ready." I felt a little weird still holding hands, but it was nice, especially given that we hadn't touched very much before. His hand was warm and a bit calloused, and his fingers curled around mine in a way I liked.

And then we met Lesley in the hallway, Claire at her heels.

Both women looked down at our joined hands, but their expressions couldn't have been more different. Claire was smiling, while Lesley looked annoyed and unhappy.

"Robert, where have you been? Claire and I have been looking all over the house for you." She looked past him to me. "I don't think we've met before. I'm Lesley Batchelor." She stuck her hand out, and I had to let go of Gerard's hand to shake it, a circumstance I'm pretty sure was intentional.

"Lesley, this is Lacey Benedict. Lacey, Lesley and I are old friends—we went to high school together." Gerard waited until we'd finished shaking hands, and then he gently caught my hand with his again. Something inside me warmed.

"Nice to meet you, Lucy." She smiled a bit insincerely, and I laughed to myself as she refocused on Gerard. "Robert, I need to speak with you for a minute. I'm trying to deal with some post-divorce business, and it's really just over my head." She looked back at me. "Robert's been my attorney for—oh, forever, right Robert? And since my divorce, he's just been a rock for me." She smiled up at him mistily, her eyes glistening. "A rock."

Claire rolled her eyes at me. "The only thing about Rob that's rock-like is his head." I snickered, and Gerard looked at me with a mock frown.

The four of us squeezed into this small hallway was a little much, as were Lesley's dramatics. I let Gerard's hand go with a squeeze. "Well, I'm sure you two have some things to talk about. Claire, how about that tour now? I'd love to see the upstairs add-on." I skirted carefully around Gerard and Lesley, talking to Claire as I walked. "Did you guys do the renovations yourselves?"

Claire had no choice but to follow me, and we walked up a stairway to the second floor, the walls covered in more family pictures and a few framed paintings I was sure were Tate's. Claire took me through the renovations that the previous homeowners had done, adding on several additional bedrooms and bathrooms behind the original second floor. There was one large, high-ceilinged kids' room, complete with a full-sized playground installation at one end. When I commented on it, she rolled her eyes and told me the boys had just this last weekend told her that they were too old for it.

"I don't think I'd have had the patience to do the renovations and live in the house at the same time, especially with kids, but the boys are getting old enough now that I think they're going to want their own rooms." She grimaced. "Caleb is already making plans." She closed the guest bathroom door behind us and faced me. "Rob told me you're the receiver on Jules and Trisha's project house." At my look, she colored a bit. "I asked him about you a few minutes ago." She started down the hall but turned to give me a sideways look. "I doubt that's why he asked you to my party."

I tried to look clueless—not difficult, since I wasn't too sure why he asked me either. We stood at the big windows in the guest room that faced the back yard, and Claire pointed out the apartment over the garage.

"It's all lovely, Claire, even more than I imagined when I drove past it these last four years." I turned to look at the beautiful room, light and airy despite the wintry evening.

She looked sad. "I'd wanted this room to be a room for the little girl I was going to have." She sighed, and I worried for a moment that something was wrong, but she continued. "Then I had the two hell-boys instead of a girl." She grinned at me. "So, I get to be a boy-mom instead of a girl-mom. Caleb's sister has a daughter, so I'll take all my girliness out on her."

I thought back to the basement. "Her name's not Calliope, is it?"

She looked at me with a frown. "No, why?"

I smiled. "I met a tiny beautiful girl named Calliope downstairs." I started to turn and then decided to warn her. "I think she and Tate may be married in a few years."

She grinned. "I'll keep an eye out." We began to walk back toward the stairs, but Claire stopped me with a hand on my arm. "Lacey, I'm just going to be blunt. Are you and my brother dating?"

I thought for a second, and then shrugged. "Hell if I know." She grinned, surprised. "He asked, I said yes, we came to your party."

"But you like him?" The question and its answer were probably not her business, but I wasn't really inclined to be argumentative.

"I do."

She turned back towards the stairs. "And he likes you, so I guess you're dating." This time it was a statement that I let float on the air as we started down.

Lesley had Gerard cornered in the living room beside the fireplace, Gerard leaning against the wall and Lesley standing less than a foot in front of him, talking earnestly to him as she gestured, occasionally putting a hand on his arm or patting his chest. Gerard had his head lowered a bit, seemingly listening intently, but as we came into the living room, he turned his head slightly to look at us from under those dark brows, and I felt the force of those eyes all the way across the room. Next to me, I heard Claire make a noise, but I was busy smiling back at Gerard, so I ignored it. He said something to Lesley and then pushed off from the wall, coming toward me and his sister. Lesley followed along behind, still talking.

"But he shouldn't have her over there when the twins are visiting, should he? Robert, I'm sure he's not supposed to do that."

Gerard stopped and gave Lesley his full attention, speaking quietly but with a certain amount of finality. "Lesley, you should ask your divorce attorney about this. I'm don't practice in that area, and I'm not your counsel." He looked at his sister. "What time does the band start up, Claire?"

"A band?" I looked at Claire as well. "You have a band?"

She nodded, smiling. "It's a country music trio. They come every year, and usually play out on the back porch." She blew out a breath and shook her head. "I don't know what we're going to do with them this time." Some people came in the front door at that moment, and she looked over with a smile. "Kris! Rick! Excuse me, guys." She started to walk off and then turned back to Gerard, walking backwards. "9. But don't feel you guys have to stay." She winked at us and then waggled her fingers in a little wave, turning back towards the newcomers.

She must have given one of the teenagers an invisible signal a few minutes before, because our coats appeared at our side almost immediately. We began to put on our jackets—with Lesley an awkward third—before Gerard turned to her. "Les, you know Claire and I are always here for you, but you need to have a chat with your attorney to see what obligations Don does or doesn't have." He side-hugged her, and she sniffled and nodded. He let her go after a brief few seconds. "Well, we're going to get out of here. You and the twins staying for a while?" He looked over her head at the media room where the teenagers were still gathered.

Lesley's red lips pouted. "I guess so." She looked over at me and then at Gerard. "Where are you guys off to?" She seemed ready to invite herself if given the chance.

I'd just about had enough of this. I held out my hand for Gerard to take, which he did, bless him. I smiled at Lesley. "Lesley, it was a pleasure to meet you. Give the twins my best." I turned to Gerard with a twinkly smile. "Ready, Gerard?"

We made it outside before we collapsed against each other, laughing. "She was coming with us, Gerard. She was about to bring herself and her twins along..."

"Over my dead body," he choked out.

I sucked in a deep, cold breath. "Oh, wow...she has a serious thing for you, Gerard."

In the porch lights, I could see him make a face. "She's just looking for the next man," he said, "and that is *not* me."

We stepped off to allow a group coming up the sidewalk to take the steps to the front door. I watched them go. "Good lord, more people? Where will she put them?"

Gerard watched as well, then turned to me. "Well, she's a professional. Don't try this at home." He took my hand, and we started to walk toward the car, dodging a couple on the sidewalk.

"What do you mean?"

"She's an event planner. Big events and parties."

I don't know why that made me feel better, but it did. "That explains it. The whole time, I was wondering how she kept all the balls in the air."

"She's always been this way, able to do things like this." He unlocked my door and opened it for me, tucking my jacket around me and gently shutting the door.

He got in and started the car and the heat, and we sat there for a few seconds, enjoying the warmth, before he spoke. "I'd like to take you somewhere. Would that be all right?"

I looked at him, but he was staring out the windshield. "Well, I don't turn back into Cinderella until midnight, and it's just 845. So, sure."

He smiled without looking at me and pulled out onto Belmont. He drove slowly and carefully, as he always did, and I relaxed. The first time I was in this car with him, we'd been traveling to visit a joint client in jail, and the two hours we were alone together I'd felt I was suffocating. This time felt so different, and I smiled at the comparison. And then I realized we'd kept going when Belmont turned into Lakewood, taking the direct road to Lawther, his street. Surely he didn't think we were going to his place...? We went under the walking trail overpass and up TeePee Hill, the road curving around into West Lawther, as I considered the issue: I was enjoying the tingle, sure, but was I ready for that to become more? The planner in me began to formulate a kind rejection when he pulled into his drive.

He turned to face me. "I know it's cold and this mist could turn to rain at any time, but how about a walk?"

CHAPTER TWENTY-ONE

White Rock Lake has walking and bike trails in an almost-unbroken loop around the entire 9.3-mile circumference. A few of the trails were first developed when CCC troops were stationed at the lake in the late 1930s. They built shelters and bridges and picnic tables, and many of the limestone structures were still around. From Gerard's house, you could see the old bathhouse across the lake, and a small bridge went over a creek feeding into the lake itself. From this point, the lake and its walking trail were almost the closest to the houses across the road.

Gerard came around to open my door as I pulled my red scarf out of my jacket pocket, digging in deeper to see if my gloves were in there. Then I remembered that I'd ripped the left one and decided they were trashed. This late in the winter in Dallas, I'd never find gloves for sale, so I'd probably be gloveless until fall. Gerard offered his hand, and I took it (even though I really didn't need it) and slid out of the Range Rover.

In the house I heard Bella barking. "You going to bring that lovely girl out for a walk too?"

"You don't mind?" He looked over toward the darkened windows, his voice slightly anxious, and my castle melted a tiny bit more.

"Of course not." I pushed him toward the house. "Go get your girlfriend." He moved off, laughing, and I stuck my hands in my jacket pockets. I wasn't really ready to go into that beautiful house. While we were on a date. In the dark. With him holding my hand.

I stamped my feet, glad I'd worn my flat-heeled 'roper' boots. Boots like these were actually really comfortable for walking—or at least more comfortable than regular cowboy boots, with their higher heels. Competitive calf ropers wore these because they had to get their feet out of stirrups quickly, jump off the horse at a run, and get to the calf to rope its feet together with all due speed. These were a light brown suede with a smooth-bottomed leather sole, and I'd had them since high school. Maybe they weren't fancy like Lesley Batchelor's boots, but they suited me.

Bella came bounding out of the house and straight for me. I braced for a full-body jump, but she was well-trained and skidded to a stop in front of me, her entire body wagging with her tail. I stooped to pet her, and we exchanged some love, me crooning and Bella whining. Gerard joined us with a leash he clipped to a belt loop, and we set off across the road. Bella did her business and then trotted down the bike path.

The cloudiness all day had kept temperatures up in the 50s, but, as the evening deepened, the clouds thinned and the air chilled. At first, it felt wonderful. Claire hadn't overheated her house, but it was still warm, so this crisp air cleared the cobwebs out of my brain. Bella danced on ahead, stopping occasionally to investigate a smell in the grass alongside the path. The clouds were low on the horizon, and, had there been a moon, we wouldn't have been able to see it. Even with all that, the tension in the air between us was lovely, and I smiled as I compared it to the overheated June nights with my high school boyfriend.

We didn't speak for the first few minutes, our thumping bootsteps the only sounds. The lake has small fishing piers and, at the first one we came to, we followed Bella to the end, where reeds choked the water on both sides. Something rustled in the reeds, and Bella's surprised bark as she ran to Gerard for safety broke the silence and the tension. We stopped so Gerard could rub her ears, and he looked up at me with a smile.

"So, what was the coonskin cap thing you mentioned a couple of weeks ago? That image has stayed with me."

As we walked, I told him about Sophia Barnstead and her chorus, but I didn't feel like making light of it. The meeting I'd had with her and her grandson still haunted my thoughts, as did Tom Terry's concern about elderly people caught in the middle of a bullish real estate market. I told Gerard about my inward argument. "What do we do about that? I mean, it's great to see neighborhoods cleaning up, but where are those people to go?"

"That's the downside of a free market," Gerard rumbled, his chin tucked into the gray-blue scarf he'd wound around his neck. "Whether it's goods or property, the economics of supply and demand mean that some people will be able to pay a higher price for things more highly in demand, and those selling to them want that higher price."

"The poor always seem to be penalized by the 'free market'." I wasn't about to take my hands out of my pockets, so I let my sarcastic tone insert the air quotes.

"Not always true—if there are more goods on the market, the price decreases." His reasonable tone irritated me.

"It's not just an *economic* discussion. There are people and their lives and livelihoods at stake." My voice rose with my annoyance. "Some of the people who are displaced by so-called 'neighborhood renewal' work nearby. Do we force them to move and then change jobs? Or drive further distances? How is that fair? And it's imposed by the wealthy on the poor!"

He stopped walking, and it took a step or two for me to stop as well. I turned back to him, but his face was unreadable in the dim light. I took a step back towards him. "What's wrong?"

He looked down into my face, and I hoped for a minute that mine was as eclipsed as his by the darkness. "Benedict, I don't disagree with what you're saying. I'm just expressing an opinion, not necessarily *my* opinion." His voice was rumbling and quiet. "It *is* just a discussion."

I pushed aside an itchy feeling of guilt. I knew I could become heated in arguments, and being an attorney was really just an extension of my sometimes-combative personality. Most of my life, I'd hidden it from people. Not anymore. "I know." I rubbed my cold nose with a slightly warmer hand and wished my gloves hadn't died the death. "The thing is, Gerard, I'm not always capable of having an academic discussion. So... if you're looking for calm, reasoned discussion devoid of all emotion or passion, you probably won't find that with me." I looked off to where Bella was sniffing at the dog blog left on a tree trunk, the leash extended completely. "I don't think I can hide that part of me anymore."

He stood motionless for a long moment looking down at me, his hands in his pockets, and I peered up into his face to see if I could gauge his reaction, but only to know how to respond. I was through trying to be what other people thought I should be. If he didn't like this Lacey Benedict, well, he could leave her be. He finally moved, taking his hands out of his pockets and lifting them to my face to cup my cold cheeks. He leaned down to kiss the end of my nose, his lips warm against my cold skin. "Don't ever hide from me. I'll learn to tell the difference, and I can take your passion."

Bella tugged us on to keep walking as my cheeks flamed, warming me for a few minutes. He took my hand and threaded our fingers together, then tucked them into his coat pocket.

THE NEXT FISHING PIER HAD NO REEDS, SO BELLA FELT FREE TO jog to the end and stick her nose into what wind was blowing. Gerard and I stood on the firm ground under a streetlight and watched her enjoy the smells off the lake. I loved these wooden structures, and sometimes, when I was on my walks, I'd stop and sit on one and look out over the water, or have a discussion with a fisherman who'd set up a camping chair to spend an afternoon with a line drooping in the water. I told Gerard about one such fisherman, who'd confessed that he didn't always put bait on the hook. He just kept the rod and line out and ready, so he had an excuse to sit on the edge of the water all day.

He laughed and squeezed my hand, then grew a more serious. "Benedict, I have a confession to make."

"You've done the same thing? You're a bait-less fisherman?" I teased, watching Bella looking down into the water, her tail wagging. I wondered if she could communicate with the fish.

"No, I can't say that. But I do have something to tell you, and the longer I go without telling you, the worse it feels." I looked up, but his expression was remote and impassive in the streetlight's glow.

He pulled our joined hands out of his pocket, looking down at them. I began to feel uneasy. "What is it?"

"When you were at my house the other day, you told me you walked around the lake on the walking path." He paused, his thumb smoothing over my knuckles, making me shiver.

"Yes, I did. I do."

"Well, I already knew that." He looked over at Bella, but I continued to watch his face. With his free hand, he ran a hand over his hair—his own personal tell—and I knew he was truly bothered.

"You already knew? What? You've watched me?" He was right—that was a little bit creepy, but the lake was a public place. "You perv." I laughed uneasily. "Well, it's not like I didn't expect to be seen."

He didn't respond or laugh as I'd hoped. "Gerard?"

The words came out in a rush. "Benedict, I had you investigated when I represented Bill Stephenson." He waited, holding my hand with his, finally looking into my face.

I felt a wave of relief. "Yes, I know."

"You *know*?" His voice rose, and now I could see his eyebrows rise as well.

"Well, at the time I assumed you would, so I looked for signs you were." While that wasn't my favorite time of my life, I was particularly proud of figuring that out back then. "They used the same two people to trail me, and I noticed they'd show up over and over in places I went." I kept my voice calm now, but I remembered a time when I was very upset by the knowledge. "Dallas isn't that small a town, and I saw the same man and woman in all kinds of different neighborhoods." I squeezed his hand with mine. "I already knew *you* knew more about me than *I* knew about me."

He shook his head, and I could see him smile tightly. "I've been dreading telling you."

"I can see that. It makes you a complete creeper." I laughed, and he chuckled, but it sounded forced. "Is there anything else you need to tell me that they reported to you?"

"They said you were pretty boring, all in all."

"Ah. Good thing I knew they were there and didn't do anything exciting."

His smile eased a bit more. "Hmmm. That puts a different spin on things. We'll have to talk about what they *could* have seen if they'd been better at their jobs." He turned my hand over to see the bandage on my palm. "Benedict, what did you do?"

I tugged my hand, but he held on. "Just grabbed a tree for balance the other day when I was walking. Remember the branch incident? That's why I have no gloves now."

He peered at the bandage in the diffused light. "Is that Cinderella?"

I tugged again, a bit harder, but I didn't want to make a big deal about it. My cheeks had begun to heat up. "I had to borrow the bandage. Sallie Shelton loves stuff like that."

He was still for a moment, and then he dipped his head and slowly, lingeringly, kissed the bandage and my palm. A liquid warmth started in my belly and began to spread, and I knew, without a doubt, that I was in over my head.

———

WE'D MOVED OUT OF THE PROTECTION OF THE TREES AND A northeasterly breeze swept in across the water, dropping the temperature of the air around us. My teeth were chattering a bit, and I wiggled my toes inside my boots.

His voice was mild. "That surprises me. I'd have thought you would be against all that."

Without saying anything about it, Gerard disengaged our hands and moved to the lake side of the path, his height giving me some protection. He caught up my left hand and tucked it inside his coat pocket, and I put my right hand in my own pocket.

"I guess I think women—or men, I guess—have a right to do whatever they need to feel confident and happy. Whether that's dyeing their hair or having plastic surgery." I happily snuggled into his side, determined not to examine the feeling too much. "My friend Carla is a beautiful woman who gets lip and skin injections on a regular basis. She was probably already beautiful before she started it all."

"Do you think you'd ever indulge?"

I considered the idea. "Maybe." Honesty compelled me to continue. "Probably not. I hate needles, and, from what I've seen, they're involved."

We could hear some ducks making low quacks, and he called Bella back from the edge of the lake. "Dallas is a city that makes far too much of people's appearance and age. I know people who've become almost addicted to the plastic surgeon's scalpel, always looking for something they can't ever get back: their youth." His voice had an air of sadness about the topic, and I wished for light to see if it reached his eyes.

I inhaled some frosty air and exhaled in a steamy huff. "That's true. All the blond-haired, blue-eyed, large-breasted women you see in Dallas can't be real, given the genetic makeup of the world's population." He chuckled under his breath, so I kept going. "I know some people who see their plastic surgeon more than their GP."

We walked for a minute more without speaking, Bella panting happily at Gerard's side, puffs of steam preceding her dancing steps.

"In fact, I think the hair dye companies are probably doing brunettes like me a big favor by supplying all the blonde highlights." I paused and kept my serious face looking forward as he glanced down at me. "Otherwise, natural selection would have gotten rid of all of us by now."

I was rewarded by a rare, un-Gerardish whoop of laughter that even surprised Bella, and I felt a grin escape at the sound.

The laugh dissolved into the more normal chuckle as we walked over a bridge, our footsteps echoing in the night air. He squeezed my hand inside his pocket. "I hope you never decide to indulge. You're beautiful just as you are."

I squeezed his hand in response, determined to accept the compliment, but not confident enough to thank him just yet.

"You've got to be kidding. I consider it the universe's joke on us. It's colorless, and tasteless."

"What about roasted? Maguire's up in Addison makes a roasted cauliflower soup that's amazing."

I made the gagging noise my brother taught me when I was four. "I can't even imagine how awful that would taste."

"You'd have to try it to know."

"You'd have to tie me down and pour it down my throat to test that theory."

He looked at me out of the corner of his eye as if he was considering the idea, and my face flamed as I realized my unconscious double entendre. Or maybe *subconscious* double entendre. An image of Gerard feeding me something as I was tied up flashed through my mind, and I swallowed hard. He cleared his throat as Bella trotted back to us.

A pair of cyclists, bundled to their eyebrows, whooshed by up on West Lawther Road as we passed in front of Mount Vernon, a huge 1929 replica of George Washington's more famous estate, and I stopped for a minute to gawk, as I always did. From where we stood, the house was at the top of a sweeping lawn atop a hill. The house and the 10 acres it sat on had been for sale for almost a decade, despite the drastically-lowered sales price. Lights placed in front of each of the six columns on the front of the house shone brightly on the white façade, but the house itself looked empty and lifeless.

"Have you ever been inside there?" I asked Gerard. He tucked my arm through his and pulled me close, and he was so warm I could have happily crawled inside his jacket and slept.

"Nope. I've seen pictures. There's a full-size bowling alley and a place for ten cars to be displayed." He whistled to Bella, who'd gotten too close to the road, and she came bounding back.

"Who needs that much space?"

He gazed up at the house as Bella sniffed around our feet. "Some people think they need all that to be happy."

"It does look like an American castle, I guess. So... you find your prince or princess and live happily ever after in a big house on the hill?" I moved closer to him, for warmth. Really. "Why does everyone want a happy ending? I'd think a happy middle would be much better."

I felt him look at me, and then he kissed the top of my head. "I think you're absolutely right."

"I WOULD SAY TORT REFORM HAS FREED UP THE COURT SYSTEM, but I have no evidence of that." His voice was mild, and this time I could tell he was taking the view as an advocate—maybe even a devil's advocate.

"Yes, but it's made it so hard for people to sue medical professionals who have really screwed up. Personal injury lawyers have to make such a cost benefit analysis that they can't take on cases that should have been pursued." I'd referred people who'd had real malpractice claims to personal injury attorneys, but the potential for damages were so low that the cases weren't prosecuted. "Bad doctors and practitioners and hospitals get away with negligence." My boots slid a bit on the moisture-slicked road, and I huffed as we climbed TeePee Hill, warmer now that we were moving. Without discussing it, we'd stayed on the walking path towards the old Filter Building.

"If that's the issue, the grievance process needs to be easier and more effective."

I stopped walking, tugging our joined hands to stop him too. Bella came back to check on us. "But it's not just that—sometimes people should receive damages for that negligence."

He looked down at me. "I don't disagree."

I stomped a foot at his calm tone. "Don't you ever get angry about things?"

He let go of my hand, and I thought he might be upset. Instead, he wrapped his arms around me in a warm hug and talked to the top of my head. "Yes, I do, Benedict. But something inside me backs away from conflict."

"You're a *litigator!*" My voice was muffled by his jacket, but he heard the disbelief.

"True. And I've seen how very ugly conflict can be. Maybe that's why I try not to have much of it personally." He squeezed a bit. "But I do *feel* things, Benedict."

I wrapped my arms around him and squeezed back.

———

"I don't see how you can believe it's appropriate to root for the Patriots when you live in Dallas." I was appalled, and my voice showed it. We'd passed the old Filter Building, a security guard on his rounds lifting a flashlight in our direction.

He raised his voice a bit, finally giving me that passion I'd asked about. "Give me a break, Benedict. Tom Brady and Bill Belichick are legends and have been for years—has there even really *been* a legend in Dallas since Roger Staubach or Tom Landry?" Bella barked at something in some bushes near the slough, and he whistled her back.

The mist had returned, but the temperature was still dropping. We were both freezing, and even Bella seemed to be feeling the cold. I didn't want the evening to end yet, though, but I think we were both leery of returning to his warm home.

"Are you kidding me? What was Troy Aikman if not a legend?"

Gerard's voice was mild. "He was good, but I'm not sure I'd put him in the 'legend' category. Brady is a GOAT." Bella tugged the leash and we followed her off the walking path and onto the road. "Are you okay for a few minutes more? We can follow Lawther to Williamson and then cut through to my place the back way on Huff and Fisher. It won't be so cold in the trees."

I scoffed. "Maybe he's great. But the 'greatest of all time'? C'mon." I squeezed his hand. "Sure. We'll get to walk below Chapel Park, right? I just found out that the man who built the Lakeway Circle house is responsible for that park."

That reminder of the hearing the week before dampened the mood some, and we walked in silence for a few minutes as the road dipped down to go under the old railroad overpass. The path was sheltered here, and it was warmer, but we stayed walking close together. Bella walked more slowly, her interest in the shrubs and trees waning as we climbed the slope coming out of the underpass, our breaths sending out puffs of steam in the cold air.

Chapel Park met West Lawther Road at the bottom of a hill, the sweeping vista dotted with trees, bounded on the road by a stone and board fence. At the top of the hill sat the O'Toole house, its second- and third-floor windows facing the lake, high above the trees shrouding the first floor below. As we came around the curve, the Park rolled out above us, broad and easy to see—as was the glow of the fire in the windows of the house above.

CHAPTER TWENTY-TWO

SATURDAY, MARCH 2 (CONTINUED)

I'd like to say I immediately reacted and knew exactly what to do, but that would be a definite overstatement. Gerard and I stood there for a full five seconds, Bella stopped next to us with her ears perked up, alerted by our stillness.

Then we both began to run straight up the hill through the park. Tokalon and Chapel Park Boulevards ran on either side of the park, but we both stayed to the middle of the parkland, running up grass coated with moisture from the day's wet mists. I cursed my decision to wear the smooth-soled boots as I slid more than once on the grass.

Once we got halfway up the hill, I veered toward the left and Chapel Park Boulevard, assuming that the homeowners on either side of the O'Toole house would have better landscaping than the back garden I'd tried to explore the day before. Because Lakeway Circle was a cul-de-sac, neither Tokalon nor Chapel Park opened onto Lakeway Circle, but a narrow alley ran between Chapel Park and the

O'Toole house these days, and there was an entry to the alley between the Allred and the O'Toole houses to allow for trash pickup and utility easements.

As we crested the hill, we could see flashing red and blue lights reflecting off the windows of the houses on the Circle. I counted three fire trucks parked outside the gates and two inside, fully-charged hoses snaking in and out, and four police cars blocking the scene. The noise was deafening: the diesel engines of the trucks were idling loudly, their hydraulic systems pumping water to the hoses; the sirens weren't wailing, but the strobe lights emitted a strange pulsing noise; men and women shouted to each other as they worked; somewhere a yelping alarm loudly protested all the activity; and the scanners in all the vehicles were a powerful running commentary to the scene.

Because we came up to the side of the scene, a police officer intercepted us almost immediately, and I identified myself, trying to quickly explain the receivership situation. She didn't quite understand what I meant, but she did seem to appreciate the information that the house should be unoccupied. She asked us to move to the outside of the yellow caution tape already draped between trees on Mrs. Allred's property and wait for her supervisor as she stepped away to speak into the mic attached to her jacket.

I could see lights on in Mrs. Allred's house, and I presumed she was awake, given the noise and activity next door. I motioned that way, and, though she continued to speak into her mic, the officer nodded at me. I shouted to Gerard over the noise. "I'm going to check on Mrs. Allred." He nodded but didn't try to answer, and he and Bella followed me across the lawn.

I didn't have to knock. Dorothea Allred, dressed in flowered flannel robe with her hair down in a long braid, opened the door as we walked across her porch. For a moment, I was afraid she hadn't recognized me, but then she opened the door wider to let me in. I introduced Gerard, who shook her hand gravely and asked if she minded Bella coming in.

"Oh, dear me, no. You all must be freezing." She motioned us into the living room, and I appreciated the gas fireplace in her living room more than I had on my other visits. The clock on the mantel said 1105, and I realized Gerard and I had been walking for more than two hours. He led Bella close to the fireplace and unhooked her from her leash.

I was alarmed to see how fragile Dorothea Allred looked. "We were out on a walk and saw the fire—did the fire engines wake you up?"

She smiled at me. "I wasn't asleep. One of the advantages of old age is the decreased need for sleep, my dear." She bent to pet Bella, who was panting after our run uphill. "This one needs some water, I think." She looked at me and Gerard, who smiled back at her. "And the rest of us need some tea." She turned back towards the kitchen, and Bella followed.

I stood at the front window watching as the firefighters continued to pull hose in through the front gates. I couldn't see any much of the house from here, and there was no way to tell how much of the house was involved or damaged. Gerard came close and put his arm around me. "Tell me how I can help you."

I leaned into him for a moment. "I can't imagine what was in there to catch fire. Between the appraiser, the real estate agent, and the security people, I've been through that house about five times now. Other than some building materials, there really wasn't anything that could cause a fire." I thought about Jerry Freeman's report. "Well, except for the old wiring in parts of the house. But it would have to be on, and nothing was left on." I thought back. "At least, I don't think so."

Gerard rubbed my arm. "Benedict, fires start from all kinds of things. You can't do anything about it now. Trying to figure out what happened without the facts is impossible."

I watched the red lights reflecting off the wet pavement and realized the glaze was probably ice forming in the chill air. "You know,

Gerard, at some point, that cool, logical thinking is going to get on my last nerve."

He was still for a moment, his arm around me. "I understand, Benedict. But you need to know that I also make the best chocolate chip cookies known to man."

From behind us, Dorothea Allred chuckled. "I'll have to test that, Mr. Gerard. As Lacey knows, I always eat the cookies these days." We turned to see her coming in with a mug of tea, and I moved forward awkwardly, unsure how I felt about Gerard's comfort in public. He let his arm fall away.

"*Carpe* cookie," I said, and we all smiled. I took the tea she offered, cupping my hands around the warm mug, and tasted tea doctored with just the right amount of sugar and cream. Clearly, Mrs. Allred's memory was not one of the things that old age affected.

"Mr. Gerard, I didn't know how you liked your tea, so if you want to doctor it up, it's ready on the counter." She smiled gently at him, but we both recognized the invitation to leave the room.

"Thank you, I'll get that. And Bella?"

"She's enjoying her water and the rug in front of the warm stove."

"Smart girl." Gerard touched my arm as he passed by, barely a brush, but I felt it and was comforted anyway.

Mrs. Allred moved to watch the activity out the front window, and I joined her. A couple dressed in formal clothes stood in front of the house opposite, and the man lifted a hand when he saw Mrs. Allred. She waved back, and I heard her sigh.

"Are you all right? I know this is so upsetting for you."

She nodded, still looking out the window, her hands twisted together tightly as if she was afraid they would fly away if let loose. "Eighty-year-old houses are not comforting to live in," she said lightly, "even if they've been updated over the years. And they *can* be firetraps." She turned and walked closer to the fireplace, her hands outstretched to the low flames. "My dear, have you had a chance to read my father's journals?"

I guiltily remembered the blue composition notebooks on my

dining table. "I'm sorry. I haven't yet." She turned to look at me, but I didn't see censure in her red-rimmed eyes, only anxiety. "I know the journals really upset you." She looked toward the front window and its view of the activity next door but didn't speak. "You don't think this fire had something to do with that?"

She looked back at me. "I don't know what to think. But when you read my father's journals, you'll understand that Jack O'Toole blamed himself for everything—for everything bad, that is—that happened to himself or anyone else. And that house is haunted with that guilt."

"Mrs. Allred." I shook my head and walked over to her to take her hands. "What you don't know is that Jules and Trisha Tarantino are out of control. Trisha Tarantino probably hired someone to set Jules's Jag on fire." I tried to smile. "She is counting on this house to bring in a lot of money—this is probably Jules's revenge for the Jag."

As I accused his best friend of arson, I heard Gerard clear his throat behind me.

———

By 1 30 am, Mrs. Allred had finally let me persuade her to curl up in an easy chair to doze, and Bella was stretched out on the rug in front of the fire, still watching everything going on. I'd spoken to a lieutenant from the fire department, showing her a copy of the receivership order on my phone when I invited her in from the icy wind outside to Mrs. Allred's warm kitchen table. Gerard had disappeared for a while as I talked to her, but I refused to feel guilty. It wasn't my fault his friend was probably an arsonist.

My nap earlier in the day was coming in handy. I was tired, but still able to function as I tried to understand what was going on. The fire had been contained in the kitchen wing, according to Lieutenant Brandt, a sturdy woman in her 60s who'd come to the door of Mrs. Allred's house in the bulky yellow jacket from her turnout gear. She refused coffee but drank deeply from the ice water I'd gotten for her.

"There's going to be water damage in most of that side of the house, but there may be some in the rest of the house as well. Smoke damage too." She coughed a little and apologized, her voice hoarse. "The first guys in noted an accelerant."

"Accelerant?" My stomach twisted, and I thought about that antique Jaguar that burned in December. So much for the easy receivership.

She nodded. "They'll run tests to see what was used." She took a sip of water and rolled her shoulders inside the heavy coat. "The point of origin was a large room on the second floor, but it looks like they used stuff that was already in the house. Most building materials are now flame retardant. What really caught was the old house itself." She adjusted the ponytail holder in her hair, tightening it a bit. She laid out the next steps of the process for me, letting me know that the arson investigator would be in touch in the morning. She headed back out only a few minutes after she'd come in.

I followed her out to watch the activity winding up and found two police officers standing just outside the iron gates, watching the firefighters dealing with the hoses and equipment they'd used. The two trucks that had been outside the gates were already gone.

The patrol officer who'd greeted us at the scene, Officer Lewey, turned out to be the one who'd responded to the alarm and called in the fire. She and her supervisor politely declined coffee, and we stood at the gates to talk, both of them in heavy winter uniforms and jackets, and me in my not-heavy-enough leather jacket. I'd lost my red scarf somewhere on the run up the hill, and I missed it as the wind blew through the jacket's open collar.

The alarm system Freddie and Kobe Blake had upgraded a few days ago had done its job when the system was tripped. The phone number the alarm company had called—not mine, as it was supposed to be—had gone to a voice mail, so they had called the police, and Officer Lewey had reported the alarm tripped and smoke showing when she arrived on-scene. She and the fire department had used bolt cutters to cut through the chain on the front gates, and she and another officer saw damage to one of the French doors in the back—but the new inner key-locks kept that door from being used. A window in the downstairs laundry room had been opened, and that had tripped the alarm. Officer Lewey had also noted that the rusted lock on the gate at the bottom of the overgrown garden had been broken, and was most likely the arsonist's point of entry. I was gratified to know exactly how difficult his trip through the jungle of the garden had been.

They made sure they had all of my information, and I'd stood in the shelter of Mrs. Allred's front porch to call Lakewood Locks and Security, who agreed to send an officer over in the next hour to stay at the property until everything could be secured. He or she would also chain up the broken back gate.

I'd also texted Karan Sullivan, explaining that there had been a fire at the house, and asking her to let Cliff Clark know, since I only had his office phone number. I'd told her that I wanted to meet with the attorneys and their clients at 10 am at a location I'd choose in the morning, and I would give them an update at that time. Then I turned my phone off and went to look for Gerard.

I found him in the library, sitting by another fireplace. His head rested on the high back of a Queen Anne armchair, and his eyes were closed. I stood in the doorway, watching him sleep for a minute, his hawkish face calm and composed without those pale blue eyes open. His hands rested on the arms of the chair, the long fingers still against the dark green velvet. We'd spent the evening holding hands, and I shivered as I remembered how his thumb had caressed my hand, how his lips had felt against my palm.

When I was five, we drove to visit my mother's aunt in Corpus Christi over the Thanksgiving weekend. We drove for days, my brother and me fighting in the back seat of the car until I cried myself to an exhausted sleep and woke up in a strange house. After a tense and unhappy two days, we drove home, but not before my dad insisted we visit a beach. My father had crouched at my feet, carefully unbuckling my sandals, and he and I had walked to the water's edge. I still remember how it felt to stand in the low surf, the warm water rushing toward me and then crashing over my feet, the cool wet sand beneath them shifting and moving, changing with each wave. I loved that feeling of insecurity, of not knowing what would come next. Somewhere over the years, I'd lost that love of the unknown, but I welcomed it now as I watched Gerard sleep. I leaned against the door frame and sighed. I was exhausted.

Unlike the child I'd watched earlier in the evening, his tense body completely filled the chair, his barely rising and falling chest the only movement. Something must have awakened him. As I watched, his fingers twitched slightly, as if electricity suddenly pulsed through him, and his eyes opened, focusing on me immediately. It was like watching a mannequin come to life.

"Hi," I said, for lack of better conversation.

"Hi." He stretched his hands out to the ends of the chair arms. Behind me, I heard Bella's nails tap the floor of the hall. She brushed past me on her way to her person, who put out a hand to stroke across her silky head as she sat at his feet. I controlled another shiver, hoping he would miss the movement. "You done for a while?"

I nodded, wishing I could be like Bella, so easy with him, so casual with affection. But I knew I wouldn't be—at least not yet, anyway. "At least until 10 am or so. I've told Karan the Tarantinos and their counsel need to meet with me."

His eyes narrowed. "Arson?" At my nod, he sighed, his eyes closing for a moment before he opened them and got up. Bella stood too, her ears going up for a signal to the next move. He walked toward me, and I wondered if we were going to have that hard conversation now—the one where he would decide to believe in his old friend over me. Instead, he smoothly slid his arms around me and pulled me close for a hug. "Benedict, you must be exhausted." I wrapped my arms around him lightly, and leaned against him for a minute, promising myself that I wouldn't get used to this, that I wouldn't rely on it, that I'd be fine when he stopped.

CHAPTER TWENTY-THREE

SUNDAY, MARCH 3

W e took Bella home, and I waited on his couch with my eyes closed while he refilled her water bowl and settled her for the night before taking me home.

I woke when the sun began to stream in the lake-facing windows. Low clouds scudded quickly across the sky, and the bare branches of alder trees across the street bent in the north wind. I lay there on the couch, covered in a sweet-smelling comforter with a velvet pillow under my head, wondering how I'd gone from sitting up to sleeping. For a moment I let myself enjoy the feeling of warmth and comfort before taking inventory: my boots were beside the couch, the laces tucked into the shafts, my jacket was laid across the arm of the chair opposite, and my phone was plugged into a charger next to the fireplace.

I sat up and sniffed. I hadn't paid attention the night before, but now I noticed a distinct air of woodsmoke around me, overlaid with an aroma of barbeque—from the party or the fire, I didn't know. I yawned and flipped the comforter back to a definite chill in the air, grateful for the socks I was still wearing as I unplugged my now fully-charged phone.

There was a small half-bath in the front entry, complete with a toothbrush still in its wrapper and a travel-sized tube of toothpaste. I took far longer in there than I had to. I washed my face and scrubbed the makeup from under my blood-shot eyes, wondering how to play the next half hour—if I should wake Gerard up or let him sleep, call an Uber or wait for him to take me home. I tried to smooth the wrinkles from my Texas flag shirt, but it was a pointless exercise—I wasn't sure it would ever be the same.

I emerged to find him leaning against the bar, his hair wet from a shower, his face freshly shaven. He wore jeans and a light blue, long-sleeved t-shirt, but his feet were bare. He had two mugs in his hands, one a latte with a light sprinkle of cinnamon (which gave me a little tingle of pleasure, I'll admit). Bella was out in the miniscule backyard doing her business, and I watched her run in a circle as I sipped the latte as if it was a life-saving IV. The raised hair on the back of my neck told me Gerard was watching me, and I pretended not to notice as I let Bella back in when she bounded up to the door. Tail wagging, she ran into the kitchen, and we could hear her crunching into her food, her tags jingling against the ceramic bowl.

"Would you like to use my conference room for the meeting with Jules and Trisha?" I turned back to him in surprise. He shrugged. "It's a neutral space. They've not ever been in it, if I recall. It'll keep them off-guard and uncomfortable." He rubbed a hand over his hair, and I smiled at the motion. He smiled back. "I don't think either one of them would do this, Benedict. I really don't."

"The Jag?" I reminded him gently.

His smile died. "I don't know what that was. I'm pretty sure it was somebody Trisha hired, but I can't imagine how." He took a swallow of coffee. "I don't need to imagine *why*." He sighed, and I noticed how strained he looked, his eyes as red as mine. "I can let you into the office and then keep myself busy upstairs."

I considered the idea and then nodded. "I'll text Karan. But would you mind staying for the meeting? I think they might be better-behaved if you're there." He grimaced. "I really do."

"I can stay." He leaned against the bar. "You hungry?"

"Starving." I checked my phone. "815. If we hurry, we can get hot cinnamon knots at Café au Lait and still have time for me to shower before we go to your office."

———

JERRY FREEMAN HAD SENT ME AN EMAIL LATE THE NIGHT before with his thoughts about the as-built appraisal. He'd not supplied numbers, but he'd let me know that he considered the architect a complete moron who'd badly underestimated the amount of funds needed to complete the house. There was no way, in his opinion, that the house could be completed with the funds borrowed. As Gerard drove in his expertly competent way, I considered how different the situation would be now, with the house damaged by fire. I tapped out a text to Jerry to let him know what had happened and copied and pasted that information into another one to Suzy.

We made it to Gerard's office by 945, and I scoped out the conference room, which had been the house's enormous formal dining room back in the 1930s. Even now, the Craftsman-style house had an aura of comfort and ease. The end on the front of the house was set up as a waiting area, with your typical Queen Anne chairs in a bay window nook, and there was a moderately-long table and ten chairs at the other end. French doors opened inward from the foyer, and a credenza with coffee cups and accoutrements was placed across from them, in between two large windows facing a side yard.

I took a few moments to rearrange the chairs, leaving my chair at one end and another chair at the other end for Gerard, putting some papers in front of our chairs so no one would sit there. Then I moved the side chairs apart, taking out all but two on each side and making sure there was a good eight inches of space between each of the side chairs; the attorneys and their clients could move the chairs closer, but they'd have to make an effort—unlikely—so they'd be more off-balance than they might have otherwise been. I relocated a water pitcher and glasses to a tray in the exact center of the long table, where everyone would have to reach for it if they wanted some.

Gerard had made coffee, and he placed the carafe with the cups on the credenza. He eyed the chair configuration and smiled, then helped me move the four extra chairs across the hall to the office area. We'd had cinnamon knots and tall slices of quiche Lorraine at Café au Lait, and, though I'd considered bringing some cookies back for the meeting, I didn't. I still hadn't forgiven Cliff Clark and Jules Taran-tino for the receivership hearing, and snickerdoodles were for people I liked.

Karan arrived first, her client nowhere in sight. "Trisha will be late," she said with a roll of only-slightly bloodshot green eyes. She went right for the coffee, filling a mug and liberally adding milk. I compared my jeans and blue blazer with her trim black slacks, turquoise sweater set, and black suede boots and tried not to feel underdressed. She sat in a chair with her back to the doors and sipped her coffee.

Cliff Clark arrived with Jules, both of them looking tired. Clark was dressed in what I assume was a typical Sunday uniform for him: golf shirt and trousers, leather driving loafers, and an expensive suede jacket. He looked my way and frowned, but I sensed he was a bit nervous. Perhaps he suspected his client too.

Jules looked like he'd thrown on clothes he'd picked up from the floor (having done that before, I recognized the wrinkles). Like Gerard, he was wearing jeans, but underneath his puffy jacket was a wrinkled and faded Texas Longhorns t-shirt with what looked like a ketchup spot giving Bevo the Longhorn a distinctly red eye. He hadn't bothered to shave, and his early morning beard was long past a shadow. I looked closer to see if he'd been scratched up from making

his way through the Lakeway Circle jungle—as he would be if he was
the arsonist—and thought perhaps he'd lost weight in the last week.
He looked around for Gerard, but he'd disappeared upstairs. They
took the seats facing the conference room door. Karan raised her
coffee cup to them, but no one spoke. I stood next to the receptionist's
desk in the hall to wait, my mind running over what I wanted to say
to the couple.

It was only a minute or two before I heard Trisha Tarantino's
rapid heel-taps coming up the main sidewalk, and I opened the door
for her. It was clear she too hadn't gotten enough sleep, but her
exhaustion was well-hidden behind some skillfully-applied cosmetics
and a typically fashionable outfit. She wore a slim black skirt and high
black leather boots I instantly envied, the end of a silky olive-green
pashmina slung artfully over one shoulder in a bit of panache I
thought might look good on me, but that I probably wouldn't
remember to imitate.

"Hi Lacey," she said softly. "Please tell me there's coffee."

I nodded towards the carafe, and she took a minute to pour a cup
before sitting next to Karan. She looked across the bit of distance at
her attorney, clearly trying to decide whether to move closer to Karan,
and then she turned toward the door as Gerard came in and moved to
sit at the end by Trisha and Jules.

"I thought Mr. Gerard wasn't welcome in this receivership," Cliff
Clark said tartly. I felt my blood begin to boil, but a wave of weariness
swept over me, taking the heat away as it went by. The little man was
sitting bolt upright in his chair, his hands gripping the edge of the
table. Suddenly I felt sorry for him, this good friend of Bill Stephenson, who felt so angry about Bill's situation that he would let his feelings about *that* lap over into his representation of Jules Tarantino. He
looked everywhere but at me, his anger so acute he didn't bother to
assess me. That was fine.

"I thought having Gerard here might make Jules and Trisha feel
more comfortable," I said gently. The couple looked at me quickly,
and then Jules flushed and looked down at his hands. "We need to

deal with some hard truths." I thought about remaining standing, but decided I was just too tired. I sat.

Karan broke in, her voice steady but measured. "I need to make sure that my client understands that nothing about this meeting or anything said is privileged." Trisha looked her way and nodded.

Cliff Clark snorted. "Nothing about this meeting is normal or appropriate." He finally looked at me, his expression sour. "And we will be pointing this out to the Court in a renewed motion to appoint a substitute receiver."

"You'll do what you need to do, I'm sure." I looked down at Gerard, but he was looking at Clark with some speculation. "I know you're aware there was a fire last night at the house."

"Which was under your care," Clark interrupted.

I acknowledged that with a head nod. "Yes, it was. New security points were installed just Friday that alerted the police to an intruder, so the fire was detected far earlier than it might otherwise have been." Now I had all their attention. "As a result, the fire was contained to where it started, and hopefully so was the damage. I'm sure we will know in the coming days." I paused—for effect, I must admit. Even I loved a little drama.

"And I'll be meeting with an arson investigator from the fire department."

———

THE SILENCE WAS ELECTRIC FOR THREE SECONDS—I KNOW, because I counted—before both Trisha and Jules erupted, jumping to their feet and hurling accusations at each other.

"I knew it! I *knew* you couldn't be trusted!"

"*Arson?* Gasoline again, Trish?"

"You know what they say about arsonists and impotence, Jules?"

"And what does that make you, Trish?!"

"How *dare* you!"

"You ball-busting *bitch!*"

They were leaning toward one another over the table, and Gerard was watching them both like an unwilling tennis spectator. Clark sat back in his chair with a bit of a smile on his face as he watched the display.

I stood. "Jules. Trisha." They shouted right over me, so I raised my voice. "Hey!" They didn't slow down at all. I thought furiously about grabbing the water pitcher Gerard had left on the table and dousing both of them, but Gerard would be the one receiving most of the water.

A whistle, loud and piercing enough to make my ears ache, cut into the flow of words. We all looked to Karan, who took a finger and thumb from her mouth with a satisfied smile. "I've been wanting to do that for months."

Trisha drew breath to speak, but I spoke quickly into the sudden quiet, aiming my words directly at the couple still standing and leaning towards each other. "If you two cannot sit down and shut up, I will file a report with the Court with my recommendation that we sell the house as-is, for salvage value." They both stared at me, their mouths open. Clark and Karan began to stand up and speak, but I cut them off with a move of my hand. "*All* of you. Sit down. Please."

They sat. Jules reached to the water pitcher tray and filled a glass —with shaking hands, I noticed. So did Trisha—I saw her watch him with narrowed eyes, and I wondered what was going on.

"Do you have *proof* of arson, or are you just trying to be dramatic?" Clark's tone was more acid than it had been, but the blood seemed to have left his face, and I noticed the shiny smoothness on his forehead that was a sure sign of plastic surgery. I hadn't seen Bill Stephenson in almost five years, and I wondered if he too was indulging in the cosmetic work I'd told Gerard earlier I didn't mind. *Must keep up appearances*, I thought.

"The firefighters reported signs of arson when they entered the scene. By now, the arson investigators will be on scene." At my words, Jules drank down the water he'd poured and refilled his glass. Clark had noticed his client's actions, and he shook his head tightly at him. Jules ignored him and continued to gulp the water.

"We can't sell the house as it is." Trisha's voice was softer but no less angry than it had been. "The loan we took out for renovations would kill us. And I can't just file bankruptcy and make it all go away." She looked over at her husband. "Not and keep my job in finance. Jules knows that."

"Neither could I," Jules said tightly, "but it doesn't matter now." There was no arrogance in his demeanor now.

Trisha stared at him. "What are you talking about?"

He shrugged, his face miserable as he looked down at his half-empty glass. "The bank is being acquired by a bigger bank. And they're not going to need me after the acquisition is completed. I'll be looking for a job."

Trisha's face softened, but her lips compressed as if she was stopping herself from uttering anything kind.

"I think both of you need this process to go well." They looked at me, but I looked at their lawyers in turn. "Counsel, please make sure I have all the insurance information necessary to report the claim and deal with the adjuster."

Trisha's voice was a bit tentative. "What happens if it's arson? Will the insurance pay?"

I shrugged. "It depends on the policy terms, I'd guess." I paused and watched Trisha and Jules as I spoke. "And who's at fault." I could see in the periphery both Karan and Cliff stiffen, and I hid a smile as I watched their clients carefully. They avoided looking at each other. I wasn't going to ask for a confession, but neither of their clients was in for a comfortable time with this process. "I'll tell you that I'd already received third-party as-is and as-built appraisals, and we were in for a difficult time anyway." I raised my hands to stop any outbursts that news might elicit. "There were several areas of the renovation that were going to have be re-done. I'll send the appraisals to your counsels, but I have no expectation of anyone's agreement or coopera-tion." I raised my eyebrows as I looked at Jules and Trisha in turn.

"Which is a shame. The fact that you both need this to go well should get you to work together. But I guess you won't?" They both looked back at me steadily, but I noticed the haggard strain on Jules' face. Perhaps life was affecting his ability to be consumed by that passionate fire Gerard had talked about.

I nodded to Gerard, and we stood. Cliff and Karan followed suit, and their clients stood slowly too. "I have to report to the Court on Friday. I'll give everyone status before then. Thanks for coming."

Cliff Clark came around the table toward the door, but his client looked over at Trisha. "Trish, can we talk for a minute?"

Clark began to object, but Jules held a hand up. "Cliff, I know. But I would like to talk to my wife for a minute. Alone." Trisha nodded at Karan, and we filed out to the foyer. Gerard shut the doors behind us, and we stood in an awkward group.

Karan finally turned to me. "How bad were the appraisals?"

"Pretty bad." I yawned. "Sorry. It looks like they began with cosmetic work before really doing renovation on the whole house, probably because they were living in the house and wanted it to be nice to live in. But the electrical on the kitchen wing would have to have been redone." I made a face. "Well, now it really will be."

"Why?"

"That was where the fire started, in the second floor, where all the supplies were stored."

Cliff Clark was silent, but I could tell he was really straining to listen to what was going on in the conference room. Gerard spoke up. "The supplies caught on fire?"

I nodded. "But with help." I leaned against the receptionist's desk, exhaustion really taking hold. "Oh, hey. Thanks for the whistle in there. I've always wanted to whistle like that."

Karan nodded with a tiny smile, then bit her bottom lip as if she was holding something back. "Lacey, is it possible that this had nothing to do with the Tarantinos? That it was about that lockbox?"

Cliff Clark suddenly focused back in. "What? I thought that was just family stuff from the previous owners." He started to puff up.

I held up a hand. "It was. There was nothing in it but family pictures and a pair of wedding rings that are more valuable for their sentiment than even the gold in the rings. I'll have an inventory with my report on Friday." I thought about the letter to Patrick O'Toole, but the only people who knew about it were me, Paige, and Patrick O'Toole, and all of us knew we'd removed the box from the house.

The conference room doors opened, and Trisha swept through the foyer to the front door, her hair disheveled and her eyes red. "Karan, I'll talk to you later, okay?" She threw the words over her shoulder, and she was gone.

Jules came out a second later, his eyes on the glass door, watching his wife as she strode down the sidewalk outside to her car. Cliff began immediately to ask him questions, but Jules held up a hand much like I had earlier. "No, Cliff, not now. Let me call you tomorrow, okay?" He focused on Gerard. "Thanks, Rob." He smiled wearily in my direction, and then he was gone, Cliff stomping out too, sputtering and posturing in his client's wake.

Karan turned to me. "You look exhausted, Lacey. I didn't want to say it in front of them, but you look like you need sleep."

I laughed. "Thanks for not saying it in front of Clark." She hugged me lightly and smiled at Gerard as she left.

He turned to me. "No offense, Benedict, but you *do* look exhausted."

"You're such a sweet talker, Gerard." I stepped up to him, and he froze. I rested my head on his chest and chuckled, stopping there for a few long moments. His arms came around me and we stood there, still, until I stepped back to find my jacket. "I'm starving. Got anything to eat here?"

———

WE PICKED UP TACOS ON THE WAY BACK TO MY APARTMENT. I'D decided Gerard might be the perfect person to help me with the whole O'Toole thing. Most of the information I had was a matter of public record, but I wanted to check in with Paige anyway. I didn't want her to hear about the fire from someone else. I texted her once we got to my apartment, and then we spoke briefly. Once she'd okayed me sharing the information about the lockbox contents with Gerard, I told her about the fire.

"They're sure it was arson?"

"Pretty sure." I watched Gerard rooting around in the bags we'd brought home, setting out the tacos and containers of black beans, rice, and *elote*, and then finding real spoons and forks in my kitchen drawers. "The firefighters are apparently trained to tell when an accelerant has been used. I had a text from the arson investigator, who asked me to meet him at the house tomorrow morning."

Paige was silent for a couple of seconds before speaking. "And you think it was the Tarantinos?"

"Or more likely someone they hired, I guess." She said nothing. "Do you think it was someone else? Is your mom back in town?" I laughed, but she didn't laugh in response, and I sobered right up. "Paige, what are you thinking?"

"No, she doesn't get back till tomorrow night. Are we still meeting tomorrow afternoon?"

I looked at my phone's calendar. "We're still planning to meet your great uncle Wednesday morning?" Gerard was digging in the cabinets for plates, and I thought uncomfortably about the mismatched set I possessed. I had an unfortunate breakage habit.

"Yes. Probably late morning. His plane gets in Tuesday about 4." She paused. "Could you meet tomorrow at 5 at your office instead of 3? I'm going in the morning to get the death certificates and whatever else I can find. I thought I might be able to get their marriage license."

I watched him arrange the plates and silverware on the table, dipping spoons for serving into the Styrofoam containers of side dishes. "Good thought. Yeah, I could do that. That'll give me time to prep for my Tuesday foreclosures." The cat had come in, and Gerard decided that petting the cat was more important than folding paper towels into napkin flowers, thank god.

Paige finally hemmed and hawed her way into goodbye, and we hung up. I tapped out a quick text to Suzy and Jerry to see if they could meet me at the Tarantino house in the morning when I went there to meet with the arson investigator. Karan had sent me the Tarantinos' insurance agent information.

Gerard was sitting in one of the four cloth-covered dining chairs at the table checking his phone, and it was clear that he'd set us up for a formal lunch, with plates and forks and knives and glasses of water. He'd moved Mr. Berenson's composition books to the couch.

I sat across from him at the table, and the overstuffed cushion of the dining chair bounced me a bit.

Gerard noted the bounce. "These chairs are a bit stiff."

I avoided his eyes as I helped myself to a soft chicken taco. "They're kind of new." I ladled on some salsa, noting with pleasure that it was studded with serrano peppers. I took a healthy bite.

He spooned some *elote* on his plate, then added a tiny bit of the salsa—not enough, in my opinion. I loved the roasted corn and *crema* dish, but it still needed some zing from something spicy. "Taco Time's *elote* is pretty bland," I said, nodding at the salsa. "You might need more."

He looked at me with a raised eyebrow. "I'm good." He put a *barbacoa* taco on his plate and added some of the sour cream he'd made sure to ask for.

I shrugged. "Suit yourself." I raised an eyebrow. "Can't handle the heat?" He just shook his head repressively at me as I laughed and pointedly ate another bite heavy with salsa.

"Hey, did you know about Jules and his job?" I tried not to talk with a full mouth, but sometimes my enthusiasm got in the way. I resolved to watch my manners more.

He finished chewing and swallowed—like the good kids do—before answering. "No. He and I haven't spoken since the hearing." He didn't look at me as he used one of the forks he'd laid the table with to pick up the leftover lettuce, tomatoes, and cheese that had fallen out of his taco.

I finished my chicken taco and chewed before I spoke. "I figured he'd be trying to apologize." I'd always used my fingers on the fallen taco innards, but I used a fork like him this time, realizing it was like an extra taco salad, which I loved.

"He has been. I've not been ready to talk to him yet." He got another taco, *carnitas* pork this round, a good idea since that was one of Taco Time's specialties.

I used the fork to pierce a couple of kernels of corn as I tried to think how to word my next question. "Is that how you deal with being mad at someone? Silent treatment?" I didn't look at him as I mixed up the black beans and *elote* and salsa with the lettuce and cheese on my plate, adding a little of the contents of one of the myriad of sour cream containers we'd asked for.

He was quiet for long enough that I finally looked up at him. He was sitting there, not eating, not saying anything, not even really looking at me, and I could tell he was thinking—and not happily. Then his eyes shifted to me, and he was back in the room. He didn't smile, though. "Maybe, Benedict."

"You still mad at him?" I took a bite of the beans and corn mixture and almost swooned at how good it tasted.

"No." He added sour cream to his taco, but no salsa, I noted.

"Then why not talk to him?" I raised my eyebrows in my best Gerard imitation. "Are you just punishing him with the silent treatment? God, it's like you two are a married couple." I finished the bite of taco 'salad' I had in my mouth while I looked back at him. His mouth finally quirked in a tiny semblance of a smile, and I inwardly cheered.

He raised the taco to his mouth but spoke before taking a bite. "Maybe I will."

I leaned over and got one of the *carnitas* tacos, and the chair bounced me a bit as I sat back down. "Then my work here is done."

Gerard barked a laugh and then shifted uncomfortably in his chair. "Benedict, how new *are* these chairs?"

I helped myself to some more black beans. "They're a few years old. The table was here when I moved in, but I bought the chairs." I looked up to see him looking at me, eyebrows raised. The whole line of questioning was making me cranky. "What?"

He shook his head and took another bite of taco without saying anything.

"Okay, Gerard. I've never actually sat at the table to eat until this week. Until then, the table was covered with work. We don't all have formal taco lunches every day." I loaded the new taco with a huge spoonful of the hot salsa and took a big bite, my eyes daring him to comment, then started coughing when the peppers hit my throat. I managed to swallow the bite, but my eyes were watering. Gerard just chewed slowly and watched me struggle. When I finally had breath, I choked out, "Are you just going to sit there and watch me die?"

He smiled as he lifted his taco to bite into it, but he didn't rub it in. I liked him a little bit more for that.

———

"So... THIS JACK O'TOOLE SHOWS UP IN 1930 IN DALLAS, marries the local 'Soaring Socialite,' bails out her father, and no one knows how rich he is, or where his money came from?" He sprawled in one of my new office chairs, facing my glass 'white' board, where I'd mapped out what I knew about the O'Tooles.

"Right. They live in Dallas for about seven years—"

He interrupted as he looked down at the pictures from the lock-box. "Living a good life, having babies."

"Check. And he builds the house to end all houses in 1937, and then two years later, his wife is dead, and no one knows why. No autopsy, family is all upset. Sister-in-law says he killed her, but there's no investigation or charges or trial."

He carefully placed the picture of Jack and Eleanor at the Lakewood Theatre back on the desk. "Benedict, they don't look miserable in December 1938."

I rolled my eyes at him. "How often do we hear about someone who kills their spouse, and no one saw it coming?"

He dipped his head in acknowledgment. "I'm sure I've heard it more than you. So, he kills her, and then lives quietly in Dallas until he dies over 40 years later, and no one ever accuses him until now?"

"Except his sister-in-law." I stood back from the glass wall and looked at all the writing I'd done. "And I'm not accusing him. If anything, what you're saying seems to me to prove my point. There's no there *there*, if you know what I mean."

He smoothed a hand over his head as he looked at the bullet points on the wall. "If you're right, he and Donal—apparently his uncle—amassed a fortune buying and selling land."

"But why lie about his age? Why say he was born in 1900?"

Gerard shrugged. "Maybe he didn't want to feel old. Maybe his wife was younger than he felt comfortable with. Maybe he committed a crime—and yes, we could probably find out if a Jack O'Toole was accused of committing a crime, but, if we don't know who that man in Dallas was, we won't know if *he* committed one."

I growled in frustration as I looked at the board. "How do you prove something about someone if you don't even know who they are at all?" Gerard was looking at me with his eyebrows raised. "What?"

"Did you just growl?"

I rubbed my eyes with the heels of my hands. "Yes." A thought occurred to me as I covered my eyes. "Wait. I haven't checked the Rosenberg Library results." I opened my eyes to find Gerard standing far too close, but, before I could move, he put an arm around my shoulders and turned me toward the door.

"Let's go sit in comfort. Those side chairs from the Sheltons are lovely, but they're only slightly more comfortable than your dining chairs."

———

I OPENED MY LAPTOP TO SEARCH THE ROSENBERG LIBRARY
records. I'd assigned Gerard the review of Mr. Berenson's notebooks after
a quick retelling of how they came to me. He began to flip through them
as I pulled up the Rosenberg Library's home page and entered Gabby's
son's library card number. I could only hope it wasn't age restricted.

I finished before Gerard did. He'd stopped me once to ask for
sticky notes or tape flags to mark the books, then went right back to
reading. He was still paging through the notebooks, stopping to read
passages written in Mr. Berenson's spidery handwriting, when I
closed the laptop.

Galveston's Rosenberg Library had an extensive collection of
materials about the Galveston Hurricane of 1900, and I read through
those first, horrified by what I found. Between 6,000 and 10,000
people died in the storm, the flooding, and the aftermath of a hurricane that hit Galveston directly on September 8, 1900. The only
reason they don't know the total number was because Galveston was
a port city, and, even with census and other records, they don't know
how many people were actually in the city on the day of the hurricane. As awful as it was, the story of the Orphanage and all the dead
children was only one of many very sad accounts: people were
drowned inside their homes, killed by flying debris, or overwhelmed
by a storm surge that was estimated to be 15 feet. Some were swept
out to sea, never to be found.

The bodies that *were* found overwhelmed any ability to deal with
them. September in south Texas can be sweltering, and I felt a wave
of nausea at the thought of all those corpses in the humid heat.
Pictures accompanying accounts showed mountains of wooden
boards that had snapped like matchsticks, and whole houses that had
imploded under the relentless pressure of the wind and the water.
Bodies were carried out for a watery burial in hopes that the sea
would claim them, only to have them come back in with the tide.
They finally burned the corpses, and accounts spoke of a smoky pall
that hung over the city for some time. No one could have lived

through that and remain unaffected. I wondered how it changed Jack O'Toole.

The Rosenberg Library had a lot of information for cardholders, including copies of city directories, newspaper archives, and links to census records. After half an hour of searching, I had to admit failure in finding this particular O'Toole family. Morrison and Fourmey's *Directory of the City of Galveston* for 1900 revealed a couple of O'Tooles, but none were Annie or Donal or Jack.

The Rosenberg's link to the 1900 U.S. Census went through the Mormons' ancestry archive. I had to open an account, and I entered the most minimal of information, hoping I wouldn't be signing up for visits from any Mormon elders. I recognized the census reports—my grandmother had pulled numerous census reports for her genealogy searches for our ancestors—but now it was much easier to find reports online.

I looked for Annie, Donal, and Jack O'Toole in the 1900 Census reports, digging through hundreds of pages, all with variations of O'Toole, some with the apostrophe, some without, some with no 'O' at all. It went pretty quick, since the search sifted through other associated relatives at the same time. The heirship affidavit I'd found a few nights before identified Jack as Donal's nephew, and the easiest interpretation was that Donal was Jack's father's brother, perhaps Annie's brother-in-law. But there was no Annie O'Toole or Jack O'Toole or Donal O'Toole listed in Texas, or anywhere else, for that matter, in the 1900 census. The previous census would have been in 1890, and I checked there briefly, but neither she nor Donal or Jack appeared then either. If they'd been poor or transient, as so many immigrants had been at that time, it wasn't really a surprise they weren't listed. They also might have emigrated in between the census years.

I had a thought and decided to look for the three surviving orphans mentioned in the reports of the destruction of the St. Mary's Orphanage in the 1900 storm: Frank Madera, William Murney, and Albert Campbell. That's when I finally got lucky. Elmer Dana, the census taker for that area, had painstakingly listed all of the orphans taking shelter at the Orphanage on June 24, 1900. Albert Campbell and William Murney were listed, but Frank Madera was not. Jack O'Toole was also not listed. Most of the children were listed as born in Texas, and there were a few from Scotland or Bohemia. None were listed as Ireland-born, although several of the sisters were Irish.

Was Jack O'Toole one of the three boys that survived the storm? Did he change his name because of the trauma or the notoriety of his survival? I thought about digging into the records for each of the boys, but I needed a break. I wiggled a bit on the stiff dining chair and looked over at Gerard, who was reviewing composition books in comfort on the love seat, damn him. I looked closer. Was he asleep? No, he turned a page as I watched, then rubbed his hand over his head. I squinted a bit at that as I yawned. That was his tell—that he was concerned. Was he finding the same thing Mrs. Allred had?

While I watched, he closed the notebook he was reading and sat still, clearly thinking.

"Gerard? Everything okay?"

He put his arm on the back of the sofa and turned towards me. "You finished?"

I nodded, unplugging my laptop and walking around to the love seat. He moved the composition books gently to the floor, and I sat next to him.

He pulled me close to his side, and I leaned in for a moment, enjoying his warmth and presence more than I thought was advisable, but enjoying it anyway. He didn't speak, but I could sense the silence wasn't a comfortable one, so I sat up and faced him. "What's up?"

He shook his head. "I think I see why Mrs. Allred is disturbed by her father's journals." He rubbed a hand over his chin.

"By the writing?"

"No." He sighed. "By the subject. According to John Berenson, Jack O'Toole was a disturbed man—maybe psychotic."

CHAPTER TWENTY-FOUR

SUNDAY, MARCH 3 (CONTINUED)

I looked closely at his face to see if he was joking, but his eyes were sad and serious. "Psychotic? That's pretty harsh. So... could he have been a murderer?"

Gerard thought for a few seconds, and then shook his head. "I really doubt it, Benedict." He picked up one of the composition books. "This is the first one—from when John Berenson went to work for O'Toole. He spent the first year trying to learn O'Toole's business."

"Which was what? No one seems to know."

"Financing of oil projects. But not bank financing. O'Toole seemed to be the person you went to when all else failed, or when your project was so risky no one else would touch it." He flipped to a blue-tabbed page halfway through. "The amounts O'Toole funded were enormous. That picture you had of him from 1943 in Venezuela?" I nodded. He looked at Berenson's spidery writing as he spoke. "In 1943-44, the government of Venezuela began to take a percentage of the oil profits in the country, and the risk of government seizure of Venezuelan assets increased exponentially. No traditional lenders wanted to risk that, so they began turning down deals for US oil exploration there. O'Toole went in and propped up the industry, and the Venezuelan government made a special deal for him. That was a typical business deal for him. In the 1950s, he began to finance exploration in the Middle East, when most US lenders didn't even understand the importance of the middle eastern oil fields yet. He was in Iran before anyone else knew to be." He looked up at me. "He was a global financing organization, all by himself."

"How do you know all this?"

He tapped the phone sitting on the couch next to him. "Google is my friend."

"Mine tooooo," I cooed with a smile. I toed off my short boots and wiggled my toes in their socks get them warm.

He opened another of Berenson's books to a blue-tabbed page. "In 1954, he made a deal in Iran just before the shah took over the oil production there, and he made millions, getting out just as most of the major oil companies were forced by the US government to sell portions of their holdings to other companies—at a loss." He put that book down and picked up a third, opening it to yet another blue-tabbed page. "Then in late 1958, he inexplicably pulled out of almost all of his investments—everywhere. Just sold his positions to other lenders, still for huge profits, but probably not as big as he could have gotten under other circumstances. And less than a year later, the market crashed from the overproduction all over the world." He shook his head. "Had O'Toole stayed in, he would have lost hundreds of millions of dollars."

I leaned against the other end of the sofa, facing him and folding one leg under the other to get comfortable. "Well, that doesn't sound like someone who is psychotic. He sounds like a good businessman."

"Oh, he was. Or really lucky. Or both." He smiled at me and moved to give me room. "That's not the psychotic part." He turned back to the first book and opened it to a page I saw he'd tabbed with a red flag. "John Berenson had a note in 1943 that he'd let O'Toole know that Patrick—who was about nine or ten, I think?" I nodded. "Patrick had fallen out of a tree and broken his leg. O'Toole cabled Berenson about it, asking after Patrick. In the same cable—randomly, Berenson thought then—O'Toole told Berenson to wire twenty percent of the profits from the Venezuelan project to a monastery in France. That was Berenson's job, you see. While O'Toole traveled the world, working, Berenson stayed in touch with the family. He was also O'Toole's man of business—today's CFO—wiring sums out and providing financial reporting."

He turned to the second book, to another red tab. "And in 1955? Just after he made all the money in Iran? Berenson had to wire O'Toole in Cairo. Patrick's young wife died in childbirth in Madrid, and the baby was lost too. O'Toole doesn't go to Madrid—he sends Berenson instructions to get Patrick home, and to bring the young woman's body home to the states for burial. A few weeks later, Berenson is told to wire almost a million dollars to a monastery."

"The same one?"

He shook his head. "This one is in Italy. And understand, I'm just giving you the highlights. In between, there are notes about conversations Berenson had with O'Toole, instructions about sending money to different religious organizations, and letters where O'Toole tells Berenson bits and pieces about his life, about big deals he's done, and how people have to pay for those."

"'Pay'? The people involved in the deals?"

"No. This is the delusional part. He believed other people were struck with *bad* fortune in exchange for his *good* fortune." He shook his head and opened to another red-tabbed page. "Once, he told Berenson that Eleanor had paid the ultimate price for his wealth."

"What? Like he was responsible?" I started to lean forward to grab the book from Gerard but stopped myself in time.

He grinned at me as if he could read my mind. "Not exactly. O'Toole was being asked for an interview by the *Dallas Morning*

News in 1945, after some huge profits in the oil fields in the Texas Panhandle, and Berenson said O'Toole seemed aghast that people would want to hear about his success, since it had come at such a steep price." He picked up the last book. "What year did you say his granddaughter was born?"

"1959? 1960? No, wait." I opened my laptop to check my notes. "1959. That was the year he stayed in Paris instead of coming home—something Judith still hasn't forgiven him for, apparently."

"Berenson and he had a bit of a falling out in 1959. O'Toole wouldn't explain why he pulled out of all of his investments, even though Berenson had written him several letters asking about O'Toole's instructions and reasons for such spur-of-the-moment sales. Berenson didn't care *why*, but he seemed upset that O'Toole had shut him out." He opened to the last red tab. "Berenson recorded what O'Toole's letter had said: 'I can no longer risk my family's well-being in my selfish pursuits. My soul's existence on this earth is hazard enough.' Berenson received instructions to begin to shut down companies and all other activities as soon as possible, and O'Toole wouldn't explain any further." He closed the book, his finger holding the place. "There are a few other entries, but it looks like by the time Berenson died, O'Toole had decided to end any profit-making businesses."

"Wow." I thought about it, but then pushed against the assumption. "But maybe he just meant his work was risky. I mean, he was traveling around the world to places that weren't that stable."

He quirked an eyebrow. "Benedict, are you taking an adverse position just for the fun of it?" I just smiled.

He grinned back and then flipped over to the last page. "I want to read you what Berenson wrote at the end of the journals: 'Once Jack asked me how my wife and I had atoned for our guilt after David's death. I explained that, of course, while we fervently wished he had not been stationed at Pearl Harbor on that horrible morning, I was proud of my son and of my family's sacrifice to help win the war. I told him that pride mitigated my sadness. He looked at me then with such fear on his face, and told me he would pray for us, and that he would help me if I ever wanted to expiate our sin and guilt in David's death. He asks after Lorna in her pregnancy but will not return to be with her. He says to do so might endanger her child, and he cannot risk another life. He vows to stay away from his family so that they will stay safe. I fear that his sanity has slipped away, brought on by religious fervor unequalled by any I have ever seen. Of course, I will do as he asks, sending the sums to the organizations as he directs me, but it is clear he believes it is not enough. I fear he will do himself harm'."

He closed the book, his expression troubled.

I didn't know quite what to say. "I don't think I understand. What did he mean, 'expiate our sin'?"

Gerard put the books on the floor and turned toward me on the love seat. "You're not a very religious person, Benedict?"

I shook my head. "Grandmother was an atheist, my father agnostic. I'm not sure where I fit, but no, not much experience with religions."

"My family is from France, heavy on the Catholicism. I barely escaped going to Jesuit—not that there's anything wrong with it, it's a very fine boys' school—but I didn't want to go there. If your Jack O'Toole was in St. Mary's Orphanage with the Sisters of Charity, he learned French Catholicism at a time when it was still a very harsh and punitive faith. Latin masses, purgatory, penance, and the impossible burden of original sin."

"Well, that fits with the hidden room in the attic."

I realized from his look that I hadn't explained much about the room, so I described the outline of the cross on the wall in candle soot. He nodded. "It sounds like a secret chapel."

"But he had a chapel—on the grounds, he had a small stone chapel built there. Why would he need another one in the attic?"

He shrugged. "Some people want to pray in secret."

I stretched my arms behind my head as I heard the heat click on. It was getting colder outside, and it had begun to drizzle as we came in from the office earlier. "Praying, maybe." I hesitated. "Gerard, only a few people know this—but there's something else about that room." I folded my arms, chilled as always by my thoughts of the closet and its presence. "Jerry Freeman, the appraiser, came to get me that day because he thought he saw blood on the wall of that room." He raised his eyebrows at me. "Spots and streaks of red stuff—really faded, so we couldn't really tell what it was. But if it was blood, something awful happened there. I wondered if he'd abused Eleanor in that room, but I'll tell you, there's no way two people could fit in there and actually move around."

"I see." He looked off to the arched windows in the back of the room that overlooked the garden Hattie was so proud of. The light was fading, and low, dark gray clouds seemed to be moving in. It was one of those days where windows for walls wasn't the best idea. "Benedict, do you know what 'mortification of the flesh' is?"

I thought. "You mean, like medieval monks? Yes, but—" The synapses connected with an almost-audible snap. "O'Toole was whipping *himself* in that room?"

———

I GOT UP FOR SOME WATER AND A BRIEF PACE AS I TOLD HIM briefly what I'd found out about Galveston and the Sisters of Charity's Orphanage. "Maybe he was one of those boys that survived the Orphanage's destruction in the hurricane. I'll check them out to see what happened to them, or if it's possible one of them changed his name to Jack O'Toole." Everything he'd been reading seemed to have dimmed Gerard's mood, or perhaps he was tired. Lord knew I was. I sat down next to him again. "I can't believe he would go to such lengths to hurt himself."

He nodded. "Don't misunderstand, Benedict. Modern Catholicism isn't known for such extreme forms of penance. But it sounds like O'Toole may have gone in for monasticism, and at that time, it's possible he undertook a darker path to what he saw as salvation. Even more so if he wasn't in good mental health anyway."

I remembered the medal I'd found behind the Lakeway Circle house, and I retrieved it to show it to him. Gerard rubbed away some dirt with his thumb, and I thought his face softened. "It's a miraculous medal. That's Mary the virgin. See how she's standing?" I sat next to him and peered at it.

"What's the inscription? Can you read it?"

Without looking at the medal, Gerard recited softly: "'O Mary, conceived without sin, pray for us who have recourse to thee.'" I shivered at the words, and he felt the movement and spared me a wan smile. He flipped the medal over. The back side had been facing down, and it was tarnished but not encrusted with dirt. "See? This is the Marian cross, with the 'M' to show Mary kneeling below the cross. It's almost been rubbed away. Someone valued it." He handed it back to me, and I looked at it and wondered—as I always do—at the things that religious people value, at what becomes precious or necessary for faith or observation.

I got up and put the medal back in my coat pocket, thinking about giving it to Paige. "If he was there during that awful storm, I wouldn't be surprised that it left a lasting mental mark. Maybe a form of PTSD." I sat back down next to Gerard, unhappy to have been the cause of any sadness.

He sighed and leaned back against the sofa back. "So, if that was him in the photo, he'd been orphaned, and ends up there, and learns about penance and punishment. And then almost everyone else in the orphanage dies. He finds himself with his uncle Donal, and they have enormous financial successes. And he decided that his success came at the cost of all those lives." He looked down at his lap. "Guilt can be a terrible thing."

I wondered at his tone but decided now might not be the time to ask any questions. Instead, I leaned forward and took his hand in mine. "The poor man lost almost everyone around him, starting with being orphaned, then the hurricane and then his uncle, Eleanor." I shook my head. "Maybe it just drove him crazy."

"Perhaps. But I think for him, his belief was compelling him toward more guilt, more pain, more penance. Even a twisted sense of responsibility. A tradeoff for his own good luck." He rubbed my thumb with his finger as he looked off to the side, as if trying to remember something. "There's some disorder or something, I can't remember...." He trailed off, thinking.

"I have a psychologist on call! I could ask Dr. Amie about it." He focused on me and raised his eyebrows. I hurried to explain. "She's a client and friend."

He grinned, and then raised my hand to his lips to kiss my thumb. "I need a nap, Benedict." He yawned hugely.

"Don't do that. I'll—" I couldn't help the yawn in response.

"Come here." He tugged, and I moved easily to his side, where he tucked me under his arm, my head against his chest, my arm sliding around his back. *Just for a minute*, I thought, before falling gently into sleep.

———

I WAS DREAMING ABOUT ELEANOR O'TOOLE WALKING UP TO A door and knocking when Gerard shook me awake.

"Benedict, one of the Shelton sisters is knocking on the connecting door," he murmured in my ear.

"Mmmph."

"Are they going to come in anyway?"

I shook my head sleepily. We'd turned around as we slept, and I was curled up and held firmly by Gerard from behind, my head resting on the back of the sofa. "Not with your car here."

"That's good," he murmured, and his breath tickled. I felt his lips touch in that hollow spot just below my ear, then slide down to where my neck and shoulder met, and I shivered. Warmth began to pool inside me, and I found I wasn't cold anymore. With my hair up, he had access to my neck, and his lips feathered my skin. I tilted my head to the other side to give him more access.

I held my breath as he took full advantage of his position behind me, his arms around me, one hand splayed across my belly. His nuzzling increased the pressure there, and I shuddered and let the breath go slowly. When his teeth grazed the skin, I gasped, and he groaned quietly, then stilled.

He tucked his head into my shoulder and sighed. "I need to go take care of Bella. It's got to be almost 6."

"Really?" I drawled, feeling lazy and tingly and sleepy and wide awake, all at the same time.

"Really." He hugged me tightly once, and then got up. I kept my head on the couch and watched him carefully stack the composition books on the dining table. He paused for a moment and then held up his Mont Blanc pen I'd been using. I just shrugged and tried to look innocent.

I got up to walk him to the door. "Isn't it usually the woman who has to 'take care of her dog' and cuts the date short?" He shot me a look and then grinned. "Truthfully, this has been the longest date I've ever had." I tightened my ponytail. While he shrugged on his jacket and tucked his pen in the pocket, I wondered if I had salsa or onion breath from the tacos at lunch. I started to surreptitiously check my breath but stopped, unwilling to be caught checking. *Did other people worry about stuff like that,* I thought, *or is it just me?*

He turned at the door. "Longest I've had too." He pulled me close. His lips met mine, a mere brush of warmth, and then they trailed down the side of my throat. I wished for a moment he could have lingered there, his mouth on my skin, his laughter in my head. But life doesn't work that way.

It was getting dark outside and a light drizzle was starting to fall, making the cold even more tangible. I shivered and wished I'd put my jacket on too as I stood there on the little porch in my sock feet.

He took four or five steps toward his car, pulling his jacket a bit tighter, before he turned back. "Benedict—" He stopped, his eyebrows beetling low as he hesitated, the mist beading on his hair.

"Hmm?" He looked at me. I stepped out under the overhang, hugging myself against the cold. "Gerard?"

He came striding back to where I was, his cold hands threading into my hair. His lips met mine hungrily, and all my thoughts about onions and salsa fled. I gripped his shoulders and kissed him back, wanting more, but it ended too soon. He kissed my lips once more, lingeringly, and then he stood looking at me for a few seconds before turning to go.

I wish it could have been longer, I thought, as I watched him walk away.

———

I PACED THE FLOOR AFTER GERARD LEFT, GOING FROM KITCHEN to sofa and back again. I turned on the television, but just as quickly turned it off. I sat for a few minutes rewinding the past 24 hours, considering the fact that I'd enjoyed Gerard so much I didn't want him to leave. For someone who'd rather see the back of just about anybody (with very few exceptions), the admission—even internally— was a pretty big deal. I got up again. Maybe I'd clean out the refrigerator.

I stood in front of the refrigerator and stared inside, thinking about the afternoon, wanting something, but not really hungry. There was a tap on the connecting door, and I opened it to find Sallie Shelton in black cashmere, her hair swept up in a bundle of thick silver curls on her head. Her eyes searched my face, and I steeled myself for her usual questions, but she just smiled. "Hattie's made chili," she said, then held out a hand. "Come have some."

I followed her through the laundry to the kitchen, where Hattie was stirring a big pot of chili on the stove. Three thick white pottery bowls were on the table, and small serving bowls of shredded cheese, chopped red onion, and chunky salsa were already placed in the middle. A small platter of cornbread squares was right in front of my usual place, and I stopped to hug first Hattie and then Sallie before sitting down.

We ate and talked a bit about my new office, the weather, and the emails they'd received from the twins, daughters of cousins third removed, and their only real living relatives. The girls were 22, and they might come stay in Dallas after they graduated from college this summer. I told them about the O'Tooles and what our research had discovered, and described John Berenson's insight into his employer.

I had two bowls of Hattie's amazing chili—which she made with regular chili beef and also the charred bits and ends of barbecued brisket—before I pushed my bowl away and faced Sallie across the table.

"I know you're dying to ask."

She lifted a delicate eyebrow. "I? What do you mean?"

I lifted mine back, the scar prickling. When would that stop? "I can't believe you waited this long." I took a sip of beer, which Hattie made sure was poured in a glass for me, and inwardly compared Hattie's nicely-laid table to Gerard's earlier. "It was a really good date."

Sallie's arch expression softened. "Was it?"

I nodded, feeling suddenly shy. "His sister lives in that great house on Belmont—you know, the big Craftsman with the wide porch and shutters?" They both nodded. "Huge party, lots of barbecue, lots of high society." I nodded to Sallie. "Probably a lot of people you know. There was this one woman, Lesley Batchelor—" Sallie puckered her mouth up and rolled her eyes, and I tipped the glass toward her before taking another sip. "Yep, you know her."

Hattie laughed and added some cream to her tea. "She's from an old Dallas family. Her grandmother went to school with us."

"Geez, who isn't?" I rolled my eyes. "Everywhere I turn this last week, I run into 'old-Dallas families' and their demon spawn." I quickly added. "Not you guys, no offense."

"None taken," Hattie said dryly, and I flushed.

"Sorry. It's just been one person lording it over me or another. Apparently, she and Gerard went to school together, and it looks like she's been pining for him ever since—even though she's been married and had kids." I avoided their eyes, looking over at the small sofa in the nook of the kitchen, where the cat was curled up watching us. "I don't even know if I like the guy, and I'm already getting the side-eye from her."

They were silent, and when I looked back at them, Sallie was watching me, a gentle smile on her face that stung. "What?"

"Nothing," she said mildly, shaking her head and sipping her tea.

I sighed. "Okay, yeah, I like him." I drank the last swallow of beer in my glass and shook my head when Hattie motioned to it. I was too tired to want another. I leaned forward on the table. "We walked for almost two hours last night in the cold and talked. I like him. But we're really different, you know?" Sallie nodded, her eyes on me. Hattie was staring off into space, and I could tell she was thinking. "I'm more of a 'right out there' kind of person—maybe more than I should be, I know—and he's really..." I trailed off, trying to think of the best word.

Hattie spoke, her voice a bit rusty. "Cold?"

I shook my head, thinking of that kiss before he left. "No. Reserved, maybe." I described in a few words the exchange we'd had about Jules and Gerard's silent treatment.

"Lacey, everyone who has been out in life at all has a bit of baggage, you know." Sallie's voice was kind, and I saw them exchange a glance. I started to ask about it, but I was too tired.

I sighed. "I *know* I have some. But how do you find out about people's baggage unless you trip over it? And then you've stubbed your toe, or maybe thrown an f-bomb or two, and yelled at whoever left it out to begin with."

Hattie was smiling at me. "You keep your eyes forward and open —if you're always looking into the past, you'll stumble over things in front of you."

I thought of Dr. Amie gently reminding me not to be weighed

down by the past. Both Hattie and Sallie were smiling at me, their beautiful eyes so much alike, despite the fact they were fraternal twins, and I wanted to tell them what had really happened over the last couple of days. I didn't know how to begin, so I just went to the most important part. "I've decided to see a therapist."

Hattie patted my shoulder, then got up to heat more water and make a cup of tea for me, as Sallie leaned across the table to take my hand.

CHAPTER TWENTY-FIVE

I woke up early on Monday morning, feeling refreshed after more than eight hours of sleep. I'd spent another hour with the Shelton sisters the night before, and then decided to visit my dad. It hadn't been a wise choice. The aide who worked at the Landover Avenue facility gently reminded me that he would have bad days along with the good ones, but I'd come to focus on the good, ignoring the rest.

This time, not only did he not recognize me, he wouldn't look at me or acknowledge me, a fact that still made my heart ache the next day. I sat with him regardless, but he simply stared ahead, lost in memories or thoughts or perhaps nothing. As I watched him, he seemed to be listening to an inner playlist I couldn't hear. He didn't seem upset by it; on the contrary, he seemed mostly peaceful. I decided I'd just sit with him with no expectations, and I found it to be restful. I let myself be just as swamped by some old memories of him and the farm and my grandmother. I still couldn't remember much about our arrival there, but I felt a bit better about the gaps. I helped the aide put him to bed, tucking him in with a kiss on the forehead, as if he were the child and I the parent.

I thought about that the next morning as I stopped off to get a latte on the way to meet everyone at the Lakeway Circle house. My father used to love coffee, and, when I was little, he'd make a cup for me on Sundays, mostly milk with a tiny bit of coffee. I'd sit across from him and carefully blow on my milky coffee just like he did as we read the paper together, me examining the comics with the same scrutiny he gave the news. The last time I remembered seeing him with a cup of coffee was several years ago, over breakfast at the farm. That was about the time I realized that, once more, things would never be the same again.

I sipped my coffee as I stopped at the intersection where I'd seen the young mom with a stroller only a week before. It was a little late in the morning for her this time, and much colder. The forecast for today didn't see us getting much above freezing, and the only people I saw out were scurrying to their cars if they were unlucky enough to have to park outside. A few of the yards with automatic sprinklers were frosted over, the pale green of the spring grass underneath.

Suzy's Lexus was already at the gates of the Lakeway Circle house, as was Jerry Freeman's pickup, both running with their drivers still inside for warmth. Freddie Blake pulled into the circle right behind me. He'd have the key to the padlock I could see was attached to a thick chain looped through the iron gates. Yellow crime scene tape was also wrapped around the chain, and I figured we'd have to wait for the arson investigator, a Lieutenant Jason Taylor. A red BMW that could only be called 'vintage' pulled up, driven by a woman I didn't recognize. She parked in front of Mrs. Allred's house and came to my window, which I grudgingly lowered.

"Hi—I'm Delaney Tatum? DCT Insurance? You left me a message this morning." Her teeth were chattering, and her lips seemed slightly blue.

"I did. I'm surprised you got it already." I moved the stuff I'd

brought with me to the passenger floorboard, and motioned her in.
She came around and got in, immediately repositioning the heater
vents for warmth.

"My car heater isn't working this morning," she said, her lips stiff.

"Oh, geez. You must be freezing." It didn't help that she was
wearing only a light suit jacket with a thin turtleneck sweater underneath. I didn't mention the fact that the hose and heels she was
wearing under the pantsuit would do nothing for warmth inside the
house, which I suspected was still without power. She'd find out soon
enough. "I expected a call, to be honest." I'd emailed her a copy of the
receivership order and left her a voicemail explaining that I was
meeting the arson investigator this morning.

"I live over in Lake Highlands, so I thought I'd stop by and meet
you." She seemed to be warming up, and her lips were finally starting
to re-pinken.

"Well, I'm glad to have you here. I have no idea what happens
next as far as the insurance claim goes."

She nodded, her eyes serious. "If it's a clear case of arson, the
insurance company will work with the fire department's investigator
to determine liability. That gets started right away. Once a claim is
filed, the insurance company has only 60 days to either pay the claim
or deny it under the the Tarantinos' policy."

"You work for the insurance company or the agency?" She
seemed really young to me, with her blond hair and big blue eyes, but
maybe you didn't have to have much experience to do this kind of
work.

"My company is an independent agent. We write policies for
insurers, like Queensland, the company that insures the Tarantinos."

"Your company?"

She smiled proudly. "Yep. All mine."

I started to ask her about that, but a Suburban wrapped in Dallas
Fire Department insignia had pulled in right in front of the gates. I
checked the clock. 915. I wondered if this was going to be a pattern
for Lieutenant Taylor.

"Why don't you stay here for a minute in the heat, while I meet this guy? And then we can talk through next steps."

"Do you hear me arguing?" She huddled in the seat, hands still outstretched toward the vents.

I got out along with Freddie, jamming my hands in my coat pockets. Although I'd dug through my closet, I didn't find any gloves to replace the ones I'd trashed last week. Freddie had a set of keys with him, but he waited at the gate for me and Taylor.

I was interested to see that Lieutenant Jason Taylor was in jeans and a dark blue peacoat much like mine, with boots that could have been ones I'd find in my own closet. He wasn't very tall—maybe a few inches taller than my 5'5"—but he was clearly a weightlifter in his spare time. He had short, spiky brown hair and sparkling chocolate-brown eyes, and a ready smile full of even white teeth. He was the kind of guy that would have been the star quarterback in your high school, all charisma and charm and good looks, who'd matured years earlier than any other boy in school. He looked around at all the cars with mock dismay.

"I'm betting you're Lacey Benedict." He stuck his hand out—in fleece-lined leather gloves that I immediately envied—and I shook it, enjoying his firm group. He leaned in close and lowered his voice. "Who are all these people?"

I grinned at him, liking him instantly. "What? You didn't want an audience?"

He smiled back. "I'm a bit of an exhibitionist myself, but I didn't know we were already onstage."

Ah, a flirt. I stuck my hands back in my pockets and tried for seriousness. "Lexus is Suzy Shapiro, real estate agent. Ford is Jerry Freeman, appraiser. BMW is Delaney Tatum, insurance agent, although she's refusing to get out of my car where the heater is. And this is Freddie Blake, who is the key to it all." Freddie grinned at me. "Or at least, he *has* the key to it all."

"Yeah, we met already. Mr. Blake, how are you?" Taylor shook Freddie's hand and then unwound the crime scene tape that wrapped around the chain and lock. "I asked him to come back this morning. Power should be restored now, and I want to see if we can get the alarm up and running." Freddie unlocked the padlock and then handed me the two keys he'd brought for the lock.

I handed one to Taylor. "How does this work?"

He took the key and tucked it into his pocket. "My team was here yesterday to collect evidence from the scene, or I wouldn't be letting you and this crowd of people in." He grinned to soften the news. "One of the other investigators will be here in about an hour to meet with your insurance agent—he is the department liaison who works with that side of it. I wanted to walk the scene first. Since you're an officer of the court, I guess I can trust you with one of the keys, but otherwise, the house and the gates should be locked, and the keys stay with me. I'll give you a receipt." I nodded. "Right now, let's leave all the vehicles outside. We took photos yesterday of the forecourt, but I'd still like to keep the cars in and out to a minimum."

"I need to visit with Jerry and Suzy, and I do want to understand the next few steps. I've got to report to the court about all this." I noticed glumly that the fire trucks and police cars had left crisscrossing mud tracks all over the forecourt, and I expected there to be a lot of mud inside the house.

"Give me a few minutes to do a quick walkthrough and talk to Mr. Blake." He flashed a quick smile and was gone with Freddie, who followed him inside.

Suzy and Jerry got out of their cars and met me in the forecourt. Both had warm coats and gloves, although Suzy wasn't wearing her usual heels. She had a beanie in a light turquoise color that blended perfectly with her teal coat, with a multicolored scarf that incorporated both colors along with several others. She side-stepped a hug as we met. "I've got a horrible cold, so you don't want to get close." She turned to look at the house. "I can't believe this happened!"

"Yeah, me either." I smiled at Jerry, who proffered a cinnamon sucker to me and another to Suzy, who took it with a smile and tucked it into a pocket. I doubted she indulged, but I unwrapped mine and started working to get it down to a manageable size.

"How much damage you think we got?" He was sucking hard on his own cinnamon cube, so his words were a bit mangled.

I pulled the sucker out and used it to point at the house. "From what the firefighters told me Saturday night, the whole kitchen wing has significant water and fire damage. The rest is going to have smoke damage at least."

"That's where it started? Second floor?" Suzy didn't sound surprised.

I nodded. "The attic section is pretty well burned. The kitchen ceiling was in bad shape, I heard."

We watched as Taylor and Freddie came out and walked towards us.

"And it was arson? They're sure?"

Taylor answered for me as he came near. "Yep. The dogs were here yesterday and went right to it. Initial tests show the guy used turpentine, probably stored here before the fire."

———

Two hours later, Suzy and Jerry had left, as had Delaney and Freddie. Suzy had been actively checking with agents she knew and had been ready to pitch for listing the house as-is until she got news of the fire.

"The Lakewood market is all about renovation right now." Her voice was a hollow rasp as she re-wound her multi-colored scarf tightly around her throat. "We probably could have gotten a pretty good price, even with the unfinished renovation. Given the amount of damage now, it would be months and a complete restoration before we can consider listing. Otherwise, you're looking at a bloodbath on price." With that sad news, she left, wiggling her fingers at me in lieu of a hug as she left.

Freddie grumbled about the laundry room window where the

intruder had entered. Apparently, the old wooden window was easily accessed. He showed me how the intruder had just used some kind of thin metal to push the lock enough to get it open. "But your alarm points did the trick," I assured him. He still cautioned me to get the property better secured, and I promised to call him as soon as Taylor released the property back to me so we could meet to discuss cameras.

Delaney wanted to be positive about the whole thing, but it was clear she was just as worried about the arson claim as her insureds were after meeting with the department liaison. She'd listened closely to Taylor as he talked to me about what he knew.

"Given that there was a broken lock on the back gate and a window was clearly the point of entry, it looks like an intruder, maybe someone who broke in to get warm," Taylor had mused to the two of us, as if it was all an academic exercise, "but the fire tells a different story."

"What do you mean by that?" I had a feeling I knew where this was going, but I wanted to make him say it.

He tilted his head and studied me, his brown eyes sharp. Then he held up a finger, counting one. "If that fire was set for warmth and just got away from an innocent person, where is he? Did he have a bedroll or belongings? If so, where are those items?" He shook his head. "There are two fire stations minutes away. Response time was minimal. Even if he ran, thinking he was going to get in trouble, we'd have found something indicating he was around." He added a finger to the first. "That was not a fire set for warmth. It was put together to burn as hot as it could, but the accelerant was all over the floor, and it burned on the floor—that's why there's so much damage on the ceiling of the kitchen."

I liked this guy, but he seemed to be leaping to some conclusions, and that was different from every law enforcement officer I knew—and yes, most arson investigators are law enforcement professionals in Texas. I couldn't help but question his thinking. "But the fire didn't really catch because the materials were flame-retardant—wouldn't that indicate a non-professional?" Delaney stood watching us, her face a picture of concern.

Taylor scoffed, his good-natured face uneasily wearing the expression. "Or someone trying to make it look like someone broke in and started an accidental fire."

I leaned in. "Sounds to me like you're assuming intent where you have no evidence, Lieutenant Taylor."

He leaned in as well. "You don't *know* what evidence I've got, Miss Benedict."

Delaney broke in, clearly a peacemaker. "Ooooookay, you two. Everything is preliminary at this point." I took a breath and relaxed, and I noticed Taylor did too. "Lieutenant Taylor, I'll be in touch, as will the company's adjuster." She smiled nervously and offered him her hand, which he shook with an apologetic smile.

I walked her out as she mapped out the process going forward. She'd be sending me policy information and would let me know what she needed from me. I was glad to know the Tarantinos had let her know the property would be vacant when they moved out, since an additional deductible would have applied if they hadn't. Then she dropped a bomb. If one of them was responsible for the fire, all bets were off: the insurance wouldn't pay a claim to someone who started a fire intentionally, or even to that person's spouse.

Jerry had trooped upstairs with Lieutenant Taylor to take a bird's eye look at the fire damage, the two men laughing and talking as they went. It never ceased to amaze me when men who seemed to have nothing in common hit it off. I saw Taylor working hard at a cinnamon sucker as Jerry made his way back to his truck.

The inside of the house was both better and worse than I imagined. Water still pooled on the marble floors of the foyer, and mud graced the floor of every room, the tracks of the firefighters criss-crossing back and forth where they'd searched in the dark and smoke for inhabitants of the massive house. Taylor told me he'd let me know when I could get restoration people in, probably in the next few days. But the living room wing of the house had suffered only slight smoke damage, with mud the only sign anything had happened in the master bedroom or bath. Upstairs, the hand-painted murals on the nursery room walls still glowed faintly in the dim morning light, a sight that made me unreasonably glad.

The kitchen wing was chaos. The long dining table had been pushed aside and the chairs with their pale green upholstery were askew, some thrown over to the other side. Several seemed to be missing. Taylor explained that the arsonist had taken at least two upstairs with him, using their upholstery to try to help him start the fire.

"So, it was clearly deliberate? Absolutely no chance it was accidental, say someone breaking in here to get warm? Maybe using the turpentine to get a fire started?" I knew it sounded crazy, but I really didn't want this to be one of the Tarantinos trying to get money from an insurance claim where they couldn't get a completely remodeled house to sell.

Taylor gave me a look that told me what he thought of that idea. We stood under the massive stained-glass window, which had survived with no visible damage. "I haven't moved to motive just yet. We just know that someone stacked a bunch of wood flooring, unfinished trim, and a couple of chairs together in a pile, doused it with turpentine, and lit a few matches to try to get it started."

"To 'try' to get it started? What do you mean?"

He shook his head and took the empty lollipop stick out of his mouth. "In my opinion, he definitely wasn't a pro. There are bits of matches all over the place in that room." I heard the front door open, and his eyes slid past me, his mouth flattening with displeasure. "Or maybe I should say 'she' wasn't a pro."

I turned to see Trisha Tarantino in the doorway, her long red hair framing her beautiful face. She wasn't looking at me—she was staring at Lieutenant Jason Taylor, her eyes wide with fear.

———

"I HAD A FANTASY WHEN WE BOUGHT THIS HOUSE," TRISHA SAID

as she ran a gloved finger over one of the miniature sailboats painted
on the wall, the deep turquoise leather a dark contrast to the light
yellow of the hull. "I'd just turned 40, and I knew any possibility of
me having a baby was fading fast." She put her hand back in the
pocket of her wool coat and turned to me, her green eyes looking as
blue-green as the turquoise of the scarf and coat. I must have looked a
bit skeptical at the thought of Trisha as maternal, because her mouth
twisted in response. "I know, doesn't seem to fit me." She sighed and
leaned against the wall. "But once I saw these rooms and the murals, I
wanted it so badly it was burning inside me."

"What happened?"

She shrugged. "Who knows? I got a promotion with more travel,
and things just seemed to get worse and worse with Jules." She
sighed. "Maybe all of that was an excuse. The fantasy I had involved
two parents who loved each other as much as they loved their child,
and that just doesn't seem to be what happens with us."

She seemed just as uncomfortable with the emotional side of life
as I was, so I decided to address the Jason Taylor-sized elephant in the
room. "You and Lieutenant Taylor seemed to know each other."

She crossed her arms over her chest. "I'm not supposed to talk
about it." I started to shrug as she had earlier, but she pushed away
abruptly from the wall. "Oh, hell. I don't care anymore. Yes, he knows
me. He was the arson investigator on the incident with Jules's Jag."

"Oh."

She nodded miserably. "It was a stupid, childish thing to do, and I
regretted it instantly." She looked out the window, where we could
see dark gray clouds scudding over White Rock Lake. On a windy
day like this, the sailboats on the wall were the only ones that could
be seen. "There was no way we were filing an insurance claim, of
course, and apparently it's really hard to prosecute someone for
torching their own property. And it was still my property too." She
rubbed at her forehead, where lines were faintly noticeable. Maybe
she wasn't one of the Dallas women staying young with injections
and surgery.

"So why is Taylor so..." I searched for the best word.

"Angry?" She laughed without much humor. "If it was up to him, I'd be in jail right now. He's like a dog with a bone."

The little I'd seen of Taylor told me much the same. He seemed like a man who took crimes involving arson personally. I said as much to Trisha as we began to walk down the second-floor stairs single file, Trisha in front of me.

She stopped on the landing outside the master bedroom and faced me. "That's what I'm afraid of, Lacey. What if Jules did this? This job change scares him—he's never been poor, unlike me—and he's feeling desperate." She bit her lip. "I'm not supposed to talk to you about any of this. But he's scared. And I'm worried about why."

"Would he try to destroy everything the two of you had done? And how reckless that would be? Surely he'd know how thorough forensic science is these days."

She shook her head, her eyes bright with unshed tears.

A voice floated up from the stairs below us. "Yes, it is, Miss Benedict." We looked down to see Taylor leaning against the wall at the bottom of the next section of stairs. His arms were crossed across his muscular chest, and his expression was deceptively pleasant. "It's very thorough—and so am I."

CHAPTER TWENTY-SIX

Lieutenant Taylor and his crew were still working in the house when Trisha Tarantino left. She'd made her way serenely down the stairs, giving him a wide berth, and she closed the front door behind her with a quiet click. I admired her restraint. Perhaps it was because I'd seen her in disagreements with her husband that I knew her face going pale was a sure sign she was upset. Unlike many redheads, she didn't flush or brighten in anger. Or perhaps she'd just learned to sublimate the emotion, like she'd done with her maternal feelings.

Either way, her restraint earned her only a scathing look from Taylor, who watched her leave with the type of expression I usually give the cauliflower Gerard seemed to love so much.

"You and she were pretty friendly." He didn't quite spit the words out, but he came close.

I shook my head as I descended the stairs. "I'm just a receiver, appointed by the court to sell the house." I stepped to the landing, intrigued as always by people's strong emotions and by when they choose to feel them. "You don't like her." I made sure it wasn't a question—I really didn't want to get another 'well, duh' look from him.

His eyes narrowed as he agreed. "I don't like her."

"She told me you didn't like the result of the Jaguar thing."

He snorted. "That's mild. People like her—especially *women* like her—they think they can buy their way out of any mess they've made." He turned and descended the main stairs in step with me. "The rest of us have to face the consequences, but not people like that."

I didn't answer, since I knew there were other consequences Trisha would be facing. Delaney Tatum had let me know that the Tarantinos' insurance policy had several exclusionary clauses, one of which would prevent payment of a claim to Trisha, if indeed Jules had been responsible for this fire. Taylor would find that out soon enough, I was sure, so I didn't bother to inform him.

He seemed to regain his good humor before I left, tossing in a dose of charm in case I'd missed it before. "I'll get back to you with our preliminary assessment in the next few days." He had a broad white twinkly smile, and this close, his eyes looked like milk chocolate. "How about we discuss them over dinner? I cook a mean steak—unless you're a vegan?" He frowned dramatically. "Or married?" His tone confirmed his contempt for both *vegan* and *married*.

"I'm not a vegan," I said, ignoring the rest of his question, "but how about we meet for coffee when you're ready?"

He eyed me speculatively. "You're no soccer mom, so I guess 'relationship'?" His tone implied the quotation marks even if he didn't make the hand gesture.

I smiled and showed some teeth. "Let's allow me to at least *attempt* to be the consummate professional, shall we?" I offered my hand, and he shook it with a 'aw shucks' expression on his face.

———

I WAS ANNOYED TO FIND IT WAS PAST 1 PM WHEN I CHECKED MY phone in the car. Fending off a good-looking flirt was time consuming, and I just didn't have the extra hours today. I headed for home, since I still had to prep for two foreclosures for tomorrow, and Paige Jensen would be showing up at 5 pm. I intended to sit and walk her through everything Gerard and I had found over the weekend, in addition to all the research I'd done during the week.

I warmed up some of Hattie's excellent chili and ate it standing at the sink, looking over the bar to the dining table where I'd eaten tacos with Gerard yesterday. I had a feeling that his dining table got regular use, unlike mine. From where I stood, I could even see one of the dining chairs still had a sale tag hanging from the underside of the cushion. I scraped up the last of the chili in my bowl, wondering if he and I were as different as we seemed to be. Or maybe the difference between us was responsible for the lovely tingle I'd felt?

And speaking of Gerard, I was a bit unreasonably disappointed that he hadn't texted or called. *The disappointment was 'unreasonable,'* the feminist in me snorted, *because you haven't texted or called him either.* As I rounded the Shelton house to get to work, I would have argued that I really hadn't had time, but she'd stopped listening to me. On my office doorstep was a box with a note in Gerard's distinctive handwriting folded and taped to the top.

I unlocked the door and disarmed the alarm before giving in to the tickle of excitement. The box was a standard white florist's box, and I cut the tape holding the flaps to release the note. And then—ignoring every piece of advice my grandmother had ever given me—I set the unread note aside and opened the box. Inside was a small African violet in a peacock blue pot that just matched the upholstery on the dining chairs I'd borrowed from the Shelton sisters. The whole thing wasn't very big, and just fit on one of the bookshelves, where I nestled it beside the books my grandmother had set aside for me.

Then I read the note, which sounded just like Gerard.

· · ·

BENEDICT:

While reforesting your living and working spaces is not my respon-sibility, providing some green for those rooms is my pleasure. You can't kill this one.

G

HA. WHAT DID HE KNOW? THERE WASN'T A PLANT AROUND THAT I couldn't send to garden heaven, and I had years of dead flora to show for it, including an African violet or two. The pot looked expen-sive, though, and I wondered if his sister deserved the praise for that instead of Gerard. I took a step back to look at the whole shelf. He was right; the bit of green helped break up the creamy white of the shelves. One side of the plant seemed flat, and I started to turn it around to the back when I stopped and felt a velvety leaf. A little *too* velvety? I leaned forward to peer at it, and then realized that Gerard had sent me a fake plant—one I truly, absolutely could not kill.

———

BY THE TIME PAIGE ARRIVED, I'D STOPPED CHUCKLING ABOUT Gerard's joke, finished all the paperwork on my foreclosures for the next day, and spent some quality time harassing my client to get the bid approvals I needed for those foreclosures. While waiting on the approvals, I'd reduced all my research on Paige's great-grandparents to bullet points so that I could give her the information quickly and easily. To my surprise, I also got a call back from Dr. Amie, who'd confirmed some of what Gerard had said, and given me a bit more to consider about possible delusional disorders.

I also was able to spend a few minutes tracing the three orphans who'd survived the hurricane. Each one of them had lived and died peacefully, two of them married with children, and the third serving honorably in the military until his death in the 1950s. Try as I might, I couldn't rearrange their public records to allow them to be Jack O'Toole. I recorded the information in my notes, happy to at least have tied that loose end.

The heating that John had rearranged to include this room was working well, thank god, so when Paige came in, she was able enjoy the room after taking off her lovely coat. I laid it over one of the chairs, smoothing the fine cream wool with a touch of envy and making a mental note that some coat hooks might be nice. She turned around the room, examining the books on the shelf, and rubbing a leaf of Gerard's African violet with some surprise. She looked far more vivid than she had the day we met, her pale green sweater dress giving her face and eyes lovely color. I noticed she had some makeup on today as well and wondered if she had other meetings besides this one. Surely she hadn't dolled up just for me.

I sat behind the desk, feeling proud of the space. Paige would be my first client-guest (because Gerard didn't count at all), and I wanted to see if it imparted the same restful feeling to her that it did to me.

For the first few minutes it clearly did not. She examined all the books, even asked about the glass wall behind me, before eventually sitting down. Then she pulled a manila envelope out of the cream-colored, pebble-leather bag that matched her boots, and took her time pulling out photocopies of legal documents. She shuffled the papers, reorganizing them and separating them into piles on my desk. In the soft light of the office, her features were so delicate, and I marveled at the changes three generations could bring. I'd stacked the photos she'd left with me on one side of the desk, and the colorized picture of Eleanor O'Toole with her plane sat on top. In it, Eleanor's short curly hair blew in the breeze during the exposure and her smile was broad and free. Paige's face had the same shape as her great-grandmother's, but her smile was more hesitant, her eyes haunted by worries and concerns I didn't understand.

She finally sat back. "I pulled Eleanor's will from the probate records. I brought you a copy, but there's nothing there. Except for a few pieces of jewelry she left to her sister or my grandmother and a watch to Uncle Patrick, she left everything to Jack." She sighed, and her eyes were troubled. "She made her will a few days before she died. Would she do that if she believed he had poisoned her or something?" She passed a document across to me, but I set it aside, making some notes on my pad. "Their marriage license and his death certificate show his birthdate as September 10, 1900." She hesitated, then looked at me directly for the first time. "Lacey, is it possible you're wrong, and he *was* born in 1900?"

I wrote 'mar lic 9/10/00' on my pad and stared at it. She started to speak again, but I held up a hand to stop her, and—bless her heart—she did. I flipped back to my notes on the lockbox. The combination had been 9-1-0. September 10. Two days after the Galveston hurricane. I rubbed my forehead as I laid down my pen.

"What is it?"

"I don't think I'm wrong." I stared off at the side chairs, where I'd rested a copy of my bar license certificate, a framed document about three feet high, in preparation for hanging it this week. "When I applied to take law school courses in pursuit of my license, I had to fill out an application and go through a background check." Paige nodded in agreement—she'd had to do the same thing. "All kinds of licenses and permissions today require birth dates, copies of records and other licenses, cards and copies and certificates. Back in 1937, social security numbers didn't even exist. Copies of identification cards with pictures were simply impossible to even dream of." I rubbed my eyes and sighed. "Let's get this out of the way." I slid the composition notebooks across the desk. "Mrs. Allred's father, who worked for your great-grandfather, kept these notebooks during the years he worked for him. Almost 20 years."

She tentatively touched the top notebook, the earliest one. "It was after Eleanor died, of course, so you're not going to find anything about her in there. Or not directly. Paige, they're not going to answer some of your questions, but they begin to answer some of mine." She looked back at me sharply, her pale eyebrows beetling. "They're —upsetting."

"What do you mean?"

I paused. There just wasn't any good way to say this. "It's possible Jack was mentally ill." I sighed when I saw her frown. "Let me explain what we found, and then you can review the books themselves."

And so I did, pointing out Gerard's tabs where John Berenson had talked about Jack O'Toole and his delusions, connecting the dates we'd found to major events in the oil and gas world where Jack had been involved, and finally pointing out the links to Paige's family history. I slid a printed page to her, where I'd done a chronology, showing all the dates I'd found.

She listened pretty quietly, interrupting only a few times to clarify something. Then she took a long look at the chronology when I finished. The silence stretched to a few minutes, so I pulled over Eleanor's will and quickly paged through it and Eleanor's death certificate, which Paige had attached to the back. Eleanor had died on August 8, 1939, and her will had been executed on July 28 of that year. I noted something and started to speak, but Paige beat me to it.

"So, my great-grandfather thought someone else suffered for his good fortune? Talk about a scarcity mindset." She placed the composition book on the desk and sat back in the chair.

"I think it's a bit more than that." I opened my pad to my notes from the call with Dr. Amie and explained my relationship with the psychologist to Paige. "She said that it's a delusional disorder. The person believes that something that happens to them is connected to another—where you or I would consider it coincidence, they see a pattern there."

She leaned forward. "I get what you're saying, but there are a lot of holes there. Who was this man? If he wasn't Jack O'Toole, who was he? What did the hurricane have to do with it?" She sounded exasperated, and I didn't blame her. "Lacey, yes, thousands of people died in that hurricane, and thousands of people survived. They didn't all start having delusions about it."

I felt slightly annoyed. Her impatience was starting to bother me. I'd been engaged for less than a week on this—over the weekend—and we were attempting to solve an 80-year-old mystery. "Who knows what they did or didn't do? Dr. Amie put it this way. You and I both went through September 11, 2001, but we react to the event differently. We come to the event from different places, both experientially and biologically."

Paige sighed. "Well, that's true. I know people who've come through a divorce or a death in totally different ways."

"Exactly. And according to Dr. Amie, everything Jack experienced just confirmed his belief. Someone gets sick or hurt or dies, and —because he did well anyway—they must be connected."

She opened one of the composition books again. "He thought if he kept succeeding, something would happen to my grandmother and my mother—like Uncle Patrick's wife." She brushed away a tear. "I didn't even know about her. I wonder if my mother does."

I looked at my notes. "How might it have changed her relationship with Jack if she'd known what he went through. Maybe she would have reached out to him, invited him to her wedding..." I trailed off. "I think he told Eleanor." Her eyes met mine. "About whoever he really was."

"What makes you think so?"

I folded Eleanor's will back to the second page. "Look at how she left her estate. I'm fairly sure you're supposed to identify people by name, just in case there are any issues."

She read the provision I'd marked aloud. "'And the rest of my estate I leave to my husband, to deal with as he sees fit.' You think she did that, knowing he wasn't Jack O'Toole?"

I shrugged. "I think you could go down a rabbit hole pretty quick on whether he was her husband or not, if he used another name."

She threw the will back on the desk, groaning. "My mother is going to kill me when she finds all this out." She closed her eyes and massaged her forehead. "I'll never hear the end of it, if she was right."

"Don't tell her." She opened her eyes to roll them at me. "I'm serious. Don't tell her. Say I found nothing but some old family photos, and I bombed out on the rest of it." I grinned. "She'd love to hear I failed and fulfilled her expectations of me."

She sent me a mock frown, but I could tell she was still troubled. "I wonder if my grandmother knew, and that's why she and my mother hated him so."

"Or your uncle Patrick." I tapped the fat envelope on my desk with a finger. "I guess we'll know about that soon enough." She nodded, and I noticed again that she seemed really tired. *In for a penny*, I thought. "Are you okay?"

She looked startled, but then she smiled, a wan smile that resembled more the one I'd seen the first day we met than any others I'd seen since then. "Just dreading some confrontations. I'm not very good at them."

"With your mother about all this?"

She nodded. "That and a lot of other things." She took a deep breath. "I'm going to tell my parents about leaving Jensen." I whistled, a soft 'wow' whistle that made her grin a bit more. "Yeah. Wow. They're going to freak."

"Is this a 'hey, I'm thinking about this' or a 'hey, I'm doing this' conversation?"

She raised her eyebrows. "The latter."

"Oh." I waded into Jensen matters a bit more. "They aren't going to approve?"

"My father knows I'm not happy, but he felt he could take care of me more if I was in the family business." She sighed. "My mother doesn't want to think about the Trust, the O'Toole side of the family, or me being anything but a good Jensen. The more things about me that are like that side of my ancestry, the happier she is." She smiled ruefully. "I can't imagine what would have happened if I hadn't been born blond. She'd probably have dyed my hair as a baby."

Hm. Well, that probably explained Judith Jensen's platinum blond hair.

"So that's all happening tonight?"

"No, tomorrow night, I guess. They get home late this evening, so I thought I'd wait." She looked down at her lap, then raised her eyes, widening them slightly. "One more night's reprieve."

I laughed, then considered the time and my state of readiness for tomorrow. "Want to get dinner and practice your technique on me?"

She grinned, that full-mouthed smile that lit up her face. "I'd love to. My treat. Maybe you can give me some advice on getting my foundation started."

———

A FEW HOURS LATER, I SHOOK SOME DRIED FOOD INTO THE CAT'S bowl and was rewarded with her running into the kitchen to eat a bite before stretching and disappearing through the cat door into the Shelton side of the house.

I'd assumed Paige would want to go to one of the Highland Park standbys, but, instead, she'd taken me to Normandie, a tiny, dark place tucked into the end of a residential area on the other side of 75. Over hearty potato soup and thick pork chops with a spicy sweet apple chutney, she'd told me about her ideas for her foundation. She'd told me she wanted to make dreams come true, and her plans for doing that were broad and sweeping and unapologetically vague. When I pressed her about specifics, she'd waved her hand and said that she'd get to all that once she got going.

If she'd had no money, I told her, she'd be out of business in a few weeks. With lots of money, she could do what she wanted and not face any consequences. That troubled her. I told her about the business plan for Blackberry Bend Farm and described how detailed Mark had been in his projections. I warned her that, even with all that work and planning, it was just as likely to fail as it was to succeed. Nonprofits had an even worse failure rate than for-profit businesses—business plans often go awry.

We discussed and argued and debated for over two hours and didn't talk at all about Jack O'Toole or her parents. By the time we got through an excellent apple tart with calvados brandy butter, we'd agreed she needed to get with someone responsible to come up with a better strategy than 'making dreams come true.' She didn't want to wait to quit her job, though. She dropped me off seeming more resolute, and I admired her ability to take risks even when she wasn't sure of the outcome. At one time in my life, I admitted to myself, I was more like that.

I'd organized all my foreclosure information for the next day, put on some comfy flannel pajamas for warmth, and was considering some television before bed when there was a tap on the connecting door. Sallie was on the other side with some printouts in her hand, and she came in when I opened the door.

"I hope I didn't wake you, dear." She was wearing a thick flannel robe, her hair twisted up in a complicated knot, and she seemed hesitant. I noted with some concern her eyes were a bit red.

"Not at all. Come on in. Everything okay?"

She smiled. "Everything is fine. I've done something I hope will be helpful, but I've never meddled in your business before." She held up the copies, and I could see they were screenshots of newspaper pages. "I just couldn't get your story about the O'Tooles out of my head. That awful hurricane and all the lives lost. It just seemed so sad. So I got on the Dallas Public Library website this evening and reread the stories about it—from the contemporaneous news stories. Imagine, being in Houston or Dallas and reading about the hurricane and the lives lost." She shook her head, and I saw there were tears in her eyes. "Being hundreds of miles away and helpless."

"Oh, hey hey," I said, and put an arm around her as I led her over to the sofa to sit.

She sniffed and took a tissue out of her robe's pocket to dab her eyes. "It's just so sad. Can you imagine? Waiting for days to hear some news, to hear from your loved ones?" She shook her head again, tears welling up.

I patted her leg. "You're thinking of what it would be like to lose Hattie."

"Yes, that too. But our news today is so immediate. Back in 1900, it took days for news to get anywhere, and the bad weather slowed it down even more." Her voice shook, and I put an arm around her again. "I started with September 9, the day after the hurricane. The Sunday *Dallas Morning News* reported that all contact with the island was cut off, and rescuers couldn't get to the island at all. By Monday, they were estimating 1,000 people dead." She swallowed hard.

I didn't know what to say to her. By this time, her evident distress was making me tear up. "Sallie—"

"No, I'm all right." She sniffled and dabbed her eyes with a fresh tissue from her pocket. "By Tuesday, they were reporting on all that was lost." She shuffled the copies around and handed me one. "They mention the Catholic Orphan's Home down the island. I'm sure that's the St. Mary's one you were talking about."

I took the page and set it aside. "Okay, that's fine, but—"

"That day, they began to see the death toll would be far greater than 1,000." She gripped my hand. "That's the day they began listing the names of the dead."

I stopped in mid-squeeze. "They began—"

"I found the O'Tooles." She spoke over me. "Annie and Patrick O'Toole." The tears began to flow in earnest, her deep brown eyes so sad. "They were listed as dead in the Dallas papers on September 12, found in a house where they'd sought refuge. Along with their two daughters. No son was listed."

CHAPTER TWENTY-SEVEN

TUESDAY, MARCH 5 (CONTINUED)

It was a chilly circus at the courthouse on Tuesday morning. The sun was shining, but the illusion of warmth ended the moment a cold breeze swept in. The area designated for crying foreclosures faced north—a happenstance I believe was intentional on the part of the county commissioners, a tactic designed to keep the crowds down to a manageable level.

I'd had three foreclosures scheduled, one with an established client and two with a new out-of-state lender I'd not worked with before, but at the last minute the new client pulled one of their two files. As a result, I was almost done with the second foreclosure before the foreclosure 'specialists' found me and began squawking to get me to slow down. These two lenders really wanted to take over the property, one for rehab and one for resale, so the credit bids started really high and no casual buyers were interested anyway. I finished my reading and credit bids with chattering teeth, the small crowd dissipating immediately to find better deals.

I made a note of the time and looked up to find Gerard lounging against the low wall that separated the foreclosure area from Commerce Street. His expensive wool coat hung open to reveal an even-more expensive suit, and in one gloved hand, he carried the red scarf I'd lost Saturday night.

"I coulda used that earlier," I said.

He walked lazily toward me, and I felt something inside—my heart? my stomach?—turn over with a thump.

"Bella found it Sunday night, but I wanted to get it cleaned yesterday. It was a bit muddy." He looped it around my neck, drawing it snug but not tight.

"You had it cleaned? Same-day service?" I couldn't imagine being on top of things enough to organize that.

He raised his eyebrows. "Sancho Panza always made sure Don Quixote's armor was ready to go before he tilted with those giants," he said, and the reference to the famous story—and the framed sketch he'd given me—made me grin inside and out.

"Those 'giants' were windmills. He didn't need the armor." I fluffed the scarf to give myself something to do.

"Windmills can be quite dangerous with all those blades whipping around in the wind," he said seriously. He looked me over. "Your lips are turning blue, Benedict. Let's go get some coffee."

My teeth chattered. "Curtis already tried to give me coffee this morning at the Café."

He winced. The coffee at the Courthouse Café was awful, and he knew it. "I was hoping for Café au Lait."

"I have to go file these deeds, but the county clerk's office will be jammed right now." I rocked up on my boot heels, as if thinking it through.

He looked off to one side, considering. "It's almost lunch time now—think of downtown traffic."

I decided to add one more incentive. "Marie has just added roasted chicken salad sandwiches on croissants to the lunch menu."

He tucked my arm through his and moved us toward the plaza and the cheap pay lot where I always parked. "You had me at croissants."

———

I BROUGHT GERARD UP TO SPEED OVER FAT CROISSANTS LOADED with chicken salad. Marie was still tinkering with the recipe, but I thought this one with walnuts and cranberries was a winner. She said she might change it around seasonally, but her husband Felix was a true Frenchman and believed that, once a recipe was deemed perfect, centuries should go by before an ingredient was changed.

"Do you think it's likely our Jack O'Toole was another child of that couple?" He used a thick paper napkin to wipe his hands. His sandwich had disappeared in record time, but then he hadn't paused to make sure each bite of sandwich was balanced with the crunch of a Café au Lait-made potato chip the way I did. He ate one or two chips, and then pushed his plate forward. I considered reaching over and snagging one of the pile he'd left, but I didn't feel comfortable eating off his plate.

I finished chewing a bite of chicken salad that had fallen to my plate from the sandwich, which I'd scooped up with my last chip. "I'm not sure we'll ever know." I dusted the crumbs from my hands.

"How did Paige take it?"

I swirled the last of my latte around in the cup, watching the dregs of the coffee darken the cooling milky liquid. I set it aside. I don't see much point in drinking cold coffee. "She was understandably upset. She's just not sure how her mother will take all this."

"Don't tell her."

I beamed at him. "I know! That's what I said. Judith doesn't have to know."

He looked off to one side. "Of course, if she finds out later, and knows her daughter didn't tell her, it could be worse than telling her now. Relationships with mothers are fraught with peril."

I wouldn't know, I thought, but didn't say it aloud. He seemed sad, and I wondered what his relationship with his mother was like. At the counter, Esther was sliding a tray of cinnamon knots under the glass. "I, uh, think I'm going to have another latte. Want one?"

He looked back at me and the sadness lifted as he smiled, a cat's satisfied smile. "I already bought a dozen of those cinnamon knots. Esther's keeping them warm for us."

I sat staring at him for a moment before deliberately sliding our plates to one side and leaning across the narrow table. Then I pulled him to me by his lapels and kissed him like he'd kissed me on Sunday night, hard and deliberate, before leaving him to go to the counter. Behind me, I could hear him laughing, a surprised, joyful belly laugh that warmed the places coffee couldn't reach.

———

PAIGE FOUND US THERE AN HOUR LATER, ARGUING THE RELATIVE merits of the different type of pizza. Gerard, of course, had taken the 'different pizza for different moods' position, but I argued for Neapolitan cracker-thin crust. Esther had come out from behind the kitchen to weigh in for a hot slice straight from the oven on the streets of New York, and some guy who was eavesdropping tried to argue for Detroit-style, which just blew my mind.

"Chicago style is bad enough, with the sauce and cheese and stuff all mixed up and in the wrong places, and now you're going to try to convince me to move them around again?"

Gerard's voice was mild. "Benedict, have you been in Chicago or Detroit in the winter?" I grudgingly nodded. "Then you know why they need hearty and filling pie. Maybe it's too much for Dallas, but..." The stranger nodded vigorously, and I thought in a moment they'd fist bump or hug or something.

"Do you two want to be alone?" They laughed and the stranger went back to his laptop while I stared at Gerard. "Chocolate chip cookies are not going to be enough, Gerard. This reasonableness is going to be trouble."

"It's because he's a Libra," Esther intoned, nodding her head so that her graying dreadlocks shook.

"Are you?" I didn't know why that might be important, but I could maybe figure it out later.

He shrugged.

"Or a Virgo," Esther added with less certainty.

Gerard shrugged again.

"Who's a virgin?" Paige said as she took off her coat. I snickered at the pained look on Gerard's face. "And Lacey, do you ever answer your phone?"

Gerard stood up. "No, she doesn't."

Paige looked from him to me and back to him, then stuck her hand out. "I'm Paige."

He shook her hand. "And I'm Rob Gerard. And this is Esther." He indicated the Gemini, who waved as she went back to the counter.

"Esther and I are well-acquainted. She is the keeper of the cinnamon knots." Paige smiled at Gerard, her polite and other-worldly smile, and then threw me her real one—the deep, wide grin. "I need coffee." She went off to the counter, a lithe figure in the tiniest jeans I'd ever seen topped by a beautifully soft, cloudy gray sweater.

I looked at Gerard. "Well, are you a book or a virgin?"

"A book?"

"Isn't that what a libra is, like in Spanish?"

He chuckled. "I have a feeling you know exactly what it is." He smiled at Paige. "It's nice to meet you, Miss Jensen. You and Benedict have a lot to talk about, I'm sure, so I'll leave you two alone."

"Oh, don't rush off." She was polite, but I think we both knew she was hoping he'd leave.

Gerard smiled at her, and then shrugged on his beautiful coat.

With a smile for me and a brush of his hand down my arm, he was gone.

Paige watched him leave, and then gave me that big smile again. "He likes you," she said, with extra emphasis on the *you*.

I felt my cheeks flame up. "You want to pass him a note in study hall for me?"

She laughed. "Okay, I'll leave you be." She smiled for a second more, and then grew serious. "I called my uncle Peter—you know, my mom's younger brother. I thought he should know what was going on."

"Did he have any relationship with your great-grandfather?"

She shook her head. "He said my grandmother—his mother—told him that her father was a devil, to be avoided at all costs. She said Jack killed Eleanor."

I gawked. "She said those words?" She nodded, eyes wide. "But you don't believe that."

She sighed and took a sip of her cappuccino. "No, I don't. And Uncle Peter doesn't either." She set her cup in the saucer with a faint clink. "He said that he didn't have much of a relationship with Jack—with my great-grandfather. By the time Peter met him, Jack was an old man, very quiet. Jack sent both Peter and my mother presents—birthdays, holidays, even saint's days, which my grandmother said was a sin."

"And your mother hated him anyway."

She nodded. "The whole time I was talking to him, I wanted to tell him about all this, but I don't feel like it's my story to tell. I think it's Patrick's." She grimaced. "Whatever story there is to tell. So my great-grandfather—who was an amazing businessman, it sounds like—had some mental problem that made him think that his good luck canceled out other people's, and they were in such danger from his good luck that he had to abandon them or leave them completely alone."

"Well, when you put it that way..."

She rolled her eyes. "It sounds just as crazy as it is." She adjusted her cup in the saucer. "I was hoping there was something—you know, a real reason for—"

"For your mother hating him?" She nodded. "Why is that important?"

Paige sighed. "My family is constantly rocked by her hatred. She and my uncle Peter don't make a big deal about it, but they barely speak. He can't take her wild, crazy swings of emotion." I didn't respond, so she kept talking. "I've tried to just live with it, adjust to it. I can't. As long as I'm working for Jensen, working with my family—"

"You have to humor her?" She nodded. "Paige, that's just an excuse. It doesn't matter what you find or don't find about your family. You have to deal with your mother and your independence." I laughed. "Your great-grandmother gave you what you needed. No excuses."

She smiled. "I always had what I needed. The money will just help me make a difference." She checked the time on her phone. "I need to leave. Patrick's flight gets in at 4, and I want to be there by the time he gets out of customs and immigration."

I reached into my bag and pulled out the thick envelope with 'Patrick' written on it. "Ready?" I asked her.

"Ready or not." She took the envelope and slid it into her bag, and then stood up and put her coat on, giving Esther a smile and wave as she left.

Esther came over to clear the cups. "That's a real nice girl." She stacked several cups within each other. "You can tell she comes from rich people, but she doesn't act like it. She's polite to everyone." She paused, balancing the cup stack and the empty cinnamon knots plate, and gave me a significant look. "We get a lot of people in here, you know, from the rich parts of town. But you can always tell quality people. Some have money, some don't, but the best ones shine regardless. My mother used to say, 'blood will tell,' and she was right." With a firm nod, she took herself off to the kitchen.

———

I WENT BACK DOWNTOWN TO RECORD THE DEEDS FROM THE morning's foreclosure, standing in line for only a few minutes now that most of the day's rush had passed. I checked my phone while I waited, noting that I had missed calls from Paige and a number I didn't recognize. The voicemail was from Bette Christensen, Shanna Barry's friend in Chicago. She'd be in town this weekend and next week and wanted to meet to discuss a new matter. She left her mobile number, so I texted her and we agreed on a time next Monday. I basked in the possible new-client glow until I got to the clerk, whose scanner wasn't working. We commiserated on the failure of technology as she rebooted her computer and the scanner a few times, until she finally gave up and used another scanner. I was her last customer of the day, and she thanked me for being patient.

As I walked away, I wondered what my blood said about me. Who knew where I came from, when it came down to it? Those first Dalton men who came from nowhere became just who they wanted to be. Did that mean they weren't 'quality people'?

Paige texted me when she dropped Patrick O'Toole off at Hotel Zaza, a quirky luxury hotel in Uptown. Apparently, he was in the Zaza Suite, the nicest suite in the hotel, and would meet us downstairs at the Dragonfly at 10 am tomorrow.

By the time I got home, Paige had called twice and texted me three times. Patrick O'Toole wanted to meet us that evening at 7 pm, and he'd told Paige to bring her mother.

———

I WAS EARLY TO THE ZAZA. I'D SPENT 30 MINUTES TRYING ON and then discarding various outfits, all of which were currently piled on my bed. Nothing seemed to be perfect for the occasion, which I'd judged to be 'dysfunctional-family-meets-to-discuss-problematic-ancestor.' Who knew what was appropriate for that? I'd finally ended up with jeans and a light blue sweater with boots, which was what I'd started with earlier. I did brush my hair and put on some makeup, although I'd lost the lipstick I'd worn Saturday night on my date with Gerard, probably somewhere in the mad dash up the hill in Chapel Park.

I spent a few minutes cleaning and polishing the medal I'd found behind the house, using some of the polish I found in the Sheltons' laundry room. The little disk was clearly silver, and I thought perhaps valuable, so I slid it into my coat pocket before leaving for the Zaza, jacket on. They were promising 80 degrees by week's end, but I didn't believe it just yet.

I thought about having a quick drink at the Dragonfly bar (for courage), but I was a bit afraid to have alcohol on my breath going into the meeting with Judith. Instead, I sat on a bench framed in longhorn horns in the lobby, flipping through messages on my phone, the blue lockbox on the bench next to me.

I texted Gerard: *About to meet with Patrick O'Toole and Judith Jensen—a day early.*

He texted back immediately: Courage.

I repeated that to myself a few times as I waited. I had a clear view of the front doors, and I didn't recognize the luxury car that pulled into the drive. Judith waited until one of the valets had opened the driver's door, and then she stepped out, a slender figure dressed completely in winter white. From the creamy cashmere two-piece sweater dress to the off-white leather knee boots, she looked like the ice-queen I think she saw herself to be. She couldn't help but see me as she swept inside but didn't look in my direction as I stood.

I walked toward the front desk as Paige followed her mother inside, and I wondered how she'd managed to get her mother here. She'd changed into black slacks from the jeans she'd been wearing earlier, but still wore the soft gray sweater. She'd pulled her hair up into a tight French twist and added pearls and black suede heels, but

I thought the whole outfit looked more like the Paige I'd been meeting with lately and less like the one I met at her mother's house a few weeks ago. It gave me hope. We exchanged significant looks and turned toward the elevator bank.

Judith had pressed the seventh-floor button and stabbed the 'up' button impatiently when we joined her. The doors opened, and she entered and turned to face the opening. Paige and I slid around her to the back wall, exchanging another look at each other behind her mother's back. I took the medal out of my pocket and handed it to Paige. *For luck,* I mouthed silently. She slid it into the pocket of her slacks as the doors opened on the seventh floor.

Rather than hanging back, Judith strode forward as soon as the doors opened, as if by getting to the door first she could move this unpleasant duty along. She rapped smartly along on the door to the Zaza Suite and waited with a tapping foot for it to be opened.

Patrick O'Toole was exactly as I expected. His white beard was closely cropped, and the waxed ends of his moustache curved upwards. He had his father's eyes: the black and white pictures hadn't done justice to the oddly silver color of the iris, with thick black lashes and brows. In Patrick's tanned face, the silver eyes were the first thing you saw when you looked at him.

"Hello, Judith." He didn't offer a hand or a hug, just dipped his head slightly and opened the door wide. When he stepped back, Judith continued her march, surging past him as if he wasn't there, saying nothing to her uncle at all.

Paige stopped to give him a hug that was warmly reciprocated, and she introduced me. He was tall, very tall, and he stooped slightly. He was 84, after all, but even so, his handclasp was strong, and he seemed much younger than his age.

"I've had coffee and tea and something stronger sent up," he said as he shut the door behind us.

This suite was huge, the rooms painted in a muted taupe, heavy drapes in deep wine velvet at the windows. The whole place looked like someone's idea of how Paris would look, if you had a vivid imagination propped up by movies from the 1930s. A full silver tea set graced the dining table, with liquid-filled crystal decanters and high-ball glasses on a silver tray, and fruit and cheese on a snowy white china plate. I'd never seen this kind of service at a hotel, but then I didn't usually stay at the four-star ones.

Judith placed herself at the far end of the table and crossed her arms with the expression you'd usually see on a teenager forced to eat dinner with the family. Paige sat a safe distance away, and I waited for Patrick to sit at the other end before I sat across from Paige. I accepted a cup of tea, and he added a tiny macaron to the saucer. Judith watched the whole process, her body held rigid.

"Why is *she* here?" No one at the table pretended not to know it was me she was referring to.

"I asked her to be here," Paige said, surprising both me and her mother. "She was responsible for finding the box." She took a deep breath. "She also discovered a lot of information about my great-grandfather that we didn't know."

Judith drew in a shaky breath, and I realized her rigidity was anger. "Paige, I specifically told you to leave it alone." She unfolded her arms and carefully placed her hands on the table. "This is a family matter, and we need to know nothing more about *that man*."

Patrick spoke. "Judith, 'that man' is my father."

She looked directly at him for what was probably the first time since we'd come into the room. "You have my sympathy for that, at least."

I looked from her face to her uncle's. While their coloring was different, it was clear they were related. The shape of Jack O'Toole's eyes that was more diluted in Paige was strong in both Judith and Patrick, and all three had versions of the wide, unsmiling mouth in Jack O'Toole's pictures.

"Mother." Paige's voice was quiet, but firm. "Patrick's father left him an envelope in the lockbox, and Patrick asked us to be here because he's read it. I think it's important."

Judith shook her head, but more in sadness this time. "This is going to change everything, Paige, *everything*. You should have left well enough alone."

Paige reached a hand out to her mother, but Judith shook her head and sat back in her chair, lips firm, her hands folded tightly together.

Patrick slid the thick sheaf of paper out of the envelope and unfolded them carefully, then handed the typed pages to Paige. "I think you should be the one to read this. Out of all of us, you are the one who can best move life forward with the knowledge." Paige gave him a look, but she accepted the letter and began to read aloud.

CHAPTER TWENTY-EIGHT

M y dearest son,
        I was born near Galveston in 1892. Or at least, I think it was 1892. As with so many things, the actual number becomes irrelevant past a certain age. My parents struggled to farm a barren plot of land, barely producing enough for us to eat, let alone extra to sell. In the early months of 1899, a fever took my father and two sisters during a killing frost that had plunged to south Texas, setting records that would last for years. The little girls went first, two pale wraiths who were delicate and lovely and good, and they died silently, their last breaths so quiet it was hard to know when they'd passed. My father fought death for days, and I believe it was because he knew that he was leaving me and my mother alone that he held out as long as he did.

There was no way my mother and I could work the farm alone, so we closed up the tiny, weather-beaten house, set the one raw-boned cow loose, and walked the miles to get to a boat to come to Galveston Island. She had no formal education and no skills—other than those required to keep a small family alive during a time of immense poverty. *Those skills were not needed in Galveston in those days. The rich loved the seaside resort, swimming in the sparkling water, sunning themselves on the beaches, driving up and down the crowded streets. I had no way to know that the beautiful buildings we passed as we walked down the lanes were simply the homes of the wealthy—I thought they were palaces with kings and queens and princesses.*

My mother was able to convince the head housekeeper at the Tremont Hotel that she was hardy enough work in the laundry, while I earned pennies running errands for the hotel's wealthy patrons. Laundry before machines was impossibly difficult work, and at the end of every day, she would come back to the tiny room we shared in Mrs. Curley's boardinghouse on Church Street looking more tired, more pale. Finally, one morning, a few months after we had come to Galveston, she was unable to rise from bed and wouldn't respond to me when I called her name. Mrs. Curley brought cold cloths and shooed me from the room, but there was no money for a doctor. She died a few days later without rousing to speak to me again. She was buried in a pauper's grave, a good woman given no reward for her life.

I was tall for my age and strong, but I was still too young to be taken aboard a ship or work on the docks or the railroad, and with no one to vouch for me, I was not able to find a job. Mrs. Curley was a devout Catholic, and she believed in Christian charity. She fed me for a few days until we decided that I should go with her and her priest to the Sisters of Charity and ask to be taken in as an orphan. The sisters asked me about my parents and my faith, but even though I could not remember being baptized, they agreed to take me.

And that is how it was, just a few months over a year later, on September 8, 1900, I was one of the boys at the Orphan Asylum when a great hurricane rolled into the harbor and claimed more than 6,000 lives on Galveston Island. Even now, almost 80 years later, it is difficult for me to think of that day and the ones that followed, much less to speak of them. With one exception, I have never spoken of them to anyone, but perhaps it is time to tell the story of that young boy, the one who became Jack O'Toole, but who was born with another name.

The nuns were good to us. They were part of an order that believed in Christian charity, and their devotion to duty was one we children did not understand. Most of the nuns had come directly from France or Canada. They spoke French or a bit of English, but the masses were said in Latin, the priests intoning the words and believing that our souls were already lost, or at least sure to face purgatory. Many of the children were the sole survivors when fevers had rolled through the community and taken their families, and almost none of us knew anything about religion or duty or love. Every day seemed to bring another punishment at first, but the sisters persevered, teaching us that life here on earth was misery and heaven would bring reward. For we children, heaven was a full belly and a warm bed, and we followed the rules so that we were allowed to stay. We were taught our lessons and how to read the Bible, and we learned to pray for our grievous sins. We didn't speak of our losses, but sometimes the little ones whimpered at night for their mothers.

The nuns usually began our day leading us in prayer before break- fast, and they ended it watching us pray kneeling next to our beds. There were two dormitory buildings right there on the beach, one for the girls and one for the boys, and our days were ordered, but not unhappy, and I enjoyed the peaceful consistency of our chores and lessons. Oftentimes, especially in the heat of the summer, the sisters would allow us to play in the sand or the tidal pools on the other side of the fence at the water's edge, and I would stand there, looking out at the water, watching the gulls wheeling as they fished. The water is terrifyingly restless, always moving, never the same from one day to the next. I never ventured into the water as it lapped the shore, but the cool breezes off the water and the endless ebb and flow of the Gulf still live in my memory.

The day of the hurricane was a Saturday. The weather had been very hot and humid for days, but that day, the air carried a heaviness that foretold of something evil. Or perhaps that is just my imagination, so many years later, knowing how the day ended. The air felt heavy all day, and the sea was angry. It was difficult to breathe. It rained off and

on for much of the day, and we kept the doors and windows open for
breezes that became gusts as the evening approached. None of the boys
were talking or laughing as usual, and it didn't take a rap from Sister
Catherine or Father Michael to quiet us. Sister Elizabeth had been in
town, but she came in just as the winds were rising and the rain
pounded hard through the open windows. Supper was a crust of bread
that most of us didn't eat. Thunder shook the buildings and lightning
flashed in the sky, sending the little girls into tears every time. The
sisters and the priests spoke together quietly, urgently, and then moved
all of us over to the girls' dormitory just as the rain began to pelt down
in the darkness. We were all terrified as the winds began to whistle
through the cracks around the outside doors. They moved us to the
second floor when water began to rush in, and they led us in hymns
and prayers as the winds began to tear the walls apart. I remember
pain and water, and then nothing.

When I awoke, I was mostly dry, but the pain was stronger, and
opening my eyes caused my stomach to heave. Someone held me as I
gave up what little I had eaten, and then I lay there and drifted in and
out. When I awoke again, I was on a sodden mattress with two other
children, one boy and one girl, and we had all been injured in one way
or another. Candles lit the sweltering darkness, and I wasn't to know
until later that I had slept the whole day through, and it was Sunday
night.

Trying to rise made me ill, so I lay there, listening to the groans of
other injured people, not knowing what had happened or where I was.
At some point, I heard the boy next to me begin to whimper and moan,
and I reached out a hand and patted him, which seemed to calm him. I
couldn't see him very well, but he seemed older than I, and I fancied
him a bit less tough, since I too was injured but had more fortitude
than to moan aloud. I lay there in a twilight sleep, and when a woman
brought me some water, I drank. I had a bandage around my head, and
I could tell by feeling that I had a gash across my forehead, just where
my hair met my brow.

The girl was carried away at some point, and I do not know if she lived or died. The boy and I slept on, but it became clear that I was becoming more sensible, while he was becoming ever more feverish. In the early morning hours, he cried out in pain, and I tried to comfort him by telling him that everything would be all right. He seemed to understand, and then he asked for his mother. I had no idea where his mother was, but I told him she was near and would come for him soon. I told him my name, and I asked him for his. He told me he was Jack O'Toole, and his parents were Patrick and Annie, his sisters Shiobhan and Meghan. For a while in the dark, he told me about his favorite times, bathing in the ocean or listening to the angel voice of his mother singing, and his fear that he was dying and would never see his mother's blue eyes again. He cried a bit, and I brushed those tears away, for he said his arms were too heavy to raise. His fever burned hot, and the woman caring for us fretted over him and said that help would come with the sunrise. He soon slept, a deep and unnatural sleep that I now know was a coma, and when morning came, he could not be roused. A priest came, one unfamiliar to me, and gave Jack O'Toole the last rites, but he was gone long before Jack breathed his last.

I stayed next to him, and I cried for him when he died, but when they came for him and asked his name, God forgive me, I told them I did not know. Worse, when they asked me for mine, I gave them the name of the boy who had cried for his mother Annie and his father Patrick.

Looking back now, I wonder at my naivete. Even then, in the Galveston of 1900, people's identities were registered and known. Galveston had for years published directories of people, with names and addresses and sometimes familial connections, and censuses were taken meticulously. I didn't think of that then. I just knew that I wanted to be Jack O'Toole, with family who would miss me, with a history and memories of swimming and singing and laughing. I even told myself that the fact that his mother and mine shared the same name was God's way of saying what I did was forgivable, if not absolutely correct. He was not so different from me, I told myself, about my age and height, and with the same dark hair and blue eyes. In my injured and exhausted mind, I was simply standing in for him, giving him and his life a little longer time in the world.

The man who spoke with me later that day and wrote Jack's name on a list of survivors told me that many had died in the storm, but I was afraid to ask questions or offer information, so I simply nodded and kept quiet. It would be days before I heard that almost all of the orphans and all of the nuns from the orphanage had perished when the gulf and the bay became one in the midst of the hurricane's wrath.

My head healed, for I was a healthy lad, and I began to help the kind couple who had found me and Jack O'Toole atop the filthy mud and debris outside their house after the storm had moved on that night. Their house had survived, but it was surrounded by lumber and the detritus that had washed up against their walls. For days we picked through the piles, finding dead animals and things I shudder to remember even now. I worked as hard as I could, and, at night on my mattress, I dreamed that they might keep me there with them, that I would have some kind of home. If they didn't want me, I would go back to the farm and live the best way I knew how, but I knew I would leave Galveston.

Those dreams were ripped apart two weeks after the hurricane, when Jack O'Toole's uncle Donal found me.

Donal O'Toole was a tough and shrewd man in his thirties, dark-headed like me and Jack, with piercing blue eyes and a rough manner. He and his brother Patrick had come to America from County Cork, Ireland in 1886, along with Patrick's wife Annie. Rather than staying in the east as so many of their countrymen did, they decided to passenger on a cargo ship to Galveston. Donal went north for work on the miles of railroad track being built in the state, while Patrick and Annie stayed in Houston. They had brought their family to Galveston only weeks before so that Patrick could work on the docks, helping to load the bales of cotton that would ship out of the harbor.

While he had exchanged letters with his brother, Donal hadn't seen his nephew Jack in almost eight years.

Word had reached him in a railroad work camp of the hurricane and its devastation, and he had left the last job he had to come see what had become of his brother's family. He'd gone to the Customs House and inquired for help with the lists of the names of the dead. Patrick and Annie and their daughters were listed, but not his nephew Jack. He'd asked and listened until he found the house where I had found refuge.

I listened to Donal O'Toole telling me about his travels to Galveston and his search for his nephew with growing alarm, for I realized that my assumption of Jack's identity, while perhaps innocent at the time, would have terrible implications now. Donal's words ceased, and he waited for me to speak, but my terror robbed me of any voice or thought. We sat and stared at each other for minutes. Finally, he slapped his thighs with his calloused hands and told me we were going back to Houston, for there was no money to be made in Galveston. I had no belongings, but I said my thanks to the couple who'd saved my life and left with Donal O'Toole.

There were as yet no clear streets in Galveston on the day we walked to the bayside docks. Debris was piled everywhere, and the stench of the smoke from the fires that consumed the bodies of the dead still hung about to make your stomach turn. Donal walked steadily without turning his head to either side, but I gawked, realizing that homes and businesses had once filled the spaces that yawned between the buildings. The Tremont Hotel where my mother had worked still stood, and I averted my head as we passed, afraid someone would recognize me and call my name. That fear never left me, and I have not returned to Galveston, even though it would be unlikely someone would see that child in the man I became.

We left Galveston on a boat, which was the only way to leave the island in that time, since the bridges had washed away with the hurricane. Donal didn't ask me if I wanted to stay in Galveston or say goodbye to anyone. Once he was ready to leave, nothing would have stopped him.

Donal was a quiet man with a gift for making things happen. Although he could neither read nor write anything but his name, he listened better than anyone I have ever known. While other men would fill their days with idle nonsense and chatter, Donal might go a full day without saying a word to me. I found the silence reassuring, since I would not have known what to say to him to avoid arousing suspicion that I was not who I claimed to be.

It was his habit of listening that made me the rich man I became. Donal had listened as travelers talked around fires on the trails we walked, at beer halls where we would drink, or at chophouses where we and other unmarried men would eat. The talk in the late days of 1900 was about Galveston's hurricane and the destruction of its wharves, which would move in the next decade to Houston, with its ship channel and weather-protected docks. He would tell employers that I was his orphaned nephew, and I would work alongside him on wharves and docks and railroad works to earn the money to eat, and we would sleep under a roof if we were given the opportunity, under the stars if we were not.

Once in Houston, Donal's listening provided a stake for us that set me on the path to millions. Out on his own looking for work, Donal overheard two men talking about a fund that had been quietly set up for survivors of the hurricane. People whose families had been wiped out could, upon the attestation of an adult, receive a cash payment to help them in their recovery. Contributions had been pouring in from all over the country, and the survivor fund, as it came to be known, would allow survivors to make a fresh start. Donal saw no reason that I should not present myself at the offices of The Houston Post, which was administering the fund. I saw every reason not to go, for my nightmares were, by this time, filled with fear that my deception would be discovered, and I would be revealed for the fraud I was. Donal insisted, however, and he accompanied me on the errand, swearing that I was indeed his nephew Jack O'Toole, and that I had lost my entire family in the storm. All these years have passed, and I still remember the sound of the running presses in the background as Donal and I met with the man charged with overseeing the funds. I can still smell the ink on his hands as he patted my shoulder and told me how fortunate I was to have survived when my family did not. I had scarce left the building before I ran to the gutter to throw up. Donal watched me but did not speak. He helped me up from my knees, and we walked on.

The talk in Houston was also of oil. The search at the time was for oil that could be used as kerosene or lamp oil or oil for lubricating machinery, and reserves in the east had petered out. We'd only been in Houston a few weeks when we heard of new wells being drilled at Beaumont. Men who discussed the goings-on over their beer were derisive about the amount of money being spent, but Donal was intrigued enough to pay for tickets for us to travel to Beaumont on the rail cars, which traveled the 90-mile trip in a frightening four hours. Once there, Donal set to listening for days to the talk of the oil drilling, and our futures were set.

Donal had an uncanny ability to find raw, undrilled land where oil was buried thousands of feet deep. He told me that land where oil was to be found had a particular 'smell,' and perhaps it did to him, but I was never able to detect it. Countless times over the next fourteen years of my life, I would watch Donal pace ground before we offered money for the land, and I became the owner of property.

For Donal bought the first parcels we purchased with the money from the survivor's fund. Without any discussion, the land would be placed in my name, with Donal as my guardian. Those first few plots of land around Beaumont were purchased for fifty-five cents an acre and sold after the discovery of oil at Spindletop for hundreds of times that amount, or even more. To my dismay, every transaction multiplied the stake amount and my shame. When we needed funds for travel or food, we would work driving wagons of goods to Houston or digging in the canals near Jefferson or even driving spikes for the thousands of miles of railroads being built, but the money we made from land speculation was saved for the purchase of more land, either for oil or for access to oil. We prospered—oh, how we prospered! And through it all, Donal watched and listened.

I could not detect oil under the land as Donal could, but I learned how things worked in the business of oil exploration. While Donal listened and collected information, I read newspapers from every city I could find, dreaming of someday leaving south Texas behind. Our stake grew as the oil boomed and the railroads spread, and we finally stopped carrying cash and gold on our persons, opening our first bank account at a big bank in Houston with more than $10,000, what we felt was a fortune. We saw the benefit of diversification, and many other accounts at other banks followed. When the papers I read began to hint in 1909 that cash reserves might be low, we withdrew our funds and held them while the rest of the country panicked. While Donal could smell oil, I could smell trouble, and we were able to find one and avoid the other for almost fifteen years.

We bought and sold land before every major oil discovery from 1901 to 1915. We never drilled ourselves, since Donal thought that the need to find and drill for oil was an addiction much like that of the opium eaters, and every oil man we saw eventually came to a bad end. We never swindled anyone, but sometimes buyers eventually found oil, and sometimes they did not. If they did not, and Donal was sure oil was beneath the land, we would buy the land back for what was paid to us. If someone was unhappy about the deal we had made, we never left town in the night, but worked the deal all the way through and then left to find the next one in another place. The one time we did not was the one time we should have.

We had made our way south in early 1915, creeping ever closer to the coast, and my sense of dread rose with every mile. We had never spoken about the hurricane, but sometimes there would be a mention Galveston or the storm, and Donal would watch me closely until the moment passed. That year was different. According to his uncle, Jack O'Toole would have turned 25 in September 1915, and for some reason, the year and the landmark it represented weighed on my shoulders like a yoke.

In July of that year, we bought forty acres outside of Brazoria from a man named Thomas Crittenden, whose family had owned the land since Texas became a state, paying him $1,000. The land was salty and dry and would never be good for farming. We resold some of the

land almost immediately to an exploration company for more than
$20,000, since drilling had started in the area. When the deed was
filed, someone told Crittenden the amount of the second sale, and he
announced in front of witnesses he would 'kill those speculators.' Two
weeks later, as Donal paced the ground in western Brazoria county,
someone fired a shot from a stand of salt cedars, hitting him in the
upper thigh. The surveyor and I tried to stop the bleeding, but to no
avail. As he died, he looked into my eyes and said, "Family is more
than blood."

I stayed long enough for the inquest and arrest of Thomas Crittenden, and to sell the rest of his land. Three days later, on August 17,
1915, another hurricane hit Galveston, and I left Texas with more
than a million dollars, all the money we had made from my $500 stake
in 1900, not to return until I came to Dallas in 1930.

The money gave me no joy or pleasure. I don't know how Donal
viewed it, but for me, the money was simply a wall, one that kept the
waves of hardship and deprivation from breaching the tiny place of
safety I had found. The few times I took part of the money in the early
days and spent it, I was drenched in anxiety, quickly replacing the
funds as if filling a hole in the wall. Later, I would gamble with God,
giving to his servants a part of the winnings I would gain. Even giving
it away did not end my suffering, for I only made more.

I would look at the financial records with only trepidation and
fear, growing more certain every year that I did not deserve such riches,
had not personally paid for the luck that came my way. You and I have
spoken of my travels but, unlike you, I was not an explorer. I ran from
place to place, trying to outrace the awful fortune that followed me,
seeking peace and an answer to God's terrible judgment on me. I am
ashamed of how I lived, how I prospered during those difficult years.
Everywhere I went, my luck held, and I became even more rich while
others did not. My secret burned inside me, but I could not confess it to
anyone. When America entered the first war, I considered volunteering, but I had no papers to show my identity, and I feared discovery.
Even more, I feared that my good luck would hold in battle and would

rob other men—more deserving men—of theirs, like it had robbed Donal of his life, and how it would rob your mother of hers.

Oil should have brought me back to Dallas. The oilmen were still rolling after the 1929 crash, but funding was not available to them. I had made a name for myself financing the riskier aspects of exploration and production, and that meant I was seen as both wealthy and willing to gamble. I was in Florida in January of 1930 when Edward Hartsfield's telegram came. Even though I had left the state, the Dallas and Houston papers were sent to me regularly, and I worked my way backwards through past issues for reports about Hartsfield to decide if I would help him.

It was in the issue for Sunday, September 1, 1929 that I found my reason to return. She was glorious, your mother. She'd completed the Women's Air Derby, an all-woman cross-country flying competition, and the newspaper had a photo of her standing next to her plane, her eyes sparkling and her hair blowing in the wind. 'Eleanor Hartsfield,' it read, 'the Soaring Socialite.' She had the loveliest smile I've ever seen, then or now. I had no romance in my heart then, so I cannot say I fell in love at the first sight I had of her face, but I know it cracked that hard rock in my chest. I was a middle-aged man by then, or so I thought, and I had no idea of love or desire. I looked through the papers I had saved for other mentions of her, but there was none, not even a society page mention. But I had made up my mind, and I would return to Texas for the first time since the second Galveston hurricane.

I met Edward Hartsfield in his office at his bank, and eagerly hoped for a picture of her, but there were none behind or on his desk. It was a tense exchange: Hartsfield was defensive and hated being in the position of seeking investment, but he truly had no choice. A group of his employees had embezzled funds to fund purchases of stock market shares totaling millions, and he had propped up the bank with his own money several times in order to keep panics from crippling the bank after the crash of '29. By the time he met me, his personal fortune was gone. To recoup it, he needed more than investment. He needed a partner.

I knew what I wanted, and I was willing to spend my fortune to get it. It was the work of a moment to be given an invitation to first dinner, and then a society event at his home. I planted myself in a hotel downtown and planned an advance worthy of any general. Eleanor was living at home, and reluctantly attended the event planned by Edward and his wife Gertrude. She was seated next to me, at my request, and was singularly unimpressed by me. I had been told I resembled Howard Hughes, who was a popular figure in Hollywood by that time, but Eleanor had met Hughes and despised him for his cavalier attitude toward women and planes. She told me so at dinner before giving me her back to speak with her other dinner companion.

I am ashamed to tell you that I bought your mother, as surely as if I had purchased her at auction. I learned her airplane was gone, sold to help sustain her family's finances, and her dreams with it. I fantasized about marrying her and presenting her with a new plane, making every one of her dreams come true. I would give her jewels and beautiful clothes and homes across the world. I proposed, but she refused. Undeterred, I proposed again, to be refused again. Finally, I appealed to her father for help, but he told me that he had long ago given up hope for his willful, independent 26-year-old daughter. I spoke with her mother, who thought me besotted, and begged her to speak with Eleanor and intercede on my behalf. It was almost my undoing, for Eleanor was angry that I would use her parents, who had been through so much.

She raged at me, and she was not a woman who was prone to rage. Her sunny disposition was known to everyone. But she raged at me, accusing me of the worst motives, and of that she was right. I was selfish and crude and cold, and she wanted nothing to do with me. I promised if she would marry me, I would help her father, and I would make her happy.

Instead, I brought her misery.

We married on Saturday, June 21, 1930 outside her parents' home in Highland Park, under a willow tree in their garden, and everyone thought she was the loveliest bride they'd ever seen. I don't think she spoke a word the entire day besides those required to legalize our union. She'd barely spoken to me since she'd agreed to marry me in April. On the Monday after we married, I had $5,000,000 deposited into an account in her name. I became her father's partner, but I didn't know about the trust your mother created for your sister until much later.

I tried to be a good husband to her. I never strayed or even looked at another woman while she was alive. I made it clear that the funds I had transferred to her were hers alone, and I made sure she never wanted for anything. We rented a home near the lake, and she would walk every day to the water, staring out over it like a lover stood on the other side.

Throughout it all, she was pleasant and detached, as if her life was not hers to live. She loved you and Leona, finding in you both some of the joy she seemed to have lost upon our marriage. Until you were born, she treated me with a distant familiarity, as if she was on the other side of a glass wall. I tried to be kind and loving, but she didn't love me, and I had never known how to inspire such an emotion in someone else. I made sure she wanted for nothing, but of course, no matter how lovely, a cage is still a cage. She never flew again, no matter that I encouraged her almost daily to find a plane to buy and fly. She didn't refuse, but she simply never engaged with me in any discussion regarding aviation.

Something changed when you were born. Perhaps it was because I had learned, ever so slightly, how hungry I was for love—your love, your mother's love—and I resolved to be worthy of it. I rarely did any financing by then. We had enough money for several lifetimes, and I simply wanted to spend all my time with your mother, trying to make her happy. She seemed to thaw towards me and would sometimes laugh with me over you and your attempts to turn over, then crawl, then walk. I soaked up each moment given me.

Life changed again the year before your sister's birth. We had attended the Exposition at Fair Park, and in the Hall of State were photographs of Texas. For the first time in more than three decades, I saw Galveston and the beaches I remembered from my childhood. That night, I cried out in my sleep from the nightmares that haunted me, and your mother comforted me, holding me while I wept. For some reason, she softened to me then, and seemed to begin to care for me. We began to spend happy days together, and I dared hope she might begin to live again. I designed and built the house in Lakeway to provide for the family—the many children—we were going to have. I hired the architect the day she told me she was pregnant with your sister, and she came home from her mother's home with Leona in her arms to a new home. For a while, it seemed that we might be happy together.

Then in 1938, Mexico seized all the foreign oil company assets in the country, and oilmen I had worked with before begged me to help them. I reluctantly did so, agreeing only to make such loans as were necessary to allow them to survive and reluctantly traveling to Mexico to negotiate compensation for the few I agreed to assist. We were able to wrest compensation from the government, and I returned home to your mother and you and your sister ready to and willing to refuse all future appeals.

But it was too late. Your mother was already becoming ill. When she finally told me about the pain, I sought the best medical advice, but she refused any treatment for the tumor they believed was growing inside her. The illness was mercifully short, and she simply decided that she would die with dignity. When she became bedridden, she allowed me to sit beside her, and we spoke of things we'd never spoken of before.

One night, when the pain caused her to cry out as I had a few years before, I held her and comforted her as she cried. My heart was breaking for her, and I wanted to share myself with her. I spoke to her of Jack O'Toole and Galveston, and I begged her forgiveness for the years of lies. She did not grant me absolution, but neither did she scold me for my duplicity. She merely listened, and when I told her of Donal's final words, she agreed, and quoted Shakespeare: "He that sheds his blood today with me shall be my brother."

I lost her only a few short weeks later, her life an awful tribute. If I had been uncertain before, her death made it clear that every victory of mine would be a loss for someone else.

Your mother had told me that if I was going to be Jack O'Toole, I should bring honor to his name, and I have tried, my son. I have been cursed with good luck and long life, watching as first your mother, then your wife and son, my dearest friends, and finally my lovely young daughter have died, while I have lived in a purgatory worse than any God could have devised. For years, as you traveled the world, I expected to hear that you were injured or worse, but you have inherited my luck. I only hope it will not cause those in your life to pay for it, as mine has.

I spent many years trying to understand how a just and merciful God had chosen me to receive the benefit of the blood that was shared. After your beautiful wife and child died, it was clear to me that the losses others endured were too great to be borne. I realized the great toll my life and my actions would take upon my family.

Your sister would never understand, and Judith and Peter are too young to comprehend what sacrifices were necessary for their protection. At her request, I have made sure that she will never be burdened with the house, but my son, I beg you to dispose of it, to sell it or raze it or burn it to the ground, but let the stones upon which it stands be scattered. It has been witness to my shame and your mother's despair, and it carries with it too many memories of loss.

I will leave it to you to share my shame or not. Judith carries her hate for me in her heart, and I must bear the blame for that. Perhaps the destruction of this house and the end of my life will end this cursed luck as well. Forgive me, my son, for the pain I caused you. Please know that I am sorry, I am most heartily sorry.

Your father

CHAPTER TWENTY-NINE

Jack's words echoed through Paige's voice, but I heard the prayer that Dorothea Allred had eavesdropped to hear so long ago: '*Mea culpa, mea culpa, mea maxima culpa.*'

I didn't realize I'd said the words aloud until Patrick looked my way and said softly: "Exactly."

"He was clearly insane." Judith's flat statement broke the spell Jack's oddly formal words had cast, and the three of us looked at her. She was rigid in her chair, her hands twisted together in her lap, and her face was pale. "He was a horrible man. He was venal and selfish. He admits he was the cause of his wife's death." A flush began to spread up her neck to her face.

"You can't have it both ways," Paige said quietly. "Either he was tragically deluded and mentally ill, or he was motivated solely by financial gain."

Her mother looked her way, and her voice dripped with scorn.

"*Of course* you can. Greed and delusion are perfectly capable of residing in the same person."

Page tilted her head, and I thought I saw sympathy in her eyes. "That's true. But I don't think that was what Jack was dealing with."

"That house—he was right about that house. It should be burned to the ground." Her tone was icy, but the heat behind it scorched us all. I looked at Judith curiously, wondering again if she had anything to do with the arson at Lakeway Circle. But I couldn't imagine this woman, this socialite, knowing an arsonist.

"That house was my home." Patrick's voice was quiet, his eyes on the letter Paige had placed back in front of him. "It's where I have the only memory of my mother." He looked up at Judith. "Why in the world would you feel that way about the house? You never even lived there."

Judith's voice was cutting. "How could you *not*? It's where she died."

"Yes, she died there, tragically young, of cancer. Like her daughter did." He was so calm in the face of her anger, but his eyes were eerily alive. "Why does it make you so angry?"

Paige spoke, her eyes on her mother. "Because you thought he killed her. Uncle Peter told me that your mother believed Jack killed Eleanor." She shook her head. "Why would she assume that?"

Judith's eyes shone, but I didn't think it was sadness causing the tears—maybe frustration or anger, but not sadness. "Delia—her aunt Delia—told her he had."

Patrick sighed, the sound loud in the room. "Aunt Delia was so jealous of my mother. And she was an angry, hateful woman. Our time with her was the worst of our lives." Judith looked shocked, but I remembered what the Shelton sisters had said about Delia Hartsfield Bock.

Judith's voice was rusty. "She thought—my mother thought—that he wasn't her father." Patrick looked shocked now, and he stared at Judith as she spoke. "She believed he couldn't possibly be her father and do what he did—what she *believed* he did." She swallowed with difficulty, her eyes on the table. "And when I told him what I knew—what I thought—he just looked at me. He told me if I wanted nothing to do with him, he understood." Her hands fisted, and she spat the words out. "He 'understood,' he said, as if that made it all right. That *bastard*."

Paige stared at her mother, but her eyes glistened as if she was ready to cry. "Mother—"

Judith looked at Paige, but she pointed at the letter as if it was the man she hated. "He tried to cut us out of the will, Paige. He wanted to disinherit my mother, and me, and you."

Patrick spoke. "Judith, that's not true."

Judith's head reared back, her eyes wild. "It is. He knew when he made his will. 'Heirs of the body,' it said. He knew—he knew—" She choked the words. I considered telling her that the archaic phrase might mean nothing, might just have been the lawyer's term of art, but I decided to keep quiet. A justice warrior I might be, but not every battle was necessary.

"Judith." Patrick's voice was quiet. "He never doubted Leona was his child. He *knew* she was." Judith and Paige looked at him, and I thought again how much they all resembled the man they discussed.

Judith just shook her head.

"Judith, I can't believe you've carried this all this time." He seemed close to tears as he laid a hand on the thick sheaf of paper. "He tried to love us the only way he knew how." Judith just shook her head again.

Paige nodded. "And when I started looking into the family—"

"Digging all that up is what has led us here." Judith cut her eyes to me, and then away. "A stranger, hearing all of this, knowing all our dirty family business." Her cheeks were flushing. "Who knows who that man was? What he was? Perhaps he killed that young boy to take his name. My mother was right. It was better if we didn't share that blood."

I wanted to ask if she'd confronted him with that, if that was why he made sure the house and this box wouldn't fall into her hands, but

I really did not want to be in the middle of this family discussion. I couldn't decide if staying or leaving was best at this point.

Paige's voice was deliberately calm. "Mother, it's all right. He was just a boy who was scared and traumatized."

Her mother cut her off again. "And look what he did, how he treated his wife, and his children, and even his grandchildren. He was *poison* for this family." She blinked hard, and I sympathized with her pain. It's difficult for a child to understand why someone stays away from you.

Patrick spoke, and I turned to him. His eyes were kind and concerned. "Judith, my dear—"

Judith surged to her feet, her face now crimson—with anger or embarrassment or indignation, I couldn't tell. "I will not sit here and discuss that—that man. We're leaving now, Paige." She gathered her bag with trembling hands.

Paige was shaking her head before her mother even finished her statement. "No, mother, I'm not. I want to learn about Jack, and Eleanor, and your mother, and you—all of this comes together in me, and I want to know." She looked at me. "Lacey will give me a ride home." It wasn't a question, but I nodded anyway.

Judith stood, looking at her daughter, her only movement the flaring of her nostrils as she inhaled and exhaled, and I wondered if she was calming herself with the deep breaths. Finally, she spoke. "So be it," she said, and then she was gone.

The door to the suite didn't slam, but the quiet click was just as powerful. The three of us looked at each other as the air in the room cleared and the tension eased. Paige reached her hand toward Patrick, and he took it, squeezing it once before letting go to take up the typed pages to read it once more.

Paige opened the lockbox and began taking out the pictures of Jack and Eleanor and their life, carefully arranging them in order, a fortune teller preparing to read her own future.

EPILOGUE

Despite all his efforts, Lieutenant Taylor was unable to establish any connection between Trisha or Jules Tarantino and the fire at the Lakeway House. The case remains open. Their insurance company paid the claim, less their deductible, because there was no evidence to show that the insureds were responsible for the fire. The Tarantinos came to an agreement as to the disposition of the house and agreed on a new architect and builder. The renovations would not be as grand as those previously planned, but the house could be finished and sold. Trisha found someone to refresh the murals on the children's rooms, and they would stay after the renovations.

A freak downburst thunderstorm hit Dallas on the afternoon of June 8, packing winds of almost 70 mph. In the short span of twenty minutes, a crane toppled in downtown, killing one person, and thousands of trees hit power lines, knocking out power to parts of the city for days. The Lakewood area was especially hard hit, and 70- and 80-year-old trees, uprooted from ground saturated with weeks of springtime rain, blocked streets and fell on cars and homes. One fifty-foot tall tree behind the Lakeway Circle house fell, hitting two more, and

all three took down the back wall of the kitchen wing, recently renovated under the new agreement between the Tarantinos.

On September 8, the anniversary of the Galveston Hurricane of
1900, I met Patrick O'Toole and Paige Jensen on Galveston Island, at
the spot where a marker commemorates the site of St. Mary's Orphan
Asylum. It was a lovely warm day, and the wind off the Gulf of
Mexico was fresh and cool. Hurricane Dorian had decimated the
Bahamas only a few days earlier, but the Gulf was relatively peaceful
at this peak in the hurricane season. A hundred yards away, a
dredging operation brought tons of sand in from the shipping channel
to the beach, and all the activity behind orange caution fences lent an
air of industry to what was usually a calm and peaceful scene. The
Labor Day crowds had slipped away a week before, and only a few
sun-worshippers lay on the sand, their bodies drenched in oil and
sunscreen.

Patrick had brought the last of the ashes of the man known as
Jack O'Toole, and he and Paige planned to drop them off the edge of
the pier when no one was looking. These days, most people don't
want to see you spreading ashes into water where people swim, but
Patrick had spread the rest of them all over the world, following the
footsteps of his father where he could. We weren't sure if what we
were going to do was illegal or not, so I'd probably act as lookout. We
stood for a few minutes on the beach below the marker, all of us
silent, all of us—I'm sure—thinking about that young boy standing on
this beach, afraid to step into the water, and the real Jack O'Toole
playing with his sisters in the surf. We watched the tide ebb and flow
for a few minutes, and then I slipped off my sandals and stepped into
the shallow water, wiggling my toes in the wet sand, delighting in the
feel of the world shifting beneath my feet.

AFTERWORD

Lakewood is indeed a beautiful jewel in Dallas and is pretty much just as described. Lakeway Circle doesn't exist, but—as any writer will tell you—it probably should. I was inspired by *Reminiscences: A Glimpse of Old East Dallas*, edited by Gerald D. Saxon, and *Dallas: The Making of a Modern City*, by Patricia Everidge Hall, and many other books and records in the Dallas Public Library.

The Galveston Hurricane of 1900 was much worse than I could have described. There are no figures for loss of life beyond a general number between 6,000 and 10,000, but it remains as the worst national disaster in the United States in terms of deaths. The St. Mary's Orphan Asylum truly existed, and the photograph of the children and the nuns is just as haunting as I hope I've described it to be. The Rosenberg Library's collection regarding the disaster is an amazing resource, and the book *Through a Night of Horrors: Voices from the 1900 Galveston Storm*, edited by Casey Edward Green and Shelly Henley Kelly, is required reading for anyone wanting to experience that particular devastation.

Many other facts herein are real, such as the Ninety-Nines and the air derbies so many of the early women pilots competed in.

Amelia Earhart was famous for her drive and desire to seek records, but many of the women of that time flew because—once they'd flown —they could simply do nothing else. Oilfield discoveries during between 1900 and 1930 were responsible for many fortunes gained and many fortunes lost—all over Texas, but especially in South Texas. Land speculators moved in as early as they could, both for land for exploration and for railroad and other access to the oilfields. The Texas State Historical Association's wonderful website is an amazing resource to all things Texas history.

I am indebted to Dr. Yvonne Fritz for advice regarding therapy, as well as psychological disorders and the symptoms thereof, and to Dr. Ronnie Shalev on medical facts. Any mistakes made herein are mine.

I'd like to thank my advance readers— Lisa Clawson, Sharon Corsentino, Neely Franklin, Mary Lyons, Heather McClure, and Kara Stoner—for their advice and feedback. Thanks to Lenny and Michael for the space to create in Galveston. I'm also indebted to my publishing partner, Jenni Tauzel, for her enthusiasm and willingness to take a leap of faith with me. Thanks also to Rachel Naldi and Alesia Cate for their publishing support for Blue Muse Books/Paris House Publishing Group.

As always, thanks to Deborah, Tracye, Gracie, and Nathan for putting up with me as I write and read and research, and loving me through the tough spots.

COMING SOON

TO HOLD THE HUMMINGBIRD
By Elizabeth Basden

PROLOGUE

"My daughter Tess committed suicide six months ago."

Bette Christensen didn't have a lovely or soft voice. It was harsh, with flattened vowels, as if she had an accent she tried to hide. As a result, her words dropped with the force of heavy stones shoved into water.

Or maybe that was just how it felt to me.

Her eyes were on mine, as if watching for a response, but I kept my face still with effort, chewing the bite of chicken enchilada I'd taken. I swallowed hard, wiped my mouth with my blue napkin, and, when I was sure I could breathe again, offered my condolences. "I'm sorry for your loss."

She waved away my sentiment—literally waved her hand—as she picked up her shrimp fork to take a bite of ceviche. I'd have thought her cold if I hadn't seen the glimmer of tears in her eyes. She speared a tiny piece of shrimp and looked at it for a few seconds. "I've learned you're not supposed to say 'committed suicide' anymore. Now you say 'died by suicide'." She ate the piece of shrimp, her face twisting. "But I can't seem to stop."

I cut another bite of enchilada, but any pleasure I'd taken from trying the dish at this new restaurant was gone. With my fork, I pulled some of the shredded chicken from inside the rapidly-disintegrating blue corn tortilla and nibbled at it. I had no idea what she wanted me to say, and no idea why I was here.

She'd asked me to meet her, and I'd agreed, since a client had referred her to me—a good, quick-paying client that I liked—and I had nowhere else to be on this cool and cloudy Thursday. She'd changed the date twice and had been almost half an hour late, but I'd not yet tried this new Tex-Mex place, so I reasoned lunch on her was worth staying to hear what legal work she needed done.

I'd been on time—an obsession of mine—and waited, munching too many blue corn chips at a table on the enclosed patio as I memorized the menu. She strode in, her high-heeled boots *thunking* sharply on the wooden floor. She was a beautiful woman, most likely in her mid-50s, with light-blond hair drawn back in a clip at the nape of her neck, highlighting her blue eyes and tanned skin. She had the look of a model—carefully-applied makeup over high cheekbones and an artfully-arranged pashmina over thin turtleneck sweater and leggings—but if she had been, it was a few years ago. She carried a few extra pounds with confidence and a definite sense of style. Her handshake had been firm but quick, and I was prepared to like her.

I'd waited to order, and she'd apologized as she waved the server over, blessing him with a dazzling smile when she interrupted his rehearsed patter. "You have ceviche?" He'd nodded, clearly a bit unhappy that she'd upset his idea of the order of things. "I'll have your house white wine and a ceviche." She'd turned the smile on me. "I'll bet you've had time to decide what you wanted." I'd nodded, and then gave the server my chicken enchiladas order, my voice apologetic to smooth over his hurt feelings.

The enchiladas had been a bit over-sauced, but new restaurants always have trouble getting recipes right in the first few weeks of business. I just scraped a bit of the thick sour-cream mixture to the side. She'd been presented with a truly beautiful mini-tower of chopped shrimp, vegetables, avocado, and herbs, but she didn't seem pleased at all. I could smell the sharp lime from across the table, and, for a moment I had second thoughts about my order, but then logic and my love of enchiladas reasserted themselves. I'd only had a couple of bites when she dropped her bomb.

Now she speared a tiny piece of avocado. "I never know how to tell people. You think you can soften it, but you really can't. There's no way to lead into it." Her chest rose and fell with a few breaths, and she put her fork down to lay her hands flat on the tabletop. "She was only 27. She'd suffered from some anxiety, but no one really saw it coming." She picked up her smartphone and turned the screen toward me. The phone's wallpaper was a picture of her and a young girl with Bette's eyes, long curly hair framing a thinner version of her mother's face. Their faces were close to each other, the broad white smiles almost identical. The screen went black, and I looked back at Bette.

"I'm very sorry. She looks like a lovely girl."

She turned the screen back towards herself and woke it with a finger tap, looking at it for the few seconds before the screen went dark again. "She was."

I put my fork down on my plate and took a long drink of iced tea, trying to think of a way to delicately move this along to whatever it was she wanted of me. Was this another matter like our common friend Shanna's, dealing with her daughter's estate?

"I don't know why she did it." Bette Christensen was looking at the darkened screen, as if she could still see her daughter's face there. "What could have been so terrible in her life that she needed to end it so early? How could she have thought there was no other option?" She looked back at me and hesitated, and my heart begin to beat a little faster.

"I know about your mother."

I felt the blood rush away from my face, and my ears began to ring. "Excuse me?"

Bette Christensen leaned forward, and I automatically leaned back and away. "I have a background check performed on everyone who works with me. Too many years of experts on the stand who haven't told me everything." Her eyes were intense, her voice strong and strident. "When I saw your mother committed suicide when you were a teenager, I felt like you'd understand the need and could help me."

My voice was raspy, and I wished desperately for another drink of iced tea, but I felt paralyzed by this woman's intensity. "What need?"

She spread her hands, those pleading eyes now filling. "The need to know *why*. Why? Why now? What happened? Why would she do this?" She stopped short, but I heard what she didn't say: *Why would she do this to me?* I looked away.

In the first year or so after my mother had taken her life, I'd felt those words beat at me almost constantly, but the years of neglect that preceded the act itself had blunted their edge, and, after time, they'd ceased to hurt much at all. Bette Christensen, I could tell, was still bleeding from the wounds.

But it wasn't my problem—her pain and anguish just made my stomach threaten to give up all those blue corn chips. The nausea seemed to break the spell. I pushed my plate forward and reached into my bag, getting out my emergency $20 bill and laying it on the table.

"I'm sorry. I can't help you." I pulled my coat from the back of the chair and put it on.

"You can. Shanna told me you're good, very good, at what you do." Her voice was heavy with displeasure, and her drying eyes were hard. "I want to know. I *need* to know. Wouldn't you want to know?"

I stood up, and she did as well. People at the tables around us looked at us curiously, but I didn't care. I stepped out into the aisle, facing a server coming toward me with a full tray on his shoulder.

Bette Christensen put her hand on my arm. "Wouldn't you do everything you could to find out? To know—if you could know—why she did it?" Her hand fell away, and I moved forward. The server dodged me, the tray dipping dangerously, my bootsteps ringing on the floor, but I heard her words clearly. "Wouldn't you *need* to know why?" I let them die in the echoes of my footsteps as I walked away.

ALSO BY ELIZABETH BASDEN

The Prodigal Daughter

Made in the USA
Middletown, DE
03 October 2022

11674947R00227